THE KING'S HAND

THE KING'S HAND

Anyone can deceive.
But there's always a price.

THE KNIGHT OF ELDARAN
BOOK 2

ANNA THAYER

LION FICTION

To
The City of Palermo

Published by Lion Fiction
an imprint of
Lion Hudson plc
Wilkinson House, Jordan Hill Road
Oxford OX2 8DR, England
www.lionhudson.com/fiction

ISBN 978 1 78264 077 6
e-ISBN 978 1 78264 078 3

This edition 2014

A catalogue record for this book is available from the British Library

Printed and bound in the UK, April 2014, LH26

Cover illustration by Jacey: www.jacey.com

CONTENTS

Map of the River Realm and its World   6

Map of the River Realm Towns and Provinces   8

Acknowledgments   11

The Story So Far   13

Prologue   21

The King's Hand   23

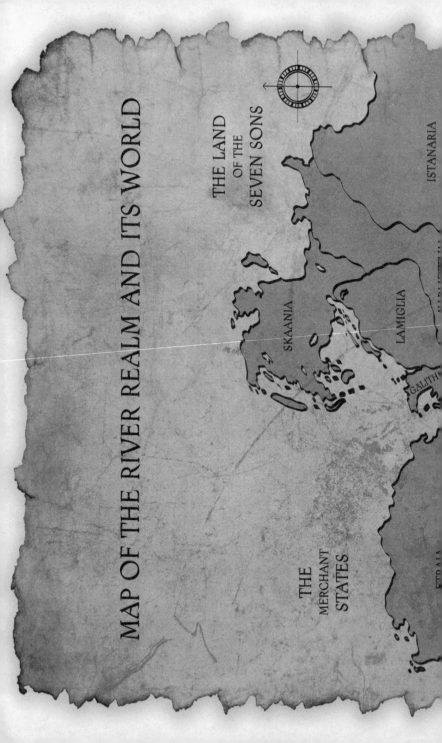

MAP OF THE RIVER REALM AND ITS WORLD

THE LAND
OF THE
SEVEN SONS

THE
MERCHANT
STATES

SKAANIA

LAMIGLIA

GALITH

ISTANARIA

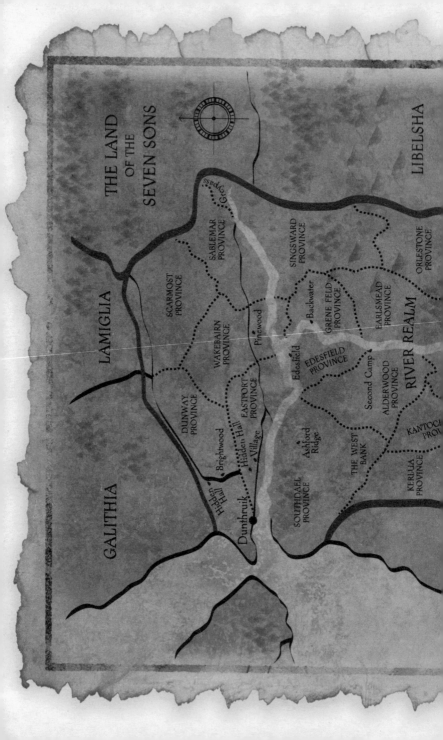

ACKNOWLEDGMENTS

Just as with its fellow, the publication of this book would not have been possible without the support of a great many people.

Thank you to Peter Gladwin, for helping to get me in touch with the right people at the right time. A real kairos moment!

I am particularly indebted to Tony, Jessica, and Julie at Lion Hudson; for their overwhelming enthusiasm for Eamon and his world, and the countless hours they have spent in the final labour of love that is editing a book (let alone three!) for publication.

Colleagues and students have for years been a source of immense encouragement, and I am grateful to them for helping to keep me going on what has, at times, been a daunting endeavour. Special mention has to go to the "Tardis crew" who, despite their changing faces, have been the best colleagues that a teacher, writer, and new mother could ask for.

Finally, I wish to thank my wonderful husband, Justin, and my son, Leopoldo – the one for his tireless dedication to reading, re-reading, thrice reading, and editorial input, and the other for sleeping just enough to let me finish the manuscripts. The discerning reader may decide which thanks goes to which gentleman!

THE STORY SO FAR

It is the 532nd year of the Master's throne. The Master is lord over the River Realm, ruling in unassailable might from his capital, Dunthruik, and asserting his authority by means of his army – the Gauntlet – and his elite servants, the Hands.

But things were not always this way. There are rumours of wayfarers up and down the River – pernicious snakes who claim that their leader is the descendent of the ancient House of Brenuin, and rightful heir to a throne stolen by the Master.

Since the death of his parents, Eamon Goodman has always longed to swear his allegiance to the Gauntlet – to dedicate his life to protecting and serving the people of the River. Living in the small town of Edesfield, his hopes for greatness – of going to Dunthruik and becoming a Hand – seem slim.

Everything changes on the day that he swears his oath to the Master. He finds his flesh marked with a fiery eagle, and his mind filled with a voice that commands his thought. Worse, Telo, the father of his childhood friend Aeryn, is revealed to be a wayfarer – as is his daughter. After Eamon has been forced to burn Telo at the stake, Aeryn reveals to him her true nature – and is captured by the Gauntlet. Compelled by his captain to interrogate her, Eamon discovers that the mark on his palm has granted him a strange new ability – that of breaching a person's mind, entering it and tearing through it to reveal their inmost thoughts and secrets. But he also discovers that Aeryn is protected from him by a mysterious blue light – a light that she attributes to her devotion to the King.

For his service in capturing wayfarers in the town, Eamon is promoted from cadet to lieutenant and sent on a holk downriver to Dunthruik to deliver his prisoner – Aeryn – to the city's greatest breachers. Torn between his friendship and his oath, Eamon attempts to discharge his duty – but finds himself troubled by Aeryn's allegiance.

On board the holk a young cadet under Eamon's command, Mathaiah Grahaven, miscarries his duty, allowing Aeryn a chance at escape. Rather than see the young man suffer, Eamon volunteers to take the punishment – a flogging – in his place, creating a strong bond between them.

Just before the holk reaches Dunthruik, it is overrun in a night-time attack by wayfarers intent on rescuing Aeryn. These men, led by a man called Giles, refuse Eamon's offer of surrender and furiously butcher all on board. Mathaiah takes a killing blow in Eamon's place, and, as Eamon cradles the dying cadet, he finds blue light in his own hands. He uses it to heal the young man, unwittingly saving his own life in the process – this light is the mark of a King's man.

Sole survivors of the holk's crew, Eamon and Mathaiah are taken back to the wayfarers' camp where Eamon makes a series of startling realizations: there is a King, Hughan Brenuin, a childhood friend of Eamon's whom he thought dead in a wayfarer attack. Hughan reveals that Eamon's ability to be both sworn to the Master and carry the blue light is an inheritance of his house – that Eben Goodman was once First Knight to the last Brenuin King, and the man who betrayed the King to the Master. Hughan invites Eamon to become First Knight once more.

Tormented by his oath to the Master and his desire to give fealty to Hughan, Eamon swears to serve the King: as part of his new oath, he will go to Dunthruik and act as Hughan's spy in the city. He concocts a subterfuge with Hughan: he returns to the city with a group of Hands who have come seeking Aeryn, carrying with him forged papers and an ancient stone, to prove his "loyalty" to the

Master. Mathaiah – who has also sworn an oath to serve the King – travels with him.

Doubly sworn, Eamon arrives in Dunthruik and is assigned to the city's West Quarter college under the leadership of Captain Waite. Persistently baited by Hands and officers, Eamon struggles to remain true to his oath to Hughan. His temptation to become a Master's man is made stronger when he is promoted to first lieutenant and becomes the lover of one of the city's most powerful women, Alessia Turnholt.

Using the stone he has brought from Hughan, Eamon leads a group of Hands into the city's ancient library. There, he and Mathaiah recover a book known as the Nightholt – one which Mathaiah feels certain he can read, despite its arcane script – and give it over to the Hands. It is a deed which fills Eamon with misgiving. He and Mathaiah arrange to send news to Hughan via their contact, Alessia's serving-girl Lillabeth.

Eamon is nominated to become a Hand; spurred on by his captain, his lover, and the Master's Right Hand, Eamon begins working against Hughan, capturing and torturing wayfarers and doing everything in his power to be formally recognized as one of the Master's elite. Mathaiah warns him that he is being baited and pulled from his true oath of service, and that Alessia is in the Master's pay. Angered and incited further by the voice which increasingly holds sway over him, Eamon shuns Mathaiah utterly.

Eamon turns his back on the King, aspiring instead to become Right Hand – a desire which he confides to Ladomer, an old friend who has won a position in Dunthruik as lieutenant to the Master's second.

After a winter of working to the Master's glory, Eamon is taken on a mission by Lord Cathair to see if rumours of an amassing wayfarer army have any truth to them. They discover that Hughan has garnered many allies. On this mission, one of Eamon's cadets is killed by Giles. The man confronts Eamon with the extent of his treachery to Hughan. Furious, Eamon violently breaches

Giles, learning the location of the King's army and many details pertaining to its logistical support and allies. It is when he sees Giles broken by his hand that Eamon realizes what he has become. Unhinged with shame and guilt, Eamon returns to the city and confesses everything to Alessia. He resolves that he should become a King's man once more.

The sensitive information that Eamon acquires from Giles clinches the decision to make him a Hand. He is given command of a mission to halt one of the King's supply convoy. What should be an easy mission ends disastrously and Eamon leads his men back to Dunthruik in disgrace.

Back in the city, Alessia invites Eamon to the theatre where the Right Hand, Arlaith, joins them unexpectedly to espouse his views on how betrayal should be answered. Alessia reveals to Eamon that she was ordered to court him by Arlaith, she has been breached, and now the Hands know everything. When she tells Eamon that Mathaiah is being arrested he spurns her and rushes to try to save his friend, but arrives too late.

Eamon realizes that Lillabeth is in danger and smuggles her out of the city. The following day Arlaith takes retribution by ordering a decimation of all those who have served under Eamon. Eamon defies him by leaping to take another man's place in the line, and demands to see the Master.

Eamon is taken before the Master. Edelred gives him seven days to leave the city and return with the head of one of Hughan's allies. If he succeeds his men will have their honour restored – if he fails, they will all be killed.

Eamon goes to the Pit where Mathaiah is imprisoned and asks for his friend's forgiveness. It is granted. With this as his only comfort, and with the lives of men that he loves resting on him, Eamon leaves Dunthruik.

Dread now seemed all his yesterdays,
Grave folly each tomorrow;
Yet courage on that blackened field
Sought he, and still he followed.

The Edelred Cycle

PROLOGUE

The chill, grey sea was to the west, its waves rolling to meet the outpour at the River's mouth. Cold drove against his face and whipped his cloak behind him. Upward glances showed him the eerie half-light, and he knew that the sun loured behind the swell of the horizon.

He cursed it.

He clung to the dark. It fled from him, unheeding. The stars, caught high in the fading black, were as faint as his hope.

A day had passed since he had challenged the command of the Master's Right Hand. Just a single day since he had seen the Lord of Dunthruik shatter the heart of the King and set him on this desperate task.

Was it really a day since he had seen the Pit riven with light?

He rode on. He could not think of rest.

It was the twentieth of February. The day pressed against his heart with the keenness of a blade.

Seven alone remained.

CHAPTER I

A grim dawn was already dunning the sky when he found himself crossing the River by ferry and then following one of its tributaries to the south. If only he could fly down the valley – ride with the force of tempests, striking clods and stones with the speed of lightning, leaving dust fulminating in his furious wake… then his task would not be so forlorn.

Ladomer had always been the rider… Why wasn't he swift and strong, like Ladomer?

Why had he been so foolish?

With soft words and a tug at the reins, Eamon bade his horse stop and then dismounted. Fatigue coursing through his limbs, he leaned for a moment against the patient creature's side. It indulged him in his weary moans.

How could he ever hope to find Hughan in time?

Eamon pressed his eyes shut. Faces lurched before his mind – of militiamen, cadets, ensigns, officers, and a dear captain…

They had all been placed in his hands by the Master, to be impossibly bartered for the head of the King's ally.

He paced, trying to force blood back into frozen limbs. He had to go on – he had to find the King.

And if he did – what then?

Hughan could never grant him the head of an ally; Eamon could not save his men without it. His task was as farcical as it was hopeless – and the Master knew it.

Groggily, Eamon took his bearings. Crossing the River he had come down into the province of Southdael. Ashford Ridge was in the heart of the region, farther south. Though Dunthruik lay a hard ride behind him, the Master's shadow was still his saddle-mate.

Eamon stared at the struggling sun, haunted by his thoughts. His failure was certain – but his return? If he did not return… he would never have to face the deaths of his men – or what Cathair left of their corpses.

He pressed his hands into his eyes as though to drive away a mist. There was no question of not returning. He had given his word, to Anderas, Manners, Mathaiah – and the throned.

He drew a deep breath. The Master's glory was forged from such things.

Quivering, he strode to the nearby stream. The smell of the Pit, dire and fetid, clung to him. As his horse watched him quizzically, he removed everything that he wore and then threw himself into the water before he could change his mind. A thousand needles pierced his skin.

His whole body pulsed with the pain of submersion, but when he came up he at last felt some touch of the sun.

The morning was not old when he set off once more. Eamon saw the sea, though more distantly, to the west. He used it as a bearing as he pressed south towards Ashford Ridge, where the King's camp had once stood. He wondered whether the King's ill-fated harriers had stalked him through these same valleys.

He rode throughout the day, stopping more regularly than he would have liked. Further south groups of fallen men, some Gauntlet, others wayfarers, littered the roadside.

He continued more cautiously then, fearful of encounter. If he did not meet the wayfarers, how would he find the King?

In the agony of his thought, he rode on.

It was nearing evening when a dark line materialized before him. Eamon made out the spires of a forest over a ridge. He recognized it, and the particular glint of the River behind him. He remembered Overbrook, lying in his own blood, and Giles, writhing.

Chapter I

He shivered.

As he approached the eaves he began weaving a slow path through the trees that guarded the hollow beyond. The trees soon grew too thick to ride through, and he dismounted. He took hold of his mount's bridle and laboriously picked his way towards the edge of the ridge. The disappearing sun elongated his shadow until it melted into the forest floor.

His horse snorted, disapproving of the terrain. Murmuring encouragement, Eamon urged it on.

They reached the ridgeline. Eamon gazed into the twilit hollow below. It took him a few moments to register what he saw. His hope fell, stillborn.

The camp was gone.

The shadowed hollow stared vacantly at the sky. It was not entirely empty. Where standards had blown but two weeks before, a long line of turned earth lay. Above it was a pole carrying a length of blue cloth, a meagre memorial to the men who had lost their lives there.

He wished he could feel sorrow at the death of men who served the King, or joy that some had lived to bury their dead in honour. But he felt only despair.

He only had seven days to return to Dunthruik. And Hughan was gone.

Trembling, Eamon led his horse down a small path on the hillside. It wound unsteadily to the hollow. As he went, the graves became clearer. Spoiled prints of man and beast, wagon and cart, were everywhere. The tracks led to the hollow's southern entrance, where Eamon had seen Easter banners joining the encampment.

In that narrow mouth were other shadows. He walked towards them.

More colours – a torn red tabard hung against a tree.

Looking beyond, Eamon saw what easily numbered a hundred mounds of earth, many more than had lain beneath the King's colour. His heart churned.

He knew that the Gauntlet had tried, and failed, to take the King's camp – he had never stopped to think of the dead. Perhaps it was a mercy that the commander of this wreckage had been killed. Cathair would have taken more than the man's head in vengeance for the humiliating defeat.

A dark copse marked the far edge of the valley. More shadows lay by it. Eamon realized that there was no turned earth there. Beneath the trees was a group of ruthlessly discarded bodies, rotting. They wore black.

The ground beneath him seemed to churn. His reeling thought conjured the cries of the dying in the gloom.

He ran his hands over his eyes and shivered. Hughan could never forgive him for the evil he had done in Dunthruik – all that he could be worthy to receive from the King was a death sentence. How could he have thought otherwise? He had been a fool to imagine that he and Hughan could be reconciled just because he had gone to Mathaiah in the Pit. His place was among the sable corpses: bruised, bloodied, broken, and with no standard to mark it.

He shook his head. Whatever Hughan might do to him when they met, his task remained that of finding the King.

But Eamon could not track the camp. It had rained, leaving the ground changed and muddy. No man could track in the sodden sludge.

Eamon looked to the trees as though they might be able to aid him. The ridges and darkening skies watched him in silence, just as the throned had watched him.

He took hold of the pouch at his neck. The heart of the King lay hidden there, the broken shards silent beneath his touch.

There had to be something he could do.

He had failed.

"I have not failed." His voice sounded frail in the grey stillness.

He had failed before he had even begun.

Eamon drew a deep breath. There was a way; there *had* to be a way.

24

He strode back into the hollow, back to the banner of the fallen King's men. The cloth stirred in the breeze, the impaled star rippling against the darkening sky.

Suddenly Eamon lifted his head to the silent ridges.

"I know you see me!"

His horse started but he persisted, raising his voice to reach the distant heavens. The stars threw his words back at him.

"I know you hear me! My name is Goodman. I would go before the King!"

He heard his voice echoing up the ridge.

The hills were silent. The trees glowered back at him.

He laid his hand against his horse's neck as the long echoes of his voice faded away.

Silently he buried his head against his horse's warm throat. What use was it? He was lost. He would never find the King in time. Why had he interfered with the Right Hand's decimation? What had he honestly thought he could save? If he had only kept still and quiet, as Cathair had told him, at least some of his men would have lived. Why had he spoken? He could have saved them better by his silence, and done so without humiliating himself. Now his men would die, and he had made himself the Right Hand's enemy. That was the price for his idiotic high-mindedness.

Suddenly his horse snorted. Eamon looked up, then gasped.

A ring of men stood around them. They were darkly dressed, with heavy hoods and masks.

Eamon's hand moved instinctively to his sword hilt. "Who are you?"

"Your name is Goodman?" The voice was indistinct.

"Yes."

"Then we will take you before the King."

Eamon stared. Was it possible?

The man who had spoken held out one hand.

"You will surrender both your sword and dagger, Goodman."

Eamon took a deep breath, then unslung sword and dagger and

held them towards the hooded man. He passed it to one of his companions. Another came and took the horse's reins. The beast tossed its head nervously.

"Do not harm him," Eamon said.

"It is not the creature's fault whom it serves. It will not suffer for that."

The man held a length of cloth. One of his fellows carried a rope.

"Am I to be a prisoner?"

"You will agree to be bound and blindfolded?"

What choice did he have?

Eamon held out his hands, trembling in the half-light. The man who tied him knew his business. The rope was taut, the knots firm. When the cloth was brought to his face, its thickness forced his eyes closed.

"You will lead me truly?"

"We will lead you to the King."

Someone took his arm. He walked forward unsteadily.

They led him a short distance and then, beneath the eaves, they helped him mount his horse. He was secured to the saddle. He heard other horses in the darkness near him. His reins were taken and the men led him away.

They pressed on hard throughout the night and much of the next day. He did not know where or how far they went. He was aware only of the tireless speed of his horse and the silence of his guides; they did not speak, either to him or to each other. His world shrank to the sounds beyond his darkened eyes.

The cold wind tore at him as they left the shelter of the ridges. From there, they passed trees that scratched Eamon's face as skeletal branches knocked overhead.

The land was mostly level, though they went through a couple of small valleys, Eamon gripping his bound hands to the saddle pommel as they went up and down. He did not know where they were, but guessed that they were still on the West Bank.

They paused from time to time. Twice he was offered food,

which he ate gratefully. When they stopped, he heard other horses and then voices speaking together. After the long silence every noise seemed as loud as thunder and startled him as much. He thought that he heard his name mentioned.

Then they were moving on again, first over earth and then over a swaying bridge. Loud water ran beneath it, but it was not wide enough to be the River itself. Perhaps they had crossed a tributary.

The wind confused and distorted the sounds around him. More horses. Tent cloth? Astonished murmurs.

A voice commanded him to dismount; other hands helped him. The men led him on as he stumbled repeatedly.

The wind stopped. He heard tent cloth drawn aside, felt the warmth of a brazier. In the sudden sheltered silence, he knew that eyes, whose gazes he could not return, stared at him.

His wrists throbbed beneath bonds that suddenly felt tight.

The man who had led him let go of his arm. Blinded, bound, and unaided, Eamon stood giddy and afraid.

"Who is this?" asked a fierce voice. Its accent was Easter. He remembered the dark-haired, clear-eyed man whom he had seen at Pinewood and shuddered.

"A Hand that surrendered to us." It was the man who had spoken to him at Ashford.

"A rare occurrence!" the first voice scoffed.

Eamon's hands were clammy with sweat.

"His name is Goodman. He asked to be brought before the King."

"This was no way to lead him."

His heart leapt joyfully into his throat: he knew that voice. It was great and stern, but kind and compassionate. While the throned assumed authority this man bore it of his own accord, of his very blood and nature. But even as Eamon rejoiced he felt shame kindling fear: for every treachery he had wilfully committed, this man could lay claim to his very life.

His sense receded from him. He felt faint. Quivering, he dropped to his knees.

"I did not deserve to be led at all," he breathed. Sobs tangled his words. "I should have been slaughtered and left to rot in the dark; thus do my deeds deserve to be repaid."

Hands came to his brow; comforting hands.

Fire leapt to his palms.

Strike him, Eben's son!

Shocked, Eamon clenched his hands, desperate to quench the flames. His teeth ground together with the effort.

There was a laugh in his mind, chill and deep. *You thought to cast me out? You thought you had? I am still here, Eben's son, and you are still mine!*

The snarling voice sought to master him. With a cry, Eamon turned from it. His only hope was in the man before him.

"Help me!" he whispered. "Please! Forgive me for what I have done! Cut me down for it if you cannot forgive it, but help me!"

The hands were still on his brow; they had not flinched. Eamon turned his whole being towards that cool touch, clinging to it against the rage of the voice.

"You have no hold on this man, voice of Edelred." The King's firm words sounded in his ear, thrilling Eamon such that he forgot his struggle. "He has turned from you and you must turn from him. I command it."

As suddenly as it had come, the voice was gone. Stunned silence hung in the air.

Shuddering, Eamon pressed his face against his bound hands. The band over his eyes grew wet.

The King touched his shoulder. "Courage, Eamon."

His eyes were unbound. Cold air brushed his face. The light seemed terribly bright. He blinked hard.

The King laid the band aside. "Now you can see," he said.

Awestruck, Eamon could bring no words to his lips, and could scarcely bear the feeling in his heart.

Hughan stepped back and gestured to Eamon's escort. "Release him. There is no call for him to be bound."

CHAPTER I

"With deepest reverence, Star of Brenuin, I hardly think that wise," said the Easter accent. Eamon looked up to see a tall man with dark hair. He bore the same emblem of a blazing sun that Eamon had seen both at Ashford Ridge and the Hidden Hall. This Easter had bright green eyes that watched him critically.

He was not the only other man in the tent. Eamon now became aware of others, some Easters and some wayfarers whom he recognized from the Hidden Hall so long ago. They seemed like vestiges of a long-forgotten past.

Eamon looked back to Hughan. "I do not deserve to be unbound," he whispered. "I am worthy of neither grace nor mercy."

Hughan met his gaze. "I know."

Grief closed about his heart. What words could he possibly speak? He would only condemn himself, just as he had condemned his men...

Trembling, he reached to the pouch at his neck. It was difficult with bound hands, but he eased the cord over his head. It held the shards of the heart of the King.

Eamon swallowed. He could not meet the King's eyes.

"I was charged to bring you this, and to perform more besides. I have betrayed you, sire, more times than can be counted. But this I return to you." The broken stone sounded as he held it forwards. "Hughan," he breathed, "I am sorry."

Hughan took the shards from him. As he did so a flash of jubilant light sparked among the pouch threads. Eamon stared in amazement then gazed up at Hughan, to whom the light bounded.

The shards grew dim, but when the King looked back to him his face seemed brilliant with light.

"I know what you have done, Eamon," Hughan said gravely. "I know that you merit death and perhaps, for a part, you came here seeking it from me. I will not give it to you."

Eamon stared in disbelief, but Hughan was undaunted.

Quietly, the King knelt beside him. Eamon flinched away, but Hughan took his hands. The King unbound him. Then Hughan reached forward and laid a kiss against his forehead.

"I rejoice at your returning, Eamon," he said, "and I welcome you."

A long silence fell. Eamon felt streams of hot tears on his cheeks. The King's kiss lay on his forehead with greater power than any mark.

"Who is this man," snapped the Easter, incredulous and angry, "that is a bloodied Hand, and you welcome him?"

Hughan rose and looked at him. "His name is Eamon Goodman." He drew Eamon up to his feet. "He is the First Knight, and defender of my house."

None spoke.

Eamon gaped. He could not bear it any longer. "First Knight! I am not worthy even to serve at your table! You cannot know what I have done! I have captured and tortured men, breached them and lied to them and led ambushes against those who should have been my fellows under your banner. I have been courted by your enemies in every quarter and given fealty to them without ever once remembering you. I have killed and broken men as wholeheartedly as any of your enemies have done." He shook fearfully. "I do not deserve to serve you; I deserve to be condemned!"

"I do not condemn you."

Eamon stared. "But you must!"

Hughan matched his gaze. "You must know this: had you worked treachery against me seven score seven times, still you would have the name by which I called you." Hughan looked deep into Eamon's eyes. "First Knight, take courage. See clearly, and serve me better henceforth."

Hughan watched him with gentleness and compassion. Eamon felt that he had never seen, nor perhaps would ever see, a truer man.

Overjoyed and overawed, Eamon slowly sank to his knee. He took Hughan's hand and touched his forehead to it.

"I will serve you with all of my heart."

The King lifted him to his feet and smiled at him. Eamon's head and heart span with emotions he barely understood.

There was a long moment of silence. Eamon slowly became aware of the others around him, their strange looks puncturing his joy. He had to say so many things… he did not have the words.

"Hughan… what day is it?"

"It is night of the twenty-first."

His heart plummeted. So they had ridden a full day. That left him only six…

"I… I–I have been sent with a terrible task –"

"I understand," Hughan said quietly, "but before you speak of it you must rest. It is late."

"Yes," Eamon breathed.

"Would you conduct him to a resting quarter, Leon?"

The man who had led Eamon from the valley nodded. He had pushed back his hood, revealing a handsome face with dark eyes. Eamon had first seen him at the Hidden Hall.

"Yes, sire," Leon answered.

"Star of Brenuin." The Easter spoke suddenly, and still his voice was hard. "I would have this man guarded."

"Very well, Lord Anastasius," Hughan answered. The Easter bowed his head, seeming better satisfied. Hughan looked again at Eamon.

"Go with Leon," he said, "and rest. I will send for you in the morning; you can speak freely of your task then."

Eamon bowed low. Forgetting every burden, he followed Leon from the tent into the cool night air.

As he was led away, Eamon heard voices rising in the tent behind him. His mouth dropped open in amazement as he took in the scale of the camp around him.

It was larger than it had been when he had seen it on the ridge in Southdael, and from what he could gather they were in a southern-facing valley. He could see no sign of any other inhabitants nearby, but there was a river branch nestled at the valley floor, around which the camp had been set. The River itself lay some distance from the camp's eastern edge. Over it, Eamon made out a bridge worked from a series of connected boats. It was being crossed by a small group of men who led carts of supplies. The pontoon snaked beneath their weight. A similar bridge spanned the tributary to the west; Eamon imagined he had been brought over the western bridge.

He was taken to a small tent, woven from dark cloth that stirred in the wind. Leon held the entryway open while Eamon passed inside. A bed had been set there, piled high with covers. Eamon wondered whether he was stealing somebody's bedding for what little of the night remained. The light led him to believe that scant hours would see them to the dawn.

"You can sleep here," Leon told him. "There will be guards posted outside, should you need anything."

"Thank you," Eamon answered. He guessed that the guards would keep a close watch on him. Leon nodded and disappeared. Eamon heard him speak to the guard detail outside.

Slowly, he got into the bed. The covers were thick over his weary limbs. Though he was exhausted he could barely still his mind.

He was in the wayfarer camp and the King had received him. But as he settled into his bed his heart was darkened by his task; its impossibility preyed on his fledgling joy.

CHAPTER II

It seemed long before he slept, and no time at all before light worked its way through the folds of his shelter. If he dreamed, he did not remember it.

At last he rose from his bed. He rued it at once as he hurried to put on his boots and fumbled for his cloak, mindful not of its colour but only of its protection from the chill. Then he stepped out.

There were four tall men in uniforms before the tent: two bore the sword and star, two the bold sun designs of two different Easter lords. As he emerged, swathed in black, Eamon saw them tense. Men and women nearby stopped and stared at him.

He shuffled uncomfortably. "Good morning," he said to his guards. His voice was dry from sleep; he swallowed. None of the guards answered him. "I must speak with the King. May I go?"

"General Leon will come for you."

"Do you mind if I stand with you until he arrives?"

"No." It was a fierce reply.

Eamon did not dare to go far from them, but stepped forward a little to stand in the early light. It was as though every eye stared at him. He steeled himself for all that lay ahead.

After what seemed an eternity, Leon walked across the damp grass towards him. The man was wrapped in his blue cloak. Eamon's heart beat faster.

"Good morning," he called as his escort approached. The man nodded but did not answer. Nor did he speak to the guards as he beckoned Eamon to follow him. Eamon felt a terrible foreboding. Every step brought him before the hateful gaze of a dozen men.

Some of them jeered him from their campfires, though a look from Leon silenced them.

They walked back towards the King's pavilion. Now that his eyes were free from both dark and band he saw it was a grand blue affair, with traces of silver along its edges. At its head blew the King's banner with the sword and star, sunlight just kissing the banner's crest.

As they approached, Eamon heard a cry to his right and turned. A woman stood there, bearing a wide tray. This she put down hastily and ran towards them, laughing and crying.

"My dear Mr Goodman! It's you!"

With a flash Eamon recognized her: Ma Mendel. Alone of all the faces that morning, she was unafraid and welcomed him.

"It's you, it's really you!" The next moment the old woman threw her arms around Eamon's neck. She hugged him with a mother's fondness.

"It's so good to see you!" Eamon answered, embracing her.

"Let her go, Hand!" someone yelled.

"Stand down!" Leon called back. The wayfarers did so, though suspiciously. "Mrs Mendel, please –"

Ma Mendel quirked a chastising eyebrow at him. "This man rescued me from the Hands, Leon. Am I not to welcome him?"

"Mrs Mendel, you're worrying the men."

"An old thing like me?" Ma Mendel gave him a wink. "It's been many a year since I worried men, sir!"

Leon sighed. "Mrs Mendel, step back."

Ma Mendel kissed Eamon's brow and fell back from Eamon's embrace to take hold of his hands. "Oh, you're frozen!" she exclaimed. "Why aren't you wearing gloves, dear?"

"I must have left them on my bed," Eamon answered. He might have felt foolish, but the kiss was warm on his forehead and her joy moved him beyond words.

"You'll go back for them!"

"He must see the King, Mrs Mendel," Leon told her.

"Then *I* shall go back for them," Ma Mendel continued. "You must wear them, dear!" She stepped back, rubbed his hands vigorously, then hurried to pick up her discarded tray. "Something warm for the King and Lord Anastasius," she explained, gesturing to it. "They both need it at this time of the morning."

"I'm sure they do," Leon muttered.

"You shall have some too, Mr Leon, and you shall be the happier for it." Her eyes were on Eamon and she beamed. "Oh, I'm so pleased you're here!" she told him again. "I was often thinking about you while you were gone."

"Thank you," Eamon answered. She never once noted either his cloak or its colour. It was a wonderful relief.

They reached the tent. Ma Mendel went in first to dispense of her tray, the contents of which steamed in the light. She emerged a few moments later.

"He is ready for you."

"Thank you, Mrs Mendel," Leon told her.

Ma Mendel smiled again at Eamon then hurried on her way, drawing a thick shawl over her head against the cold. Eamon followed Leon into the tent.

Hughan was there, framed by the banner of the sword and star. He sipped at the small mug brought by Ma Mendel. Another man stood by him. His face wan, he had not drawn any drink. Eamon remembered him to be Lord Anastasius.

"Eamon." Hughan set his cup down and came forward. "Good morning, Leon."

"Sire," Leon acknowledged, then turned to the Easter. "Lord Anastasius, Lord Feltumadas."

Eamon blinked, realizing then that there was a third man in the room. Like Anastasius, he was dressed in the blazing sun of the Easter armies. The man was young, likely in his late twenties, and looked uncannily like Anastasius.

"Will you join us, Leon?" Hughan asked.

"Certainly, sire." He relaxed a little and took a place at the table.

35

Eamon swallowed. The two Easters and Leon watched him darkly. Only Hughan smiled at him.

"How are you feeling, Eamon?" the King asked.

"Tired," Eamon answered truthfully. "I didn't sleep well." One of the Easters snorted, but Hughan nodded compassionately.

"I'm sorry to hear that. Few of us sleep well in these times." The King gestured the Easters to the table. "Please do sit, lords."

"You would have me sit with a Hand, Star of Brenuin?" Anastasius's voice was scathing; Eamon feared the man's anger at once. The second Easter said nothing, but Eamon was sure there would be no kinder response there.

"I would have you sit at a table with me and with my First Knight," Hughan answered, an undeniable strength in his voice.

With silent acquiescence the two Easters sat, and Hughan gestured for Eamon to do the same. He sat nervously next to Leon.

"I am sure that you have news of the city for us, Eamon," Hughan began. "May I ask you about it?"

"Yes," Eamon breathed. Everything about Hughan inspired loyalty and devotion. He would gladly kneel before such a man, and give his life for him without a thought. It was Hughan's justice and his compassion that made him strong.

He drew breath to speak. "The throned is culling the city, trying to rid it of his enemies. The pyres burn constantly." Eamon shuddered at the memory of them. "He does it because he fears you." Why else should the throned move with such a hand against the people of the River Realm?

"And what of Pinewood?" It was the younger Easter that spoke, his voice baleful in its anger. "Tell me of that, *Hand*."

"It was a mistake," Eamon answered carefully.

"Lord Feltumadas." Hughan spoke the name as a caution, but the Easter relented little.

"You know that he was in command of that mission, Star," he said angrily. "He is both our enemy and yours, and I cannot stand for him to be seated here. He is a Hand and a Hand cannot serve you."

"He is my First Knight," Hughan answered calmly.

Eamon sighed. "That may be so," he said, "but Lord Feltumadas is right: I served you most foully that day."

"And on many others," Leon added.

"I am sorry for it," Eamon whispered, meeting his gaze. "It is not the least of what I have failed to do."

"Then why did you come here?" Anastasius spoke now. His voice had a calculated tone that reminded him of Cathair. "Was it to renounce your cloak and city?" the man added sarcastically.

"I cannot renounce Dunthruik," Eamon replied. His answer surprised him, but it was true. He knew its streets, its people, its towering palaces. They all formed a part of him. "It is where I belong."

"A traitor by his own admission!" Feltumadas cried, casting Hughan a dreadful, triumphant glance. "Do not endure him, Star! Let Leon kill him where he sits." As Leon stiffened beside him, Eamon wondered if he would do it.

"This man went to Dunthruik at my request, Lord Feltumadas," Hughan spoke firmly, "and, whatever his misdeeds there, he has had my pardon and he has my faith."

The Easter grimaced. "Then perhaps it would be wise not to let him return to the city, Star."

"But I must return," Eamon interjected. "That is why I came."

"There is little logic in that, young Hand," Anastasius told him with a patronizing smile.

"I have been charged with it by the Mast… *throned*," Eamon faltered. Leon and Feltumadas stared at him; Anastasius simply watched him. He looked to Hughan for support. "If I do not do what he sent me to do, a hundred men, who have done nothing deserving such a punishment, will pay for my absence with their lives. I must be back in Dunthruik by nightfall on the twenty-seventh."

"Do you think you alone suffered losses at Pinewood?" Anastasius snapped. "What of the villagers that these men of yours slaughtered without mercy?"

Eamon gazed at him, appalled. How did the Easter know of that?

"You cannot let him return!" Feltumadas called, turning to Hughan.

Hughan motioned for silence. "What is your charge, Eamon?"

Eamon drew a deep breath. This, then, was the moment he had dreaded.

"He bade me to bring back to him the head of the commander of the Easters' army, as proof of my allegiance and a bartering piece by which to redeem the honour and lives of my men."

His words were met with a long silence. He saw Feltumadas staring at him in astonishment, as though his words were brazen beyond compare. Was there a touch of fear to the man's face?

"You were charged with taking back the head of my son?" Anastasius's voice was thick with anger. "You will not have it."

"Men will die if I don't," Eamon answered, knowing that the answer was not good enough.

"A hundred of the throned's men, yes," Anastasius retorted quietly. "And you?"

"No." Eamon felt ashamed.

"I am sorry to disappoint you, Lord Goodman, but I am rather attached to my head!" snarled Feltumadas. Eamon gasped, alarmed.

"I –"

"It's all right, Eamon." Hughan looked to the Easter lords, both red with anger. Eamon's task was horrific, and he saw how difficult a position it left Hughan in with his allies. Was that what the throned had intended? Were his words, and his presence, all that was needed? It might be enough to shatter alliances, if Hughan defended him.

"I would have you curb your tempers, lords," Hughan said.

"And give over my head?" Feltumadas asked acridly. "To salve the conscience of a man who has betrayed you?"

"We do not know that he tells the truth, sire," Leon added.

"You have no cause to trust this man, Star of Brenuin," Anastasius continued. "He has long persecuted your servants, as he himself admits. His charge is abhorrent, and he may well have been sent with designs on your own life. If you will take my advice," he said, glancing coolly at Eamon, "you will have him killed."

"If that is what the King wills, then I will go willingly to it," Eamon answered hotly. His words surprised Anastasius.

"I trust this man, lords," Hughan said, "and I do not decree death lightly to any man. Neither will I condone the sending of Lord Feltumadas's head back to my enemy, so be at peace." Eamon felt his hope falling – without a head, his men were lost. "Perhaps, however, we may find a resolution," Hughan added. "I would be grateful if you would inform Lords Ithel and Ylonous of this matter, and return to me."

"Very well, Star of Brenuin." Anastasius rose from the table and his son followed him. Both bowed to Hughan, and saluted Leon cordially. Eamon felt reduced to nothing as, without glancing at him, they left. After a few quiet words with Hughan, Leon went also.

Eamon sat uncomfortably in the following silence. Hughan cupped his drink in his hands again. He watched it for a few moments. At last he set it down and rose. Eamon saw a thin silver circlet in the King's hair. Awe washed over him anew.

"Will you walk with me, Eamon?"

"Yes."

Hughan moved from the tent. Hesitating, Eamon followed him. Hughan stopped and turned to him.

"I asked you to walk with me, First Knight," he said. "Will you not walk by me?"

Trembling, Eamon met the King's gaze. "Do you not fear me? Do you not fear that what the Easters say is true?"

"That you have been sent to harm me?" Hughan shook his head. "No. I do not fear you, Eamon; I love you."

Eamon was astounded. Tears blinded him. "How can you love me?"

"You are my First Knight, Eamon," Hughan countered. "More than that, and long before we set our feet to the paths laid out for us, you were my friend. You are that still."

"Eben was Ede's First Knight and friend." Eamon shook his head again in disbelief. "Just like him, Hughan, *I betrayed you*."

"I do not deny it, and I will not deny that there were times when I feared that Edelred had truly broken you." Eamon saw gravity on the King's face. He imagined the fear that had been in the King's heart. "Mathaiah sent news to me during the winter."

Eamon lowered his head in shame. "Everything I have done since I went to that city has been against you."

"No." Hughan spoke with surprising firmness. "You have been a better servant for me in Dunthruik than you know, or than the throned would have you believe. Every kindness that you have done to any man was a service to me. Striving against your own doubts and fears was a service to me. Sending Lillabeth was a service to me. Going to Mathaiah in the Pit was a service to me."

Eamon's eyes widened. "How do you know about that?"

"I heard you singing," he said simply. "Like Mathaiah, I always believed that you would see clearly again."

"I am sorry that my clear sight comes so late."

"But it has come."

Eamon looked at him in silence. Then, at Hughan's gesture, he stepped to the King's side.

They walked together. Eamon felt as though every man watched him. But the soldiers bowed to the King, greeting him as he passed.

As they went by a group of Easters a man started forward, a curious look on his face. Eamon gasped, recognizing him at once: the Easter who had spared him at Pinewood.

"Good morning, Star of Brenuin." The Easter bowed deeply to Hughan.

"Good morning, Lord Ithel," Hughan answered.

"I can tarry but a moment – Lord Anastasius wishes to see me – but I must ask, Bright One: who is it that walks with you?" The Easter looked intently at Eamon.

"His name is Eamon Goodman."

The Easter's dark eyes took in Eamon for a long moment. Then he shook his head and laughed – a piercing sound that broke through the morning air and made Eamon jump.

Chapter II

"You take me by surprise, Lord Goodman!" the Easter said. Eamon was thrown by the use of his title. The Easter smiled broadly at Hughan. "Star, you must know that the man walking with you was born of folly and courage. It was he who braved our archers at Pinewood, and all to rescue one injured man! In his bravery he is worthy of your banner, and it pleases me to see him here."

"He is of my banner," Hughan answered with a small smile. "He is my First Knight."

Ithel laughed again and thrust out his hand. He took Eamon's and clasped it. "I am glad to meet you in better circumstances, First Knight," he said. "I thought it strange that a Hand should dare so much for so little. Now I understand it. What became of your injured man?"

"He is faring better, Lord Ithel," Eamon answered.

"He survived to reach Dunthruik?" The Easter was astonished.

"By some luck, yes," Eamon answered.

The Easter looked briefly across at Hughan. "I find it more likely that he reached it by the prayers of a King's man." He released Eamon's hand and stepped back. "I am glad that I spared you."

"So am I," Eamon replied. He was relieved that at least one of the strange men in Hughan's camp should smile at him.

They exchanged farewells and continued on their way. Eamon saw dozens of Easters, some of them likely men whom he had met at Pinewood, watching him as he passed in the King's company.

"You have many Easters here," he observed. He remembered Cathair saying that Hughan had been in Istanaria garnering support from the Easters during the winter and that there had been a failed attempt on the King's life.

"They are my allies," Hughan answered. "And they are valuable. They pressed in over the eastern border just before the winter, drawing many of Edelred's men towards it, which allowed us to move more freely both on the East and West Bank. The Easters built the bridge on the River here, and every day they send us more supplies. Such things are hard to come by in these months."

Eamon nodded, marvelling at the fruit that the King's winter work had borne.

Hughan continued: "There are wayfarers all over the River Realm, but I have long known that we do not have the strength to take Dunthruik alone. It took a good deal of negotiating to gain their aid, but it has been well worth the effort. In part, the Seven Sons feel responsible for the throned's mastery and hope that, by aiding me, they will atone for it."

"What part did they play?" Eamon asked.

"He came from Istanaria long ago."

Eamon fell silent.

Hughan led him to a small tent. "Come inside," he said.

There was an occupied bed inside the tent. An empty chair stood by it. Hughan led Eamon to the bedside. Eamon gasped.

Giles lay there, quietly watching them as they approached. Eamon felt every muscle in his limbs tense to run. He trembled with the memory of what he had done to this man.

"Good morning, Giles," Hughan said.

"Good morning, sire," he answered, smiling and rising to his feet. The big man's voice was strangely gentle and he bowed with difficulty.

Overcome with sorrow, Eamon stepped forward. "Giles, I'm so sorry –"

Giles looked at him curiously. "Who is this, sire?"

"His name is Eamon," Hughan answered. "He was there when you were hurt."

"Ah!" Giles nodded and turned to smile at him. Eamon wanted to weep. "I am getting better. Hughan has been very kind. I don't remember much of what happened to me, but perhaps you can tell me?"

Eamon stared, dumbstruck. "You... you don't remember?"

"I don't remember many things about before," Giles answered. "I remember being hurt in a battle, on the north borders. Near..." He fumbled. "Galithia. That was maybe three years ago. That's where I met Hughan. I remember Galithia." He frowned. "I'm afraid I don't remember you. Have we met before?"

"Yes."

"Did I hurt you?" Giles paused reflectively. "I'm sorry, if I did."

"Thank you." Eamon could barely comprehend what he was hearing. "Giles, I… You have to know that I… I did this to you."

Giles looked at him curiously. "Did what?"

Eamon glanced guiltily at his hands. "You don't remember anything because of me. I did this to you. I'm sorry."

"Did I make you angry?" Giles smiled. "People tell me things, sometimes, about before. Most of them seem to agree that I often made people angry."

"You did, but I shouldn't have… Giles, I am so sorry."

"Were we friends before?" The question was sudden; Eamon thought he caught a glimpse of the man's old suspicion.

"I'm afraid that we weren't," he answered slowly.

"And was there a reason for that?"

"Yes."

"Well I don't remember it!" Giles laughed out loud. Eamon offered a timid smile.

"I will forget it," he said. Relief washed over him.

"Good. Why are you wearing black?" Giles asked.

"I came from Dunthruik. I was serving there."

"Oh! What is Dunthruik like?"

Eamon looked to Hughan. "You must have many things that you need to do," he said. "May I stay with Giles for a while?"

The King watched with a smile. "Of course."

Eamon stayed with Giles for a long time. He told the man about Dunthruik, about the towers, the city streets, and the Four Quarters, about the Hands and the Gauntlet. Giles listened intensely and asked questions about almost everything.

"Are you a Hand?" he asked at last.

"Yes," Eamon told him.

"But you serve Hughan?"

"Yes."

Giles nodded, as though the idea was entirely acceptable. Eamon laughed.

During the morning, Ma Mendel passed to bring Eamon his gloves. She stayed until he had put them on before leaving to tend to other business. A servant, sent by the King, brought them food at midday, and they ate together. Giles spoke about the borders and the cities that he remembered: crowded streets full of markets and small, lithe ships that danced along the coast to trade with the River Realm and the other merchant states. He told Eamon about the long years of unrest and war at the north borders, and about the day when he had first met the Gauntlet in battle. The enemy had surrounded a convoy of wood and demanded it. When the merchants refused, the Gauntlet had destroyed the line and taken everything.

"It's mountainous country there," Giles said, "and not easy terrain for a fight. I think I killed a lot of men that day." He frowned and flexed his big hands, his fingers still showing good memory of holding a sword. But the gesture seemed strange to him; he shook it away. "There were many battles. I was injured in one and that's when I met Hughan. I don't know why he was there." He lowered his voice. "They say he's a king. Sometimes I'm not sure if I believe that – or if he should be King." He looked curiously at Eamon. "What do you think?"

Eamon met his gaze. "I believe he is the King."

Giles fell asleep during the early afternoon and Eamon sat beside him. Speaking with the man was a humbling experience. He wondered how it was that Giles had any part of his mind left after what he had done to him. Eamon gazed down at his hands, remembering the red light. Surely only Hughan could have brought the broken man back from the brink to which he had pressed him?

He fell asleep until a noise drew him back. Through sleep-fogged eyes he saw a young woman enter the tent. A moment later he recognized her.

"Lillabeth!" he breathed, rising quietly. She could not have reached the camp much before him.

"Mr Goodman," she greeted, and smiled.

"How are you?" Eamon asked, feeling the question was woefully inadequate.

"Safe," she told him. He watched her for a moment, and then she spoke again. "I came to find you. Lady Connara wants to see you."

Eamon gasped. "Aeryn is here?"

"Yes, sir."

"Don't call me sir!" Eamon answered. He noticed a glint of silver on her hand. "What is that?"

"A ring, sir," she began – but before she could finish Eamon took her hand. Trembling, he stared at the silver ring. It looked familiar, so familiar…

"Who gave you this?" he whispered, but he knew the answer as well as he knew the ring. He had but two days ago pressed its fellow into Mathaiah's hand.

"My husband."

Eamon reeled.

Of course she was Mathaiah's wife – how could he have been so dull as not to have guessed it? Had he but had the eyes to see past his own tempests he would have seen long ago that his ward adored her.

He had condemned Mathaiah to the Pit.

Guilt quivered through him. "Lillabeth –"

Mindful of Giles, she caught his hand and led him out of the tent. The setting sun covered their faces. Eamon began shivering.

Lillabeth pressed his hands between hers. "Please, Mr Goodman," she whispered, her voice alive with urgency. "How is he? How is Mathaiah?"

"Lillabeth, I…" Her eyes searched his. Eamon struggled to find words that might strengthen her. "He knows that you are safe. I am… I am so proud of him, Lillabeth. He has stood firm and true, even against the throned himself." He paused, and swallowed. "They took him to the Pit."

Lillabeth clenched her eyes. "Oh Mathaiah –"

"He is not dead," Eamon hastened. "I went to him. I saw him two days ago. He is alive; they cannot break him."

"You went to him…" Awe filled her face. "You… went down… to the Pit?"

"Yes."

"For him?"

"Yes."

She stared, stunned.

Eamon took her hand. "When I go back to the city I mean to free him. I'll bring him to you," he said. "I swear it."

"No, Eamon." Lillabeth offered him a sad, quivering smile. "Do not swear it. Do not bind yourself to sorrow. He… he may not live."

There was wisdom in her words. He tried to hear it.

"Very well; I'll not swear it. But do not resign yourself to sorrow – he may not die."

Lillabeth nodded. As she pressed tears from her eyes she pressed her other hand across her belly, and shuddered.

The gesture shook him with the force of deafening thunder. She had been so pale and weary when he took her from Alessia's house…

Seizing the girl's hand once more he looked deep into her eyes. "Lillabeth?"

She seemed to know his question before he asked it. There was no need for a word to be spoken. She nodded.

Joy and sorrow pulsed through him with wild force. Before him stood Mathaiah's wife, the one who would bear Mathaiah's child. He had no words to say.

Footsteps passed nearby; he became aware of soldiers. Turning, he saw Lord Feltumadas. The Easter glared at him.

"Lord Feltumadas," Eamon said carefully, and bowed low.

"Why aren't you being guarded?" the Easter demanded.

"I do not need guarding, my lord."

Feltumadas came forward, his face dark. "I would guard my tone, if I were you, *Hand*." His eyes fell on Lillabeth. She had shrunk to

Eamon's side at his fierce approach. Feltumadas jeered. "Here less than a day, and already you procure yourself a wench?"

Eamon stared incredulously. "I am accustomed to hearing such things in Dunthruik, my lord, but scarcely thought that I should hear them from the lips of one allied to the King!"

"I scarcely thought to find the Star of Brenuin allying himself to a treacherous slave of the Usurper," Feltumadas countered.

"That's enough."

Eamon looked up as Lord Ithel walked towards them.

Feltumadas scowled. "Tell me that the truth is otherwise than as I see it!" he hissed.

Ithel fixed him with a firm gaze. "I shall not gainsay you, but do not speak from rage."

Feltumadas shot Eamon a dark look, and laughed disparagingly. "My head!" he exclaimed. Glowering, he stalked away.

Eamon watched him go, blood returning to his veins.

"I apologize to you both," Ithel said.

"Thank you, my lord," Lillabeth whispered.

Eamon glanced at Ithel. "Lord Feltumadas is the commander of the Easter army?"

"He answers to his father," Ithel sighed. "His uncle commanded it before him. Lord Feltumadas was in charge of a cavalry banner. Not two weeks ago there was a battle, and Feltumadas was surprised and in danger. His uncle led the charge that rescued him, but lost his life. Lord Anastasius, rightfully, put his son in his brother's place. Feltumadas has a fine mind but a grieved temper – he was as fond of his uncle as of his own brothers. It was a Hand who killed his uncle." Ithel offered Eamon an apologetic smile. "Feltumadas killed the Hand."

Eamon's blood ran cold. "Thank you for your intervention."

"I know my brother well," Ithel replied.

Ithel excused himself and returned to his duties. Eamon turned back to Lillabeth. As the Easters retreated, she drew herself upright and let out a long breath.

"Are you well?"

Lillabeth nodded. "They remind me of the Hands," she answered with a small smile. Eamon laughed; he had thought the same.

Lillabeth began leading the way across the camp.

"Sir," she said, "have you any news of Lady Turnholt?"

Eamon felt his face darkening. "I'm sorry, Lillabeth," he said at last. "I do not."

She did not ask again.

They passed the King's tent – Eamon wondered if he heard raised voices within – before arriving at another. It was also blue, rimmed with silver, a banner waving at its top. Several guards stood outside, and they looked at him suspiciously as they approached. On speaking with Lillabeth, however, they permitted entrance.

The tent was large, much like the King's, and a figure sat at a desk within it. She was writing with a gracious and steady hand.

"Lady Connara," Lillabeth began, curtseying as the lady turned. "I've brought Lord Goodman."

"Thank you, Lillabeth," Aeryn answered, rising. Eamon stared, marvelling at both her beauty and her grace.

"You are truly worthy to be a queen," he breathed as she approached.

She took his hands. "You've grown strangely eloquent since you went away," she told him.

"I wasn't before?"

"I had forgotten it," Aeryn conceded.

They embraced and, for a moment, Eamon imagined they were back in Edesfield, exulting in some petty victory at the Star. But when he opened his eyes they were still in the tent, and the victory was far away.

"By your leave, my lady." A nod from her, and Lillabeth left.

"Come and sit down," Aeryn told him. Encouraged by her gentleness, Eamon followed.

They sat together and she watched him for a long time. "I don't believe it," she said at last, and shook her head. "You're a Hand."

Eamon blushed. He wished that he could tear the cloak off and burn it. Aeryn touched his arm in comfort.

"It's all right."

"I don't know how Hughan can see fit to trust me," Eamon told her. How could anybody trust him?

"But he does."

"What if he's making a mistake?"

"He isn't."

"How do you know?"

Aeryn smiled at him, and he tried to let himself fall into the two blue pools of confidence that were her eyes. But he could not. Looking at her, he suddenly remembered Alessia.

"*If you ever loved me you will hear me now…*"

He turned sharply away.

"Eamon?" Aeryn touched his arm again. "Eamon, what is it?"

He drew a shuddering breath; he had to stay calm. It was not Aeryn's fault…

But his hurt would not be quelled. "They know everything!" he cried at last. "The throned knows everything. If I don't take back Feltumadas's head he'll kill every man who has ever served under me. And how does the throned know everything?" He grew quiet and looked away. "I let myself be seduced, Aeryn. I let myself believe that a woman… *loved* me, and I told her everything. *I had to.*" His voice shook. "You have to understand I… I couldn't bear it alone. I had already lost Mathaiah." Ravenous grief rose inside him.

Aeryn pressed his arm.

"Now Mathaiah is in the Pit," Eamon wept, "and I learn that his wife and unborn child are here. For my treachery, she will be widowed and her child fatherless. And I have to go back to Dunthruik, where I can bring only death, and I have failed the King." Sobs swallowed him. He plunged his face into his hands. "I was supposed to be the First Knight, Aeryn. First *blight* is more like it!"

"You have not failed the King," Aeryn told him. "He loves you. He trusts you."

He tried to believe her. It was true, wasn't it? Hadn't Hughan shown how true it was?

It grew dark outside. After a time, Aeryn rose.

"Do you want to walk?"

Eamon looked at her. It was a question he had often asked her when they were young and she was upset. She smiled. He nodded.

They left the tent. The cool evening air soothed his face; he was glad that none could see the grief marks there. Aeryn led him through the quieter parts of the camp, where most men were absorbed in finding supper. For a long time they walked in silence.

"What was her name?" she asked at last.

"Alessia. Alessia Turnholt." A shiver ran through him. He sought her gaze. "How could you not know her name?"

"I knew her name," Aeryn answered, "but I had yet to hear it spoken by one who knows her."

"I knew her," Eamon whispered. His heart began to ache.

"Did you love her?"

He didn't answer – he didn't know.

Aeryn listened to his silence, and understood it. She slipped her hand into his. "What was she like?"

For a long time he could not answer her. "She was beautiful, Aeryn," he said at last. "Oh, she was dawn in a dark land, dawn to me." He thought longingly of Alessia's long hair, her deep eyes, her silken touch –

Her tears. Her treachery.

"I wish I had never told her!" he snarled.

There was a flash of bright light against the eastern sky, followed by a loud crack. Startled, they both looked towards it.

"What was that?"

"I don't know."

They watched the sky together for a few moments. The echo of the sound died away into the distance.

Aeryn pressed his hand. "Have you heard from Ladomer recently?"

"He was posted to Dunthruik not long after I arrived."

Aeryn looked at him in surprise. "What for?"

"He has become the Right Hand's lieutenant," Eamon answered. "He's always carrying paper."

"I always imagined him becoming a Hand, not a paper-boy," Aeryn mused. She looked up at him with a smile. "He was certainly the more likely candidate for being Handed, out of the pair of you."

"That's what I always told him," Eamon agreed with a laugh. "Did you ever try to warn him?" he asked suddenly.

"About joining the Gauntlet?" Aeryn's brow furrowed. "I tried," she whispered. "He didn't seem to understand. Maybe he didn't want to. He told me not to worry myself with wayfarer talk. Something about what he said frightened me." She drew a deep breath. "I never spoke to him about it after that. I think it was because he frightened me that I didn't speak to you sooner. You are so alike... I was worried what you would think, of it and of me."

Eamon matched her gaze. "I'm sorry. I doubt that I would have had kind words for you then."

They paused for a moment by a tall tree. Eamon heard the tributary running nearby in the dark. The camp was lit like a field of blossoming stars. Indistinct calls ran along the more distant River water. He remembered Hughan's words from that morning, and wondered if another convoy of supplies was coming into the camp. Where did the Easters manage to find the supplies at this time of the year?

"I'm glad that you came," Aeryn said quietly. "I'm sorry for what you've been through in Dunthruik for us. After all that, you're still you."

"It was a near thing," Eamon confided.

Suddenly they heard cries and looked up. A group of guards surged through the camp towards them. The men – a mix of wayfarers and Easters – bore torches.

Eamon looked across at Aeryn in surprise. "What's happening?"

"I don't know," she began, looking as surprised as he felt. As she spoke, the men reached them and nocked arrows to their bows.

"Step away from her, *Hand!*" snarled one.

Eamon and Aeryn stared.

"I'm sorry?"

"You heard me, bloody trumped-up Glove! Step away or we will loose!"

Eamon stepped to the side. Bewildered, Aeryn walked to the soldiers. One snatched her and pushed her behind them. They demanded to know if she was hurt.

"No –"

"Give yourself up, Hand!"

"Give myself up?"

"*Do it now!*"

"I give myself up," Eamon said incredulously. Hadn't he already given himself up? He felt the urge to point this out, but the glinting arrowheads suggested this might not be wise.

A band of men surged forward and bound him. They seemed afraid to touch him.

"Stop!" Aeryn cried. "Whose authority do you have for this?"

If they answered her he did not hear them do so; she was bustled away to safety and he could not see more past the men who bound him. The ropes pulled tight. One man struck him.

"I'm hardly resisting!" he cried, but they didn't hear him. He was hit again.

The men dragged him forward and took him to the heart of the camp. They hauled him bodily to the King's tent, and hurled him inside.

Hughan was not there, but Eamon did not go ungreeted. Anastasius stood by the long table, his shadow cast eerily on the ground by the brazier. His eyes flashed with anger.

"Lord Anastasius," Eamon began.

"You treacherous, black-clad bastard!" The Easter came forward and struck him hard across the face.

"What is the meaning of this?" Eamon yelled.

"I told him to have you guarded!" Anastasius exploded. Eamon cowered before his fury. "I told him that you could not be trusted and that you were here for evil purpose. I counselled your execution and he defended you. Now perhaps you will get what you deserve."

"What have I done?" Eamon demanded. His head swimming, he could barely focus his eyes on the man.

Anastasius stared icily at him. "How very typical of a Hand," he spat. "What have you done? You spend the whole day harping on the value of the lives of your men, and then, in a moment, you obliterate thirty of mine!"

Eamon's heart slowed sickeningly. "What?"

Anastasius struck him again. Blood trickled down his face.

"You dare deny it?" the Easter cried. "I saw you with my own eyes."

"What did I do?" Eamon cried.

"You knew that men were bringing supplies over the bridge tonight," Anastasius howled. "You killed them all when you destroyed it!"

Eamon stared. He remembered the River bridge. It was vital to the camp's logistics.

Suddenly he remembered the light and crack that he had heard with Aeryn.

His stomach churned. He looked at Anastasius and shook his head.

"I-I knew nothing of it," he stammered. "Of this charge, my lord, I am innocent!"

Anastasius glowered. "Even the Star of Brenuin has not the power to make you innocent of this, Hand. He is coming here and he will denounce you, renounce you, and cast your corpse back to the filth-ridden city from whence it came. I will see to it!"

Eamon stared in terror. He had done nothing. Anastasius towered over him. It was only the King's edict that kept the Easter from exacting the vengeance he violently desired to take.

The voice in his mind exulted in his fear. *Your faith is broken, Eben's son!*

And, as Eamon trembled and waited for the King, he believed it.

CHAPTER III

Blood trickled down his face. His heart pounded. Anastasius stood over him, a dark edifice, his green eyes glinting fiercely, forbidding defiance.

Eamon matched that glare. The more he considered the situation, the more ridiculous it seemed to him. He had done nothing and could prove that he had been nowhere near the bridge. Could they cast doubt on him when they found that he had been with Aeryn? And yet…

How was it that he had been seen?

Eamon fixed the Easter with a sudden and suspicious glance. The Easters had built the bridge. What if – however unlikely it might be – the bridge had been poorly made? What if the fault belonged to the Easters and they were simply looking for someone to blame? They distrusted and hated him – perhaps they meant to scapegoat him.

Though he knew little about Anastasius, already he felt sure the man was no liar. The smouldering Easter lord was an ally of the King – Hughan would not ally himself to evil men. If Anastasius *said* that he had seen Eamon destroy the bridge, it would be the truth… but how could it be?

Whatever the case, Hughan could not choose to sacrifice his alliance with the Easters by believing a Hand over an Easter lord. Eamon and Anastasius both knew it, just as they both knew that the price of Eamon's treachery would be death. Anastasius sneered with triumphant disgust.

Run, the voice told him. *Break your bonds, strike down this witless fool, and return to me. I will give you the strength, Eben's son.* The words made him shiver. *I will show you mercy.*

Eamon shook his head. He felt his vision flickering as though he neared the plain – he would *not* go.

"The King's grace protects me!" He did not care who heard him. "You can no longer counsel me, voice of Edelred!" He called it by the name that Hughan had given it. Though there was treachery afoot, he had not committed it. There was no need to run; he would face the King.

The voice fell silent, as though it reviled being recognized and loathed Eamon's submission to the King. Then it was gone.

Eamon looked up with clearer sight to see Anastasius again. The Easter watched him still, but now Eamon felt able to bear the accusatory stare.

He heard cries outside. As men passed into the tent, the smell of burning wood wafted in on the wind.

It was then that Hughan came, wet and muddied, smoke caught in his clothes. As he saw Eamon, bound and kneeling before Anastasius, anger filled his face. Eamon bade his heart hold firm.

"This is the man responsible, Star of Brenuin." Anastasius sounded calmer. His statement was presented factually to the King. "I saw him with my own eyes."

Hughan shot his ally a fearsome look. Anastasius received it, barely flinching, and then both men looked at Eamon, the lord with anger and the King with unreadable blue eyes. Eamon pinned all his hope on the latter.

"Follow me, Eamon," Hughan said, his voice quiet.

Why hasn't he unbound you? He thinks you guilty, Eben's son!

Eamon turned from it. Steadying himself, he rose to his feet and followed Hughan out of the tent. Anastasius stayed close behind him.

The King led him into the night air. The reek of burning was strong now. Eamon was struck by a sudden, painful memory of the pyre where Aeryn's father had been bound. He remembered the feel of the faggots in his hands.

Not far away he saw light. Hughan led him towards it. He followed until the King halted but paces from the site of the destruction with which he was charged. Eamon stopped and stared.

Where the bridge – a broad line of planked and anchored boats – had stood but hours before, Eamon saw ruins and flames. Broken timbers lay everywhere, shattered as though a tremendous force had ripped them apart. The spokes of a cartwheel lay forlorn on the far bank. Flames still burned on the splintered wood, and screams and moans filled the air, for the banks were flooded not just with water but with men. Some bore torches, necessary now that the initial blaze had died down. Others stood half in the freezing water, dragging out men who had fallen from the pontoon. Men lay shrieking and burned on the bank; others lay pale and still. They would never call again. Eamon guessed that a number had been dragged away by the River, though he could not guess how many. He saw the wretched body of a horse snagged in a tangle of trees and branches, its mane bloodied and blackened. His stomach turned.

He looked back to the rescue efforts in the water and saw a man surging up out of it, dragging with him the broken body of a soldier. Eamon could not help but stare as he recognized the rescuer: Feltumadas. His dark hair was slicked back with sweat and muddy water.

The Easter lord passed the soldier he was half-carrying to one of Hughan's men, then waded back into the water, calling for help as he spotted more men struggling in the cold.

Eamon's being was filled with the howls of the wounded, the smell of smouldering flesh and wood, and another bitter smell which he did not know. They choked him.

For a moment he doubted himself. What if the voice of Edelred had usurped him utterly, even just for a moment…?

No. He would not have destroyed the bridge – he could not and did not do it. As his racing thoughts stilled he felt Anastasius glowering. Dimly, he became aware of Hughan watching him.

"Did you do this, Eamon?" The King's voice was soft, neither accusing nor excusing him.

Eamon turned to look at him.

"No, sire." He did not falter. "I did not."

There was a long silence. Anastasius watched him with a glare that might shred flesh, but he would not retract what he had said. He had told the truth.

Hughan held his gaze for what seemed an interminably long time. Eamon matched it, feeling as though the King was searching and testing his soul. Doubtless Hughan had also heard – and maybe seen – that a Hand had destroyed the bridge, and that the only Hand in the camp was also the King's First Knight.

As First Knight, Eamon was answerable to the King alone. Still, he was painfully aware of the men on the banks staring at him and his heavy black cloak.

"Murdering, black-robed bastard!" one screamed.

"Murderer!"

Others joined the chorus until the air was rife with cursing. Eamon could not hide from the words; each utterance fell upon him like a blow. He tried to steady himself against them. Every man believed that he was guilty, that his innocence was inconceivable. He had been tainted by Dunthruik and could never be redeemed.

"Death to you, and your bastard house!"

"Enough!" Hughan's voice cut across the air, his eyes filled with anger. "Wish death on no man's house. Even if he is guilty, his sons are not."

Silence fell. None answered the King.

Awed, Eamon held his breath as the King turned to him.

"I did not do this, Hughan," he whispered. "I swear it to you."

At last, the look in Hughan's eyes softened. Eamon breathed out in relief. For the King, his word was enough.

"You believe him?" Anastasius stood, ashen with anger. "You believe him!"

"Yes, Lord Anastasius. I do."

"He was seen at the bridge by dozens of men – scores of men…
yet you believe *him*?"

Eamon turned to him. "You question the King?" he cried. The
words had left his mouth before he even knew what he was saying.

"Peace, Eamon," Hughan told him softly. "It is his right to speak
just as it is yours."

Eamon hung his head in disbelief. The throned would never
offer such words. In Dunthruik, Anastasius would have easily lost
his life for such insolence.

"And I speak this," Anastasius answered grimly. "He is a Hand.
He is responsible for what has happened here. Perhaps you have no
care for the lives of your allies," he added darkly, "but you should
have a care for your own dead, Star of Brenuin."

Eamon turned cold. He was a divisive element in the King's
camp. While he remained in it, he was a threat to Hughan's alliance
with the Easters.

Leon appeared, wet and stinking, at Hughan's side. Eamon
marvelled that the men with the power of command had themselves
been aiding the dead and wounded. He could not imagine Cathair
or Ashway doing the like.

"You sent for me, sire?"

"Yes, thank you." Hughan's voice was quiet. He and Anastasius
watched each other. "Please escort Eamon to some secure quarters."

"Yes, sire." Leon did not sound enthused with his charge.

Anastasius came forward suddenly. "He will be bound," he
snarled. "He will be guarded. He will be killed if he so much as
steps out of place."

Hughan looked across at him. "Eamon, will you agree to be
bound and guarded?"

"Yes," Eamon replied, shaking in the face of Anastasius's anger.
"I will, if you ask it."

"I ask it," Hughan answered. The firelight touched their faces,
but Eamon felt chilled to his core.

"I will go with Leon," he said quietly.

Hughan laid his hand on Eamon's shoulder for a moment. "I promise you that you will not be harmed, First Knight," he said, and looked firmly at the Easter lord. Anastasius bristled.

"Come with me," Leon said.

Eamon nodded to the King and then allowed Leon to lead him away from the hellish remains of the bridge. Anastasius raised violent protests behind them. He wondered what Hughan could ever say to allay that anger.

As they walked he knew that every man they passed watched him, some murderously. It seemed to make no difference whether he strode through the streets of Dunthruik or whether he was led through the heart of the King's camp: looks of anger, jealousy, suspicion, and fear followed him. The sensation gnawed at him.

He glanced at Leon, who was drenched and muddied up to his shoulders. Eamon wished the man would say something to him – anything. Away from Hughan's support and even Anastasius's outrage, his confidence quailed.

Leon led him to the tent where he had slept the night before. Guards approached it – doubtless his guards. Their number was now greater – and grimmer – than it had been before.

"One will sit inside with you," Leon said quietly. His voice was hoarse.

Eamon nodded. He did not speak for fear of betraying the terror that marked his limbs.

"The others will wait outside. Stay here until the King sends for you."

Eamon swallowed. Leon's civility chilled him. He felt the man's sharp eyes driving into him. Did Leon think he was guilty?

Leon escorted him inside and gestured to the bed. Eamon went across to it, his hands still bound. Still, he counted himself fortunate that he was to be permitted to rest there, rather than being chained to the tent's central pillar for the night.

Another soldier, this an Easter, entered. Leon acknowledged him, bade Eamon a curt good night, and left.

CHAPTER III

Eamon stood for a few moments, staring at his guard. The man was tall and slim, with an angered look. Could he trust such a character not to kill him in his sleep?

The King's protection was over him. Surely, as long as the King's name held, none would dare to touch him or do him harm?

He offered the Easter a tired smile, uncomfortably twisted his bound hands, and tried to settle to sleep.

CHAPTER IV

He heard crying. While not broken, the voice was not as defiant as it had been when it had last touched his ears. It was burdened with the unyielding press of pain.

He was on the plain. Mist moved round him, obscuring his sight yet sharpening none of his senses in return. There were eyes in the dark, foes in the mere, watching him. A voice spoke to him, but he could not hear it clearly. There was no light.

Shadows passed; some jeered. One wore his own face, like a mask.

The mist parted, revealing a line of broken, bleeding bodies. They were cadets and soldiers, each familiar to him. As he gaped at them, a flaming river appeared and swallowed them, whirlpooling them away with the blackened remains of a bridge.

He reeled before that churning tide. The distant, crying voice was Mathaiah's.

He woke with a terrible start, drenched and shuddering. He murmured a name and reached out for something that was not there: her hand. He fell still in the heavy dark.

She was not there. She would never be again.

Somewhere nearby, he heard his guard breathing – the quiet breathing of an attentive watchman. He was glad the man could not see his face, for hot tears streamed down it. His hands throbbing against his bonds, he drew them up to where he had once kept the heart of the King.

He had grown accustomed to dreadful dreams, but this one lingered. His face marred with tears, he waited for the dawn.

The light outside grew grey. He did not know how long he lay there, clutching his breast and staring at the doorway – a threshold that he could not cross. His whole world was held in walls of canvas. In the half-light he saw the guard watching him. What thoughts passed behind the man's steady face?

You can discover them, the voice urged.

He rolled over and clenched his eyes shut. He would not breach the man. His stomach turned at the thought of it. He never wanted to breach any man again.

But you will, Eben's son. And you will glorify me.

At last he heard movement outside but still he did not move. He did not want to get out of bed until he was sure that he was being summoned. He did not want to face his guard. He could speak no word without it being misconstrued.

The man who came for him was not Leon. His face was grim. Neither fact was encouraging.

The man looked at the guard. The Easter rose to his feet. Eamon noticed with a start that it was a different soldier from the one who had watched over him the night before. How could he not have heard a change in the watch?

"Has he given you any trouble?" The newcomer's voice was gravelled, as though he had not slept.

"No, sir."

The man looked keenly across at Eamon. "Follow me, Lord Goodman."

Eamon drew a deep breath and followed his escort.

They went again to the King's tent, Eamon conspicuous in his black trappings. He looked up at the fading stars and felt his blood run cold: it was the twenty-third of February.

In silence he followed the man into Hughan's tent, where a row of stony faces awaited him, all in the varying colours of the sun-marked Easter lords. He recognized Anastasius, Feltumadas, and Ithel – the former two struck him with a lethal glare.

Hughan stood at the head of the group, his face stern. He

did not smile as he met Eamon's gaze. Eamon grew even more uncomfortable. Most of those in the tent were strangers to him, and Eamon was alarmed to see that some of them shook as he was brought before them. He suspected the source of their fear.

His escort dismissed, Eamon stood, alone, before the enemies of the throned.

Silently, he bowed down on one knee before Hughan. All words left him, but one thing he knew: he would not say that he was guilty.

"Sire," he breathed.

The King was before him. "Will you stand, Eamon?"

Eamon looked up. Something about the King's face induced a sweeping wave of terror. "Is this a trial?" His voice was faint even in his own ears.

"It is a hearing," Hughan answered. He nodded encouragingly, and Eamon rose slowly.

The King turned to the other men. "I know that this exercise will seem fruitless to many of you," he began. "To most, this man was seen working treachery against us and that should be reason enough for me to command his death without delay."

Eamon could see Anastasius bristling angrily and wondered how many times the Easter had brought those very words against Hughan during the night. He held his breath, as though his life hung by a thread.

Hughan's firm gaze passed over them. "To all of you, this man is a Hand, and a Hand alone. But still would I have you hear his words, treating them as you would treat the word of any man here." The King turned to him. Eamon's heart raced. "Eamon, tell us where you were yesterday evening."

"I was with Giles during the day. Yesterday evening, I was walking with Lady Connara."

Shocked looks passed through the gathered men.

"What business does a Hand have with the Star's bride?" Feltumadas spat indignantly, his gaze smouldering.

Eamon drew a deep breath. Feltumadas's powerful gaze drilled into him. Meeting it, he knew that much rested on his answer.

"She knew me long before I first knelt to the throned," he answered softly.

"Your queen would count a Hand among her friends?" Anastasius's chilling voice rose above the outrage of the crowd.

"He is my friend also," Hughan told him evenly.

Anastasius gave no reply.

King and Easter watched each other for a fractious moment. Panic welled inside Eamon.

"My lords," he hastened, "any bonds of friendship between Lady Connara and me, or between me and the King himself, do not cloud this matter. That I was with Lady Connara is proof that I was not near the bridge and proof that I am innocent of the charges you bring against me."

"Innocent?" Feltumadas answered with a snapping sneer. "Yes, innocent. As this is a 'hearing', let us also hear this man's opinion." He matched gazes with one of the unknown Easters by him. "Is this the man that destroyed the bridge?"

"Yes, my lord."

"And what did you see?"

"Red light, and an explosion, lord," the soldier answered. He shook. "I was struck by debris when the bridge was hit, lord. Many with me were hit, too. While I was tending to them, I saw a man dressed in black running from the River to the camp." The man faltered.

"And of what stature was this black-clad man?" Feltumadas asked, staring acridly at Hughan. "Was it, by any chance, equivalent to that of the man before you?"

The soldier nodded. "It was, noble lord."

Eamon gaped open-mouthed. "Lord Feltumadas –"

"And you," Feltumadas continued, calling forward another man; "what did you see?"

"I saw him going to the River just before the bridge collapsed, lord."

"And you," Feltumadas turned to the next man; "what did you see?"

The soldier looked nervously back at him. "I saw him standing at the bridge with the Star, after the fires," the man said quietly. "I never saw him before that."

Feltumadas scowled.

One by one, a further seven gave their accounts. Most had witnessed the explosion of red light that had broken the bridge. Some of them had seen Eamon at a distance; some hadn't seen him at all.

"Anyone could have dressed themselves in black," Eamon cried at last. "I swear I did not do it!"

"Anyone?" Feltumadas turned to him, a cold look in his eye. He laughed, and looked at Hughan. The King said nothing. "He tells me it could have been anyone, Star of Brenuin. But I say it was he. My men say the same – as would yours, if you had not silenced them!"

A heavy quiet fell. Eamon looked across at Hughan in alarm. Was that why there were no wayfarers at the hearing?

Hughan matched Feltumadas's gaze. "My men have not been silenced, Lord Feltumadas."

"Then why are they not here?" Feltumadas cried, slamming one fist into the other.

"When my men speak of what they saw and heard, Lord Feltumadas, they will speak only of what they saw and heard," Hughan replied. "They will not be influenced by other accounts."

Feltumadas shook his head. "This is a charade!" he snapped. "You do not mean to bring any man of yours to speak against this Hand. You mean to let him go, with blood on his hands."

"Whether I acquit him or not, Lord Feltumadas, I will do so impartially," Hughan answered. "Summon General Leon."

Eamon watched as an aide left the tent. In the silence that followed, Feltumadas glared at the King.

The guard returned with Leon, his clothes still muddied from the night before. He was grim-faced as he bowed.

"Sire." He did not look at Eamon.

"Leon," Hughan said firmly, "I would have you give your account of what you saw and heard last night, omitting nothing."

"Yes, sire." Leon rose. "Last night I went to meet the incoming supplies; my duty was to lead them back to the camp. My men and I were among the first to cross the River bridge.

"As I crossed I saw two things: a great mass of woods coming down the River, and a man, standing a little farther along the bank." Leon's voice grew quiet. "I am not a man of poor sight. The man that I saw was wearing black. I saw light gathering in his hands – red light.

"I have seen this light before, and I know its power." He paused. When he spoke again his voice was strained. "I immediately ordered my men off the bridge, but there was little time. I ran towards the man. The light had left his hand before I could reach him. It struck the barge of flotsam just as the barge collided with the bridge. Everything erupted into flame. After the explosion, the bridge collapsed in a mass of fire, with men and supplies caught in the flames. A few made it to the water; most made it dead."

Eamon thought again of the crack and the light... he shuddered.

"That was when I reached the man. He lowered his hands and turned to me. I saw him as clearly as I see him now. The man looked me in the eye and smiled." Leon looked grimly at Eamon. "That man is before me. He struck me. I fell into the water. He ran." Leon stared balefully at Eamon, his voice harsh and his gaze cold. "This is my account."

Silence. A look of triumph was on Feltumadas's face.

"Thank you, Leon," Hughan said.

Eamon gaped. "It is not true! I wasn't anywhere near the River! How could I possibly be in two places at once?"

"You are a Hand, Lord Goodman," Ithel's voice broke in. His face was grim, though not as hostile as many others. "Hands have been known to have stranger abilities for the working of their Master's will."

Eamon fell silent. What the Easter said was true.

He met the King's gaze. "Breach me," he said suddenly.

Many grew tense. A number of Easters passed their hands over their breasts in a sign to ward off evil.

"We do not condone such things here, Lord Goodman," Leon said gruffly.

"If my own account is not enough then tell me how else I can prove that I am innocent!" Eamon cried.

"If the Star of Brenuin is reluctant to condemn you, even in the face of evidence from his own," Anastasius growled, "you will stay in this camp, a prisoner of war, until all this is concluded."

Eamon stared at him in horror. "I can't!" he cried. "My men –"

"The destruction of this bridge, Lord Goodman, has cost more than the lives of men," Anastasius retorted icily. As his glare worked into Eamon's own, understanding wormed into him. The bridge had been the camp's pass over the River to the East Bank, and the way by which supplies were brought to the King's army. Cut off from vital supplies, those who meant to stand against the throned stood in true peril.

Eamon looked desperately at Hughan. "Please – I see the loss that this has brought you, and I am grieved by it, but do not make innocent men answer for it."

"*Innocent men?*" Feltumadas roared. "No man of Edelred's is innocent!" He surged wrathfully towards Eamon. Ithel grabbed him.

"Peace, brother."

"Then who would you have answer?" Anastasius demanded. "To take the lives of your men in exchange for the lives of mine lost at the bridge – and to demand no further price – is more generosity than you deserve."

"Lords." When the King spoke all others fell silent. Hughan turned to him. "Eamon."

Eamon looked up, tears in his eyes. He trembled. "I will abide by your judgment, sire."

"Thank you," Hughan nodded. "I know that you have answered me this question before, but I would have you answer it again, in the presence of all these men." Hughan watched him; Eamon felt unspoken power in that look. "Are you innocent of this work?"

"This is outrageous!" Feltumadas spat. "Have you not heard the evidence?"

"Peace, Feltumadas," Ithel told him again. Feltumadas shook his brother's restraining hand away and glowered, unable to speak.

But Eamon almost did not see them. In the hold of the King's eyes the world slipped away.

"Are you innocent?" Hughan asked.

Eamon nodded quietly. "Yes, sire," he said. "I am innocent."

The Easter lords erupted in cries of outrage. Feltumadas surged at Hughan. The Easter towered over the King in his anger.

"Would you stake your alliance with Istanaria, and the Land of the Seven Sons, on a Hand's claim of innocence?" he screamed.

Hughan's face was calm. Eamon watched in horror as Hughan nodded.

"Yes, Lord Feltumadas. I would."

"No!" Eamon rushed forward to place himself between the Easter and the King. "You can't, Hughan! You need the Easters, to defeat the throned. Your alliance is more important than my innocence!" As his words grew louder he felt their stares. He gave them no heed. "I am one man – many here are finer men, men who will serve you better than I."

Hughan touched his arm. Eamon stepped silently aside.

The King looked again at his allies.

"I would stake my alliance on this man's innocence," he said. "In this hearing, lords, you have slurred the honour of my First Knight. In his supposed treacheries you have also involved the honour of the lady whom I would call my queen."

Each man's mouth hung open in stunned silence. When Hughan next spoke, his voice was fierce with the strength of his conviction. "I would stake my alliance on this man's innocence because, if he is false and fills his time in working to our destruction and I see it not, then I am a man beset by blindness and folly. A man privy to such vices is worthy of no alliance; all his endeavours are doomed to failure.

"In accusing my First Knight of treachery, you charge me with darkened sight. If my sight is dark, my lords, then you must take your alliance and go, before I doom us all to death and suffering in Dunthruik's darkest halls."

His voice grew quiet again. His words stirred in the sudden stillness of the tent. "But if my sight is clear, and this man is true, then, lords, you would honour me much by staying."

Eamon gazed in awe. Even Feltumadas fell back in amazement.

Hughan watched for a moment and then looked to Anastasius. There was no trace of fear in the King's eyes.

"We see the wisdom in sparing a man's life in any case of doubt." Anastasius's voice was harsh, only a little cowed by the King's words. "We will not retract our alliance, Star of Brenuin. But," he added angrily, "a resolution on this man must be reached before we are brought to that juncture." He looked coldly at Eamon. "You have the Star's goodwill," he growled, "and I shall grudgingly lend you mine.

"But know this, Lord Goodman: it is loaned, not given, and if the Star will heed me, you will be bound and watched this day."

Strengthened by the King's words, Eamon matched the Easter's iron glare.

"I will submit to that," he said. He looked across at Hughan to see that the King nodded once to him.

"Thank you, First Knight."

Eamon emerged from the meeting exhausted, willing for the night to wrap him in sleep, but when Leon escorted him from the tent again Eamon saw that the sun had barely climbed beyond the horizon. He shuddered, and rubbed at his hands where the ropes bound them. His cloak snapped about him.

"Leon," he said quietly, "I'm sorry for what happened."

The man did not answer, his gaze fixed firmly ahead. He simply escorted Eamon back to his tent and left him under the supervision of several guards – four outside the tent and one within.

Eamon sat down heavily.

He could do little but lie and wait, pretending to rest. The waiting was the worst part. The guards changed every couple of hours. He wondered how many men were charged with watching him. Perhaps they were grateful for the work; perhaps, without the bridge, there was little else for them to do. He imagined what it was like to be one of them, to be charged with guarding a Hand. Were they terrified as the others had been? Did they worry that he would escape?

What would they do to him if he tried?

Eamon looked at his bound hands. Escape was certainly within his grasp.

Surely you do not think that your life is safe here? You cannot trust a Serpent. Go now.

He could run and be gone. Would not Hughan's allies, even the King himself, thank him for that? He was a nuisance; he could remove himself.

But it was the voice's suggestion. That, Eamon told himself, was precisely why he would not heed it. The voice was a liar. Eamon trusted Hughan. More than that: the King understood that Eamon was a piece in a larger work. He still needed Eamon in Dunthruik.

The thought emboldened him. That was the task of the First Knight.

Lunch was brought to him and he ate quietly, slowed by his bonds. He was grateful for the hindrance; it gave him something to do. The guard on duty watched him curiously, as though he doubted Hands ate and drank like normal men. Eamon smiled, wondering if he might be able to engage the man in talk. But his gesture was met with a scowl. Lowering his eyes, Eamon settled back to his lunch. Outside, he heard the camp going about its business. The familiar sound of moving horses drifted in the air.

After he had eaten he fell asleep. In the darkness of his mind the voice was clearer. He held against it.

You still turn from me, Eben's son? The words crept through him.

He did not answer. The voice laughed and suddenly the darkness was broken by a cry. Eamon stiffened as he recognized it. Still he said nothing.

The cry grew louder: Mathaiah. Howls reverberated in the darkness, clawing at him.

Do you hear it, Eben's son? the voice laughed. *Do you? Perhaps you think that he is safe, because your Serpent wills it. But he is not.*

"You lie." Eamon forced his whole will into his answer, but terror pounded in him. What if it was true?

Vision flashed in his eyes. The dark spread apart. He saw the book that he and Mathaiah had retrieved from Ellenswell laid open on a table. The twisted, hidden letters flickered on the page with the clarity of carved stone.

He heard the cry again. His blood froze.

The voice rejoiced in his fear. He felt it seep into his thought. *It troubles you? Turn to me, Eben's son, and his pain will cease.*

"No." Eamon shook in the dark. The King protected him and the King's grace was over Mathaiah. He would not bind himself to that voice again.

The cry was unleashed on his ears again, twisted sounds forming his name.

"Eamon!"

He shook his head. It was not the voice of his friend.

You would defy me? the voice hissed. *Then you make him suffer.*

Fierce anger filled his heart. He would not heed this voice!

As he stood in the cloying dark, he called out in words that he did not understand. He saw a faint blue light about himself. As the words continued the light grew, reaching out to his hand where it shimmered into a sword.

"Mathaiah is covered by the King," he called at last, "and so am I."

The voice spat at him. *Then let him cover you!*

Eamon opened his eyes. His breathing was harsh; sweat dripped from every pore. Shaking, he pressed it away. He could see only little in the shade but saw it was late afternoon. Through the tent folds he caught a glimpse of the westering sun.

A shadow passed over him. He blinked and pressed his bound hands to his eyes. Nothing. Even his eyes were beginning to play tricks on him. How long could he endure this war of wills?

With a sudden hiss something lunged at him – a glinting blade. He rolled to one side, barely avoiding its downward slash. He tried to leap to his feet, but his bindings hindered him.

A fist struck him in the gut. As he drew breath to cry out, a blow to his ribs stole it from him. He collapsed. He scarcely had the strength to move.

He would die if he did not.

His hands beneath him, he tried to sit up. He heard his assailant coming for him. Before he could roll out of the way heavy knees slammed into his ribs, crushing him down. A fierce hand grabbed his hair and yanked his head backwards. He wanted to cry out but his constricted throat made no sound.

The blade came for his neck; he would die, never having seen the face of his attacker.

Suddenly he heard a noise behind him. The hand holding the blade froze as a voice called out in surprise.

"Stop!" it cried from no more than a couple of yards away.

Abruptly Eamon was dragged to his feet, the blade still against his throat. The man who held him was taller than Eamon. The assailant seized his arms and wrenched him round to face the newcomer.

It was then that he saw who had kept him from the knife thrust. Giles.

The man bore a look of surprise, though his muscles had tensed. They remembered a history of violence, even if Giles did not.

"Let him go." Giles spoke softly, carefully.

"Leave!" The voice of Eamon's attacker burst out behind his ear, deafening him. He glanced at Giles's determined face, the blade at his throat pressing tighter. He suppressed a cry as it drew blood. He could do nothing.

"Let him go."

"Leave, or I'll kill him!"

Giles pulled a curious face. "Isn't that what you intend in any case?"

"Then try and stop me!"

Eamon braced himself for the thrust. Giles could never reach him in time.

But he did.

Eamon was never quite sure what happened. He knew only that at the moment when the blade should have severed his throat and sent him to his knees in a haze of blood, his attacker screamed. Somehow, Giles had crossed the short distance between them and spun the blade away. The big man dealt a single blow to the attacker. Cast aside in the ensuing struggle, Eamon staggered to his knees and crawled away a few paces.

A knife in Giles's hands swept across the back of the attacker's knees. The man sank with a cry. It was only then that Eamon saw him: his would-be murderer was an Easter, and bore on his breast the same green insignia that Eamon had previously seen on Feltumadas and Anastasius.

Giles stood over the screaming man, bloodied blade in hand. He blinked hard, looked at it in surprise, then looked to Eamon.

"Are you all right?"

Eamon felt wet blood clinging to his throat but knew the cut was shallow. He nodded silently. They both looked back to the Easter.

More men rushed into the tent, drawn by the attacker's cries. Leon was the first – pale-faced and angry. He looked at Giles.

"This man attacked Goodman," Giles said simply.

For a moment, nobody moved: they could only stare at the fallen man. There was a wild look to his eyes, and the Easter cursed Giles loudly in his own tongue. An Easter soldier who had entered with Leon paled. Giles looked at Leon with confusion then offered the dagger to him with a shaking hand. He took it.

"Help him up," Leon barked, gesturing at Eamon. Eamon

gasped as he was helped to his feet. He saw an anxious look pass over Leon's face. "Are you injured, Goodman?"

"Not badly." His own voice sounded quiet. He feared to speak too loudly lest it should encourage the blood that still slid down his neck.

Leon rounded on the man whom Giles had disabled. "Who sent you?"

The man didn't answer. The wild look in the Easter's eyes was one that Eamon had seen before – in First Lieutenant Alben.

Leon seized the man by the scruff of his coat. "Answer me," he growled.

"Don't hurt him!" Eamon gasped as pain shot through him. Leon looked back at him, astonished.

"Don't hurt him," Eamon repeated.

Leon nodded. Suddenly the attacker cried out as though choked, though no man touched him. His eyes grew wide and Eamon saw clarity in them.

"Help me!" the Easter choked, his white eyes fixed on Leon.

Eamon lurched forward, not knowing what to do, only hoping to do something. As he moved, the Easter collapsed; Eamon dropped beside him. Led by his heart's instinct, he laid his bound hands to the man's brow, closed his eyes, and slipped onto the plain.

There was no red light, no sear of hellish power in his hands. Eamon looked about himself. This man's mind was dark, cloaked in shadows. He heard the Easter calling piteously in his native tongue. Eamon followed the sound and saw the man.

The Easter was on his knees. The darkness around him was struck through with red that pierced him. Eamon had never really understood the things that he saw on the plain, but he understood this well enough: the man was transfixed by the red light, and he was dying.

"No!" Eamon screamed, outraged.

In a heartbeat he was by the Easter, and in his hand was the sword that he rarely bore. It flashed silver and cut swathes of light through the dark. As he brought it over the Easter it shattered the red.

"You will not take this man!" Eamon cried.

His vision changed, but he hardly dared look back to the world where he now knelt. He panted hard. His neck felt sticky and slick with blood. He opened his eyes.

The Easter lay still on the ground before him, eyes closed. No sound left the man's throat. Nothing on the pale face indicated either life or death.

"What have you done?" breathed a voice quietly behind him: Giles's.

Eamon blinked hard and shuffled the heavy cloak on his shoulders. He did not know what he had done, only that he had done it too late.

Leon knelt beside him and looked at the Easter. After a moment of stillness he swiftly drew a length of cloth from a pouch at his waist.

"He's alive," he said.

Eamon blinked in disbelief then watched as Leon bound the cloth about the man's leg. The Easter still bled, but he lived.

A wave of relief flooded Eamon. He rested on his haunches, overcome by trembling.

Leon turned to one of the other soldiers. "We will escort them both to the infirmary."

Eamon rose unsteadily and stumbled. He had not lost much blood, but he reeled with shock. Giles steadied him. He looked up at the man with deep gratitude.

"What were you doing here?" he asked. As the collapsed Easter was taken out of the tent, Giles led Eamon from it.

"I asked after you this morning," he said quietly. His face seemed perplexed. "Mrs Mendel told me that you were being confined, so I decided to come and offer you some company. I'm supposed to be recovering, but Hughan lets me walk about the camp, helping with jobs sometimes. So I thought that sitting with you wouldn't be too taxing." He flexed his hands. His eyes flicked back and forth slowly, remembering what he had done.

"Was I a good fighter before?" he asked.

"One of the best I ever met," Eamon answered.

Giles nodded soberly.

It took all of Eamon's will to keep still while one of the infirmary's doctors daubed his wound with skin-searing alcohol. It was like returning to the *Lark*, and his treatment following his flogging. Giles stayed to see that Eamon was properly assisted and then quietly excused himself. Eamon watched him go.

The Easter was laid in another bed not far away, his face pale. Eamon saw Leon standing nearby. The man watched him with interest.

The doctor was finishing his work when the King arrived. Hughan came swiftly to the bedside.

"How are you?"

Eamon smiled. "I'm fine."

A moment later the doctor finished. Hughan thanked him. The doctor bowed once before the King and left.

Eamon watched him go and then looked quizzically at Hughan. "I'm surprised – but not displeased – that you have an infirmary," he said, his mind on the blue light and the power of healing that he knew it bore. "Surely, with the King's grace, you have little need for doctors or for infirmaries?"

"The nature of grace is to meet each man at the pass where he stands," Hughan told him quietly. "Many prefer the skill and hand of a doctor or a surgeon; they too bring healing."

Eamon looked at him in surprise. "But it would heal them," he said, "just like it healed Mathaiah."

"The grace cannot be commanded," Hughan told him. "The wise cannot fathom what it does," he added, "and so to trust in it is difficult, even for the best of men."

There was a moment of quiet. Hughan sighed deeply. "What happened?"

Eamon lowered his gaze. How could he tell Hughan that an Easter had tried to kill him without endangering the fragile alliance even more?

78

"I…"

"An Easter tried to kill him, sire. Had the look of a hired hand, if you'll pardon the idiom." Leon shot a deft look at Eamon. "The man in question is one of Feltumadas's guard. Feltumadas is hot-headed, sire, and I could believe that he sent the man, given this morning's altercation."

"I don't believe that even Feltumadas would try to kill a man under my explicit protection," Hughan answered heavily.

"He didn't," Eamon interrupted.

"Then who did, Goodman?" Leon's voice was stony.

"You believe he acted alone?" Hughan asked quietly. "Without Feltumadas's approval?"

"Certainly without Lord Feltumadas's approval." Eamon paused. How could he explain? "Hughan, I went into his mind." Leon stiffened, but he persisted. "It was dark… When I found him, he was surrounded by red light, calling for help. I have seen its like before. I do not believe that this man acted from his own volition." How the red light had taken hold of the man, he did not know.

Hughan watched him for a moment. "I'm sorry, Eamon," he said at last. "You're in danger here."

Eamon offered him a wry smile. "No more than in Dunthruik. But here, I endanger you." His smiled faded. The Easters would not take this latest occurrence well. Feltumadas would likely claim that Eamon had staged the affair to mire the King in treachery.

Everything he did – and even the things he didn't do – was being played against the King. None of the fractures in Hughan's vital alliances would have been caused if he had not come to the camp.

When he looked up to meet Hughan's glance, he saw the King read his thought.

"He's using me, Hughan," he whispered. "That's why he sent me. I can't stay here."

"Stay or go, First Knight; but do not do it for fear of Edelred. That is how he uses you."

Eamon knew that it was true.

Hughan watched him. "Eamon, I can't give you a head to take back."

"I know." Eamon's heart waxed heavy, grieving. His men would die. His only achievement would be discord among Hughan's allies. The throned would reap a great victory.

Silently, he laid his head down in his hands. How could he not act in fear of the throned, when the throned held so much over him?

"I know what grief it is to lose men." Hughan spoke softly. "I do not rejoice that you will know that grief, whatever colour your men wear."

"Thank you." It seemed of small comfort.

"Eamon." Hughan touched his shoulder. "I know that I have asked much of you and that Dunthruik weighs on you. There are many men who serve me, and perhaps it is true that, measured against their service, yours is the most difficult of all. But I should not have asked it of you if I did not think that you could bear it. I believe," he added, "that you can bear it still. Even so, if you would bear it no longer, tell me."

Eamon's mind turned. He could be free to not go back to Dunthruik? The thought was strange. He could leave? Hughan offered him release – such sweet, simple release! – from all that tormented him.

And yet...

He could not renounce Dunthruik. He knew and loved the city. He was needed there.

Hughan watched him with confidence.

"You will need me there," Eamon said quietly. "Dunthruik is the place of my service. I will go there for you, to prepare the way."

"That is why the throned strikes you much," Hughan told him gently. "Make no mistake – he will keep striking at you. When you return to the city he may strike at those close to you."

"Those close to me?" Eamon frowned. Who was there left in Dunthruik at whom the throned might strike?

Then he understood. "Mathaiah." His heart churned as he thought of Lillabeth. But Mathaiah had known that risk; they had both known it. He knew it.

He looked up at the King once more. "Should it come to pass," he breathed, "I will bear it. I am your First Knight."

"I know you are." Hughan paused. "Your heart, Eamon, is your great strength, and the foundation of all that you do. It is a gift of your house. Men see it and are drawn to you, for it looks to them like a great light; it gives them hope and courage." Hughan looked firmly at him. "Though you are First Knight your battles are not yet on an open field; they are in your heart, and it is your heart that the throned will strike, because it is there that he must conquer you. Should the worst befall Mathaiah, do not bear it alone. Do not let the throned work your love against you. As it has been with others of your house, your heart is both your strength and your weakness."

Amazed, Eamon nodded. "Yes, sire," he whispered.

Hughan smiled. "I will speak to the Easters. We must arrange for you to go. I do not think that you should leave before tomorrow; you need time to rest."

"Yes." His throat throbbed.

Hughan pressed his shoulder. "Courage, Eamon," he said. "These days are dark, but they are not without end."

CHAPTER V

The rest of the day passed slowly, Eamon spending much of it under a doctor's vigilant charge. After his initial treatment he was kept well apart from others in the infirmary and supposed that the precaution was wise – in part because he most likely terrified them, and in part because any one of them might possibly try to finish what the Easter had begun. Of the man who had attacked him, he heard nothing. He wondered what Hughan had told the Easters about the event and whether it had shaken them at all.

Towards evening Leon returned and silently performed his accustomed escort duty. They did not go to the same shelter as before – Eamon guessed that the risk of attack was still thought too high.

"How are you?" Leon asked as they walked.

Eamon was startled – Leon never spoke to him! "Better," he said at last.

Leon nodded, seemingly contented.

At last they reached the tent. Leon gestured for him to go inside. Eamon was about to, then turned. "Will you not bind me?"

Leon shook his head. "The King does not wish it. Good night, Goodman."

Entering, Eamon was comforted to see that Leon remained outside; he hoped that the man would remain there throughout the night.

He slipped into the welcoming warmth of the bed and soon fell into a dreamless sleep.

He woke suddenly, for no reason. He was alone. Grey light showed outside. All around him was silence, and still, cold air.

Eamon rubbed sleepily at his face and sat up. He rose slowly, thinking to pull on his cloak and speak to Leon; he wanted to know what had been decided.

As he rose he heard someone entering behind him. Assuming it to be Leon he turned with a greeting on his lips, and then stopped in surprise.

Standing before him was Feltumadas. The Easter lord glared at him sourly, his face a picture of terrible rage. He held a curved dagger. Eamon could not imagine how he had passed the guards, and, as he thought it, he realized there were no guards outside the tent. The blade glinted in the grey light.

Panic welled inside him.

The lord advanced, his lips pulled back in a sneer. Eamon backed away but there was nowhere for him to go. He looked straight into the eyes of the Easter and then stopped cold. His eyes saw Feltumadas; his heart saw something else.

Scarcely daring to breathe, he held his place while the man advanced dangerously close. There was a flicker – faint, so faint! – about his form.

With a start, Eamon remembered his dream: men wearing his own face, like a mask. Then he understood.

The man before him was not Feltumadas.

A memory from a day long before came to his aid. Lord Cathair had spoken of one who had won the Master's masque by attending "as a woman". Looking at "Feltumadas", Eamon became eerily certain that the same man stood before him.

He dared to watch the armed man come closer. A smile crept to his face.

He, too, could wear a mask.

"Good morning!" he said. "Tell me, Lord Rendolet – have you come to finish your botched work?"

The man bearing the form of the Easter lord froze and stared at him.

"The West tells that you are a breacher, not a seer." The voice was in every detail that of Feltumadas, but it was not he. The man standing before him was a Hand.

Changer. The word leapt into Eamon's mind. He understood at last how so many men had seen him at the burning bridge.

His enraged blood curdled, but still he smiled.

"The Master greatly blesses those who greatly serve him," he answered. He turned his gaze to the knife, and then let his eyes fall coolly on the startled Hand. "You intend me some injury?" he asked politely.

Feltumadas's stolen lips parted to give an answer.

"You are a traitor to the Master," Rendolet snarled. "Besides," he added, a fresh smile passing over his face, "there is much damage that I can do to the Serpent by killing you."

"There is much damage we can do to the Serpent together." Taking his courage in both hands, and drawing onto himself every detail of Cathair's inflection and mannerism that he could muster, Eamon stepped forward conspiratorially. He was within the Hand's striking distance and was painfully aware that error meant death.

The Hand hesitated at his boldness. He laughed.

"Lord Rendolet, have you heard nothing about me? Need I refresh your memory about the man who saved the life of Lord Cathair, or the man who obtained the location of the Serpent's lair and delivered it to the Master? Have you not been told," he asked, "in what way I serve the Master?"

"The man who surrendered his sword? You do not serve him, Goodman!" Rendolet growled. "You think I have not seen you in these days, and not seen your true allegiance?"

Eamon pressed fear aside. He laughed scornfully. "You have seen nothing!" he countered. "And neither has the Serpent, which is *precisely* how it must be. But you give me great encouragement by your words: I fooled even you." He looked at the stolen face, saw new doubt cross it, and an idea came to him.

He would wear his mask for the King.

"How I came to be here, I know," he said. "But you?" He cocked his head curiously. "How came you here, Lord Rendolet? Were you sent by the Master, as I was?" The face before him faltered. "No," Eamon discerned. "You were sent to Ashford Ridge." The Hand froze. "And what failure you had there, Lord Rendolet. Why! All Dunthruik knows of it; of how you, and those with you, sullied the Master's glory in pitiful defeat."

The Hand gaped. "How do you –?"

"All Dunthruik knows of your shameful, scattered retreat, of how the Serpent crushed you in his jaws," Eamon told him. Barely hidden terror flashed across the man's face. "I am an eloquent man, but even I find myself at a loss for words enough to describe Lord Cathair's displeasure. You fear it," he said, fixing a grinding glare on the Hand, "and you fear the ire that he, and the Master, will rightly pour on you for returning in disgrace. Perhaps that is why you attacked the Serpent's bridge – to allay their scorn? But you have not bettered your lot, Lord Rendolet: now I will tell them of how you interfered with my work."

The face of Feltumadas grew pale.

Drawing all his wits about him, Eamon laughed and laid one hand across the man's shoulder. The Hand stiffened beneath his touch. "Come, Lord Rendolet!" Eamon said lightly. "I am a generous man. A great reward has been promised to me should I succeed in my task. Perhaps I may be persuaded to let you share a little of it, if you aid me."

The Hand's blade-grip tensed angrily. "Why should I share any reward?"

"You are a witness of the terrible loss at Ashford Ridge," Eamon told him simply. He smiled. "Make no mistake, Lord Rendolet; if you return to Dunthruik you will be breached."

The words had the desired effect. The face looked at him, terrified.

Eamon allowed the anxiety to grow for a few moments before fortifying himself with further memories of Cathair – of which he had many – and speaking again. "You do not wish to be breached? It is true to say that it is painful. Perhaps you have seen it done?

Perhaps there was some fault in your actions at Ashford Ridge that you would rather not be revealed?" The Hand did not answer him. Eamon looked at him with a smile. "Of course, I would not hurt you, Lord Rendolet, if I breached you. I might even assist you to cover any particularly embarrassing blemishes. Indeed, I will help you – if you will help me."

Rendolet stared at him in silence. Eamon knew that the Hand was ambitious, and terrified, yet perhaps might not be moved to grant him his life unless the flames of that ambition were fanned further.

"Do you know how they speak of you at court, Lord Rendolet?" He lowered his tone and fixed pitifully on the Hand. "They speak of you as a Hand that won a woman's prize at the Master's masque."

Rendolet cast him a withering look. "Speak for yourself, Lord Goodman," he sneered. "You also won it."

"I did," Eamon acknowledged, "but they do not speak of that as my crowning achievement. The same cannot be said for you. It is such a pity – it is hardly the accolade that you deserve! Add to that your defeat at Ashford Ridge, and your hindrance to me, who does the Master's work, and what have you? Shame and dishonour. Lend me your help," he said, "and you will receive the Master's praise. It will bring a rich harvest, blotting out all that has gone before."

The Hand's grip on the weapon relaxed.

"Come," Eamon told him, "and make a name for yourself with me. Come and be counted among the Master's nearest, as I shall be when my task is done."

At last, a smile appeared before him. It seemed grotesquely out of place on Feltumadas's face. Eamon felt revulsion. He knew by the smile that, though outwardly acquiescing, Rendolet thought that he might yet gain the upper hand.

"Tell me, Lord Goodman, what is your task?" Rendolet's voice was thick with sudden eagerness.

"I was to savage this Serpent's alliance with the Suns by taking a life and a severed head back to the Master. It is to be a trophy to bathe him in splendour and glory." The eyes before him went wide.

"Whose head, Lord Goodman?"

Eamon smiled, but he trembled within. This was the testing point.

"That of Feltumadas." He paused. "You present yourself to me by some strange fortune, Lord Rendolet. For I feel that we may do even more for the Master. We shall kill Feltumadas now, together, and you will go in his stead. What havoc you shall wreck in this pitiable camp! Why, they shall make songs of it – how you brought the Serpent to his knees, to the Master's glory."

The face before him broke into a long smile. Eamon breathed. The Hand had taken the bait.

"I knew that you had a certain style, Lord Goodman," Rendolet said smoothly. "I tried to mimic that when I moved their little bridge. But I see that I was not nearly stylish enough!"

Nauseous unease coursed through him. He swallowed it down. The cries of the burned and drowning men, and the impaling glares of the Easters flew into his mind. His unease was unhorsed by rage. How he longed to strike the Hand!

Instead, he smiled.

"You compliment me well, Lord Rendolet, and I trust that you will complement me also. I have, as you might imagine," he added, "no weapon to hand. May I take yours?"

"Of course, Lord Goodman," Rendolet answered, freely rendering his blade into Eamon's hand. "I have others at my disposal."

"Good." Eamon felt a wave of relief as the dagger passed into his hand. "Where did you leave Feltumadas?" He had to hope that the Hand had not already killed the Easter lord.

"Resting in his tent," Rendolet answered snidely, then laughed. "They would have charged him with your murder and he would have denied everything."

Eamon saw at once how close to disaster they had come. After Hughan's firm defence of his First Knight the previous day, to have that knight killed by an Easter who then denied the murder could well have spelled the end of the King's alliance with the Land of the Seven Sons. Without them, Hughan could not have made a successful attempt on Dunthruik, nor kept up his skirmishes in the other regions and provinces of the River Realm. The broken alliance would, at best, have slowed the wayfarers to a near halt – allowing the throned to weed them out at greater leisure – and, at worst, have culminated in the elimination of the King's men.

Eamon looked at the Hand again. "A masterful stroke," he cooed. "I see that you have a style of your own, Lord Rendolet."

The Hand smiled. Biting down his anger and the fear that touched his limbs, Eamon bade the Hand lead the way and followed him from the tent.

There were no guards outside.

"My guardians, Lord Rendolet?" he asked, softly and innocently, as they left. "Another stroke of yours?"

"Sent away by the Serpent's sycophant," the Hand answered. Eamon was chilled. Had Rendolet impersonated Leon, too?

They walked swiftly and silently across the camp, past the majority of wayfarer shelters, and on towards the large tents at the camp's centre where both the Easter and wayfarer lords had their resting places. Eamon caught sight of Hughan's tent to his left; Feltumadas's was ahead and to the right. If he could just get Rendolet to Feltumadas, the Easter would see the changer and be able to help him in containing the venomous Hand.

Suddenly, Rendolet stopped. Eamon's heart pounded as the sly face turned and smiled at him.

"I have heard it said, Lord Goodman, that the Serpent keeps some wench by him that he intends to make the fount of his bastard house," he said. Eamon followed the Hand's glance towards Hughan's tent; Aeryn's had been placed next to it. He froze, but still he had to smile.

"I have seen her, Lord Rendolet," he answered.

"Is she worth some sport, Lord Goodman?" There was a terrible glint to the Hand's eye.

"Perhaps to the Serpent," Eamon answered with a forced snicker. The look in Rendolet's eye did not diminish, and, as Eamon tried to think, from the corner of his eye he saw something that terrified him more.

Men began to stir. Hughan, Leon, and Anastasius walked towards the King's tent. Any moment now they would see him. His opportunity would be lost, and this Hand could easily disappear to dispose of the Easter, or Aeryn, or perhaps even Hughan himself.

"Why strike just once, Lord Goodman?" Rendolet's voice dripped foully from the stolen mouth. "Why just once, when a second strike can be more pleasurable than the first?"

"You would rape his queen?" The words spilled indignantly from Eamon's lips.

Rendolet looked at him curiously. "You would not?"

Eamon did not answer.

A dark look passed over the face of Feltumadas and, as curiosity became suspicion, that same face turned vilely on him.

"Reluctance does not serve the Master, Goodman." Eamon caught a glimpse of red in the man's palm.

The King's party could see him now, but he had no choice. He dropped all pretence and looked the Hand straight in the eye.

"No, Lord Rendolet," he answered. "It does not; and neither do I."

Rendolet's eyes flared with rage. Eamon saw the red light gathering in the Hand's palm. There was a frantic race of hands, Eamon's to his blade and Rendolet's to the foul red light.

With crushing force Eamon whipped the dagger round and drove it hard and deep into the Hand's chest. The false Feltumadas's lips opened in a horrendous, wrathful scream. Eamon persisted, drove the dagger down to the hilt, twisted sharply, then dragged it heavily out of the gushing flesh.

"Traitor!" The Hand's voice – Feltumadas's voice – screeched as reddened hands reached out for Eamon. Eamon dodged the clawing grasp, stepped to one side and then drove his knife down into the flailing man's undefended neck. The scream became a frothing gargle and the Hand crumpled to the ground.

"Eamon!" Hughan's cry coursed through him, the depth of its grief felling every sense. Eamon reeled.

Gasping and covered in blood, he held the dripping blade in his hand. All the eyes that watched saw that Feltumadas lay dead on the ground before him. As he turned, his gaze met that of his stricken King.

Suddenly the air erupted in shouts. He saw a man stringing a bow and seconds later an arrow struck the sodden ground by the corpse.

He hurled down the dagger and ran. Arrows hissed at him both from in front and behind. At the cries dozens of men emerged from their tents. Faced with a bloodied Hand careering towards them they fell back in fear. Eamon did not believe that he could clear the camp but he could not stop – he could not count on Hughan's name to protect him.

Men snatched at him as he hurtled past but they could not catch him. Still he ran.

His pulse pounded in his sutured throat. Gasps for breath unsettled his wound and it bled again. The cries were strong behind him and he could not stop.

"Stop him! Halt him!" yelled a voice, dangerously close. Eamon risked a glance over his shoulder and recoiled.

Leon tailed him, his face full of fury, his hands ready to exact vengeance.

Terrified, he tore through the camp, pressing on in a desperate pelt to the tributary. A group of soldiers leapt at him as he came to the banks, but he darted past them and hurled himself into the water. It was deep, and the shingle was treacherous. He stumbled on debris as he waded; the water behind him grew red as it drew the Hand's blood off him. He swam.

As he staggered out on the other bank, shivering, he heard sounds in the water behind him. Gasping, he saw Leon in the water, determination driving him ever closer.

Crossbowmen wearing Easter colours drew up on the opposite bank and set arrows to their strings. With a cry, Eamon turned and fled. He had to get away, but he could not outrun Leon. Surely they would see that he had not killed Feltumadas?

By the time they saw it, he would be a corpse.

An arrow struck at him, piercing a fold of his cloak and missing his flesh by little. He ran.

Woodland lay before him, the ground thick with hollows and bushes. He turned and looked over his shoulder again: Leon was there.

He plunged into the trees, looking wildly for cover. Suddenly he saw some thick bushes on his left, next to a small clearing. The plants were overgrown with barbed thistles, but he had no choice. He drove down into them, scrambled underneath the pronged leaves, and pressed his starved lungs deep against the forest floor.

He lay trembling in the dank tangle of leaves, forcing his ragged breath to silence. His soaking hair trailed over his face and he anxiously pushed it away.

Suddenly a shadow moved among the trees. He fell completely still: so much as a sound, and Leon would find him.

He peered between the leaves. Where was the shadow? He had seen someone, he knew he had, and yet now…

He froze. There, hidden in the thick maze of trees across the small clearing, he saw the shadow again. He *had* seen someone, but not Leon. For the shadow set among the trees wore black and beside it were three others, similarly clad.

Hands: four of them. Eamon repressed the urge to swear viciously. He could only guess that they had not seen him. Why were they there?

He had no time to reason an answer: Leon entered the clearing. The wayfarer stopped, his own breath ragged as he searched the trees for his hidden quarry.

"I know you're here, Goodman!" he yelled. Eamon flinched at the rage in that voice. "Treacherous murderer! I know you're here!"

Eamon didn't answer. He looked across again. The hidden Hands watched Leon intently; one whispered to another. What were they saying?

Leon filled his lungs: "Out!" His words, yelled at the top of his ample voice, were full of wrath, and his hands trembled with uncontainable fury. Leon stared with ashen face about the clearing and summoned him again. "*Traitor!* Out!"

Eamon felt the words striking at him as he lay there. Then he saw the shadows move and suddenly he realized that either he must strike at Leon, or they would.

There was no time to think. With a terrible cry he rose to his feet and lunged at the King's man.

CHAPTER VI

The world slowed. Thorns ripped at his arms and face and then fell back from his terrible forward motion with rending snaps. He tore out of his hiding place.

Leon heard his cry and turned, rage ingrained on his face. Fuelled by terror, Eamon surged forward with all the speed and strength he had.

He grabbed Leon's arms and then, stepping to the side, kicked the back of the man's knees.

The King's man crumpled. Eamon snatched the dagger that glinted at Leon's belt and dropped on his back. He grimly drove his knees against the man's arms, pinning him down. Leon gasped for breath as Eamon brought the dagger round to his throat.

"Traitor!" he howled, trying to hurl him off. Eamon almost lost his grip, but held firm. He forced the blade closer to the man's neck.

"Lie still, snake," he hissed, "or I'll slit your throat like I did that of your precious sunny princeling."

In the silence that followed they both breathed heavily. Leon's chest heaved as he sought to regain his strength. Eamon knew that the King's man would be a capable fighter, and feared that he would lose his scant advantage if he delayed too long. Discreetly, he flicked his eyes to the Hands in the shadows. They had not moved. Indeed, he could no longer see them. As he held Leon pinned he tried to think.

What could he do now? He realized with a lurch that his plan had been only half thought through. Leon was held, that was true, but there was no telling whether, even now, there were other wayfarers charging over the River. If such men arrived and found this scene, they would cry traitor and run him through. How long would it take them to realize that Feltumadas was alive and well? About the same amount of time, Eamon imagined, as it would take them to realize that they had killed him without cause.

He looked back at the wayfarer beneath him. Leon seemed to have been following a similar train of thought to his own.

"Now what, Lord Goodman?" he asked grimly. "Kill me and have done with it! You have done your work."

"Not quite." Eamon smiled sweetly. "Not quite, *dear* Leon. But I think you must agree that the work I have already completed, I have done *extraordinarily* well."

Leon gaped with utter hatred. "He trusted you." His voice was grieved, barely more than a whisper.

"And you trusted him," Eamon countered. "Which of you was more foolish?"

With a cry Leon tried to break free but, with an unpleasant chuckle, Eamon crushed him back hard.

"You must face the truth, Leon: you have been outdone!"

Leon fell silent. What could he say? Eamon was sorry to treat the man in such a way, but had no choice. He leaned in close to Leon's face. "Now you will have the honour of assisting me in the last stage of my work. It is more than you deserve!"

Leon gaped – and found no words to say.

Eamon was coming to the breaking point of his bluff; he drove himself forward. "But console yourself, Leon. It is difficult to match my genius. Wouldn't you agree, gentlemen?" He called the last loudly, to the silent woods.

For a moment nothing happened. Leon stared at him.

Eamon held his nerve. He needed the Hands out where he could see them. He gave an amused laugh.

"Ah! There are several explanations, dear Leon, why these lords might refuse my summons. The first charge is cowardice." He cocked a sarcastic smile at the wayfarer. "Given as you are subdued, I cannot lay that against them. The second might be that they claim not to hear me. But I can hear them, so I find this solution as fault-ridden as the first. They may, of course, be in awe of my brilliance – something to which I have become modestly accustomed in the Master's city, Leon – but I find it more likely that they hide themselves for the simplest reason: that they were not to be seen by me."

It was logical, though quite what they had been doing, he did not know. Had they been sent to watch him in the camp? His heart chilled. How long had they spied on him?

They would have had something to watch now, at any rate.

Turning his gaze to the shadows he raised his voice again. "And if they don't reveal themselves to me now, Leon, do you know what I shall have to do? I will have to report their indiscretion to the Master. He will not look kindly on them for that – because, unlike me, they will have failed."

"You are mad, Goodman," Leon countered, disgusted.

"You would find that satisfying, I am sure, but I must disappoint you," Eamon returned. For the shadows moved, the threat of shame forcing his enemies to play their hand. "See what a snake this is, lords? He would like to excuse me my allegiance on account of madness. Do you not think that generous of him, Lord Febian?"

"Yes, Lord Goodman." Febian's face was downcast. Eamon didn't recognize the three Hands with him, but he did not need to; he would know them again in the city.

Leon froze.

"A pleasure to see you, gentlemen," Eamon told the Hands, offering them his warmest smile. "How have these last few days been treating you? Well, I trust?" He glared straight at Febian – the Hand who had incited the massacre on the return from Pinewood. His tone hardened. "I want rope, Lord Febian."

Febian started. "Lord Goodman, we cannot –"

"Cannot what?" It was not hard to make his tone harsher.

" – *interfere*. The Right Hand commanded that we observe."

The Right Hand? Eamon glared; the Hand flinched. Eamon felt a chill within.

The Right Hand – not the throned?

He cast the thought as best as he could from his mind. Eamon knew that performing the will of the Right Hand was as vital to Febian as performing the will of the throned was to him – both of them had to make amends for their failures at Pinewood. He needed rope to bind Leon so that he could take him back to the King's camp – he had to get Leon safely away from the Hands. But he also needed a plausible reason to do so...

As he glared irately at Febian, the answer came to him: what better reason to go back than for the head he had been sent to obtain?

He made a harsh sound at the gathered Hands and rose suddenly to his feet, dragging Leon with him. He yanked one of the wayfarer's arms painfully up behind his back, all the while keeping the blade firmly to Leon's neck. The King's man made no sound and, though defiant, complied.

"Give me rope, snake," Eamon told him.

"Will you hang yourself with it?" Leon asked acridly.

"I fear not."

"Then I am afraid that I have none I can spare."

Eamon tensed his muscles as though to knife across the throat; Leon gasped. Eamon laughed cruelly.

"Next time you will not have the chance to gasp. Get the rope," he commanded.

Leon drew a length of rope from where it was wound about his belt. The gesture was slow and cumbersome, for Eamon allowed him to use only one hand.

At last the coil of rope was in Leon's hand. "Good," Eamon told him. "Hold it, and kneel down."

Leon stiffened.

"Kneel!" Eamon hissed.

Leon knelt. Setting his foot heavily on one of the man's legs to keep him from bolting, Eamon tucked the knife into his belt before binding Leon's hands together so tightly that the man winced when the knots were drawn firm. Eamon regretted it, but it had to be done.

The Hands watched him with strange awe as he stood back from his work. Leon knelt, bound, on the ground before them. Though the sight sickened him, Eamon smiled. He turned pejoratively to the Hands.

"You may go back to the Right Hand," he said smoothly, "and tell him that I shall be in the city with my charge before nightfall tomorrow. For with Leon's most genteel assistance guaranteed, the Serpent cannot but give me what I ask."

"I will take no part with you, traitor!" Leon tried to leap to his feet, but Eamon struck him back harshly.

"Down, snake!" he snarled, and turned back to Febian. "I will discharge my business and you may yours."

As he turned his back on the Hands and their pale and astonished faces, he trembled. He looked at Leon with a sarcastic smile.

"When you're ready, *snake*."

Leon answered him with a look that might crack stone, and rose in silence to his feet. Eamon seized his hands where they were bound behind his back, and pressed the blade of the dagger between the man's shoulder blades.

"It is such a beautiful camp – it would be a shame not to see it one more time," he said. "Good day, gentlemen. To his glory!"

"His glory!" the Hands answered. One laughed nastily as Leon stumbled before the blade. Eamon knew that they watched as he made Leon walk back to the edge of the woodland, towards the River and the camp perimeter.

"When you see your men, you will tell them not to come near," he told the King's man. "Do you understand?"

"Perfectly." Leon's voice was harsh. What must the man be feeling? As far as Leon was concerned, he was in the hands of a traitor and was going to be used against the King, a man whom Eamon was sure Leon loved. He could imagine the agony of being made a weapon against his lord; he knew that pain himself. How often he had known it! He was sorry that Leon had to endure it, but he could not say a word – the Hands were watching. Leon had to believe that it was a traitor who drove him pace by pace to the camp.

Eamon forced Leon a little downstream to where the Easters had erected a small bridge over the tributary. He had avoided it in his flight, fearing to be trapped on it. A group of men stood guard there. As they approached, the first soldier saw them and cried out:

"Leon!" Then he saw Eamon.

The man's hand flew to his sword. "Archers!"

"Tell him to stop," Eamon growled in Leon's ear, pressing the blade closer.

"No." Leon's response was calmly defiant.

Eamon swore. The bridge guards were readying their weapons. He stopped and drove the blade distressingly close to Leon's neck.

"Disarm!" he called. "Disarm, or he dies."

The guards hesitated and then fell back. Eamon forced Leon across the bridge. The soldiers stared.

"You," Eamon called to one of them, "go to your Serpent and tell him that I demand to see him. If he does not grant me my request, this man will pay for it."

The soldier looked at Leon. The wayfarer shook his head slightly. The soldier paled. Eamon cursed. Damn Leon's nobility!

"Go *now!*" he yelled.

Terrified, the soldier ran.

The moments while he waited there by the bridge, surrounded by men who thought him an enemy, were excruciating. Eamon kept Leon close by him and the knife tight by the man's throat. The soldiers watched him in silence. He smiled. He had to give the Hands something to see. He did not know how long they stood there. A group of men approached. At the head walked Hughan, Anastasius by his side. Eamon sought the King's eyes; he saw strain on the man's face and felt grief in his heart, for he felt sure that he was the cause of it. Even so, as they met gazes, a weary, welcoming look passed the King's brow.

"Eamon," he called. "All is well."

Eamon turned cold. If Hughan knew some of what had really happened, and announced it, all was lost.

"You can let him go," Hughan continued, "these men will not –"

"Stay back! Stay back, or I will kill him."

Hughan frowned, and Eamon saw Anastasius stare at him. He laughed sharply.

"Are you insane?" he snapped.

"Eamon," Hughan began softly. The King had come to within a few yards. "You will not be harmed. You can let him go."

"Sire, you must not do as he asks," Leon called suddenly. "There are Hands just beyond the perimeter. This man is working some new mischief –"

"There are indeed Hands in these woods, Serpent," Eamon rejoined with a laugh. But then he looked straight at Hughan. He spoke again, quietly; his affected arrogance disappeared. Leon fell still in his hands.

"There are Hands here. I'm sure they were sent to watch me. I'm sorry, Hughan, for now they know where you are. You may be strong enough to stave off their attacks, but you are cut off from your convoys and you will have to be alert and cautious in the days ahead."

"Thank you," Hughan answered. He also spoke quietly. Had he already understood what was happening?

"Sire –" Leon began again.

"Leon is one who would go to the very ends of the earth in your service," Eamon said, and Leon fell quiet. "I am glad that such men are with you."

"You really are insane." Leon struggled with the ropes about his hands. "Sire, don't trust him!"

Eamon looked back up at them and raised his voice. Again, he changed it.

"Bring me the body."

His demand resounded coldly over the field. The gathered men stared incredulously.

"Are you simpletons?" Eamon sneered. "Or do you want this man to die? Bring Feltumadas's body, and lay it before me."

"Sire, no –"

"Do it." Hughan gestured to nearby soldiers. Reluctantly they left, and returned soon after, hauling the body between them. Relief coursed through Eamon's veins: in death, Rendolet had retained the form he had been holding in his last moments of life. He did not dare to think what he could have done if the Hand had not.

The soldiers laid the body in front of him. The sun blazed still on the bloodied chest and the stolen face was frozen in a hideous cry of pain. The man's hands were rigid, contorted by the red light that had died there. Eamon shuddered.

As the soldiers stepped back, Hughan looked at Eamon.

"Let my man go," he said, "and you will be permitted to leave."

"My Master's work is not yet complete," Eamon answered snidely. "Lord Anastasius."

The Easter met his gaze. From the calculating look that he saw in the man's eyes, Eamon imagined that the Easter lord had at last understood his plan.

"Dear Anastasius, this is your office." Eamon smiled, and tilted his head down towards the body. "Strike off his head."

He heard gasps among the soldiers, and knew then that they did not know what Hughan and Anastasius knew – that the body before them was that of a Hand, not that of the Easter's son.

"You would not dare me to do such a thing," Anastasius answered, his voice chilling in its intensity.

"You dare not refuse me," Eamon replied with a laugh. "Do it now or I will take this man's head instead." Leon went rigid.

Anastasius gave a cry of rage and snatched a curved dagger from his belt. Howling words in his own language, he dropped to one knee and severed the body's head with a practised hand. At last he rose from his grisly task, and cast the blade beside the bloody corpse.

"Good," Eamon told him. He looked up and matched Hughan's gaze. "The head will be put in a bag and given to me. You will bring me my horse, my cloak, my sword, and my dagger, and let me leave. When I am beyond the perimeter of the camp I will release your man to you. Any interference and his life will be forfeit."

"Do not, sire!" Leon called out again, something close to grief in his voice. "This is no –"

"Do you understand?" Eamon demanded.

"Yes." It was Hughan who answered. Eamon's heart churned with a strange, guilty sorrow. Who was he to command the King? And yet, he told himself, he did not command Hughan; he played a game in which Hughan played a part.

At Hughan's command, soldiers slowly brought the bag, horse, cloak, and other effects out of the camp. Eamon made Anastasius place the bloodied head in the sack and watched as the lord balled his ruddy hands angrily together.

"I swear, Goodman, my house shall repay you for what you have done!" he cried. As Eamon met his glance, he wondered if the words were a threat or a promise – or both.

"I shall look forward to that day," he answered. The horse they brought him was his own. The creature seemed pleased to see him, tossing its head and pressing its muzzle to his arm. Eamon made them fix the bag firmly to the saddle and had them lay his cloak on the horse. The soldiers complied uncertainly, unable to believe that the King was allowing the Hand to leave.

Eamon waited as patiently as he could while they finished their work. Finally, they stepped back.

"Take your prize and go!" Anastasius's voice ripped through the air. Eamon smiled.

"Thank you, Lord Anastasius. I believe that I shall."

"The next time we meet, Goodman –"

"Next time we meet, Lord Anastasius, I shall wear my true colours clearly," Eamon replied.

A faint smile passed the man's lips.

"Go," Hughan told him.

They could say nothing more. It was not the parting he would have chosen.

Turning his back on the King he crossed the river again, leading the horse and driving Leon. He saw traces of black in the woods, and a shudder passed through him. He had done right to hold as he had: they had seen everything.

They walked beyond the perimeter into the silence of the forest. Somewhere, high in the canopy, a bird sang. None hindered them. Leon was silent. Eamon thought he glimpsed wrathful tears in the man's eyes.

They walked some time alone. At last, Eamon judged it to be safe.

"Stop."

Leon did so.

"I cannot unbind you," Eamon added quietly. "I am sorry for that, just as I am sorry for how I have used you today."

"I don't believe you," Leon hissed.

Eamon smiled sadly. "I didn't think that you would."

He took the end of Leon's rope and bound it to a nearby tree. The knot was sturdy, but could be unpicked with a little time. Leon would be able to free himself.

He belted his sword and dagger back to his side before throwing his cloak over his shoulders and mounting his horse. The bagged head was heavy at the beast's side, but the smell of blood did not agitate the horse. It was well trained.

Eamon looked once more to Leon. The man ceased straining against his bonds and now stared at him in stunned silence.

"Give my regards to the King," Eamon told him, and spurred his horse away.

He rode for a long time in silence, his thoughts blurred. The memories of the last few days jostled and mixed with disconcerting ease in his mind. He had made a good Hand – indeed, he had found it easy to play the part. It was an ease born from both the treacheries he had committed in Dunthruik and his familiarity with Lord Cathair.

But he knew also that his service was to the King; he was strengthened by Hughan's continuous trust in him. His place truly was in Dunthruik. As he rode farther, his thoughts cleared.

Yes, he had been a traitor. He had worked against the King; he had been framed by the throned to be Eben's son, a man to betray the King. The throned had always intended for Eamon to strike at Hughan. If he had done so inadvertently that was the same, to the Master, as if he had done so with purpose.

He rode on. He would return to Dunthruik.

"Why aren't we staying in the city?"

He was a boy, barely ten years old, sitting before his father astride a horse which, at the time, seemed the most beautiful creature in the world. It startled him at first, for it was a huge beast. But his father swept him up in his arms and held him close. Eamon had loved the city; it was full of life. They had left it a few short days after his mother's death.

"Why are we leaving? Are we in trouble?"

His father had looked at him and smiled. *"Sometimes, Eamon, it is not what we've done,"* he answered. Eamon heard it as clearly as he had on that horse nearly fourteen years ago. *"It is who we are."*

The motion of the horse brought him back to the present and his father's voice faded away. He had never really understood what his father had meant. He wondered how much Elior Goodman had known about the wayfarers. Had he known the history of his house?

Eamon exhaled deeply. The head in the saddlebag would be accepted by the Master as indelible proof of Eamon's allegiance. His blood was tied to the battle between the house of Brenuin and the throned. In that moment he was certain that Hughan would reclaim what the throned had stolen.

You delude yourself, Eben's son. The voice laughed at him. *The Serpent will fail, and you will witness it. You will serve me until the day of your death, and that shall be a day of my choosing.*

"I am not Eben's son," Eamon replied.

The voice did not answer. He laid a reassuring hand to his horse's mane, and rode on.

CHAPTER VII

It was the evening of the twenty-fifth of February when he reached the main stretch of the River. The water ran away westwards, running at its end past the gates of Dunthruik to the sea.

A small village lay nestled there in the curve of the river. Eamon had lost his bearings more than once on his journey – and lost valuable time with them – but was certain now that he had reached Eastport, one of the River's ferry points. The village had a barge for crossing the River's wide strait. He was a day's ride from Dunthruik.

As he descended the shallow valley to the River, a surge of amazement overcame him. He would return in time: his men would live.

The bag hung limply by his horse's side. How recognizable would the head be by the time he reached the throned?

He reassured himself that it couldn't matter more than a little. He had the head, and that was what mattered.

It drizzled all afternoon. With the coming of evening, the clouds let forth a torrent of water. Eamon slowed his horse, cursing the sky for its outpouring. The horse whinnied in apparent agreement, and Eamon laughed. He drew his cloak and hood up about him as a stark wind, one of the death throes of the cold winter, rattled along the valley floor, bringing with it the bite of the sea. Still the horse carried on steadily, loyal even to him. He might not be a good rider, but the beast was a good companion to him and he had grown fond of it.

Carefully they made their way down to the hamlet on the riverside. Some of the shutters over the tall windows twisted back as he approached, and he saw people peering at him through the hazing rain.

As he neared the hamlet, a middle-aged man with thick, dark hair dared to meet him. He watched as Eamon halted on the path.

"Good evening, my lord," the man said, and bowed before Eamon's dark cloak. "How may we be of service?"

"I must cross the River." Once, Eamon might have spoken the words in arrogance, or in the assurance of his black robes. Once, he would have revelled in the man's obsequious gestures or the flecks of fear in his eyes. But neither of those things mattered to him now. Kind and simple words were truer, both to himself and to the King. "Is the ferry here?"

"Yes, my lord." The man watched Eamon curiously, though with no trace of suspicion.

"I would use it."

"I am one of the ferry-runners, my lord. It is just here. If you would follow me, my lord."

Eamon followed the man as he led the way through the village towards the River. The buildings, mostly of stone, were quiet, though Eamon heard voices between the slanted shutters. The rain was heavy, drumming against the River's skin. Eamon's cloak was becoming cumbersome with wet weight.

A wooden jetty stood at the riverside, its planks darkened by water and its feet reed-encircled. Moored to it was the broad barge, oars tucked neatly inside. The River was wide there. The winter had swollen its banks so that grasses trailed lugubriously beneath the grey waters. The ferry was large enough for two men and a horse, and looked sturdy. Another jetty waited on the far side of the River. From there, Eamon need only follow the water west along the valleys to Dunthruik. He would have a day to spare! His heart leapt as he dismounted.

The man stepped down onto the ferry. Together they convinced the horse to step onto the wooden platform. Uncertain at first, with coaxing the creature stepped down. Eamon followed it, glad of the deep sides to the craft.

Slowly, the ferryman pulled them across the water. The rain grew heavier, wind snatching across disturbed water. But the ferryman seemed unperturbed. The farther bank neared.

When they reached the other side the ferryman deftly launched his ropes and tacked the vessel to the mooring post. Even in the rain the gesture came easily. Eamon admired the man's skill as he disembarked and steadied the craft against the jetty.

"If you'll pass me the reins, my lord, I'll get him down," the ferryman said, gesturing to the horse.

Eamon passed him the reins. Murmuring words of encouragement, the ferryman drew the horse from the ferry. The creature gingerly laid hooves to the jetty.

But the planks were wet, and as the horse brought its hindquarters to the muddy, sodden wood, it slipped. With a frenzied neigh, it lost its footing.

"No!" Eamon cried, as the horse tumbled half into the water, striking the ferry sharply away from the mooring posts. The ferryman dragged at the reins to draw the flailing creature back onto the banks, narrowly avoiding tumbling into the river.

Eamon counted himself lucky that the mooring ropes held. Recovering from the jolt of the strike, he took hold of the cord with wet hands and dragged himself back to the jetty. Cursing quietly he stumbled onto the jetty and then the bank, where the ferryman quieted the shivering horse.

"Are you well, my lord?" the man called anxiously.

"Yes," he answered. "My horse?"

"Took a sharp knock, lord." His voice shook. Eamon realized that the saddlebag had torn open in the scuffle, and the severed head showed through the opening.

Eamon walked up to the horse and quickly closed the bag. When he looked up he saw the ferryman examining the horse's legs. As he reached the hind right he suddenly froze. The stallion's leg was bruised, and a deep cut ran along it. The horse stumbled as they looked, and held its weight uncomfortably.

Eamon felt himself paling. He looked back to the ferryman. In terror, the man dropped to his knees.

"Please, my lord," he whispered, clenching his hands together.

Eamon reached into his pouch and drew out a couple of coins. They felt heavy in his soaking hand.

"Hold out your hand," he said.

Trembling, the ferryman closed his eyes.

"Please, lord," the man breathed, stretching out a shaking hand, "have pity on my livelihood –"

His words were broken by a gasp as the two coins dropped into his palm. Feeling their chink, he looked up in amazement. Eamon watched him.

"You rendered me good service, ferryman."

"Thank you, my lord." The man barely raised his voice above a whisper. Perhaps he feared that he was living in a terrible dream. Watching him, Eamon grew strangely angry – but not towards the ferryman. Who were the Hands, that they should make men fear for their livelihoods?

"Stand up," he said.

Shaking, the man did so. Eamon firmly took hold of the man's shoulder. "Ferryman," he said, "no man has the right to take from you your hand or prop or life for such an error. Do you understand?"

The oarsman stared at him in utter amazement, rain coursing down his face. Eamon held the man's gaze. After a moment, the shaken ferryman nodded.

"Yes, my lord." Eamon smiled, but the oarsman gestured weakly to the bleeding horse. "Your horse, lord –"

"Has been saved from death." Eamon looked down and saw the horse, still tossing its head in pain. Its hind leg bled heartily. He suspected the poor beast had also sprained its muscles in its wild flail for the bank.

"Will he still walk?" he asked, trying not to let his anxiety fill his voice. He was so close to Dunthruik!

"Yes, my lord," the oarsman told him. "But he will be slow, and it will hurt him. He will take no weight."

Eamon's heart sank. His calculation had been to arrive in Dunthruik sometime on the following day, the twenty-sixth, and have a whole day of his time left. With his horse injured he would have to walk the distance himself. He filled with dread. He did not know if he could still arrive in time, and one thing was certain: he would have to leave the horse.

"There are no horses here that I might take?"

"No, my lord," the ferryman replied. "We have some mules, farm animals mostly, but none can bear you onwards swiftly. The horses have all been taken by the Master's messengers."

Eamon drew a deep breath. Eastport was both a ferry and a relay post; if all of its horses were already in use, then it spoke of the dispatch of a huge number of messengers. Most likely they had been sent out to the regions with commands from the throned. It also implied that matters in the River Realm were not as secure as most in Dunthruik were led to believe. Perhaps the defeats at Ashford Ridge and Pinewood were not isolated incidents.

Slowly, Eamon reached up and stroked the horse's nose.

"Rest well," he told it, and proceeded to unfasten the bagged head from the saddle. He took the reins and turned to the ferryman. "What is your name?"

"Marilio Bellis, my lord."

Eamon pressed the reins firmly into his hands. "I must speed to Dunthruik, so I will kindly ask you to care for this poor beast. He has been a faithful servant to me."

"Yes, my lord."

"Thank you, Mr Bellis." Eamon touched the horse's muzzle reassuringly, and drew his belongings together.

"My lord!" The man spoke as Eamon turned to leave, a touch of wonder in his voice. "My lord, who are you?"

"I am Lord Goodman, of the city of Dunthruik."

Marilio Bellis tugged gently at the horse's reins. "I will bring him back to you, my lord," he said, his face a picture of sudden but immutable fidelity.

Eamon watched in utter surprise. He smiled. "That would be a great kindness."

"It would be one well deserved," the ferryman answered.

Eamon hefted the bag and, taking a firm grip upon it, stroked his horse's neck one last time. "I leave you in good hands," he told it. "I bid you farewell, Mr Bellis."

"Farewell, Lord Goodman."

Eamon turned and, wishing the rain to wash him of the anxiety dogging his steps, climbed up to the path that ran along the riverside.

He walked until deep into the night. Though the rain all but obscured his sight, he followed the road from Eastport to the East Road. The way grew broader, and the knotted valleys widened out into open plains that ran along the River. Some of them bore fields, and Eamon saw small lights nestled at the field edges, marking villages. He had no light, his travelling companion was a severed head, and the road was desperately dark. Footsore, he pressed on. He had to see Dunthruik's walls before nightfall on the twenty-seventh.

You will not be in time. They will all pay, the voice sneered at him, but he did not heed it.

The rain grew heavier, and he was forced to seek shelter beneath a large copse of trees. He stood, wrapped thickly in his cloak, his precious cargo held firmly against him. While the rain cascaded through the leaves, he turned his hands up to gather a drink. It was sweet. He was not hungry, and, as the rain clouds thinned to reveal a slim moon, he realized suddenly that he was not tired.

Laughing, he let his sodden cloak fly freely behind him in the cold. He took to the road again. The fields stretched out by him, and the River grew to a torrent to the south. As he walked he sang to himself, quietly at first, to melodies that he did not recognize and in words more beautiful than those of any song he had ever sung.

They spoke of the King, and though he'd forgotten them as soon as they left his lips, they comforted him.

He rested a little in the morning, then went on. All that day and most of the following night, he walked, water creeping into his boots at every muddy puddle. As the dawn appeared he saw the thin grey line of the sea marking the horizon, and before it a thick bannered mark which he knew to be Dunthruik. The moon slimmed away overhead.

It was the morning of the twenty-seventh. He took firmer hold of the bag in his hand, and strode on.

By mid-morning the wind pushed the dawn mist away and the city was clear before him. He remembered the road – he had walked it with Cathair and again with his broken men when he returned from Pinewood. Now he walked it alone, and his heart felt unburdened. The day had dawned clear, and his cloak felt warm over his shoulders.

He soon met the first groups of travellers – merchants with bags of discoloured grain and bakers offering dry bread at prices more than a little too high, but the winter had been harsh and it was all there was to be had. Eamon saw dying pyres to the north-east, still sending smoke into the sky. What work had they done during the night? He could at least take comfort in the certainty that his men would not be laid on them that day.

On he walked. People bowed before him, felled by his black cloak. As he went on they stared, and as they stared he felt the smile on his face growing.

The Blind Gate rose before him. None of it had changed. The stone eagles and the Gauntlet were on duty there, checking all who passed. The sun struck at Eamon's eyes, temporarily blinding him from the identities of the faces he approached. As he reached the gate, a road-worn Hand with a sodden bag, the ensign on duty looked up and grew pale.

"Lord Goodman," he breathed, and bowed. Every man in the checking line followed his gaze and gesture.

"May I pass?" Eamon asked gently.

The ensign glanced at the bag, and nodded dumbly.

Eamon thanked him and moved past. As he did so he heard his name on other lips.

"Lord Goodman!" they cried. Turning, he saw cadet Manners emerging from the shadow of the gate, his face wide with elation.

"You're here!" He laughed out loud and turned to the streets by him. "He's here!" he called. The whole street echoed it. "Lord Goodman is here!"

Commotion stirred around him. His name ran on the wind. Heads turned. Eyes watched in awe.

With a broad smile, Eamon looked at Manners. It was the twenty-seventh of February, and he was in Dunthruik.

"I am going to the palace," he said. "Will you walk with me, cadet?"

Manners fell into step beside him with a delirious grin as Eamon walked the length of the Coll. Each stone seemed familiar to him and from every window, every door, every balcony – from every place where a face could look – a face watched. For many had heard of the task he had been set, and as the watching eyes saw the bag he bore and the look on his face, his name passed their lips.

"Lord Goodman!"

He heard people walking behind him, drawn by his return and the way his name was spoken, following him to the palace. Other cadets and soldiers, men who had served him in the city or at Pinewood, were on the Coll. His name went through the city before him and called them out of the places where they had lain and feared the breaking of that day. Each greeted him with a cry of joy and he greeted them each in turn, by name when he could. They joined the train of people walking with him.

Soon the palace gates rose before them. The nobles and their ladies who strolled there turned to stare. Before such a mass of men, they had no choice but to draw up their skirts and cloaks and fall back to the edges of the road.

The Hands at the Hands' Gate did not stop him. They gazed at the crowd of men who followed him into the yard. Only a week before, those same men had been gathered to face the wrath of the Right Hand.

He strode firmly to the hall's colonnade. A group of Hands stood by the doors to the hall, their heads bent attentively towards a familiar face: Cathair. How long it had been since he had seen Cathair! But where once he would have quaked at the piercing power of those green eyes, Eamon now stood tall. A victorious smile passed over his face. He knew what was happening: the Hand was diligently preparing to round up all of Eamon's men to administer the Master's justice.

"I want them all brought, do you understand?" Cathair's eyes flashed with a grisly anticipation of slaughter as he spoke. "To a man."

"You need not trouble yourself, Lord Cathair." Eamon was surprised by his own firm tone, but he did not rue it. He had done the task they had given him to do. Though they had sought to trap him in it, he had escaped. He had seen the King, and he knew that the King loved him. It gave him indelible strength. "I have brought my men." And he had: the jubilant mass filed into the courtyard behind him. Seeing the Hands, they smartly took to ranks.

Cathair looked up and stared at him. The Hand's eyes dropped slowly to the bag Eamon held. The pallid face grew paler.

Could it be that Cathair had not known of Eamon's success? To whom, then, was Febian reporting?

"It's impossible!" one of the other Hands muttered. Cathair glared at him before smothering the glare under a sinister scowl.

"Lord Goodman," he said. "I was told that you might answer me regarding an incident in the Pit last week –"

"Summon the Right Hand."

The Hand blinked in astonishment.

"What?"

A deafening silence fell.

"Summon the Right Hand," Eamon repeated. "I have performed a mighty task for the Master."

"He sees it."

Eamon's blood curdled. The sudden silence had been caused not by his audacity, but by the presence of another. Every man behind him had fallen to his knees. Before him the Hands fell to theirs.

Eamon turned to find himself looking up into the steely eyes of the throned.

Fear cracked at his frozen courage. He stared, remembering the terrible moment but a week before when the Master's hands had reached out and torn the heart of the King from his neck.

Now he met the Master's eyes. He alone remained standing.

Slowly, he raised the bag in his hand.

"Master," he said, "I bring you the head of Feltumadas, heir to Anastasius of Istanaria, ally to the Serpent, and commander of an army that dared to stand against you." He reached into the bag. His fingers touched the hair, grizzled by rain and travel, but he did not flinch. What if…?

Momentary terror assailed him. What if the head had not retained its disguise? What if he drew out the head of a Hand?

Wordlessly, he held the throned's gaze. It took all of his courage. He drew out what was concealed and, showing it, bent his knee before the throned.

"Your glory, Master."

Silence hung. Eamon did not dare look up. His knees trembled. As he held the heavy, bloodied head high he forced his arm to be strong.

"Your service is accepted." The throned's voice spoke at last, a clap of thunder in the stillness. Eamon looked up. The Master smiled on him. It chilled his core.

The throned nodded once to the Right Hand, who stood beside him. Eamon did not know how he could not have seen the Hand before.

The Master turned and left, his will imparted to his Right Hand.

Eamon watched as the Hand raised his voice to the stunned body of gathered men.

"Let it be known that all those men who stood to lose their lives are, by the will of the Master, pardoned and restored to honour. This trophy," he added, indicating the head, "will be set at the Blind Gate. To his glory."

"To his glory!" The courtyard erupted into a mass of rejoicing men.

"An impressive feat, Lord Goodman." The Right Hand's voice was suddenly in his ear.

"Thank you, my lord," he answered, holding the head to one side as he bowed low.

"You will come to the Hands' Hall tomorrow."

Before he could answer, the Right Hand turned and left. Cathair half scowled at him before snatching the head from his hands and stalking after the Right Hand.

As he watched them go, a cold sweat broke suddenly across his brow.

Had they seen? Did they know?

Surely they would never have pardoned his men if they had known the truth.

A group of Third Banner cadets, led by Manners, surged up around him.

"Long live Lord Goodman!" cried one, and it was not long before they had all taken up the cry. Eamon found himself laughing as the cadets, *his* cadets, ran up one by one and seized his hands.

"Lord Goodman!"

"How did you get the head?"

"Did you see the Serpent?"

"Now is not the time for me to answer these questions," Eamon told them gently. The cadets shrugged off his answer without a shred of disappointment and his name ran around the yard on their lips. Eyes watched him from the upper windows of the Hands' Hall, but he did not care. These men loved him, and he had proved that he loved them. He had saved them.

Eventually the men began to leave the courtyard, eager to carry the news to any who still awaited the outcome of the day. The cadets, mindful that Waite would be waiting for them back at the college, were eventually persuaded to leave also. Eamon watched them go, deep contentment in his heart.

"You shall be the talk of the whole city tonight, Lord Goodman," said a voice.

Eamon felt joy wash over him.

"Anderas!"

The East Quarter captain was still pale, but able to walk once again. He bore no stick and no aid.

"Of course, I was expecting you to come at sunset, just as they had lined us up." Anderas's blue eyes twinkled mischievously. "I was half hoping that you would burst in, framed by the setting sun, and thunderously cry '*Stop!*' just as they were setting sword to the first man." He laughed. "That is how they'll tell it in a hundred inns throughout the city tonight. It would have been very much in your style."

Eamon smiled broadly. "Some things cannot be left to style, captain."

"That is precisely where your style lies, lord," Anderas replied. The blue eyes watched Eamon for a moment. He wished suddenly that he could tell the captain everything that had befallen him in the last seven days: if only Anderas knew the King!

Anderas reached out and clasped hands with him like a brother. "Welcome home, Lord Goodman."

Home. The word no longer seemed strange to him. Yes, Dunthruik was home, and Eamon knew at last that he could live in the city and serve the King.

"Thank you, captain," he said.

CHAPTER VIII

The day of his triumphant return to Dunthruik was a day that Eamon knew he would never forget. Every man, woman, and child answered his look with open-mouthed stares of awe. He was the man who had been made a lieutenant on the whim of a captain, surrendered his sword and escaped the wayfarers, become a first lieutenant in the West Quarter in three days, and a Hand in months. Now, he had brought back the head of the throned's enemy and saved the lives of many. The people called his name in jubilation, for in all he did, he brought glory to the Master who ruled the city of Dunthruik. They shared in his triumph.

And yet, in moments of quiet, Eamon wondered what the city's wayfarers would think when they heard the news. They would not rejoice. They would weep. He was sure that Cathair would use the beheading of Feltumadas to sour the minds of the King's men held in the Pit.

The Right Hand granted him the remainder of the day to rest and to reorient himself. He was grateful for it, but found himself at a loss. He wandered, basking in praise from every quarter. On that day every man knew his name.

It was about mid-afternoon when a familiar voice greeted him as he passed the Brand.

"Hail, wanderer returned!"

Eamon smiled. "Ladomer," he answered, catching his breath as his friend embraced him enthusiastically.

"I can't believe that you did it!" Ladomer cried, slapping Eamon's shoulder so hard that Eamon had to take a moment to recover.

"I see being a paper carrier hasn't dulled your arm!"

"If I had to spar you now, like we used to in Edesfield, I'd still beat you in about three seconds," Ladomer told him with a friendly wink.

"I believe it!"

"And I really can't believe that you did what you've done," Ladomer replied with a reckless grin. "I was there when Cathair brought the head into the Hands' Hall. Ratbag, you should have *seen* his face! He was *fuming*."

"He was looking forward to killing them?"

"Yes." Ladomer shrugged. "Lord Cathair is disgusted with you, but the Master…" He gave a low whistle, smiled, and jogged Eamon's arm. "He is impressed."

A chill ran down Eamon's spine. "He is?"

"He *is*. You forget that you address the one, only, and *impeccably* dressed servant of the Right Hand. He confides many things to me, Lord Goodman."

What kind of things? Eamon wondered.

Ladomer grinned. "Cathair sent the head down to the Blind Gate to be hung up. The Right Hand had a meeting with the Master so told me that I could be spared for an hour. I want to see it," Ladomer enthused, catching Eamon's arm with a great-lunged laugh. "And, when I look at it, I want the man who brought it from the Serpent's grasp to stand beside me and tell me how it came to be there."

"Ladomer," Eamon began, "I haven't given any official testimony of that to anyone. I don't think it would be –"

"Then you can tell me all the parts that you intend to omit!" he added greedily.

Eamon allowed himself to be convinced to return down the Coll to the Blind Gate. People hollered his name as he passed, congratulating him on his service to the city. Eamon smiled, suddenly uncomfortable under the collar of his thick cloak. There had been a time when this kind of praise had been the very substance on which he lived. Now, they praised him for striking a blow against their enemy, not knowing he had struck against the one who now dealt in dark counsels with the Right Hand.

Eamon glanced uncertainly back towards the palace as they moved down the Coll.

"A sight for sore eyes, isn't it, Ratbag?"

"What do they do?" Eamon asked suddenly.

"What do you mean?" Ladomer quizzically cocked his head.

"The Master and the Right Hand," Eamon answered slowly. It was a strange question he asked. "I understand that there is much work to be done in governing the River Realm, and I don't doubt that much of it is beyond what I can understand, but…"

"They rule," Ladomer answered, as though that were enough.

"Then what of the city?" Eamon asked, deciding to change tack. "Tell me, O most impeccably dressed! What has been happening here while I was away?"

"You missed not a thing. Some noble or other challenged another to a duel at a state function. You'd have liked it," he added with a cheeky grin. "It was over the honour of a woman. They were both drunk, of course, and the challenger withdrew the next morning when, as I understand it, his lady wife had been kind enough to tell him exactly whom he could and could not duel for!"

They paused at the Four Quarters to allow some traffic to pass by. Eamon's eyes turned east. He wondered where Anderas was.

The traffic quelled, and as they passed the city wall the Blind Gate came into view. "The cull has continued very successfully," Ladomer continued.

"Yes?" Eamon prompted, feeling his heart sink.

"Oh yes, some excellent work has been done, especially by that captain… I can't think of his name… East Quarter…" He waved wildly east with his arm, as though to aid his flailing memory.

"Anderas?" Eamon's sunken heart grew heavy. Anderas was a man who did his duty. Eamon could not fault him for that. And yet…

"Anderas! That's him. Oh, he's filled whole pyres by himself. A slight exaggeration, I'll confess, but all founded in truth, I assure you. Did you know his first name is *Andreas*? Cruellest parents on the River, if you ask me!" Eamon was grateful that his friend laughed so hard that his own discomfort was hidden.

Anderas has lead the cull? It was abhorrent to him; a splintering wound lodged in his chest.

"In other news," Ladomer said, lowering his voice, "there's been a bit of gossip flying about concerning that Turnholt woman of yours."

"Lady Turnholt," Eamon told him, surprised by his own ferocity.

"*Lady* Turnholt," Ladomer corrected himself. Eamon noted a careful look to his friend's eye. "Did something happen between the two of you?"

Eamon didn't answer.

"They're saying that she's gone back to her father's lands, to the north. The Master himself bade her farewell – who knows what new service the house gave to afford such honour!"

"The Right Hand didn't tell you?"

"He told me that she left bearing a message to her ailing father and that she was in the company of Lord Fleance," Ladomer replied, "whose lands adjoin his. There was talk of…" He fixed Eamon strangely. "No," he said at last, a touch of sorrow to him. He took Eamon's shoulder. "Perhaps you needn't know it all."

Eamon stared. He understood.

All her words and pleas, tearfully given as she knelt before him… she had promised – nay, *sworn* – that she loved him, *him and no other*, and that she always would. She had no ailing father. No – she had left the city with another.

She had lied to him.

"Something did happen, didn't it?" Ladomer looked carefully at him. "Are you all right? Eamon?"

Eamon drew a deep breath and walked on. Ladomer followed him. They continued to the Blind Gate. After a few minutes of silence, Ladomer spoke again. "I heard something just after you left," he said. Eamon felt his friend's keen, almost baiting, interest. "Something about the Pit."

Eamon went cold. He tried not to show any trace of emotion as he met Ladomer's gaze.

"What about it?"

"I should rephrase that." Ladomer spoke more quietly this time. He fixed Eamon firmly in his gaze. "I saw the Pit – what was left of it."

Eamon met his look unflinchingly. His friend searched his eyes; Eamon thought that he saw a trace of fear in Ladomer's face.

"They say it happened while you were there. That there was a storm of light… The Pit certainly suffered for it! What happened, Eamon?"

"Ladomer, sometimes the servants of the Serpent are strong. But faced with the Master, they are less than creatures blinded by dust and wasted with hunger."

"This Grahaven, your ward… he is a strong one?"

"Yes. He did what you saw."

"He has paid for it," Ladomer answered with an arrogant sniff. "He pays for it often."

Eamon's heart wrenched.

Ladomer laughed nastily. "Between them, Lords Ashway and Cathair have been grinding him down."

"Good." Never had a more hateful word left Eamon's lips.

They had reached the far end of the Coll now, the Blind Gate tall before them. Eamon felt the eyes of countless carved eagles glaring down at him. As they approached he caught sight of a group of Gauntlet soldiers atop the gate-tower. The men were setting a head – *the* head – upon a pike. A crowd gathered to watch the work. As the grisly token was raised it was met by a great cheer and clapping.

Ladomer and Eamon watched silently. Ladomer laughed and gestured exultantly at the newly impaled head. "Look at your work, Lord Goodman!"

Eamon looked, wondering how well Lord Rendolet enjoyed his new view of the city.

They walked back to the palace together and Ladomer hurried off, eager not to be missing when the Right Hand emerged.

It was early evening. Without orders from the other Hands or from the throned, and without even Ladomer's company, Eamon felt strangely purposeless. His thoughts returned to Hughan, to the preparations that the King would even then be making to protect and reconnect the camp to its Easter allies. He wondered about Leon – would the man forgive him when he learned the truth? And what of Feltumadas – was he safe and well? Had he been told what had happened?

He rehearsed their faces before his mind, fearing that those memories, so powerful while he lived them, would fade. He had not been able to say farewell to Aeryn or Lillabeth, or Giles, or Ma Mendel. He knew that they were far safer with the King than he was in the city.

He took to strolling in the Royal Plaza and then returned to the Coll. The odd passer-by stopped to congratulate him, but the wave of praise died down as the sun slipped away.

He wandered, lost in his thoughts. None bothered him. It was turning dark when at last he emerged from his reverie.

He stood before the gates to Alessia's house. But the doors were shut, the windows barred, and no lights burned in welcome.

It came softly, unbidden: the memory of her touch, of her hand in his – the smell of her hair, lying between them in the bed they had shared. The music of her laughter. The tenderness of her embrace. The sincerity and strength of her hands when she had found him, kneeling, by her fireside, his own blood on his hands. She had bound him, soothed him, cherished him. Surely he had… surely he had loved her?

She was gone.

He felt something burn hot against his face. He struck the tear away.

Hadn't she loved him? Anger in place of sorrow. *Hadn't she?*

No; she had whored herself to him, on the whim of another. Her adulation was nothing but falsehood. Now she had whored herself to Fleance. She had been rewarded – Ladomer had seen it with his own eyes – the throned had bid her farewell in person! It was a reward for her treachery, for her beguilement of his weak heart – it had to be. He saw how it would have been, how Ladomer would have seen her – her teasing smile, her lips lingering on Fleance's cheek, her arms twined lithely about another.

No; he would feel no sorrow. She had scorned him. She had betrayed him.

If Lillabeth's child grew never having met its father, it would be Alessia's doing.

He shivered, though he was not cold. He drove his hurt deep inside. She was gone. Part of him had gone with her, shattered and torn as her faith had been.

With a bitter taste in his mouth, he turned and made his way back to the Hands' Hall.

He woke long before dawn, to see the throned's banner hanging over him. It seemed a strange guardian. Cold clung to him as he rose, washed, and dressed. His room, still and empty, seemed as unwelcoming as a tomb. He left it swiftly. He was wanted by the Hands that morning.

His footsteps sounded dead in the courtyard as he passed along the colonnade to the Hands' Hall. Its posts framed the pastel sky like an obsidian relic. Their sharply carved letters cut his eyes like knives. He turned from them and went inside.

Cathair was in the atrium. His green eyes flashed, but he remained disturbingly civil.

"Lord Goodman."

"Lord Cathair."

"You slept well, I trust?"

"I did. Yourself?"

"Well indeed."

The doors to the greater hall opened. They passed within.

The Right Hand was seated upon the raised chair in the hall, his shadow long across the floor. He rose and came forward to greet them. Eamon bowed.

"My lord."

"Your work has been well done, Lord Goodman," the Right Hand told him. "The Master passes on his congratulations once again."

"Thank you, my lord," Eamon answered. He did not meet the Right Hand's eyes – this was the man he had brashly defied before leaving the city. As the Right Hand watched him, he knew that the throned's closest had not forgotten it.

"It is the Master's desire for you to serve Lord Cathair over the coming weeks."

Eamon saw Cathair look up sharply.

"Lord Cathair still has much to teach you, if you will learn it," the Right Hand continued. "He has been a master of men, and a servant of the Master, for years uncounted."

"His glory." Eamon risked a discreet glance at Cathair. The Hand's eyes raged green fire, but he held his tongue.

"Tell me of your mission," the Right Hand continued. "I would hear how you accomplished it."

At the Right Hand's gesture Eamon rose and spoke of what he had done. He spoke of how he had been to the King's camp and endeared himself to them, how the pontoon bridge had been destroyed – for which he claimed the credit – creating a rift between the Serpent and his allies which, even if it did not destroy the alliance, would severely damage it. Last of all, he told how he had used that rift to kill Feltumadas and then forced the Serpent to trade the life of one of his own men for the head which now so richly adorned the Blind Gate.

"You let this man live?" the Right Hand asked quietly.

Eamon met his gaze, sensing that the incident at the village on the way back from Pinewood lurked in the Right Hand's mind.

"Yes, my lord," Eamon answered, and smiled. "He will be of no trouble to us again. He has been bettered by me, and cannot hope to overcome that shame, either for himself or to those under him.

As for the Easters, I do not expect them to maintain their crumbling alliance too long, given how short-sighted their ally proved to be."

"Is it so, Lord Febian?" the Right Hand called.

The summoned Hand emerged from the shadows where he had hidden throughout the meeting. Eamon felt a chill go through him.

"Lord Febian." He allowed himself to sound surprised – Cathair looked it. So the Lord of the West Quarter had not known of Febian's mission. Like Cathair, Eamon turned to the Right Hand as though to ask how it was that Febian could give any answer. The Right Hand smiled. Eamon tried hard not to do the same. He surmised that Febian had not spoken of their encounter in the woods near the King's camp: so much the better.

Febian did not blink. Instead, he bowed to the Right Hand. "My lord."

"What say you, Lord Febian?" the Right Hand asked. "Is it as he tells it?"

"Yes, my lord." The Hand's answer was firm. "It is."

The Right Hand gave a satisfied nod before turning back to Eamon. "I believe that Lord Cathair has some matters of business this morning. You will accompany him, Lord Goodman."

"Yes, my lord."

Eamon bowed once more; Cathair did the same. In silence, they left together.

Outside the hall Eamon welcomed the cool morning air, inhaling deeply to clear his head. He paused and glanced at Cathair. The Lord of the West Quarter matched his gaze. He smiled icily.

"It seems that you have been pressed into my service, Lord Goodman," he said.

"I would not say pressed, my lord –" Eamon began.

"What happened in the Pit?"

The question was ferociously direct. Eamon stared.

"My lord?"

"I am reliably informed that before you went head-hunting you went down to the Pit. It may interest you to know, Lord Goodman, that since that day the Pit has been rendered somewhat inoperable."

"I surmised as much when I left it," Eamon told him. In his mind he heard again the singing, felt his joy at Mathaiah's forgiveness, saw light cracking along the walls...

Cathair glared at him with a look that might grind blood from a stone. "Learn this, and learn it well, Lord Goodman: none descend to the Pit without my foreknowing."

"I am sorry, Lord Cathair," Eamon answered demurely. "It was late, and I had need of information before I left." Though tempted, he did not add that with the Pit inoperable, there was no danger of a repeated offence. "I had no wish to disturb you at such a time."

"The Pit is half collapsed," Cathair continued bluntly. "I am told this occurred after you descended into it."

"What are you suggesting, Lord Cathair?" Eamon demanded.

Cathair stared at him, saying nothing. Then he smiled.

"Tell me, Lord Goodman; have you seen your ward since you returned?"

The shift in subject almost caught Eamon off guard. He laughed nastily. "No, my lord."

Cathair smiled – a long, creeping, spine-chilling smile. "I think you should."

It was to the Pit that Cathair led him. Fear crept into Eamon's limbs as he followed down the long, familiar steps. The torches guttered, the air thick with dust. It was not long before the smell reached them and Eamon nearly retched. How could he have forgotten that smell in so short a time? It had only been a week. It felt an eternity.

The Pit was as he remembered it, with rubble strewn everywhere. The narrow hole through which he had initially been lowered was a gaping orifice. The apparatus for the lowering and retrieving of prisoners hung brokenly to one side.

Eamon noticed Cathair shudder, but euphoria touched him as he remembered his visit with Mathaiah. It was almost as though some echo of the song lingered in the walls. The stones, forced so long to witness torment, could do nothing but witness to the strength of the blue light.

A couple of Hands on duty made their respectful greetings to Cathair. One of them stared at Eamon – was it one of the Hands who had been there a week ago?

Cathair took him to one of the rooms off the central chamber, one that he had not been to before. A red stone guarded its entrance. It was cracked and singed. Had the blue light done that, too?

The door opened into a room that might hold two dozen people, its walls dimly lit by torches. Between the torchlight, Eamon glimpsed the angular writing that also marked the doors to the throne room and the Hands' Hall. It turned his stomach. The harsh words seared his eyes, imprinting themselves in his mind so that when he looked away he could see them still.

The same letters marked the Nightholt.

Near the centre of the room was a table covered in sheets of parchment, an inkwell and quill perched on one side. There were a couple of chairs but only one, on the far side, was occupied. In it sat Mathaiah, his arms bound to the arms of the chair and his legs to its legs. The cadet was deathly pale. Deep marks rimmed his eyes like enormous bruises; slashes and cuts covered his bare arms. Eamon's dream – of Mathaiah, crying out – returned to him.

Around Mathaiah several Hands were gathered. One held the cadet's head, forcing him to look at the papers scattered on the table. A couple of Hands were positioned at either side of him, armed with small blades that glinted red – as did the fresher wounds on Mathaiah's arms. Blood laced the floor and table.

As Cathair entered, one of the Hands towered over Mathaiah. The cadet's eyes were pressed shut as he fought to wrest his head free from the Hands.

"For the last time, you wretched snake!" the Hand yelled, his voice swollen with rage. Eamon realized with a start that it was Ashway. "Or I will tear your eyes out!" The Hand holding Mathaiah's head wrenched it sharply to the side. For a horrible moment, Eamon feared that the cadet's neck would be broken. But the Hand knew his trade: Mathaiah only gasped.

"If there is any gouging to be done then I think you will find, Lord Ashway, that such delights fall under my jurisdiction," Cathair interrupted soberly. Eamon wondered at the perilous tone to his voice.

Ashway rounded on him. "This whole wretched affair is your jurisdiction! If you hadn't –"

"Lord Ashway," Cathair said.

Ashway fell silent. The Hand looked paler than usual. As Eamon watched, Ashway pressed a hand to the side of his head; his fingers shook where his dark gloves encased them. He glared darkly at Cathair.

"I'll not waste any more of my –"

"Outside."

Cathair's rage was a serpent, coiled and ready to strike.

Ashway glared. "You would dare to –?"

"I said outside."

Panting a little, Ashway drew himself up straight and strode from the room. Cathair followed him. Both Hands went into the main chamber and pulled the door closed behind them. Eamon heard raised voices, but could not make out their words.

He looked at Mathaiah. As Ashway had stormed out of the room the Hand holding the cadet's head had thumped it hard against the back of the chair. Now he laughed as the cadet moaned. The Hand moved to strike the young man again.

"Hold!" Eamon commanded. As he spoke he saw Mathaiah's eyes drawing open. Pale and bloodshot, as they rested on Eamon a glimpse of light returned to them.

The Hand looked up at him. "Hold?"

Eamon strode over. "This is no way to use a prisoner, lord," Eamon told him. "This is a matter requiring a certain finesse."

"Lord Ashway has tried finesse," the Hand retorted testily. As he spoke, Eamon saw the other Hands retreat from him.

"You are Lord Goodman," one of them said.

"Yes, I am." The eyes of the Hand before him grew wide with trepidation. "And I shall show you why my name is feared."

Slowly he leaned himself against the table to look squarely into Mathaiah's eyes. "Mr Grahaven, I find you in a somewhat poorer condition than when we last met."

"I am no poorer," Mathaiah answered simply. Eamon idly scooped up the papers on the table and scoured them. It was clear to him that Mathaiah was being made to read something. But what?

The pages all bore the same thing – the hideous lettering from the Hands' Hall. As Eamon nonchalantly perused it, foreboding crossed his heart. The papers had the look of something copied, the letters rushed and misshapen, as though scribed by a less expert hand. They had none of the bold and angular incisiveness of the letters he knew.

The answer came to him like a blow: the Nightholt. They were copies of pages from the book that they had found in Ellenswell – the book that, on Eamon's insistence, they had delivered to the Hands. Mathaiah had said then that he could almost read it; Eamon had said as much to Alessia.

She had told the Right Hand.

He looked up at Mathaiah, saw his unscathed face – his *untouched* eyes – and understood. They needed the young man's eyes because they were making him read the Nightholt. But why would they need him to?

In silence Eamon laid the papers down. "Have they told you of my latest exploit, Mr Grahaven?"

Mathaiah did not answer, but Eamon saw the other Hands staring at him. He laughed arrogantly.

"You may well be the last person in the city to hear of it," he said, "but I relish the telling to you especially. I have destroyed the Serpent's alliance with the Easter houses. The head of Feltumadas, heir to the house of Istanaria, even now stands impaled upon the Blind Gate. But you are, perhaps," he added indolently, "uninterested in that?"

"You cannot destroy the King," Mathaiah retorted fiercely. "Nor can you extinguish the light brought by the house of Brenuin!"

The other Hands seemed startled that he had spoken. They glanced at each other and then at Eamon nervously.

"Do not let him sing, Lord Goodman!" one of them hissed.

Eamon looked back to Mathaiah. "Always you think of the house of Brenuin. But what of the house of Grahaven?"

Mathaiah fell still. It was not how he wanted to bring such news to his friend, but there was no other way. He laughed. "Your father is old, your brother is dead. Only you remain, and on my travels, *snake*, I had the pleasure of meeting your charming wife." Mathaiah's eyes widened, but he remained silent. "She bears the last heir of your line. Be assured, Grahaven," he said, lowering his voice, "that unless you render unto Lord Ashway everything that he needs, I will hunt down your wife and base-born child and, finding them, will serve them suffering, torment, and death."

"Then you may bear my wife a message," Mathaiah said weakly.

Eamon fixed Mathaiah with his most arrogant glare.

"You would make a messenger of me, snake?" he sneered.

Mathaiah met his gaze with a small smile.

"Tell her that if my son is to be base-born, then she shall name him Eamon."

Breath failed him.

"What?" His voice came as a whisper, which the Hands, judging by their faces, took to be deep anger.

"You are not deaf, Lord Goodman," Mathaiah answered. As Eamon stared Mathaiah gave him a simple, slight nod.

The door opened. Cathair entered, eyes flashing. He took in the room at a glance.

"Lord Goodman."

"My lord?"

"There is work to be done."

"Yes, my lord." Eamon looked at Mathaiah one last time.

The cadet's eyes were steady. Eamon wondered that such a heart could be in one so young and marvelled that he had the honour of calling such a man his friend.

Cathair called his name again. Without hesitating, Eamon followed.

Back in the open air, Eamon realized just how hot he felt. He was flushed with emotions that he didn't understand, with senses of obligation and foreboding and the sudden memory of a promise he had made to Lillabeth.

He had to try to get Mathaiah out, but how could he? He could not go down to the Pit without Cathair knowing of it. Even if he could, he did not know how he might get Mathaiah out of it or whether it would be safe to take him to the Serpentine…

Ashway stood in the courtyard, pacing ferociously around the flagstones. He might have been tracing patterns on them and avoiding the cracks while he muttered to himself. Eamon wondered what words the two Hands had exchanged.

Ashway looked up as they emerged. He was red, as though he might explode into a tirade, but on seeing Eamon, fell silent. Eamon feigned not to notice.

"Lord Goodman, please accompany Lord Ashway back to the East Quarter," Cathair said. "He has copies of some notes which I need. Bring them to me."

"Yes, Lord Cathair."

"Do you think that I need to be – ?" Ashway began, but a look from Cathair silenced him. "I will send you the notes, Lord Cathair," he hissed.

"Thank you, Lord Ashway."

Tangible ire passed between the two. With a great sigh, Ashway turned on his heel and stalked off. Eamon bowed once to Cathair and then hurried after the Lord of the East Quarter.

Ashway did not wait for him. Keeping pace with the Hand was like chasing a wrathful beast as it darted and wheeled down the colonnade, through the Hands' Gate and onto the streets of Dunthruik. Eventually Eamon managed to set his step in time with

Ashway's. He caught a glimpse of the man's face, its accustomed pallor disguised by rage.

Ashway walked in silence all the way to the Four Quarters and then strode abruptly down Coronet Rise towards the Ashen and his own Handquarters. Soldiers and Gauntlet and civilians froze before him and bowed as he passed, but Ashway scowled angrily at most of them. To the others he barked that they should remove their sodden carcasses from his path or join the next pyre wagon.

Eamon came after him as though in the wake of a devastating wind.

Ashway's Handquarters were an impressive set of buildings in the quarter's main square. A broad marble slab set into the wall announced that the square was known as the Ashen and a token collection of ash trees were growing in one of its corners. The buildings were tall and well kept, and the square was clean, crawling with Gauntlet soldiers who all looked busy. Just to the right of the Handquarters Eamon saw a low arch that bore the crown: the East Quarter Gauntlet College. Anderas would be there, performing the duties of his captaincy. Had the man really sent as many wayfarers to the pyres as Ladomer claimed?

Ashway marched to the Handquarter doors. His guards leapt aside with well-practised agility and bowed as Eamon passed, following ever in Ashway's steps. The Hand led him through the entrance hall, in which a tall statue of the throned gazed austerely over a red marble floor, down a corridor with several connecting stairs and passages to a large door. Ashway threw it open, revealing a long, grand study with an arched window overlooking a garden. Workers were out among the plants. As they saw Ashway enter his room, they fled from view of the window.

Ashway went straight to his desk, littered high with papers; there was a tall bookshelf to one side, also strewn with parchments. The Hand rifled through the sheets on his desk and then went to the case with a loud and angry sigh. Eamon stood awkwardly, feeling not unlike a boy summoned in ire to his schoolmaster's table, and tried to ignore Ashway's evident rage.

At last the Hand pulled down a slim collection of papers. These he folded in three before sealing them. He used the ring on his finger to put his mark into the wax: an owl. Eamon tried to catch sight of the writing as the Hand worked, but saw little of the narrow script.

Ashway rose and turned to him.

"These are the papers that Lord Cathair requires," he said. "Take them and go."

"Yes, Lord Ashway." Eamon let the Hand slam the papers into his outstretched palm, trying not to flinch. Ashway's hand went back to his forehead. He drew a sharp, seething breath.

Eamon looked at him in alarm. "Lord Ashway, are you –?"

"I said *go*."

Eamon bowed and left.

The papers seemed heavy to him as he made his way back through the streets to the palace. He wondered what they were, but knew that he could not remove the seal.

It was late afternoon when he came at last to Cathair's quarters in the Hands' Hall. In comparison to the dark wood and red marble in the East Quarter, Cathair's rooms were exotic. Eamon was admitted without hesitation, and when he knocked at Cathair's door he was summoned swiftly inside, to be greeted by his dogs. He restrained any sudden movements while they barked and snarled, daring him, as always, to defy them and merit a mauling.

"Lord Cathair, I have brought your papers," he called.

Cathair appeared from one of the side chambers. He snatched the papers and looked carefully at the seal.

"I see that there is some shred of honesty in you, Lord Goodman," he said, proceeding to tear it away.

"Lord Cathair –"

"You know well that there is work to do," Cathair answered him. "Do not waste my time with your petty endearments."

"Then do not you waste mine with your accusations of treachery," Eamon retorted.

Cathair looked sharply at him.

"You are too bold, Goodman." Something in his voice made Eamon fall very still. "Should your allegiance ever be shown to be against the Master, know that I will make you pay for every word that you have ever uttered. There are certain parts of my learning, Goodman, that cannot be understood unless you experience them for yourself," he added with a long smile.

"Then I fear that I will always remain ignorant of the full extent of your greatness, Lord Cathair."

Cathair did not answer him. His eyes ran hungrily over the paper, which he held in such a way that Eamon could never hope to see what was written there. As Cathair read, one of his dogs came to him. The Hand rested a palm on the beast's head.

"Lord Goodman, I have had a small office set up for you," Cathair said at last, "and I have a matter of great importance for you to attend to."

"Yes, my lord."

"The port waterfront is a vital part of the West Quarter's jurisdiction," Cathair told him. His eyes took on a melodramatic, sarcastic sheen. "The storehouses must be counted and the ships inspected before the start of the trading season reaches us in force. Most importantly of all, the main roads must be resurfaced, all according to regulation, of course. It is, as I am sure you will agree, a desperately important role, which can only be entrusted to a man of *quality*."

Eamon matched his gaze. The overseeing of port and waterfront maintenance was a role normally given to lieutenants in the North and West Quarters. Eamon was fairly sure that Lieutenant Best had been in charge the previous year and seemed to recall the man giving account of how he had hated every minute of the assignment. His hatred had been alleviated only by knowledge of the fact that, in being assigned to the port, he had avoided being assigned to the sewers.

Lord Cathair intended to give him as crushing and humiliating a role as he could. Eamon refused to be deterred.

"It is an especially important task," he agreed.

"I am *so* glad that you see it as I do," Cathair answered. "I've had the regulations taken down to your study so that you can look at them before you begin work. I've taken the liberty of sending some notice to Captain Waite on your behalf, to put together a team of workers for you. You can collect them tomorrow and begin taking up the old stones."

"Yes, Lord Cathair," Eamon said. "Thank you."

"No, no, Lord Goodman," Cathair answered with a grand smile. "Thank *you*."

One of Cathair's servants showed him to his "study". Eamon was not surprised that the servant led him first into a hall and then to a small, dusty side corridor, then to a short, and not entirely stable, wooden staircase that led down into what seemed to be a small cellar. The air was dank and musty, and the stones crumbled underfoot. A large wooden door, such as might be found in a barn, was set in the wall and led outside – cracks of light passed through it. Mice scurried in the corners and, beyond the door, horses stamped. Eamon smelled their dung. He suspected he was in one of the series of servants' rooms below the main part of the Hands' Hall.

The room had a small table and chair, as well as a lopsided candle. There was a fireplace to one side, thickly blackened. When Eamon went to inspect it he wondered how many decades it had been since the place was last used. The table bore a thick volume, its edges frayed; he couldn't even make out a title on the dull cover.

The tattered state of the book's bindings spoke eloquently as to its age and the extent of its use. On looking at the first few pages he saw outlines of the rules and regulations to be followed in the setting down, and taking up, of roads in the city, with long sections of maps and illustrations.

He set the book down and looked around the room. Clearly Cathair had not taken well to the Right Hand's choice of his assistant.

"Is that all, Lord Goodman?" the servant's voice sounded in the empty room. Eamon drew his eyes from the tome.

"Thank you, yes."

The servant nodded and hurried quickly away, his footsteps soon fading into silence.

Eamon surveyed the room again. The situation was a little ridiculous, but if it was how Cathair wanted to begin, then it was how they would begin. He had nothing to lose.

Slowly, he sat. The chair felt unstable, and was more than a little uncomfortable. Pulling his hood over his head in an attempt to block out the sound and smell of the horses and singing stablehands, he drew the lit candle closer to him and began studying the book.

CHAPTER IX

When Eamon finally emerged from his new lair, stiff and bleary-eyed, he bumped into Ladomer. Amused by Eamon's apparent disorientation, his friend raised an eyebrow.

"Cathair?" Ladomer asked.

"Cathair," Eamon answered, and they laughed. One word had been enough.

Eamon slept fitfully that night. Waking, the banner of the throned stared eerily back at him in the moonlight and, sleeping, it was Mathaiah's pale face. The young man's words went round his mind countless times – he could not comprehend the love and respect and joy that had been in them. He would take the message to Lillabeth – but would rather be present to see Mathaiah deliver it himself. He wrestled with how to free the young man, but no viable plan came to him.

The next morning was the first day of March and he rose early. Mindful of Cathair's instructions he made his way down to the West Quarter College, arriving just as Waite's morning parade was filing out of the yard to its duties. As Eamon entered, the captain greeted him.

"Lord Goodman." He took Eamon's hand and clasped it warmly. "I heard all about it," Waite added, smiling. "You've made us all very proud."

"Thank you," Eamon answered. He watched the last cadets leaving the courtyard, then looked back to Waite. "Lord Cathair told me that he had sent you a message –"

"Yes." Waite's face seemed to darken a little, but the look passed.

"I've gathered the men he asked for. They'll be in the entrance hall for you in a few minutes."

"Thank you, captain."

Waite offered him an apologetic smile.

Eamon was therefore not surprised to find his digging contingent composed of the Third Banner cadets. The young men waited merrily in the hall, chatting happily to one another. When they saw Eamon they broke into spontaneous applause.

"Lord Goodman!"

"Show a little restraint, gentlemen!" Waite called, though the attempt was half-hearted.

"I'm sure the work I have for them will restrain them well enough, captain," Eamon answered.

"We'll be working for you?" A young face – Cadet Barde – spoke the common question.

"Yes, though I'm afraid you won't be needing your swords today. Please go and ransack the college tool store," Eamon added loudly. "I want each of you back here in two minutes, armed with something fit to carve up a road."

The cadets looked at him in surprise for a moment, but then Manners beamed.

"His glory, Lord Goodman!" he cried, and the others followed suit before the cadets filed out of the hall. Eamon watched them and laughed quietly.

"They're good lads," Waite said. He looked at Eamon with a peculiarly paternal face. "They're glad you came back. So am I."

Eamon didn't know how to answer, but nodded, accepting the compliment. As he did so a thought crossed his mind. "What became of the others?" he asked quietly.

"Others?"

"The ones… the ones who were killed in the line." Eamon remembered the first man from the decimation line falling, his blood red at his breast beneath the dark swathe of the Hand's strike.

"Their bodies were thrown to the pyre."

Eamon stared. The man's face was deliberately nondescript. "Pyre?" he repeated dumbly.

"Died in dishonour, Lord Goodman. No better than snakes."

"What were their names?"

"Morell, Yarrow, and Doublen," Waite answered. "Two were quarter militia. Mr Morell was a West Quarter cadet."

"And they went to the pyre?"

Waite nodded.

Eamon gulped back nauseating anger as the Third Banner cadets poured back into the hall, carrying picks and shovels. Men of his had been sent to the pyre like criminals or the diseased, like the victims of the cull. He seethed with anger.

The cadets formed a neat line before him, giving him a formal salute. Driving down his ire, Eamon addressed them.

"Gentlemen, today you shall be having a little bit of sea air. They tell me that it's terribly good for the constitution."

As the cadets grinned back at him Eamon felt a strange swell of emotion. These men did not seem to care what they did; their joy came from serving him, the man who had saved their lives. Their merry eagerness poured burning coals on Cathair and his petty strike at all their honours.

Eamon laughed, bade farewell to Waite, and led the cadets out through the Brand into the streets of Dunthruik.

People stopped and stared at them as they passed, for they made an unusual sight: a group of Gauntlet cadets led by a Hand, each carrying not sword or banner but pick and shovel. Eamon took them towards the harbour, which was set just beyond the city's west wall.

The Sea Gate was wider than the Blind Gate; through it peered curiously bobbing spires of ships which fretted at the moorings that had held them the whole winter long. The seafront was loaded with lodgings and storehouses and there was a highly visible Gauntlet presence. Many of the ships flew the colours of merchant states. Eamon wondered how such men had found the winter. Of the ships that bore the eagle and the crown, some were part of the throned's small fleet of warships. Those ships were laden with guards and militia. Eamon wondered if the holk that had once tried to bear him to Dunthruik had ever been moored there.

The waterfront road was in a poor state of repair. The winter winds, rains, and beating waves had driven potholes into much of it and had sunk large areas of the dock's paving.

As they spilled through the gate onto the waterfront Eamon saw a tall cart loaded with dirt. Lord Febian stood near it, a piece of paper in his hand and a bemused expression on his face. At that moment Febian noticed Eamon, looked at the paper, then came over.

"Lord Febian," Eamon acknowledged civilly.

"Lord Cathair... sends his regards." Febian gestured to a tall wagon filled with dirt and stones, and then noticed the group of cadets for the first time. Their gazes met again. "Surely, Lord Goodman, there's been some mistake –?"

"None whatsoever. Please thank Lord Cathair for his foresight and pass him my best wishes for the day." Eamon looked down at the rugged, broken stones beneath his feet, then back at the cadets. So far as his reading the day before had indicated, the best way to start was in removing the stones and levelling the road surface, using the dirt to do so.

"Third Banners, to work!" he called.

"His glory, Lord Goodman!"

They worked at the port and dock roads for over a week and Eamon was pleased with how the cadets applied themselves. Their laughing and joking made light of any hardships, and when he doffed his cloak to help them they cheered and handed him what was universally considered to be the best shovel. Groups of militia from the West and North Quarters were also sent to the work. Eamon split the men into teams, assigning them to different parts of the waterfront.

On the second day, Eamon was sure he caught sight of Cathair watching them from the shadow of the gate. He had been tempted to offer the Hand a cheerful wave, but had decided against it.

The road grew steadily smoother. The sailors and captains, waiting in the waterfront inns for the first sailable weather, watched their work with tacit appreciation. Some of them, having nothing better to do, brought tools of their own and joined in. The cadets' favourite such worker was a heavily bearded man from one of the southern merchant states. The man was habitually drunk, but his swing was good, and he cheerfully yelled obscenities at the road when it refused to cooperate with him. He reminded Eamon of Giles.

On the fourth of March, as Eamon inspected the latest stretch of the road repairs, he heard singing among the cadets. This in itself was not unusual, and for a while he took no notice of it, but at last he caught some of the words:

> *"Tell, O tell! The Gauntlet cry,*
> *Tell us of this man!*
> *The surrendered sword, the fallen pine,*
> *The noblest of the Hands!"*

Eamon went across to them. "What is that you're singing, gentlemen?"

The group of cadets, tools in their hands, fell silent. Manners looked up at him.

"It is something that Cadet Ostler made up, my lord."

"Really?" Eamon looked along the dock – Ostler was in one of the other groups farther down, and was currently helping to set a great stone. The bearded merchant worked with him.

"Yes." Manners looked a little sheepish. "It's about you, Lord Goodman."

"So I hear."

"That's not the best verse," the cadet added apologetically.

Eamon looked carefully at the cadets. He was deeply touched by their show of respect for him, but surely it was a dangerous thing – what if the other Hands heard of it? They would not react well to such loyalty.

"Mr Manners," he asked, "was Cadet Ostler drunk at that time?"

"No, Lord Goodman –"

"Drunken men aren't always well inspired," Eamon told him firmly, and with a discreet nod. Manners met his gaze.

"Yes, Lord Goodman."

The work continued well. Eamon found that after spending an hour or so helping with it each day he slept much better at night. But his sleep was still haunted by Mathaiah's plight. When he woke, he felt cracking pressure at his breast. He was running out of time: Mathaiah had to be freed. But how could he do it?

He tried to think about it while he worked, but the work drove thought from him, and when he lay down at night to rest, he slept before he could think. In those rare moments when he was able to consider the problem he would turn it back and forth a hundred times, seeking for a way to pass into the Pit and safely bring Mathaiah out of it. However much he wrestled, no answer came to him, and when no answer came, his thought drifted from Mathaiah to chilling visions of the Nightholt.

By the end of the eighth of March the majority of the work was done – and done well. The cadets knew it.

"It's been done by the book, my lord!" Manners laughed cheerily.

"Indeed it has, Mr Manners," Eamon answered. Having finished most of their work for that day the cadets were on their way back to the West Quarter College. Eamon walked with them, meaning to speak briefly with Captain Waite.

"You've all worked exceptionally," he told them.

Grinning, Manners turned to those nearest to him. "If only good road work counted towards Gauntlet records!"

Cadet Ford cast Manners a partially disgusted look. "I don't see why you're worrying about that. You're on the captain's list!"

"On the list?" The words tumbled out of Eamon's startled mouth.

"There are few Third Ravens who can say as much." Ford offered Manners a broad smile.

"He'll be 'Lieutenant Manners' before anyone can stop him, my lord," Ostler added. "He says that he wants to follow the West's finest example."

"Mr Manners has his eye on a captaincy?" Eamon asked.

"No, my lord." Manners' face had grown red with embarrassment.

"He's looking to follow in your footsteps, my lord," Ostler explained.

Manners flushed a deeper red, but did not deny it.

Eamon clenched his fist closed over the mark on his palm. "It is a noble goal, Mr Manners."

"Th-thank you, my lord."

It was then that the skies opened and rain began to pelt the stones of the Coll, making the road slippery and a little treacherous. They hurried back to the Brand and college. Once in the hall, Eamon dismissed the dripping cadets back to their other duties. He watched them going, laughing and talking among themselves. It was a strange sight. Soon, all of them would be marked men.

"Lord Goodman?"

Eamon looked up in surprise to see Manners. His drenched brow was knitted.

"Mr Manners?"

Manners looked at him uncertainly. "My lord, it might seem an odd question to ask…"

"I shall not know that, Mr Manners, until you ask it."

"My lord." Manners drew a deep breath. "Did you go straight to lieutenant?"

"Almost," Eamon replied. "I was sworn in on the eighth of September and made a lieutenant on the ninth."

Manners met his gaze. "Was it difficult, my lord?"

Eamon swallowed. What should he say? He did not for a moment hope to see Cadet Manners put forward for a lieutenantship and he did not want to see the man kneel to receive the eagle's burning mark upon his hand.

Flexing his own hand quietly, he looked at Manners. "Even as a cadet you've had some officer training," he said. "They give you more when you are sworn in, because they know that men like you make good officers." He faltered. Manners watched him intently. "Mr Manners," Eamon said gently, "being a lieutenant isn't difficult – and I am sure that you would make a fine one. What is difficult is being a good man."

"What makes you a good man?" Manners watched him still, with an intense, piercing curiosity.

"Duty," Eamon answered. "Honour. The Master's –"

"No," Manners interrupted. "I'm sorry, Lord Goodman. I know that all those things are important. What I wanted to know was what makes *you* a good man."

"Apart from my name, you intend?" Eamon asked with a smile. Manners laughed and Eamon looked at him seriously. "Apart from my name, Mr Manners, it is the one I serve who makes me a good man. In fact," he added, "my name has little meaning without him."

Manners watched him in silence for a moment and Eamon matched that gaze. Had he gone too far? He bit the inside of his lip.

At last, Manners smiled and nodded. "Yes, my lord… Lord Goodman, do you –"

A howl rent the air.

They froze. Nothing could be heard except the rain. Eamon shook his head. Was he going insane?

The shrieking cry repeated, clearer and more terrible.

Waite appeared in the hall. His face showed that he had heard it too.

"Captain?" Eamon asked.

"It's coming from the Brand, Lord Goodman."

Another long cry shattered the air. Wordlessly, they rushed down the college steps and out into the pelting rain.

In the square, a fearsome sight met their eyes. The Brand was crowded at its edges with people, their eyes fixed on the figures on the raised platform of stones at the square's centre. Eamon recognized the men immediately. He saw Anderas being cast violently from the plinth by the other man. This same man then tore away, to roam ferally between the plinth's statues. As Eamon, Waite, and Manners halted breathlessly at the edge of the Brand the man came forward among the statues. His black cloak rode wildly about him as he hurled back his head.

"Woe, woe!" he yelled. His voice carried inhumanly far. "Woe to you, Dunthruik, city of open graves and whitewashed faces! Woe to you who bow before a painted, bloodied throne!" The man flung his arms wide. "There is blood on the streets, and fire in the air! The Blind Gate sees – it opens to him! The house that was fallen takes back its own.

"The King is come! The King is come and his man rides before him, clothed in stars…" The figure covered his eyes with a miserable cry. Streams of sorrow ran freely down his face. "Woe to you, Dunthruik, unless you heed him!"

Waves of chill terror buffeted Eamon. For there on the platform, his robes dishevelled where frenzied hands had torn them, his hair undone and wild in the heavy rain, his pale face grizzled with bitter weeping, his eyes thrown back to the open heavens, and his voice raised with the roar of thunder, was Lord Ashway. And the seer saw.

"Master, save us," Waite whispered.

None could move as Ashway continued howling. The people stared at him, petrified. They called to each other, aghast.

At the foot of the stone plinth, Anderas climbed to his feet and tried to bring the Hand to reason – but Ashway would not be calmed.

The seer lowered his head and surveyed the crowd. He looked straight at Eamon.

"See, the Sword and Star are coming! The one is here, and the other close behind." Ashway whirled where he stood among the stones, and laughed. He cast his hands out and spun so that all could hear him.

"The city rises!" he called. "The city rises, with a new name!" His voice, touched with fear and awe, rose as he trembled, calling out the words again and again: "*A new name!*"

There was a flurry of movement in a corner of the square. People were thrust aside as a group of Hands rushed into its centre. Cathair was among their number, his face a picture of rage and horror. The Hands hurled themselves at Ashway, trying to bring him down from the stones or somehow restrain him. But the Hand threw them off with ease.

"The one is here! He opens the gate!"

Horror coursed through Eamon. His legs propelled him forward. The crowd parted before him.

He joined with the Hands in moments – indeed, was there to catch one as Ashway hurled the man from the platform. Eamon saw Anderas climbing up from the drenched stones where he had again been hurled.

Eamon reached the steps to the platform as Cathair climbed up onto it. The Hand took hold of Ashway's arm.

"Ashway!" Cathair cried.

Suddenly the Hand turned and seized him. "Your ways will come on your head, Cathair. The blade will break and turn true – and it will fall on you."

Cathair stared. Eamon had never seen such fear in a man's eyes, but he did not have long to watch it. The next moment Ashway struck Cathair aside and leapt from the plinth.

"Hold him!"

Eamon recognized the Right Hand's voice. Anderas tried desperately to stop Ashway as he careered away, but Hand brushed captain aside with a wrathful cry.

The next thing Eamon knew was that Ashway stood before him. The Hand surged at him, an odd light in his eyes.

Time froze. The rain thudded into them like drums. Ashway's sight pierced him.

"I know who you are," he whispered. The Hand began to tremble with indescribable emotion. "I know who you are and what you will become!"

Eamon felt the world watching him. Terror was in the air. Malice and awe waxed in Ashway's face.

"I know."

Eamon looked straight into Ashway's eyes. The world fell away.

"Be silent," he commanded.

The Hand fell still and his lips, parted to speak, hung open. Trembling, Ashway closed his mouth and sank slowly to his knees. With a sob he pressed his head deep into his hands.

Silence. Behind the kneeling Hand, Eamon saw Anderas, gaping, quaking. The captain was not the only one who looked at him thus.

Suddenly Hands were all about him – a limping Cathair among them. Eamon felt them watching him with stunned, sickened silence.

He stepped to the side as the Hands drew Ashway to his feet. Looking up, he realized that the whole Brand stared at him. People pointed, shuddered, shrank away. He swallowed with a dry throat.

Slowly he turned. The Right Hand towered before him, his dark eyes watching Eamon intently. Eamon said nothing.

"Lord Cathair, see to Lord Ashway," the Right Hand commanded.

"Yes, my lord."

"Lord Goodman."

"My lord?" Eamon's heart pounded.

"Return to your work."

CHAPTER X

Fear froze his limbs. Ashway *knew*. As they returned to the hall of West Quarter College, Eamon sensed Manners watching him with a curious expression. Trembling, he concentrated his will on climbing the college steps. But the thoughts growing in his mind were terrifying and he was not able to press them away. If Ashway knew, then surely it was only a matter of time before the other Hands knew too.

He looked up. Waite's Hand-board hung in the rainy gloom. A sudden streak of lightning illuminated his name: *Eamon Goodman, Handed, 9th February 533rd Year of the Master's Throne*.

Quietly, he dismissed Manners and left the college. The rain struck hard as he made for the Hands' Hall. He let it: he felt as though he might slip from the world were there not something to keep him in it.

The rainstorm continued throughout the night, piercing his dreams with thunder. The hangings in his room swung silently as wind crept between the stones.

When morning came the roads were still too wet to continue work, though the day dawned fine. Eamon made his way back to the port to inspect the road and see what damage the rain might have caused. To his relief, bar some deep muddy puddles, most of the work was intact. He tried not to notice the men who stopped and stared at him as he passed.

"I hear you've become an expert in way-laying," said a voice beside him. Eamon looked up from his inspection of the muddy ditches.

"I've read the whole book," he answered. "Fearsome knowledge it is, too."

Ladomer laughed. "Well, I have come to waylay *you*."

"You've become a highwayman?" Eamon asked, sceptically and bad-naturedly. It was good to see Ladomer, but he had a hundred things weighing on his mind and had hoped to slip off along the docks to think. He mused wryly that, since he had returned from the King's camp, he seemed incapable of going anywhere without being noticed.

"No, though I'm sure I would make a very good one," Ladomer told him. "You silly ass! I've not seen you for days – what with one thing and another – and the Right Hand is busy all morning. I thought I'd find you and see if I could persuade you to join me for a drink."

"I'd rather –"

"Stand and look at mud you can't do anything with?" Ladomer quirked an eyebrow. "Eamon, you are an awful, boring relic."

"You are talking to a Hand," Eamon reminded him firmly, though he felt a smile creeping onto his face.

"And you," Ladomer answered, drawing himself up proudly, "are talking to the Right Hand's... right hand!"

"Is that official?" Eamon laughed.

"No." Ladomer pulled a face. "But it sounds good, doesn't it?"

"I wouldn't say it in front of the Right Hand if I were you."

"Come now!" Ladomer answered. "You say all sorts in front of him. Why shouldn't I?"

Eamon didn't answer him. "Sense of self-preservation?" he tried at last. Ladomer just laughed.

In the end he allowed Ladomer to persuade him and, assuring him that he would not be taken far from his beloved mud, Ladomer led him to one of the inns on the waterfront. A grotesquely hewn dolphin advertised the locale that his friend chose, and, though Eamon was unconvinced, Ladomer assumed command. Though he was of the higher rank, when with Ladomer Eamon often felt overshadowed and uncertain. Ladomer had always been brighter, faster, stronger, and more tactically inclined than he. It was Ladomer who had always been destined for great things – Ladomer who should be wearing black.

Ladomer directed him to sit at a table near one of the tall windows and returned to it not long later with a couple of broad mugs. One he handed firmly to Eamon, with the insistence that he drink from it. Reluctantly Eamon set the thing to his lips. The brew was reasonable, but his mind wandered to the first time he had met Hughan in the Hidden Hall; this drink was nothing compared with that.

"So tell me about yesterday."

Eamon looked up, drawn with hideous suddenness from his memory. Ladomer watched him with an inquisitive look.

"What about it?"

Ladomer threw his hands up in despair. "What about it, he says to me. *Eamon!*"

Eamon swallowed, and lowered his voice. "Something was wrong with Lord Ashway –"

"For throne's sake! I *know* that!" Ladomer looked at him as though he was the densest person in the whole of the River Realm. "You think that I didn't *see* him when they brought him in? They've taken him back to his quarters and confined him under his captain's care."

Eamon was stunned. "Who's directing the quarter?"

"Temporarily, the captain." Ladomer grimaced at the change in subject. "Lord Ashway ran a tight ship, so there isn't much to do."

"And the captain?"

"What do you want me to say?" Ladomer demanded. "He's as bright as an eagle's eye and as fit as the hand that downed the Serpent. Satisfied?" Eamon was about to interject when Ladomer spoke again. "*Now* will you answer me my question?"

"You seem to have answered most of it yourself," Eamon observed carefully.

"You are very cagey with me sometimes, Lord Goodman. Do you know that? It never used to happen at the Star."

"That was the Star, Ladomer." Memories of Edesfield ran sharply through him – incisive, like a blade.

Ladomer took a long draught of his drink and then leaned more calmly across the table. "I'm sorry."

"It's all right."

"You miss it?"

"I miss how things used to be. Before any of this happened. It all seemed easier then."

"Maybe it was." Ladomer was silent for a moment. "Will you tell me what happened yesterday?"

"I told him to be quiet," Eamon answered. He met Ladomer's searching gaze. "That was all."

"No other Hand there was able to stop him. Have you thought about that, Eamon?"

"Yes." And he had wondered why he had not been summoned to give account of it. If Ladomer had an explanation for this fact, he did not give it.

There was a long silence. Both of them sipped at their drinks in the quiet inn.

The inn door was pushed open. Eamon thought nothing of it until a shadow passed over the table.

Manners stood there, a stern expression on his face.

"Mr Manners?" Eamon asked.

The cadet did not answer. Slowly he set something down on the table.

"For my life, Lord Goodman."

Eamon stared at him, not understanding. Manners bowed to him, acknowledged Ladomer, and left. On the table was a golden coin.

"What was that?" Ladomer asked.

Eamon was about to answer that he didn't know when he saw another one of the cadets at the door: Ford. Barde and Ostler were behind him. They also came to the table and each set a coin there. "For my life, Lord Goodman," they said, and left without a further word. There were more behind them.

Eamon could only watch as, man by man, men from Pinewood and from Dunthruik – the men he had seen trembling before the might of the Right Hand in the decimation line – came into the inn and each one of them laid the same coin before him with the same words. As man after man – ensigns, cadets, and militiamen – came in a seemingly endless stream, neither Eamon nor Ladomer spoke. There were no knights, Hands, or officers – just men. Some remained after laying their coins, watching him.

Last of all came the man whom he had saved from the line. Eamon recognized his face and remembered how it had lain before him, riddled with fear and awe at a Hand who would save a simple man. Eamon remembered his name: Redmound.

The man laid a coin at the edge of the large pile.

"For my life, Lord Goodman." There were tears in his eyes as he spoke.

Eamon looked at him, astounded. At last, he found his voice. "You – none of you, owe any of this to me," he said. Ladomer stared at him and he knew he had to speak. "Please, take these back." He looked at the faces of his men. "Take them back." His voice was a whisper.

Redmound smiled at him. "By a good man we were redeemed and made good men again. What is a coin to that?"

Eamon could only gaze as, one by one, the cadets and men filed from the inn. The innkeeper looked after them in amazement, but seemed more amazed by the golden mass in front of Eamon. Eamon looked back to the coins, tears welling in his eyes.

Ladomer leaned towards him. "It would be well," he said, and his voice was oddly quiet, "if the Master did not hear of this."

Eamon looked at him, speechless.

As the day drew on it clouded over once again, but Eamon took the Third Banners, and men from the North and West Quarters, back to the road to finish working. They had all but completed the most important stretch of the waterfront road, and, as they worked, the sailors and merchants – many of them by now familiar faces – stopped to speak to the men and encourage them. The stones were laid together with precision; Eamon watched Ford perform a victorious walk over the first completed section of road, encouraged by riotous applause from the other workers.

Eamon helped with the work, but kept to himself, still overwhelmed by their generosity.

That evening he went to the college with them.

"Will you join us for a meal, Lord Goodman?" It was Manners who asked. Had any other Hand in the whole history of Dunthruik ever been addressed in the loving, free way that these men addressed him?

"It is kind of you to offer, but I have other duties."

Manners nodded. "Yes, Lord Goodman."

The cadets began to go. After a moment Eamon called out after them. "Mr Manners."

Manners paused in the darkening hall and returned to him with a bow. "My lord?"

"Your service… must be to the Master."

Manners smiled. "So it must." He bowed. "Good night, Lord Goodman."

Eamon watched him go. Thoughts churned in his mind, of the men whom he had saved, and the men whom he had lost. With deepening resolve he turned and went to Waite's offices.

The captain was there, sorting through papers. A lamp, dwindled by long service, burned by him, casting light over the wood. As Eamon entered, the captain looked up, then stood smartly.

"Lord Goodman. I wasn't expecting you."

"What was said to the families?" An angry edge came into Eamon's voice and he tried to soothe it.

Waite looked at him seriously. "The men who were executed?"

"Yes."

"The Right Hand dealt with it, Lord Goodman." His tone warned. Eamon ignored it.

"Do you know where these families live?"

"Yes, Lord Goodman."

"Tell me."

Waite looked at him as though he were insane. "Lord Goodman –"

"Where do they live, captain?"

"Would you have me work against the Right Hand?" Waite demanded.

"Has he set a restriction against my knowing this information?"

"No, Lord Goodman."

"Then I would have you do as I have requested."

After a short pause the captain looked at him and nodded. "The families live in the city, Lord Goodman."

"Would you show me?"

Reluctantly, Waite led him into the hall and to Overbrook's map of the city. The detail was exquisite. The young man's death ripped through him like a barb.

"One on the Ermine off the Coll; one near the Four Quarters; one at the waterfront." Waite pointed out the places on the road. "What do you intend to do?"

"Thank you for your assistance." Eamon offered him a smile and then left, knowing that Waite stared.

The streets of the city were settling under darkness. He returned briefly to his room in the Hands' Hall and examined the bag where he had put the money given to him that morning. Almost eighty crowns glittered inside. It was a great deal, but it could never be enough.

Silently, he divided the money.

When darkness fell completely, he was just another Hand in black, moving through the city unnoticed. The city lights ran all along the Coll to the Blind Gate, where Rendolet's head had no doubt received its first winged visitors. Eamon shivered. He went to the house of the first fallen man.

Even though it faced onto the Coll it was small. It looked as though it might once have been part of a larger property, now divided between several families. The entrance was down a cobbled side street. Eamon heard music in a nearby inn as he followed the street into a tiny courtyard. In it he saw a boy and several old men;

they sat and listened to strains of music. When they saw Eamon, the boy leapt to his feet.

"His glory!" he called. None of the older men moved.

"I'm looking for the house of Morell," Eamon said quietly. The boy pointed at a sunken doorway in one of the walls. Light crept through the misshapen timbers.

"There, my lord."

Eamon went to the door and knocked gently.

It was a long time before there was any answer. At last the door opened, letting a thick, smoky light into the street. A young woman stood there, hair collapsed in tangled tresses about her face. Eamon's heart sank. She trembled as she saw the black he wore.

"Mrs Morell?" His words felt futile.

"My lord." She did not know who he was, but, even in her grief, she would honour a Hand. His heart went out to her, yet, looking at her, he found that he did not know how to do what he had come to do.

"Mrs Morell," he began, "I am Lord Goodman."

Her eyes widened with terror and hatred.

"Was killing my husband not enough for you? It was your defeat – *yours*. Why should you live, and not him?"

Eamon recoiled. He brought a bag of coins from under his cloak. It was awkward in his hand. "Mrs Morell –"

The woman's eyes fell on his offer. She spoke with disgust. "I will take no coin from you. My lord, please leave." Her voice shook.

"Mrs Morell –"

With a grieved bow the woman turned and fled, weeping, into the house. Without her to hold it, the door swung closed.

As Eamon stood there, stunned, he heard someone stepping up by him. One of the old men, leaning heavily on a cane, came to bow to him.

"Did you come to buy our silence, Lord Goodman?" he asked. Only age quelled his fury.

"I did not come to buy anything," Eamon retorted. The old man did not flinch. Eamon took a deep breath. "Mr Morell?" he guessed.

"My lord."

"Mr Morell, I came to offer something that can never take the place of the son who has been taken from you and your house. Your son served me and he served the Master even with his life. He fought at Pinewood with honour, never once abandoning his oaths. He did not deserve death as he received it. He deserved to be honoured, and he should have rested better in a noble tomb than on a wretched pyre."

Mr Morell stared. They were not the words that the Right Hand would have spoken.

"In whose name do you come, my lord?" Morell asked carefully.

"My own," Eamon answered wretchedly. "Just my own."

Sorrow poured into his heart. How could he assuage their grief? Perhaps he could not.

In the silence, he offered the bag again.

At last, Morell took it. He met Eamon's gaze. "We will accept what you bring."

"I am sorry for what was done."

"So are we, my lord." The old man bowed once, and entered the house.

Eamon watched him go. Grief surfaced, raw and red. This was what he had to do, for every man whose life had been given in the line for his shame.

Turning, he went back to the Coll, away from the music, and on to the next house.

His reception in each house was much the same, consisting of suspicion and wary acceptance. It was a bloody coin that he brought, never able to give back what had been taken. Those who remained behind were widows, aging mothers, fatherless children. Their grief was green, budding, and seeding hatred of which he was the object.

It was late evening when Eamon arrived at the Four Quarters, his errand concluded. He felt heavy of heart, desperately so, but he had done all he could. Maybe one day the families would understand the truth of what had happened – maybe that day would never come. He reminded himself that though men had died in the Right Hand's decimation line, and died because of him, many more had lived – and that was his doing also.

He stood, drawing deeply of the air, when he heard footsteps approach. Someone halted by him.

"Lord Goodman?"

"Yes?" He did not recognize the man before him, but saw that he was a first lieutenant.

The man bowed. "First Lieutenant Greenwood, East Quarter."

"Good evening, Mr Greenwood."

"I'm sorry to trouble you, my lord – Captain Anderas implores your assistance."

Eamon frowned. "Has something happened?"

"I believe it has to do with Lord Ashway. My lord, would you come with me to the Ashen?"

"Of course."

Eamon accompanied the first lieutenant along Coronet Rise and then across the Ashen. The square was moonlight-mottled, and tall braziers stood at the Handquarter doors. As they approached, Eamon made out a figure on the steps who peered anxiously into the square.

Greenwood vaulted the steps and saluted. "Sir."

"Thank you, Mr Greenwood," the captain replied.

The first lieutenant saluted again, bowed to Eamon, and left.

"Lord Goodman," Anderas said formally.

"Captain."

The moonlight illuminated a tense, gaunt look to the captain. Eamon at once remembered what Ladomer had told him: Anderas was holding the reins of the East Quarter for the time being. "Is everything well, captain?"

A flicker of strain ran across the captain's face. "No, Lord Goodman. My men looked everywhere for you, but couldn't…"

Eamon suddenly saw that the captain shook like a brittle leaf. Eamon reached out to steady him.

"Courage, captain."

Anderas looked strangely at him, biting his lip. At last, he drew breath.

"Lord Goodman, I sent after you because… it is about Lord Ashway. I…" He faltered and closed his eyes. "I cannot control him."

Eamon stared. "What do you mean?"

At a loss for words, Anderas shook his head. "The Right Hand commanded that he be kept confined in his quarters, as befits his station, until I receive further notice," he said, "and I have done so. But this evening… This evening he is howling, calling down curses. I cannot stop him."

Eamon remembered Ashway in the Brand, and shuddered.

"Will you help me, Lord Goodman?"

What could he do? He met Anderas's gaze. "I will do all that I can, captain."

They went together into the Handquarters, its corridors and rooms eerie in the moonlight, like the chambers of a forgotten keep.

The captain led Eamon to Ashway's quarters and on towards his study. Eamon saw the internal courtyard through the tall windows lining the corridor. A tall ash tree was engraved on Ashway's door, its leaves lined with emerald traces.

There, Anderas reached to his belt. He drew out some keys and unlocked the door.

The study was dimly lit and lined with bookshelves, as Eamon had seen the week before. They were grim and forbidding in the shadowy light. One wall was dominated by a tall painting framed with gold. It showed a tangled mass of men, some under the banner of an eagle, some under the banner of a tattered star.

Ashway sat in a great chair by the windows, his clothes torn, his face bruised and unshaven, and his long hair lank about his jowls. Ropes lashed him to his place. He watched the courtyard trees as they swayed in the night breeze. At first glance he seemed calm and in his right mind.

Anderas led Eamon to the window. At their approach Ashway looked up sharply. His eyes and tone were cool.

"Lord Goodman," he said.

"Lord Ashway," Eamon answered with a bow. He wondered what help Anderas had needed; the Quarter Hand seemed as placid as a sea becalmed.

He glanced at Anderas. The captain looked both terrified and ashamed.

"Lord Goodman, I am sorry to waste your –"

"There has been no waste. All is well, captain," Eamon replied.

He looked back to Ashway. The Hand watched him intently.

"Have you come to kill me?" Ashway said. Fear glimmered in his hollow eyes.

"Your sight is dimmed, Lord Ashway," Eamon answered gently. "I have not come to kill you."

Ashway shook his head slowly. "No, no; it will not be you to kill me. But you will kill him."

For a moment Eamon wondered whether the Hand meant Anderas. Ashway's eyes took on a faraway look.

"You will kill him for what has already been done this night. I have seen it." Ashway looked back at Eamon. His voice changed. "I too am bound," he said quietly. "I too will die tonight."

"Lord Ashway," Anderas began, stepping to the Hand's side. "You only hurt yourself to take such notions to heart."

Ashway looked at him witheringly. Anderas fell back. Ashway fixed Eamon with a grave face.

"I tell you, Lord Goodman, that this captain loves you more than he has ever loved me."

Anderas stopped in his tracks, alarmed. Ashway laughed.

"Do you see so little? It is true, just as it is true that he will serve you, Lord Goodman, more heartily than he shall ever love or serve the throned. I have long known it."

"You mean the Master, Lord Ashway," Eamon countered quietly.

"I mean the throned," Ashway spat. His eyes passed up to the painting on the wall and a scowl darkened his face. When he next spoke, Ashway's voice was caustic. "I mean Edelred. Thus he named himself, and thus I call him."

Eamon froze. What could he say?

Ashway's eyes were fixed on the painting, his bruised and bloodied face coloured with distant remembrance. "He thinks himself safe. But it is not only the Star of Brenuin that he should fear."

"The Serpent," Eamon corrected.

Ashway fixed him with a blistering gaze. "You cannot feign before me, Eamon Goodman," he sneered. "You know his name better than I." He turned his gaze to the window once more. Suddenly, Eamon saw a tear moving down his mottled cheek.

"Anderas?" Ashway whispered faintly. Suddenly he cried: "Anderas!"

The captain was already at the Hand's side. "I am here, my lord."

Ashway searched the space before him. "I can no longer see, Anderas," he breathed. Tears marked his pale face and his eyes took on a faraway look. "I saw the star shining in the streets. And now I see nothing else."

There was a long silence. Anderas trembled. Eamon felt gagging hesitation. What should they do?

"All that I have done…" Ashway half-spoke, half-sang. He laughed sadly. "All that I have done will come upon me."

"No, lord –" Anderas began.

With a wordless screech, Ashway rounded on the captain.

"What do you know of it?" he howled. Anderas leapt back before his overwhelming rage. "Were you there when Edelred drove his sword through the heart of Ede? Were you there to see the Serpent's house scattered in ruins? Were you there when Edelred took the throne? Were you there to see the founding of this city, and the dressing of the throne in blood?"

"No." Eamon spoke quietly. "He was not – but you were."

Ashway fell silent and stared at him. Eamon felt the chill move through him.

"Yes," Ashway said at last. "Yes. I was there." He fell heavily back, and turned his unseeing gaze to the moonlit garden. "I was there."

There was a long silence.

Courage, Eamon.

Filled suddenly with deep conviction, Eamon stepped before the Hand.

"You have seen how this will end," Eamon told him. "What would you choose?"

"The throne is built on my blood also," Ashway answered. His words were bitter, regretful. "I have nothing left – no sight, no choice."

Agony wracked Ashway's face. Eamon saw, and knew what stirred it.

"It is the voice of Edelred who counsels you thus," he said.

"My choices have brought me here," Ashway answered fiercely. He looked up with proud eyes and smiled. "I rue none of them! I will die as I have lived. Save your words; they will avail you nothing. You will not live to see what was shown to me. You will perish, impaled and writhing, before your enemy. You will drown, gagging, in your own blood. But you will suffer much before that day. You will suffer this very night! Ah, how you will suffer. And you will crumble before the throne that you malign!" Ashway's voice grew strange and strong, his eyes wild in the moonlight as he laughed. "Benighted and forlorn you shall be, Eben's son!"

Eamon fixed him with a stony glare. "Hence, voice of Edelred!"

Ashway gave a horrendous cry and tried to grip his head with his hands. As he thrashed, Eamon laid his hand on his shoulder.

"Tureon."

Ashway froze. Hooded eyes searched Eamon's face, and then grew round with tears. "What?" he breathed.

"That is your name." Eamon did not know how he knew it. He knelt down by the Hand, grasping his hands in his own. "Peace, Tureon."

Ashway watched him for a long time, face torn by long remembrance.

"I may not turn, Eamon," he whispered at last, gesturing ironically to the cords on his arms. "I am bound, just as you are."

He wept freely. Eamon pressed his hands.

"I will not be bound," he said, "and you need not be."

Ashway did not answer him.

Eamon did not know how long he knelt there, holding Ashway's hands. Suddenly the Lord of the East Quarter looked up sharply.

"Lord Goodman, you must go."

Eamon frowned. "I will not –"

"Fool and simpleton!" Ashway snarled. "He is coming – can you not feel it?" The Hand trembled wildly. "He comes to take my life for what I have done – and he does not know the half of that. He will take the lives of any he finds here." He fixed Eamon in a fierce gaze. "I will say nothing to him of you, *but only if you go*."

Eamon stared.

"Go now, or lose all that you seek!" Ashway yelled. The Hand's eyes filled with tears – yet they were clear.

Eamon rose and turned to Anderas.

"Come with me, captain."

Anderas shivered, as though disturbed from some terrible dream.

"Lord Goodman –"

"We will go." Eamon looked once more at Ashway. The Hand met his gaze.

Without another word, Eamon drew Anderas from the room.

They staggered out of the Handquarters into the night air. Anderas still shook when they stopped in the Ashen.

"Lord Goodman…"

"Are you afraid, Anderas?"

"After the things that I have seen and heard, these days and this last night…? I am afraid of many things, Lord Goodman – of war and death and famine, of this city falling in ruin to the Serpent, and of the Serpent himself. I am afraid for this quarter," he added quietly, "entrusted to a captain when a Hand should hold it. I am afraid for the men under me and for the Hand over me. He is a seer, and he…"

He looked at Eamon in terror. "What he has howled fills me with fear. And yet all of this is but nothing compared to how much I fear you."

Eamon gaped. Anderas tried to steady his uncertain breathing.

"Anderas, do not be afraid – least of all of me." Eamon laid a light hand on Anderas's shoulder. "Go and rest, captain. The quarter will have need of you in the morning. I will come and find you when my duties permit me to do so, and we will speak of all of this."

"Yes, Lord Goodman," Anderas answered, and bowed low. "Thank you."

Eamon watched the captain return to the East Quarter College. Anderas supported himself a moment on the threshold and then went inside.

Drawing a deep breath, Eamon walked back to the Four Quarters. He desperately needed rest.

The streets were quiet and the music from distant alley inns was faint. Ashway's words burned in his mind. As he considered them he felt himself turn cold.

How could Ashway have been there at the battle where Ede had fallen? And when the voice of Edelred had spoken, what exactly had the seer seen? Was he truly to die – in his own blood?

I spoke it, Eben's son! the voice proclaimed, with such force that Eamon staggered. *You shall see how truly I did so!*

Eamon turned from the voice, shivered it away. He pressed his hands into his eyes, drew deep breath. He would not choose to believe it. He would choose the King's way. He was the First Knight.

Have courage, Eamon. The other, quieter, voice stirred in his mind. He wondered at it. *Courage.*

He looked up. Something came down the Coll towards him. At first he could not make out what it was, but it became clearer as torchlight pooled upon it. He stopped.

It was a low, open-topped, horse-drawn wagon whose driver, a militiaman, yawned as he urged his beast on. Eamon realized what grisly load the wagon bore through the streets in the dead of night: bodies, for the pyre.

Chapter X

The wagon reached the Four Quarters and the driver turned his vehicle towards the North Gate. Eamon stepped back to let him pass, shadows shifting over man and beast. As the driver spoke quietly to his horse, the voice drew Eamon's attention. He looked up to measure the man, and doing so, saw the wagon's burden clearly.

Suddenly his eyes were caught, his breath stolen. He rushed forward and, as he saw, his heart was torn in two.

"Stop!" His cry throbbed in the empty street. "*Stop!*"

The driver halted and turned to stare at him, his lips parted to the platitudes of lordship to which a Hand was entitled. Eamon did not care. He saw nothing – nothing except that one face, lying among a dozen others.

"Stop!" he cried, as though he could somehow undo what had been done. He could not.

The driver stared at him, his mouth voicing words. Eamon did not hear them.

With shaking hands Eamon tore down the back latch of the wagon. But the face before him did not change – it was still *that* face, a face he had long loved.

It was unreal. It could *not* be true…

He reached, touched the pale forehead, traced bloodied hollows where bright eyes had once lived and laughed, reached for hands that had once clasped his own in friendship. They were hewn at the wrist.

Eamon's chest heaved with grief as his shaking fingers confirmed what his eyes saw so unwillingly. It would never, could never, be *un*-seen. He opened his lips to cry out – but no cry came, and no tears could unbind his eyes.

It was Mathaiah.

He reeled. His breath came in ragged gasps through the constricted, contorted passageways of his breast. That this could be done… that this could be done to any man, had been done to many a man before, was known to him. But that this could be done to *him*…

Again and again he looked – the eyeless hollows violated his sight. Robbed of their light, they mocked him. Grief lay thick in his stomach.

The voice of Edelred crawled amidst his thoughts.

Look, it told him.

Eamon looked, and the dull, blackened voids consumed him.

With a cry he reached out. He could not look, he could not, and with his hands he sought the face and covered the hateful hollows. Suddenly there was blood and gore on his hands and it seemed to slip inside of him and work its grisly way into his very heart. He cried out again and clenched his eyes shut. But the hollows were there and met him in the darkness, and the voice taunted him with the story of their making.

He retched. He tore his hands away, forced his eyes open. His whole body shook as the maelstrom gripped him.

"Who did this?" His voice was nearly a scream. The driver shook before him.

"My lord, I do not –"

"*Who did this?*"

"My lord –"

His rage crumbled into helpless grief, and, taking Mathaiah's head between his hands, he laid his quaking face next to his friend's. The mess of the sockets smeared him.

The words pronounced by Ashway's tongue came to him: "*You will suffer this very night.*"

He had delayed too long: it was his doing. He could have endured any grief, any treachery, any accusation…

Any but this.

"Lord Goodman."

He looked up from his place among the corpses.

Ladomer was there. The Right Hand's lieutenant watched him.

Trembling, Eamon choked back the feelings surging in him. He could not weep, he could not cry, he could not howl. He was watched. He said nothing.

"Come down, Lord Goodman." Ladomer's voice was cold.

It was also a warning. Ladomer's harsh, unyielding stare drove into him. He knew that the Right Hand also watched him through those eyes. Ladomer was right: for his own sake, he had to come down. He knew it as surely as he knew that his place was there, cradling the broken corpse.

What a man you are, Eben's son! The voice wove deftly among his tormented thoughts. *Twice you would betray and abandon your wretched ward – once to the Pit, again to the pyre.*

The jaws of the trap that held him were strong. He could not stay and yet… how could he go?

Where is your brazen courage, Eben's son? the voice sneered.

A shudder ran through Eamon with the intensity of a blow. As the voice mocked him, it snatched from him even the smallest victory he had ever won against it.

How little it takes to subdue you! But then, son of Eben, there never was much of you to subdue.

The voice deadened his thought and senses. It had to be true: he was defeated, had been from the start. What other explanation could there be? He had been a fool to pit himself against the powers that strove in him. Mathaiah had paid for it – for his folly. Surely there was nothing left except surrender to the voice of the throned?

But the idea of surrendering stoked some last reserve of courage in his heart. Had he not faced this voice before? Had it not been cast down in Hughan's name? Was the voice not, by nature, that of a liar? Hughan had said as much, and, as Eamon grappled for his sense, the King's words came clearly into his mind:

"*It is your heart that the throned will strike, because it is there that he must conquer you…*"

The voice might have held sway over him once, and he did not doubt that it would try to sway him again, but its power lay in his own choice. Choosing to heed it now would be the true betrayal of his friend and obeisance of his courage. Eamon realized that, until he yielded, he was neither a traitor nor defeated.

He looked back at the face between his hands. Fresh doubt assailed him. He could choose to renounce the voice and its insidious counsel, but could he truly choose to leave his friend? His throat was taut with grief and he stared at the hollows, their darkness reaching for him.

How could he go?

You would not be leaving him, Eamon.

The words washed over his heart. This voice called him by his name – his true name – and he trusted it. It called him on to courage. *You would not be leaving him; he is not there. Even unto his last hour, he loved you. He loves you still.*

The whispered comfort faded. Strange quiet stilled his heavy heart.

Yes, he would go down; it was right and necessary for him to do so. But he would not do so for Ladomer or for Edelred.

Slowly, Eamon bowed and kissed Mathaiah's forehead. It was cold and bloodied, and though that grieved him still it held less fear for him than when first he had seen it. It was not the farewell he would have chosen, was scarcely a farewell at all – but he chose it.

Silently, he stepped down and met Ladomer's hard gaze. The Right Hand's lieutenant crisply closed the back of the wagon before stepping back and gesturing for the alarmed driver to move on.

The driver did not need to be asked twice. Eamon watched as Mathaiah's broken, eyeless body was taken away to feed a pyre where it would be reduced to nothing.

"Lord Goodman, he was a traitor." Ladomer had followed his gaze. His voice was deathly quiet. Eamon did not flinch from it.

"He was my ward, Ladomer," he answered simply, turning to face his friend. Emotion surged from him with power and grief he did not understand. "He was my ward, *and I loved him.*"

Ladomer stepped towards him with an ireful look. "You tread dangerous ground, Eamon," he said, pressing something into Eamon's fingers. It was cold and sharp. As it rested in his hand Ladomer watched him, daring him to move. He stood still. "You are summoned to see the Master in the morning."

"Yes."

At last the wagon was gone. Ladomer nodded once to him. "Good night, Lord Goodman."

Eamon watched him, a shadow that melted into the streets. Then he looked down.

A signet ring was in his palm. The seal that it bore was an owl.

He wept.

CHAPTER XI

The Coll seemed unreal beneath Eamon's feet, the whole road both familiar and alien to him. The doorways that lined the road, each darkened by the tenebrous night, were beyond his wit and sight, as was any man whom he passed.

Ashway and Mathaiah were dead.

His exhausted limbs grew desperate and heavy. His hands shook and he was unable to muster strength enough to raise his head to face the gates. Mathaiah was dead. As Eamon walked, sorrow and grief fell into step with him, threatening to trip him or crush him with the weight of their burdens.

He passed the Hands' Gate, the long colonnade, the posts of the Hands' Hall, and at last climbed the stairway to his own room. None stirred in the hall – no man met him and none heard him pass. His hands shook as he tried to open his door, the handle slipping between his bloody fingers. He gagged and tore at the handle.

With a silenced sob he pushed the door open. He had to clean the blood from his hands and face, but it would not help him. The bloody witness penetrated him like poison.

You will not wash it away! The voice laughed at his dull simplicity. *You have not the skill, Eben's son! No man lives who can free you from what you bear.*

He closed his door. The very wood watched him. The hateful walls that hemmed him round were dark, for the moon had shifted. Only pale starlight reached him. It was cold and bitter. He looked up at the distant flickers. Stars. Swords and stars.

For a moment bitterness masked his grief. Had Hughan known

that he would have to bear this? Had Hughan known, the day he drew Mathaiah into his service, what cost that service would demand? Had he known and yet allowed the boy to go?

Rage reared archly in his breast: rage against the King and against himself. Hughan had known – and done nothing. Eamon had known – had *always* known – that Dunthruik was no place for Mathaiah. Eamon had betrayed the young man to Alessia, and she had drawn Mathaiah's name from her lover, amidst a silken lair of pillows and firelight.

She had done it. She – the one who had spoken out his secrets and betrayed him to his enemies – had done it.

Anguish clawed in his throat. *She* had given Mathaiah to the throned.

And you did not save him. The voice was there again, cased in the coils of his rage. *Even thus did you betray him, Eben's son. You did it willingly.*

"No!" Eamon heard his own voice, a desperate whisper in the dark room. The walls closed around him and the stars grew faint. His throat constricted so that he could barely breathe, and, all the while, the voice laughed and the broken hollows of Mathaiah's dead face rose up before him.

You made no plan, no attempt, to save him. You let her treachery go unchallenged. You let her beguile you. So he burns.

Bile came to Eamon's throat, the smell of burning flesh to his nose, and suddenly he saw the pyre in Edesfield. When he looked up it was not Telo's face upon that pyre but blackened pits where eyes had once been – he saw Mathaiah's face horrifically twisted by the scourging tongues of flame.

He drove his face into his hands with a cry, but still the image ground at him. Suddenly Ashway's voice screamed in his mind; Overbrook's blood touched his feet; Alben's hands were at his throat, and Giles's bloodied sword swooped overhead while young men screamed. In the furious scream he heard Mathaiah shriek also, and the boy's agony ripped through him.

You did all these things.

"No!"

He could not bear it. His grief and rage bred bitter progeny in his heart.

But he could not cry – he could not. The Master's banner hung over him, watching, listening, waiting. He could not howl out his grief into the narrow walls of that room; he would be heard and then be lost.

So had he been heard when he had confided in her.

It was the weakness of your heart that day that condemned him, son of Eben.

His legs lost their strength. He sank to his knees but they could not hold him; he sank until his whole body was prostrate on the frozen, stony floor. The chill met every inch of him and he feebly dashed his bloodied hands against the stone, clawing at it with his quivering fingers. There was no comfort for him – no one to unburden him from his woe – and there could be no grieving and no tears. He could not remain silent, and yet he could not speak.

No man could be asked to bear it.

The Serpent demanded it of you, Eben's son. You are as nothing to him. Your grief is his delight.

Eamon shook his head. It was not true! Hughan would never…

But he did, son of Eben. So did she.

He had no strength to answer. His grief closed round him and his heart screamed silently where he lay, trembling, on the stone floor.

He did not know if he slept. As the grey dawn stole into his chamber he barely knew who he was. His right arm was dead beneath him, crushed between his weight and the ground. His cloak swamped him. He smelled dry blood.

Eamon.

The voice in his heart was gentle. It knew his burden.

His eyes were crusted with grime. He forced them open.

Shivering, he stirred. His head swam as he rose upright. He

should wash and eat – how long had it been since he had eaten? – but he could do neither. His whole being reviled both. How could he wash and eat, when Mathaiah…?

She had done it. Alessia. In that moment, her name was to him like a ghoulish, bloodied harlot, and he hated it.

He stumbled painfully to his feet, flexed his hands, and walked over to his basin. As he did so he caught sight of himself in the water. The face that looked back at him was shrouded in a Hand's cloak, and it was pale beneath the blood.

He stood for a long time over the water. If he washed away the blood, with what could he ever hope to hold the memory of Mathaiah – except her hateful treachery?

Eamon.

Shaking, he plunged his hands into the water. It struck at him like ice. He rubbed his fingers together, colouring the water black-red. He worked at them until they seemed clear, then lowered his trembling face to the cold. His eyes burnt as he washed. At last he raised his head, the freezing, mottled water trickling down his neck.

As he patted his face dry, he saw something glinting on the floor. It had tumbled from his hands as he rose, and now, seeing it again, he froze.

The ring.

It was Ashway's. The Hand was dead.

For a long time he stood and stared at the ring, lost. Then Ladomer's words returned to him: he was to see the Master that morning, and it was now morning.

He weighed the ring in his hand. It was cold and heavy. He shuddered.

To the Master he would go.

His footsteps echoed dully in the halls. Slivers of early morning light cut through the corridors. The smell of the sea was strong, the cobbled courtyard stones slippery. It had rained during the night. Smoke from the distant pyres was thick, black from the dampened wood.

He passed the guards at the entrance into the East Wing, and they bowed low before him. Had any of them seen him during the night, a blood-harried ghost? He did not stop to speak to them; his voice was shrunken.

He followed the corridors of the wing, corridors down which Captain Waite had brought him but six months before, and allowed his eyes to rest on the tall pillars and crowned ceiling. They were cold and brittle before him.

Slowly he went towards the throne room. The banners and crests shivered, whispering about him as he passed.

The Master's doorkeeper was at the door. He bowed.

"You must wait, Lord Goodman."

"Where shall I wait?" Eamon whispered.

"Here, my lord," the doorkeeper answered him, gesturing to the right. There were small waiting rooms to either side, one for the Quarter Hands and one for all others. It was to the former that the doorkeeper indicated.

Eamon stepped through the doorway, heart pounding. He clenched his fingers about the ring. The waiting room of the Quarter Hands was ringed by the emblems of the quarters, and the Right Hand's eagle was marked boldly onto the ceiling. But Eamon did not see it; his sight was fixed on owl and ash.

There was a sound in the corridor behind him – footsteps that swiftly reached the throne room's doors. Eamon peered through the waiting room door. The walker stopped. A look of surprise filled the green eyes beyond.

"Lord Cathair," Eamon bowed.

"Here a little early, are we not, Lord Goodman?" Curious delight passed over the Hand's face. "One might go so far as to call you the 'early bird'." He laughed, glancing up for a moment at the banners along the hall. It was then that Eamon realized that Cathair was accompanied by several of the West Quarter's Hands, Febian among them. With them were three other Hands whom Eamon did not recognize. Perhaps from the East Quarter?

Eamon swallowed. "The Master desires to see me, Lord Cathair."

Cathair laughed again.

"Oh, he does, but you shall have to wait for a short while. Would that be an inconvenience for you at all, Lord Goodman?"

Eamon felt unnerved. "No, Lord Cathair."

"How right you are, Lord Goodman!" Cathair smiled. His voice took on the lyrical tone of a poetic citation. "After all, 'there is glory to be gained when times of waiting wane'." The Lord of the West Quarter looked to his followers. "Come, gentlemen."

Cathair and his Hands continued on past the doorkeeper. The Lord of the West Quarter whistled. Eamon's blood curdled.

He did not know how long he stood there, surrounded by the birds of the waiting room and gazed at by the crowns of the hall. Anxiety gnawed at him. He waited.

At last a group of Hands came down the corridor. He recognized them all: Tramist, Dehelt, and the Right Hand, the former two accompanied by Hands from their own quarters. All favoured him with an odd glare as they passed before him into the throne room. He realized that the Quarter Hands – just as Cathair before them – all wore the full ceremonial regalia of their quarters and positions.

"You will be summoned," the Right Hand said as he passed, his voice thick and wrathful. Eamon bowed.

"Yes, my lord."

The Hands entered, the doors closing heavily behind them. Eamon's pulse raced. He felt sick.

What did they want with him?

He stood and waited.

At last, the doorkeeper stirred and turned to him.

"You may go in, Lord Goodman."

Eamon stepped forward. The doors opened before him. He entered.

The long hall was broad and ruddy. The great pictures that had seemed so bright on the night of the ball were dull in the grey dawn. The trappings of the daised throne glowered in the gloom.

The throned sat there, a great crown circling his fiery head. Eamon met his grey gaze across that long room and all courage failed him.

The Master *knew*.

How could he not know? Ashway had spoken so much in his frenzy – and whether by force or not, he would have reaffirmed it before his death. Eamon was deliriously certain of it.

The Master smiled at him. Eamon remembered the heart of the King shattering over him on that dais. With trembling feet, he carried himself forward.

To the throned's right stood the Right Hand, regal in black. His eagle was embossed in red at his breast, his face as shadowy as his robes. The man watched him closely. Had Ladomer spoken to him? But what Ladomer had said didn't matter – Ashway would have confessed it all. The Lord of the East Quarter had had no reason to lie to them. The Right Hand would know.

Gathered at the foot of the dais steps were the other Quarter Hands: Cathair, Dehelt, and Tramist. On their breasts he saw their emblems – the raven, falcon, and harrier – and on their hands their gold rings. He recognized at once their likeness to the one he held. His heart faltered. Behind the Quarter Hands knelt all the others who had accompanied them to the hall.

But Eamon's eyes were drawn past the gathered Hands to the keen, grey eyes of the Master. Caught in that gaze he found that he had not the strength to stand.

He halted. Then slowly, painfully, he shuddered down to his knees before the throne and lowered his head.

There is still time, Eben's son.

Yes, there was still time. He could still renounce the King. They would not kill him if he offered his unreserved allegiance. It was what they expected and deserved. That was surely why he had been summoned: to reveal the folly of his disguise to them. They would kill him, just as they had killed Ashway, and Mathaiah, and Eben...

Kneeling in silence, he made one final effort to drive such

thoughts from him. He would not speak before they accused him. It would come soon enough.

"Lord Goodman, you are here to answer the Master's will." It was the Right Hand who spoke. His voice rang sharply in the long room.

"Yes, my lord." Eamon forced his tongue to words. "I will answer."

The shadows round him moved, and the Hands, their faces solemn and pale, stepped into a line behind him. He was aware of the Right Hand and the Master coming down the steps towards him. The whole earth quivered beneath those steps. He dared not look up.

"Give me the ring of the East Quarter's lord, Eben's son," spoke the Master. His voice drowned all thought.

Eamon stretched out his hand. The throned took the ring. It was small in the Master's palm, the owl engulfed by powerful fingers. Ashway's pale face came to Eamon's mind. He pushed it away in silence.

"A master has servants." The throned spoke quietly but his voice was thunder in that room and a deafening tempest in Eamon's mind. "Those who serve me well are given to greater service." He smiled, and Eamon saw that he cast his eyes for a moment to the other Hands before looking back at him. That gaze was swollen with pride.

"These Hands, son of Eben, have served me faithfully. One has served me since the day the Serpent's house fell. He has seen this city founded and has been given power of life and death over it in my name and with my authority. The others have served me for a lesser time, but their service is not less. All serve me and me alone. We have made Dunthruik strong, a name to be feared throughout the River Realm. We have subdued north and west beneath our crown. We have broken the house of the Serpent – as he is crushed, we are made bold."

Eamon looked up. The dying unicorn was before him on the high wall, the snake fleeing from its bloody cove.

The Master's eyes rested on him. "You also are my servant. More than any of these, your house is bound to mine. Now you will be bound to me."

Eamon's heart quailed. What further bond could he endure?

As he met the throned's gaze the weight of gloved hands fell on his shoulders. There were two on his right and those on his left – Cathair's – gripped him fiercely. Fear shocked through him. He flinched as the Right Hand stepped up behind him, setting a hand on his left shoulder. With a smile, the Lord of Dunthruik came forward and laid his great hands on both Eamon's shoulders.

There was a long moment of silence. In that cage of hands, Eamon shook.

Cathair's voice suddenly broke the silence. "I am the raven and vine, Lord Cathair of the West Quarter. I witnessed the fall of the Serpent and rise of the Eagle. My blood is the Master's, his mark is my strength. As it is the Master's will, so is it mine: this man shall serve."

A terrible chill speared through Eamon, but the mark on his brow felt warm and the eagle on his hand – still and silent for so long – ached deep. Both drew force from the grief and anger he hid.

Another voice spoke. "I am the falcon and oak, Lord Dehelt of the North Quarter. I saw neither fall nor rise but my blood is the Master's, his mark is my strength. As it is his will, so is it mine: this man shall serve."

"I am the harrier and yew" – the third voice was brittle – "Lord Tramist of the South Quarter. I saw neither fall nor rise but my blood is the Master's, his mark is my strength. As it is his will, so is it mine: this man shall serve."

"I am the black eagle." Now it was the Right Hand who spoke. His hand, cruel and hard, gripped Eamon's shoulder. "My blood is the Master's, his mark is my strength. I am his right hand. As it is his will, so is it mine: this man will serve."

Eamon felt something in him, but knew it not; in their voices he heard the echo of a time long ago. For a moment he saw an image of the throne room. Five men knelt, as he knelt even then, before the throned. They were robed in black and one of them, Eamon understood, was Eben.

Eamon looked up. The Master's eyes were on him.

"It is my will," the throned said, a slow smile on his face. "Hold out your hand, Eben's son."

Eamon held out his shaking hand and watched in silence as the throned took his fingers. His grip was huge, powerful, and crushing – it made Eamon's skin crawl. But he could no more flee from it than he could draw his eyes from the pools of molten iron that devoured him.

Suddenly the cold, golden clasp of the ring was round his finger. The chill of it crept into his bone. The throned held the ring there, pressing it into his flesh. It was heavy and hurt him, but still he did not understand.

The throned smiled at him. "Rise, Lord Goodman."

Eamon clenched his eyes shut, and, quivering, rose to his feet. The Hands still crowded him. Their hands weighed on his shoulders like an immovable burden. His own hand hung heavy with the ring; it felt both too tight and too large for him.

Suddenly the hands on his shoulders were gone. Eamon gasped as the Right Hand reached around from behind him and undid the clasp at Eamon's neck, from which his cloak hung. The pressure of hands and cloth seemed enough to choke, but Eamon forced himself to keep still as the Right Hand pulled his cloak from him.

Cold air rushed at him. Though he wore both shirt and jacket beneath the heavy garment, bereft of his cloak he felt vulnerable. He shivered. Panic flowered in his heart, and his chest rose and fell with nervous, unsteady breath.

The Master stepped up to him, a black robe hanging menacingly from his hands. It was heavy, of the same quality as the ones worn by the other Quarter Hands. The Master came so close that Eamon felt the man's breath on his down-turned face. He battled every nerve to keep his trembling limbs in order as the Master's arms reached round him and, in a terrifying half-embrace, laid the new robe upon him. It settled over his shoulders, touching his back and arms. Last of all, its rich weight touched his chest, laying over his heart an emblem that he knew. It consumed his sight. No words reached his throat.

A cloak was laid over the robe and fixed upon him, and then the Quarter Hands stepped back to stand behind him. Eamon finally understood.

"You will serve me, Eben's son." The throned's voice blasted his ears like fire. "For treachery, for defiance, for insolence, for any grievance, you will receive my wrath. For loyalty, you will receive my pleasure." Eamon couldn't breathe. The words struck like hammers to an anvil.

The Master's hand was on him, taking his jaw in a pincer-hold and forcing his chin up. Their eyes met. The man's flaming face was lit by an indulgent smile. The Master held him, the grey eyes searching every part of him. Eamon wanted to howl and tear himself away, to throw back the ring and cast off the robes and cloak bestowed upon him. He could not.

The Master knew it.

"You are the owl and ash." The Master's words drummed into Eamon's soul. "You are the Lord of the East Quarter. Your blood and strength please me. You are mine."

The grip on his jaw tightened; Eamon could see nothing but the twin pools of grey, could hear nothing but the words that axed his stricken heart.

They had made him a lord of Dunthruik.

"As is your will," he heard himself whisper, "so is it mine."

The throned laughed. His great hand caressed Eamon's cheek.

"You will serve, Eben's son."

The hand released him and tossed his chin away. Eamon staggered, his mind in turmoil. As he stepped back he felt hands on his arms. The Quarter Hands were around him again.

"Your glory, Master." They spoke in unison, bowing. Eamon stumbled to keep with them. The throned nodded. At some unspoken signal, Cathair, Dehelt, and Tramist bowed even more deeply before leaving the hall in silence, taking with them every other Hand present. Eamon saw the Right Hand towering nearby, and waited.

The throned's eyes were on him. The touch of the Master's hand lingered on Eamon's cheek.

"Lord Arlaith," the Master said.

"Master."

"Conduct Lord Goodman to his quarter."

The words rushed over Eamon with stomach-turning speed. *His* quarter…

"Your glory be ever first in my heart," the Right Hand replied, bowing low. Eamon followed his lead. When he rose it was to find the Master's eyes still watching him, the glint of victory shining through the grey.

I have made you mine, son of Eben. Now honour me.

Eamon followed the Right Hand from the room. Even when the door closed behind them, he felt the eyes on him.

The Right Hand led him out of the palace and across the enormous Royal Plaza. The Gauntlet on duty snapped to attention as they passed. They stared at him in awe, for his robes were marked with the ash and owl and his hand bore the ring that had for countless years belonged to the seer of Dunthruik.

They passed out of the palace's great gates, Eamon following dumbly in the Right Hand's steps. As the palace fell behind him, his insides churned with a sour mix of conflicting emotions and broken loyalties. They had killed Mathaiah and Ashway, and rather than kill him – why had they not killed him? They surely knew his heart! – they had made him a lord of Dunthruik. From her treachery – and their deaths – he had been made a Quarter Hand. It delighted and appalled him, terrified and enraged him.

He resolved to keep his eyes on the paving stones – he could not look at the Right Hand.

They soon reached the Four Quarters. The Coll's shop fronts glistened in the morning light while the statues over the quarters, players on a stage of light and shadow, took their turns in the changing arcs of sunlight. Eamon's eye was drawn to a giant crowned eagle, a stone shield at its breast, which towered over the top of one of the quarters. The shield bore both the ash and owl.

"Ash trees drive away serpents."

Eamon twitched in alarm as the Right Hand's voice spoke in his ear. He realized that he had been looking at the emblem for a long time.

"An appropriate symbol for a lord of Dunthruik." The Right Hand paused for a long time. "For you in particular, Lord Goodman."

Eamon's heart tremored. Slowly, he forced himself to meet the Right Hand's gaze. The formidable face watched him incisively.

"Feltumadas's shall not be the last head that I bring to the Blind Gate, my lord." With a gut-crushing effort, Eamon forced an arrogant laugh to his lips. "There will be no snakes in this quarter by the time I have done."

"It has been long since there were many," the Right Hand answered with mock thoughtfulness. "They seem, Lord Goodman, to have migrated west in recent months."

He meant Mathaiah. Eamon choked back his heart. "You should perhaps speak with Lord Cathair regarding that matter, my lord."

The Right Hand smiled. "Wise counsel, Lord Goodman! Wise indeed!"

They passed into Coronet Rise and Eamon recognized buildings that he had dimly glimpsed the previous night. Soon the broad street leading to the Ashen appeared on their right, and they took it. Faces peered curiously from the doorways, and voices murmured as they passed.

Suddenly the Ashen, its trees swaying lightly in the morning breeze, opened before them. As they stepped into the sunlit square, Eamon gasped.

It was lined with rank after rank of Gauntlet soldiers, officers, and militiamen. By them were quarter officials. Every man was impeccably uniformed or dressed, and, as Eamon and the Right Hand came to a halt at the square's heart, two hundred hands raised two hundred swords to two hundred faces in the Gauntlet's formal salute.

"I come in the name of the Master," the Right Hand called. Eamon realized there was still some ceremony to be undergone. "Let none gainsay me. I bring to you a man after the Master's heart, chosen by him."

The words shredded Eamon. How could he be like Edelred? He remembered the feel of the hand at his chin and fought the urge to rip his nails across his jaw. He longed to eradicate that loathsome touch!

"In the Master's name," the Right Hand thundered, "I declare that this man shall henceforth be Lord of the East Quarter."

The eyes of the attentive men turned to him. He saw other onlookers, ordinary men and women, hidden in the shadowy streets.

"Declare yourself, lord."

Eamon felt that it was a voice familiar to him, yet he could not grasp it. His own voice seemed rusted to his throat. At last he raised his head to face the assembled men.

"I am Lord Goodman," he called. As his name rippled across the courtyard, strange silence descended. Since Pinewood, his name had gone before him into the East Quarter.

"Lord Goodman, choice of the Master, be his Hand among us."

Through the mire of his thoughts, Eamon recognized the voice with sudden clarity. He looked up, and found that a face he loved was there.

As their eyes met, Captain Anderas smiled.

"Lord Goodman for the East!" the captain called jubilantly. Every man assembled took up his acclamation with one voice:

"Lord Goodman for the East!"

Some called it in fear, some in thin hope, some in awe, some in uncertainty, but they all called it. The wave of his name washed over him, and Eamon sensed the Right Hand, a dark and furious presence, beside him.

See how I repay those whom I love, Eben's son? With adulation and with power. More of it shall come to you, serving me.

With odd reluctance, Eamon forced his thought from the enticing words and sought Anderas again. The captain's face was pale with fatigue, but he smiled.

"The East Quarter welcomes you, my lord," he said.

To my glory, son of Eben.

"*To his glory.*"

They were the words that he had to say, the words on the tip of his tongue – but there they froze. Eamon felt something stir with forgotten gentleness in his breast.

"Thank you," he said.

The Right Hand stiffened blackly beside him, but Eamon did not turn. Strange expressions passed over the faces that watched him.

Captain Anderas stepped out of the ranks and marched smartly up to them. He bowed low. "My lords."

"Captain," the Right Hand answered, his gaze falling hard on Eamon, his hands tensing within their black gloves. Eamon wondered – not for the first time – whether the man might be considering doing him some violence. But then the Master's closest looked back to the captain with a small smile. "I leave Lord Goodman in your capable hands."

Silently he left. Eamon felt a little weight pass from his breast and turned to Anderas. The captain smiled and held out his hand.

"The East Quarter welcomes you," he said with a quiet laugh.

Their hands clasped together. Eamon felt the shape of Ashway's ring bound about his finger.

Dismissed, the men in the square went in an orderly fashion back to their duties. Anderas led Eamon to the Handquarters and Ashway's own rooms. Eamon remembered following Ashway along the corridors on the morning he had come to collect papers for Cathair. Everything was the same as it had been then, the stone corridors still engraved with leaves. Sometimes the angular, haunting script from the Hands' Hall appeared, hidden among the top-most parts of the stone.

They were met with silence everywhere. Eamon saw nobody.

When they reached the more private halls of the Handquarters, Anderas turned to him. Eamon silently nodded to permit the captain to speak. He could not trust himself to do more.

"The Right Hand sent a message to me this morning," he said, "directing that the East could expect a new lord…" His worried eyes sought Eamon's. "What happened to Lord Ashway?"

Eamon's mind cast itself back to the hours of darkness and to Ashway, bound in his chair… Had it only been last night?

"I don't know," he said at last. "I do not believe, captain, that it would be wise to ask." The words came out more harshly than he had meant them to. He could not speak of the manner of Ashway's death, nor his thoughts as to how or why it might have occurred. Had he not seen what happened when he entrusted himself to others – as he had done to her?

"You are tired, I expect," Anderas answered. "I will show you to your chambers."

Anderas guided him to the great doors of the study. The captain pushed them open. Eamon followed him inside.

The room was exactly as the previous night. The bay window looked out over the immaculate garden and tall shelves hung imposingly from the walls. The painting stared at Eamon. He heard the sounds of the mêlée in his mind. He heard Mathaiah screaming.

He gasped.

Anderas looked carefully at him. "Lord Goodman –"

"I am sorry, captain." Eamon looked at the man. He remembered Pinewood and the decimation line. This captain trusted him, and he trusted and loved the captain –

He had trusted and loved *her*.

He could not speak to Anderas.

"I am tired," he said. "I came from the palace. It's a long way."

How ludicrous that sounded! A green cadet could march from the East Quarter to the palace in less than half an hour.

"The journey to the East Quarter is a long way to go before breakfast," Anderas answered quietly. There was a small pile of paper on the desk. Anderas cleared it before gesturing to the table. "If it would please you to sit, Lord Goodman, I'll have something sent to you."

Eamon moved obediently forward then stopped. The chair stared back at him. He saw Ashway bound to it, and then Mathaiah, bound in torment in the Pit.

His hands shook.

"Captain –" His voice was a partial sob. He bit it back.

Anderas glanced at him in surprise. "Breakfast is not usually a cause for grief in this quarter, my lord," he said gently. "You will find that your cook knows his trade well."

"My... my cook?" Eamon stared, then watched in disbelief as Anderas nodded. With a deep breath, he steadied himself. "Captain, I..." His eyes fell on Ashway's chair. There were no marks of death or struggle on it. It haunted him.

Anderas followed his gaze.

"Please accept my apologies, my lord," he said. "This seat is certainly too low to the table; you would find it most uncomfortable. I will have the servants bring you another."

Eamon met his gaze. Anderas's tone was light, but his eyes saw well. "Thank you."

The captain smiled. "You shall be less inclined to thank me, I think, when you realize that you shall have to sit in your chair to read, sanction, sign, and distribute all of those papers," he said, gesturing at the load on the desk. "But we can discuss a fitting punishment for my deception later. Would you eat alone?"

"Yes," Eamon answered. "I would eat alone."

Anderas was true to his word. Barely had he left when servants arrived to remove the chair. They kept their gazes lowered and moved with a disconcerting silence. Eamon did not feel it in himself to speak to them. He stared out of the window and tried to occupy his mind with the twisting branches and climbing leaves that dappled the morning.

When he turned back it was to find that a new, much taller, chair had been set at the desk, and a tray, filled with bread and cheese, had been left next to the papers. There was also a pitcher of water, its neck elegantly traced round with a circlet of leaves.

He ate slowly, each mouthful agony. His body wholly rejected the notion of food, and yet he broke the bread and pressed it to his sealed lips. With each piece he swallowed, he felt that he might choke. The ring on his hand was heavy and it drove his arm back down to the desk.

He ate a third of what had been presented to him, then rose. The painting on the wall drew his gaze, seeming both clear and distant. As he looked about the room at the long shelves of books and ornaments, he wondered.

What had happened to Ashway? Had they killed him there? His blood ran cold. If the room had been witness to the lord's death, it was too dull to speak of it. Who, he wondered, had made the stroke?

Had the hands that had taken Ashway's life taken Mathaiah's also? His grief gagged in his throat until it choked him.

He did not know how long it was until Anderas returned.

The captain showed him the rest of the Handquarters, detailing its every room and use. Eamon was shown his bedroom, a grand affair wrought in dark wood with green drapes surrounding its four posts and a long view across the garden. He met some of his servants. He saw the reception room and dining room, the countless corridors, the kitchens and the servants' quarters, the washroom, the cellars, and the stables. Anderas spoke to him about each, but he barely heard what the captain told him.

After the Handquarters, Anderas took him to the East Quarter College. It was very similar to Waite's college, but the insignia over the gate was slightly different, bearing the expected ash tree.

Anderas seemed utterly at his ease there and Eamon was impressed by how smoothly it ran. The cadets, ensigns, and officers on duty saluted smartly, calling the captain's name with pride; others bowed. The men watched Eamon oddly as he passed, almost as though they feared for the safety of their captain with the new Hand.

The captain smiled at him. "You have a fearsome reputation in this quarter, my lord," he said. "There isn't a man in the whole city who hasn't heard about the Easter head." He lowered his voice. "There isn't a man in this college who hasn't heard of your boldness before the Right Hand."

Eamon imagined how the college must have lived in fear the whole time he strove for Feltumadas's head in Hughan's camp. Apart from the many East Quarter Gauntlet and militia who had stood in peril, Anderas himself would have lost his life – and the East Quarter College its clearly beloved captain – had Eamon failed.

"What do they say about me?" Eamon asked.

Anderas laughed gently. "Much," the captain confessed, "and very little exaggerated."

It was a long day. Eamon wondered how it was that it seemed to him so much longer than the time it took for the sun to rise and cross to the western skies. Anderas took him through some of the papers he had to sign, ranging from trading licences to permissions to release or imprison men, and orders for detachments from the East Quarter College for the following weeks. There was a list of candidates from the college who were to be sworn in, a list of families seeking permission to leave the city, and requests for various cases to be taken from the Crown Courts and set under the jurisdiction of the Quarter Hand. Some Gauntlet units still needed reshuffling and their numbers adjusting after the losses sustained at Pinewood; new cadets needed to be gathered from the quarter, and death warrants needed authorization. There were reports on the progress of the quarter's culling efforts, accompanied by a list of those sent to the pyre that night. This Eamon quickly pushed away, fearing to read what he knew would be there. There were papers for the distribution of food and drink to be reviewed and passed on to the logistics draybant, invitations to a dozen minor events in the quarter itself, requests for clemency or vengeance, notices of buildings and roads that needed repair, or of suspicious behaviour that needed to be investigated.

Eamon looked at the papers, all of which wanted his signature. He drowned as he surveyed them.

Anderas lit lamps at the desk to aid the failing daylight.

"Which ones should I sign, which should I seal, and which… should I mark?" Eamon asked. Anderas had already explained it to him, but he hadn't been listening.

Anderas picked up the first paper from the pile. He moved slowly, perhaps aware of the odd nature of his position. "This one needs signature and seal, Lord Goodman. The rest can wait until the morning."

Eamon looked at the parchment – an order authorizing one of the college's lieutenants and his unit to carry out the arrest of suspected wayfarers in the nether parts of the quarter. Two families were named.

Eamon stared at the paper. Suddenly, he was watching Dorien Lorentide racing across into the arms of his horrified father.

"What did they do?" He tried to make his voice neutral.

"Hindered the Gauntlet in the rightful extraction of a known wayfarer," Anderas answered. There was no emotion to his voice. As Eamon looked up, he remembered Ladomer's praise of the East Quarter captain who had filled whole pyres by himself.

Slowly Eamon took up the quill. He could scarcely feel it in his hand – his mind already spun with so much grief. He could not refuse to sign. That could not be his first act as the Lord of the East Quarter.

Dipping the quill into the inkpot he signed his name and laid the instrument aside. He remained still for a long moment. Anderas watched him.

"Forgive me, Lord Goodman," the captain said at last. "Your seal is needed."

Eamon took the candle and allowed some of the wax to drip down onto the paper. It was thick like blood. Awkwardly, he turned his hand and pressed the ring down. He felt heat in his hand, and for a moment caught sight of the red light between it and the paper.

He pulled sharply away to see an owl embedded in the wax. Eamon stared.

Slowly, Anderas took the paper. "I'll see to this, Lord Goodman. Shall I have the servants see you to your bed?"

"No," Eamon answered weakly. He could not endure anyone watching him. The papers that had condemned Mathaiah had been signed and sealed just as this one. His hand shook. He set it discreetly beneath the desk.

If Anderas saw his hands, he said nothing. Instead, the captain nodded. "Very well. Good night, Lord Goodman."

"Good night, captain."

Eamon watched as the captain left, his heart silently begging the man to stay. He needed solace; he needed the freedom to speak out everything that had tormented him since he had seen Ashway bound and Mathaiah blinded.

But Captain Anderas could not hear him. Even if he could, even were he to ask for his ear, Eamon knew that he could not speak. The man served the Master by filling pyres.

The door closed. Eamon stared at it.

He seized the quill. With a cry he crushed it in his hand before hurling it brutally across the room. It struck the painting, disfiguring a soldier's face before falling pathetically to the floor.

Eamon sank back into his chair. His chest heaved and sobbed, but still no sound came from him and no tear touched his eye. He curled his limbs together in the high-backed, deep-seated chair, and drove his face down into his shaking hands and arms.

He would not go to a bed. In her bed had he been poisoned and betrayed.

He did not sleep that night. When the dawn stirred him, he was still in the chair, his cheek marked by the ring against which it had lain.

CHAPTER XII

The days that followed seemed interminably long, the hours of light marked by a hundred things he could not grasp, and those of night by memories he could not bury. He could not eat, he could barely sleep, and during the nights he sat in the tall-backed chair until he could no longer feel his limbs.

Anderas showed him the quarter's streets and buildings, many them steeped in significance. He met the Hands who worked for him and answered to him in and beyond the quarter. They stood in relation to him much as he had stood in relation to Lord Cathair. Seeing them fawn filled him with disgust. Eamon met First Lieutenant Greenwood and the quarter's officers, as well as many of the cadets and ensigns. He heard their names as Anderas introduced their faces. Each seemed anxious to please him but he seemed unable to keep hold of them; they turned into so many staring faces which meant nothing to him, unless it was to remind him of the face that he had lost, and the one that had caused him to lose it.

When he walked through the Handquarters he sometimes heard the servants flee before him. Where once he would have sought them out, he now preferred their absence. He often sat alone, a prisoner of his thoughts. No escape came to him unless it was the hated voice that counselled him to bury his grief and rage all the deeper, to turn them against the Serpent that had allowed Mathaiah to die.

One evening it grew unseasonably cold. Eamon sat in his office, staring at the papers that he should sign, seal, and mark. Anderas usually came to collect them in the evening, and signed any that were left on his behalf.

That night Eamon had neither read nor signed any of them. His cold, vacant eyes saw nothing. He barely heard the captain when he entered. He did not even know if the man had greeted him, for he saw and heard nothing until a sudden smell touched him. It drove him to his feet with a furious cry.

"What are you doing?" he demanded.

Anderas was standing by him, checking various papers, and a small boy knelt in the corner by the fireplace. He had stacked some logs together and a fire now licked at the dry wood. The boy had frozen, his hands suspended by the grate that he was setting back. He cowered before Eamon's anger, but Eamon did not see it: he saw only the fire – the all-consuming, man-eating fire.

"It is cold, Lord Goodman," Anderas spoke quietly. "I think if you feel your hands, you will find that you are, too."

"Do not presume to tell me whether the temperature is to my liking, *captain!*" Eamon's voice quivered with rage. He turned ireful eyes on the boy. "Put it out!"

The boy hesitated. Eamon's voice rose almost to a scream.

"*Put it out!*"

Anderas laid down the papers he held. He moved to the boy and touched the child's shoulder to send him from the room. Eamon did not know whether either of them spoke; all he knew was that he shook, grief writhing inside him like a wild beast. The smell of the flames threatened to draw it, retching and clawing, from him.

Anderas doused the flames in silence, his face pale. Eamon knew that fear had to be in the man's mind, but he did not care. He drew his cloak up around him and strode from the room, out, out into the garden where the servants and stars fled from him. He needed air, space, help…

Help? Eamon drove the word away in disgust. There was no help for him, and he needed none. Silence was all that could cover him.

He pressed deeper into the garden's inky dark. Captain Anderas did not follow him.

It was mid-March. Eamon sat, as was his custom, in his chair. It had been six days since he laid himself down in a bed to sleep – his whole body ached for it. Each day the lines about his eyes grew broader, thicker, deeper. But there was no peace for him, no rest. There was nothing for him anywhere but in his chair. It was the only thing that could hold him and the only thing that could bear the whisperings of his virulent, wretched heart.

At about mid-morning there was a knock at his door. Wearily he granted entrance. One of the servants came in and bowed low. Eamon recognized the man, the major-domo in charge of ensuring the smooth working of the Handquarters' many servants.

"Forgive my intrusion, Lord Goodman." He was tall and thin, with grey wispy hair and a timid face. "I wondered if I might ask you a few questions about the supper?"

"Supper?" Eamon looked at him, struggling to gain any memory of either his name or the supper he mentioned.

There must have been anger in his voice, for the servant flinched. "The formal supper to welcome you to the quarter. I believe that Captain Anderas –"

"What does that require I do?" Eamon said more brusquely than he meant. The servant froze. Annoyed, Eamon sighed heavily and gestured for the man to approach. "Tell me what I have to do," he repeated. The man held a piece of paper on which a list was written in rough script. He laid it gingerly in front of Eamon.

"My lord, it is not often that the quarter has the honour of celebrating a new Hand. It is traditional for the one being feasted to choose the meal. If it is too much trouble, I can –"

"I will choose," Eamon answered. He swooped the paper up from the table and steadied it in front of his eyes. He had to squint at the script to make any sense out of it, but eventually words suggested themselves from the tangled strokes.

"There are five services to choose, my lord." The butler, emboldened by Eamon's taking of the paper, continued. "There's the starter, soup, principal, dessert, and cheeses, and of course wines."

Eamon peered at the different suggestions for each service. A frown creased his face.

"I want to change the order of the courses." The major-domo looked alarmed. Eamon ignored it. "I have never held with this odd notion that cheese should be eaten after something sweet," he said flatly, setting the paper down again. "Put it before."

There was the briefest hesitation on the butler's part. "Yes, lord," he said, hastily making an amendment to the paper. He pointed to the starters. "Would you prefer dried fruits or nuts to begin?"

Eamon sighed. Surely there could not be much fruit in the city to dry after a harsh winter? "I have no preference," he answered.

"But, my lord –"

"I have to choose? Very well: nuts." He watched as the major-domo made a note.

"For soups –"

"The thickest one," Eamon answered, jabbing at the paper. "I cannot abide the thin, watery kinds of which this city seems so fond."

"I'm sorry that you feel that way, my lord. It will be the Crown Medley – a seasonal speciality of this quarter." The butler made another note. "And for your principal?"

Eamon looked hard at the menu, wanting nothing better than for the torture to be concluded. His choice was between various red meats – a selection called the "Crown Platter" – and dozens of different kinds of fish. He chose one of the former.

"My lord, wouldn't the fish be a higher complement to –?"

"I have made my choice," Eamon interrupted, aggravated. "Please make sure that it is well cooked," he added as the butler jotted once again on the paper. His face paled slightly.

"My lord, it is supposed to be served rare; it then more closely resembles the Master's colour –"

"Well cooked," Eamon insisted. "Followed by the cheeses and then dessert, which you may choose yourself." The major-domo's jaw dropped, but Eamon carried on. "What wines are there to choose from?"

"They are all Ravensill." The wines came from land that belonged to Lord Cathair, and the revenue from the trade was fed back into the West Quarter and maintenance of the port; Eamon had seen the numbers and the details when he had served as a quarter's Hand under Cathair. Ravensill wines were highly sought after in the merchant states; he wondered what the Easters made of it. He remembered the red that he had tasted as a first lieutenant in the West Quarter, and the way that Lieutenant Fields had cooed at him while he poured.

He had enjoyed that wine. But he did not want it.

"The white," he said, tapping the page. The major-domo looked horrified, then vaguely distasteful.

"The white?" he asked, as though he hoped repeating it would change Eamon's mind.

"*The white.*"

"Let me see if I have understood correctly, my lord." The major-domo drew himself up. "You want the nuts, followed by the *Crown* Medley, then the *Crown* Platter – which, despite being red meats, are not to be red. This is to be served with a white wine, to be followed not by dessert but by cheeses, to be followed by something to be chosen by someone other than yourself?"

Eamon nodded. "Yes," he said.

"My lord… you realize that you are choosing a two-crown dinner? In many circles this will be considered an ins –"

Eamon didn't care how many crowns were involved. "That is what I command," he said slowly.

The major-domo bowed swiftly. "As you wish, my lord."

"When is the supper?" Eamon asked.

"Tomorrow evening," the man answered. "The invitations will be seen to. Thank you, Lord Goodman."

That evening he sat at his desk. It had come to be his entire world. He stared out of the window over the garden. Anderas came earlier than usual and checked the day's papers. Eventually, Eamon noticed that the man watched him. He turned to face him.

"Captain?"

"Forgive me, Lord Goodman," Anderas inclined his head, then matched Eamon's gaze. "Mean you to look at these papers?"

"Aren't you already doing that?"

"Lord Goodman..." Anderas closed his eyes, then drew a careful breath. "Lord Goodman, I cannot authorize them all."

"Have you not done so thus far?"

"I should *not* authorize them." He paused. "I am but the captain of the East Quarter. My men want to see the hand of their Hand on these papers. You must –"

"*Must*, Anderas?" Eamon's tone was virile.

The captain fell silent. Eamon watched him. Why did he suddenly feel so estranged from this man?

His haunting thoughts returned to him. He raised his hands to his head with a deep breath.

Anderas watched him. Then he gathered up the papers, bowed, and left.

The heavens stayed clear during the day, and as the evening set in, a chill breeze blew in from the sea.

In the late afternoon, Anderas took Eamon to the grand dining hall in the Handquarters. The room was long though not too narrow, and great tables lined it, meeting a high table at one end on a dais. The room had been prepared for over a hundred guests, among whom would be the quarter's officers, some selected ensigns, the Hands under Eamon's jurisdiction (whom he had met several times, but remembered none of them), and representatives from each of the other quarters, accompanied by their own men. Eamon saw the guest list and was relieved to learn that the other Quarter Hands did not intend to put in a personal appearance. This fact should perhaps have perturbed him, but he did not rue their absence, nor take any hint of warning from it. The only names on the list he recognized were those of Waite, who would be coming on behalf of Lord Cathair, Anderas, and a handful of officers from the North Quarter whom he had met when working at the port.

Eamon stood in the hall with Anderas, watching as the servants laid the places to the tables and set carefully written name tags by each place. The cutlery was impeccably polished and arranged, and the glasses shone where they stood; he had caught scent of the cooking when they had passed the kitchens earlier and it had boded well.

"As you are aware, my lord, this supper will be your formal reception as the Lord of the East Quarter." Eamon allowed his attention to be drawn by Anderas's words. "You greet your guests in the hall outside when they arrive, and after the servants let you know that all is ready, you can bring everyone in. They find their seats. There is a toast to the Master, then the meal. At its end you bid farewell to your guests as they leave by this door."

"Is that all?" Eamon didn't feel much intrigued by the description of his evening's activities. He wanted to sit in his chair and stare at the familiar, gaunt hollowness inside himself.

"Yes, my lord, it is."

Eamon looked across at the captain and almost allowed himself to be concerned by the man's pale face and tense tone. The moment passed.

Anderas bowed. "If you'll excuse me, my lord."

"Of course."

The evening came swiftly, and Eamon again donned the ceremonial robes that had been given to him by the Master. He hated them, just as he hated the ring on his finger, and he hated that he could not sit alone with his grief and rage but must instead put himself on show to scores of people whom he also hated. He consoled himself that it was but one evening and that they would have to leave when he told them to.

The sun sank below the horizon when he made his way into the reception room. Some of the quarter's lieutenants and two draybants were already there, their uniforms smartly presented. A couple of token ensigns walked with them, their uniforms even more sharply primed and their eyes wide as they took in the great alternate banners bearing the owl and Master's eagle. Servants passed among those gathered there, serving drinks. As soon as he appeared, Eamon was greeted by a room of rustling fabric and silent, bowing men.

Eamon greeted them but stood aloof as they resumed conversation. He barely heard what was being said, his mind far away. His glass chinked against the ring in his hand as he moved.

"Lord Goodman, good evening." Eamon turned and saw Waite. The captain rose from a deep bow and stood at his elbow. He smiled. "How are you, Lord Goodman?"

"Well, thank you, captain."

The captain's perceptive eyes rested on him for a moment. "I bring you Lord Cathair's regards, but, unfortunately, not Lord Cathair himself. He has sent a case of wines for your cellar, by means of an apology and as a token of his esteem."

"Were they poisoned?" Eamon asked abstractly. Waite blinked in surprise, then laughed.

"No, Lord Goodman – at least, not that Lord Cathair told me. He did, however, ask me to advise you that the wines come from a noble rot crop, and that he felt these would be most fitting for your feast."

Eamon looked at the captain. He saw the insult and Cathair's intent, but he could not feel it. There was nothing left in him capable of feeling.

Waite spoke again. "So far as it concerns me, a good wine is one that sits well in the stomach, and it can rot or not as it chooses." He smiled. "How do you find yourself as a Quarter Hand, my lord?"

"I find myself well, captain."

"I find you much changed."

It was a sudden and unexpected stroke.

Eamon looked at him sharply. "I find you much too bold."

Waite smiled, a small smile, then laughed quietly. "I found you as a lieutenant," he said. "You had a strange look to you in those first days, Lord Goodman. It was after Alben died that I first noticed it." The captain fixed him with a firm stare. Eamon felt hideously vulnerable, as though the angry casings of his grief would crack under the gaze of the man before him. "I see that look again now," Waite added, "and I wonder why it is you bear it."

Eamon's hand clenched tighter about his glass. He willed the captain to dissolve into the ground, and to take his wretched curiosity with him.

He was saved by a servant who came forward and bowed beside him.

"When you wish to go in, Lord Goodman," he said, "we are ready."

Eamon summoned them all to dinner.

The long dining hall was brightly lit and welcoming. Not a thing was out of place. On the wall over the high table hung a banner bearing the owl and ash. The Master's eagle framed it. Eamon felt its regal gaze on him as he took his place at the high table. Waite was to sit to his left and Anderas to his right. Neither man met his gaze as they took their places, and part of him thought less of them for that.

He watched as those invited came into the hall and took their seats. He saw the servants by the doors at the back of the hall, standing as inconspicuously as they could. As the guests stood by their chairs, their eyes turned to him, but he was not able to discern the intention behind the stares. He was a prisoner, and anything beyond the walls of his cell ceased to interest him.

The goblets at his place were filled, the cutlery wrought in a golden sheen, and small crowns marked the stems of the goblets. Eamon took one and raised it in his hand. As he did so, every man in the room did likewise. He marvelled that his gestures should have such effect.

"To the East Quarter," he called, "and to his glory."

"His glory," the room echoed. The hundred voices spoke and drank in unison. The guests set their glasses down and seated themselves, as the first servants stepped into action, silent and flawless. They bore the nuts to the table.

Conversation surrounded him as the meal progressed. Some of it may have been aimed at him, as an attempt to engage him, but he was never certain. He responded to little or none of it, and ate swiftly, enjoying less than little of it. It was a business that had merely to be endured and dispensed with. He found some pleasure in the fact that the wine was white and that the soup, a deep red colour, was thick. It tasted good, though he would not have liked to admit it.

Soon the Crown Platter, an exquisite selection of red meats, was brought out. Eamon was dimly aware of a stunned silence as it was laid before the guests. One or two of them glanced at him in horror, but he did not understand it. Perhaps they preferred their meat bloody. He did not.

Anderas stared at him. He ignored it. Even Waite seemed a little disturbed as the plate was laid before him. In silence and with uncertainty, the men began eating.

There was another odd silence when the cheeses were brought, though most seemed content with the major-domo's choice of dessert – a rich pastry served with honey. Eamon found it ironic that the part of the meal he enjoyed the most was that in which he had had no part. He wondered idly whether he should have let the major-domo choose everything.

The meal drew to its close. At Anderas's whispered instruction, Eamon rose and went to the door for the formal leave-taking of his guests. He made himself smile and bid farewell to each of them. Anderas stood at his elbow, discreetly whispering their names to him as they approached. Eamon cared about none of them, not even those he knew.

"Thank you, Lord Goodman," Waite said as he took his turn. Eamon wondered why the captain looked pale.

"Thank you, captain," he answered. "Please give my regards to Lord Cathair," he added, as the men representing the other Quarter Hands also approached, "and to Dehelt and Tramist. Thank you all for your company." He was lying with every utterance, and well he knew it. Perhaps they did, too. They bowed to him and left.

"Lieutenant Mers, East Quarter," Anderas muttered, and Eamon looked up to the next man, one of the last in the long line of leaving guests. He was red in the face and his eyes did not seem entirely clear. He laughed. It seemed to Eamon a strange, mocking laugh.

"A *two-crown* dinner," Mers sneered, bowing ridiculously low.

"Lieutenant." Anderas's voice was harsh and full of warning.

"Very fine, Lord Goodman. You have my thanks. A two-crown dinner for a backhanded quarter." As the lieutenant spoke he looked slyly at Anderas.

"Hold your tongue, lieutenant."

Anderas's voice was terribly loud in the emptying dining hall, causing a couple of the servants to glance at him. The outburst stirred even Eamon from his stupor. Anderas's cheeks coloured with anger. Faced with such a look from his captain, the inebriated lieutenant grew a little pale.

"Yes, captain. I know that you have his papers to deal –"

"Leave," Anderas told him. "*Now.*"

The lieutenant left. Eamon watched him go before looking back at Anderas. The captain's hands shook as he leaned forward to speak once more, his voice bearing its customary whisper.

"Lieutenant Smith," he said quietly. Obediently, Eamon bade the remaining men farewell.

Anderas walked with him back to his quarters. As they crossed the main hall to the study, the captain was curiously quiet. At the door, the captain bowed and made to leave.

"You're forgetting your papers, captain," Eamon told him. "Fetch them, and you may go."

Anderas's eyes closed a moment. He sighed. "Yes, Lord Goodman."

The captain followed him into the room and strode to the desk to collect the papers. As he did so, Eamon gently closed the door.

Anderas looked up. His eyes recognized a coming storm. He paused by the desk, the papers in his hands.

"My lord?" Anderas's voice was tense.

Eamon waited for him to speak further, but the captain remained silent. Eamon's chair, the ennobling throne of his grief, called to him from behind the dimly lit table. He walked across and sat down in it, feeling its wooden arms holding his own. Anderas watched him sit.

"For such words as he uttered," Eamon began, "you should have rendered the lieutenant some punishment."

The captain's face was still and pale. Eamon wondered that the man did not answer him, but his wondering did not last long. Soon, his eyes drifted to the window, his body assuming its accustomed rigid repose.

There was silence.

"I will not punish him," Anderas said at last. His voice was strained. "If, in so doing, I act or speak out of turn, it is because the lieutenant did not do so."

Eamon looked up, annoyed that entry to his brooding thought had been thus disturbed. Then he understood what the captain had said.

"What?" he snarled.

Anderas's jaw trembled, but there was clear thought in his blue eyes. Eamon envied it.

"You put two 'crown' dishes in the dinner," Anderas told him. His voice grew more heated as he went on, "Two crowns. *Two crowns!* No dinner in Dunthruik has two crowns – Dunthruik is ruled by one crown alone!"

Eamon felt his gaze hardening and vile, acidic words bubbling up into his throat.

"You would criticize a lord of Dunthruik over a menu?" he hissed.

"You are no lord!" Anderas exploded at last, his voice roaring with something near rage.

Eamon stared, stunned beyond words. "What?"

"Are you dull or blind, that still you cannot see?" Anderas yelled. "Your eyes were good once. Now you see *nothing*! You are no lord, you are no Hand, barely are you a man!" Anderas leaned furiously across the table and slammed the papers down.

"These men, this quarter, welcomed you with joy!" he cried, gesturing towards the college. "*I* welcomed you with joy. What a man like him could do, I thought! But you are not the man who marched to Pinewood, you are not the man who stood against the Easter cavalry, you are *not* the man who defied the Right Hand. You are not the man," he added more quietly, "who saved me."

He fell silent for a moment as his voice caught. "This quarter waited for *that* man, and he never came. Now they mock you, you who sit enthroned in your dull thoughts night and day! They mock him who gives all his work to his captain, who knows not enough to say that his captain *cannot* sign every paper, who has not the *wit* to remember the names of the men *who serve him*, who is *fickle* enough to terrify a boy for lighting a fire and *reckless* enough to insult the Master by serving a meal with two crowns!" The captain shouted the last at the top of his lungs, his hand driven against the wood of the desk as he beat it with his palm, and then fell back.

Eamon stared at him. The captain's words rang dizzyingly about him. For a moment those words lodged near his heart, crying out their truth. His heart froze in fear.

Was that what they said about him? How could he have been so blind?

He has no right to speak to you thus, Eben's son.

Eamon rounded darkly on his trembling captain. "Do you not fear me, Anderas?" His voice seemed deathly quiet, but all the force of his blockaded rage was behind it.

"Your goodness gave me cause to fear, and to hope, once," Anderas replied quietly. He shook. "I fear you still, but not for that."

"Your life will be forfeit for what you say." The words passed Eamon's lips, but he knew it was not really he who spoke them.

Anderas met his gaze. "If you hear but one word, then I will pay that price."

Eamon stared at him. He meant to draw his blade to strike the man down, to see his blood run into the cracks in the stone floor. Anderas understood *nothing*.

Eamon rose to his feet and surged around the desk. Still Anderas held his gaze, and he held it without flinching.

The captain's resolve shook him. At the last moment, Eamon turned and stalked to the window. He turned his back on Anderas. Surely the captain would leave. He had to leave Eamon and his baleful grief alone. It was the only way.

Eamon. The gentle voice passed through his heart, strangely close. It took his breath.

He closed his eyes and set his head in his hands, broiling with a million thoughts and hurts. He could not hold them… but he could not let them go, or give them over to any other. He had done that once, and *she*…

"Lord Goodman." Anderas, his voice filled with immeasurable courage, stood next to him. Eamon felt a light touch on his shoulder. It was bold – too bold – but he had not the strength to throw it from him. He knew he had heard truth in Anderas's words. It terrified him just as his wicked grief consumed him.

Do not speak, Eben's son! He will betray you and rend your heart – just as she did!

"I cannot speak to you, captain." Eamon's voice, wrathful and afraid, spilled from the hands over his face. Terror seized him. He staggered against the window frame and dropped down to the floor. "Do you understand?" he howled. "*I cannot.*"

"Then let me speak to you." Anderas sank to one knee at Eamon's side. The gesture tore Eamon's heart from him in a cry of grief.

"Do not kneel!" he cried, trying to force the captain away. "Not to me."

Obligingly, Anderas shifted and sat instead. He reached out and took Eamon's shaking hand. Eamon stared at him, incredulous at his audacity.

"You dare to take my hand?" he asked, anger seeping into his voice. Anderas flinched at the tone, but held.

"Once, I saw one dare to offer such a comfort to a lord of Dunthruik," he answered. "It is his example that I follow."

Eamon stared at Anderas. "You speak of myself and Lord Ashway."

Anderas nodded.

There was a moment of silence before the captain spoke again. "Lord Goodman, there is a weight on you." The captain's hand quivered with fear as it held Eamon's, but it held fast. "There has been a weight on you since first you came to this quarter. I believe that it is that weight which has taken from you everything that you are. Tell me its name."

Horror churned through Eamon. His monstrous emotions clamoured to remain undisturbed.

He shut his eyes. "You cannot ask me to do that."

"Then let me guess at its root," Anderas answered. "I know you, Lord Goodman, and have some sense of the depth of your heart. I witnessed that when you bore me back from Pinewood, when you put your life in the line. I am honoured by that witness – and by the fact that, when I was very small, my mother taught me to read."

Eamon looked up, caught out by what seemed illogical to him. But Anderas held his gaze. When he next spoke, the captain's eyes were grave.

"I read the reports that the palace sends," he said quietly. "Every day, I receive a list of names – men and women who have been sent to the pyres. I know, Lord Goodman, who they sent the night that you sat here and comforted Ashway. I think you know it also."

Eamon's eyes burned. His grief raced up his throat and seared his mouth; rage rattled his heart and lungs. As the captain gently pressed his hand, Eamon suddenly remembered Alessia – he saw her kneeling by him, binding the wound on his injured palm as he drew breath to speak out the whole truth of who he was…

He will betray you, son of Eben. Just as she did.

Eamon shuddered violently. "I cannot speak to you."

"No." Anderas shook his head gently. "It is not that you cannot speak, my lord. You choose not to speak because you are afraid, and deathly angry."

209

Eamon looked at Anderas. The captain's eyes were sincere and the grip of his hand on Eamon's own was firm.

"I am stricken with anger, Anderas," Eamon told him. His heart ground with its burden as he said it. "And I am afraid that you…" He pressed his eyes shut. "That is why I cannot speak to you."

"My lord," Anderas spoke quietly. "Do not be afraid. Least of all of me."

A sob ripped through Eamon's throat. His hand was on the latch of the cart. The face was before him, and he was screaming at the driver and crushing his cheeks down into the terrible gore…

His voice was overcome and broke. All the rage within him howled out of his throat in a shredding cry. All his insidious and wrathful grief tore at him, striving with tooth and claw to keep hold of its precious lair in his heart and drive him back to silence. But bitter tears were in his eyes; they rushed over his face and hands.

"Mathaiah!" he cried. His voice brought the room – the whole world – crashing down around them, but the captain held his hand. "*They took Mathaiah!*"

"They took you with him," Anderas whispered. "My lord, do not carry this alone! You need not speak its whole. Let me bear it with you."

Eamon lowered his sobbing face into his hands. Long was the time that he wept, deep the angry and harrowing grief he had to spend; but Anderas sat beside him until long after his weeping ceased.

CHAPTER XIII

Dawn crept into the chamber. As the light reached across the walls it touched the pennants in the painting, illuminating the King's star.

He breathed deeply. It was quiet. For a moment he waited for the darkness of thought, the horror of disaffection. But they did not come. His breathing eased, his heart lightened, and as the first quivers of tentative birdsong sounded, Eamon opened his eyes and smiled with gentle delight.

The deep hopelessness was gone. It had been taken when his eyes had unburdened all their tears and his heart its grief. It was true that he was still in Dunthruik – and that brought terrors of its own – but the image of Mathaiah's cruelly defiled face no longer held such terrible power over him.

Slowly he arched his back; he still sat against the window's embrasure. It was uncomfortable, but as he looked to his left he saw the whole garden laid before him, green and dappled gold in the rising sun. It stole his breath.

At last he stirred his limbs. His black cloak was wrapped around him and it fell in long folds, almost tripping him as he sought his feet.

Anderas was there. The captain lay on the ground, asleep, one arm gathered under his head to cushion it against the cold floor. Eamon looked at him in awe. The captain had put his life before the fury of a Hand, and then sat watch through a vigil of tears until the dawn. He had freed Eamon from the grip of his crippling grief.

Looking up, he saw the star on the wall, and he thought of Hughan. Mathaiah had died in the King's service. Eamon realized that, were he to lose his own life, he would not want to die for less.

Peace settled on him in the silence. He watched the painted star-banner on the study wall. Like that banner, he had to go through the city before Hughan.

He drew another deep breath. How could he go before Hughan when he wore black? How could he be a Quarter Hand and serve the King – and live?

It seemed an impossible task. It was true that he was a lord of Dunthruik, but in the grip of his horror he had allowed himself to be seen in weakness and woe. Who could follow the commands of such a Hand as he had been? He had sown seeds of bitterness – in his house, his college and, no doubt, his quarter – in his angry despair. It was bitterness and hurt that he had to undo before he could begin to serve the King.

You must start with your house, First Knight.

The gentle voice and the name by which it called him touched him with forgotten clarity. It was a name that, unlike the colours of Dunthruik, he could not wear clearly. Though he might bear sorrow and anger still, he would not allow those things to hold sway over him.

It was time to be Hughan's First Knight.

Stepping carefully past the sleeping captain, Eamon rose and left the study.

The corridors were palely dashed with light from the tall windows and tinged with green from the new-budded leaves. Eamon passed swiftly through the shadows, his footsteps echoing in the passageway. He saw no one, but, as he walked, he heard soft feet fleeing before him. The servants must have been up for an hour or more already and none dared meet him. How could a servant serve without knowing his master? What kind of service was it, rendered in fear of distant footsteps?

He turned towards the servants' quarters and to the kitchens which lay buried in one wing of the building. The smell of cooking emanated from it. As Eamon approached he felt almost as though he smelled fresh bread for the first time; there was no sensation like it in the world.

He heard the master cook singing softly to himself, his deep voice drifting in the morning air, mixing with the birdsong. Eamon paused in the corridor to listen to it. The cook was singing an old River ballad. Eamon recognized the words, and remembered how his mother's sweet, clear voice lifted up in the same song while she laid him in his bed to sleep.

> *"The green blade rises, the sparrow sings,*
> *My heart rejoices with the spring."*

Quietly he stepped down into the kitchen, trying to mask the sound of his feet. He measured his success by the fact that the singing continued undisturbed.

Many of the Handquarters' servants were there, either eating meagre morsels or preparing to turn their hands to further work. The kitchen was filled with tables and cupboards stacked high with cooking instruments. At the end of the room was a large door that opened out into the garden. The door was open, the morning air and birdsong mingling with the smell of the baking bread and the harmony of the cook's voice.

As Eamon came in, one servant, then another after another, looked up and froze in horror, their faces still dull with sleep. Only the cook, working with his back towards the door, did not see him. It was the awkward silence of the other servants that caught his attention. Eamon watched as the man turned, the song falling from his lips. The cook bowed low.

"Lord Goodman," he said. Though he alone of all those gathered found the strength to speak, his voice cracked with fear.

Eamon looked at the men and women standing before him. They all served him and yet he had seen almost none of them before. His gaze passed over them, and as he looked, he saw among those gathered at one of the tables the boy at whom he had shouted; he could be little more than ten years old. As their gazes met, the child gave a half-cry and shied his head and hands into the skirts of the girl next to him. She could not be his mother – she was too young – yet the two had similar faces. The girl wrapped one arm firmly about the child while she curtseyed.

It was clear that they feared him. How could he possibly show himself to be a good lord? That he had not treated any of them with respect or lenience filled him with shame.

The table where the servants ate was covered in stale and broken table scraps from previous days. Other tables stood nearby, where the cooks prepared the day's meals. On one of them stood the fresh bread, cooling in the morning air. It seemed a harsh arrangement.

He walked to the bread. He examined it for a long moment and then chose three of the largest loaves. They were still warm. He turned back to the servants, who stood rooted to their places.

"Are they to your liking, Lord Goodman?" The cook, his hands still covered with dough, watched him nervously. Eamon nodded.

"Yes, Mr Cook," he answered sincerely, "they are."

Eamon stepped across to the servants' table and laid the bread there. None dared move. Perhaps they feared he laid a trap for them.

He still held one of the loaves in his hand. With gentle steps he moved about the table to the bench where the quivering boy stood. The child watched him fearfully around the flimsy folds of the girl's dress. The girl also watched him, with the terrified gaze of one who knew that, should Eamon choose to do or say anything, either to her or to the boy, she was powerless to stop him.

Eamon offered the girl a smile. She stared at him in horror. He crouched down until he was level with the boy's half-hidden eyes. His cloak trailed in flour and dust, but he did not care. The whole room watched him as he met the child's gaze.

"I am sorry that I shouted at you."

Eamon's voice was swallowed by the silence. The servants gaped at him.

"It was unfair of me," Eamon added.

Slowly, the boy emerged from his hiding place. He frowned. "Then why did you –?" he began.

"*Shhh!*" the girl hissed.

Eamon smiled kindly at her, then looked back to the boy.

"Why did I shout at you? That's a very fair question, and I would like to answer it." He paused. "When you lit the fire, I remembered something that had happened to me that hurt me. It made me angry. But that wasn't your fault. So I was unfair to you in being angry with you."

As he mulled on this information, the boy's eyes flicked across Eamon's face.

"What's your name?" Eamon asked.

The boy curled his fingers into his sleeves and pinched the cuffs between them. "Callum, my lord."

"Callum," Eamon repeated. He wondered how long the child had worked in the Handquarters. Had he been born of one of the servants? Did he know no other life but this?

The last thought was a grim one, but he knew that he could not change it – at least, not yet.

He held out the loaf of bread. "Callum, this is for you."

"Me?" The boy looked once at the bread, then at Eamon again.

"You."

Slowly Callum reached out and took the loaf from Eamon's hands. Eamon watched as the warmth and smell filled the boy's face with delight. "Thank you, Lord Goodman!"

Eamon was about to rise when he saw the table again.

"Callum, is this what you eat every day?" he asked, gesturing to the stale foods. The boy looked dolefully at the table, and then back to his own hands with an expression of sorrow.

"Yes, Lord Goodman." He chewed his lip, looked guiltily up, then held the bread back towards Eamon. "Lord Goodman, it isn't fair for me to –"

"Will you do something for me, Callum?" Eamon interrupted. The boy nodded. "I'd like you to tell the master cook that this food is not fit for the servants, because you work very hard – probably harder than I do." A tiny smile escaped the boy's lips. "Tell the master cook that you must eat food fresh each day, as the Gauntlet do."

The boy gaped. "Won't we be punished for that?"

Eamon's heart moved in compassion. Ashway had run a tight ship, he knew: household servants caught eating anything due for higher tables received lashes, and Ashway's house had been no exception.

It would not be so in his house.

"A servant who betrays me – or my trust – should be punished," Eamon told the boy quietly. "A servant who keeps up his strength, and sets to his tasks with that strength, should not." Eamon cast a glance at the cook himself. The man stood agog. "Do you think that's fair, Callum?"

It could so easily have been a barbed question, a trap laid for an unwilling victim to be torn by dogs. On Cathair's lips it would have been. But the boy knew nothing of the sinister plots and subtleties of such men. After a moment's ponderance, he nodded.

"I think so, Lord Goodman."

"You are a wise man," Eamon answered, "and a great builder of fires. I want you to tell the servants that they will all eat fresh bread, not just this morning, but every morning." The boy smiled. "One more thing, Callum: does the master cook sing often?"

"Yes, Lord Goodman."

"It is not the least of his talents. Tell him that he sings well."

"Yes, Lord Goodman."

Eamon smiled at the boy once more, and rose to his feet. The whole kitchen, which contained a large proportion of the household – *his* household – gawked. He met their looks in silence one by one, and smiled.

"Good morning," he called to them at last. A halting chorus of good mornings stumbled back to him. "Mr Cook," he added.

"Lord Goodman?"

"I'd like breakfast in my study as soon as you can manage. Please send breakfast for Captain Anderas also. He and I have some business to conduct this morning."

"Of course, Lord Goodman."

"Thank you."

The words were the final blow in a catalogue of astonishment for the household. The cook's jaw fell open, but was swiftly shut.

Eamon smiled again. With a heart bursting with joy, he turned and left the kitchens.

He made his way back through the still corridors. The sun was higher now and filtered down through the windows. Eamon walked back towards his study, marvelling at how the light lived on the deep wood. He had not noticed it before.

His meeting with the servants had given him hope. If he could have peace there, then perhaps he could also bring peace to the quarter. Peace would honour the King.

As he walked down the corridor, he came across an elegant archway. It was met by a path that led out into the garden. The place was thick with budding greens. Some of them would suffer in Dunthruik's late chills, but spring followed swiftly behind them. Eamon's heart surged at the thought. *Spring.*

Would the King come in the spring?

He set his hand to the door and stepped out onto the path. The light stones beneath his feet led into an open courtyard where a small and impeccably kept fountain cast out a delicate stream. The buildings that rimmed the garden were faint shadows behind the trailing leaves. That the city was not so tainted that it could not bear things of beauty gave him cause for more than hope.

Footsteps came down the path towards him. He looked up to see a figure pause on the other side of the fountain: Anderas. His brow was knit together. Catching sight of Eamon, the captain changed the direction of his steps and walked quickly to him.

"Lord Goodman –"

"You feared for me, captain?"

Anderas looked at him a little uncertainly. "I… Yes." He met Eamon's gaze. "Are you well, Lord Goodman?"

Eamon felt the light on his face and listened for a moment to the running water. He thought of the servants, of Anderas's words of comfort, of the city that he loved and to which he had been sent by the King.

He looked back to Anderas with a small smile. "I am."

Anderas watched him for a moment and judged his words. At last, Anderas nodded. "I am glad of it, my lord," he said, and buried his face behind one hand as he was interrupted by a yawn.

"You are in need of sustenance," Eamon told him. "Fortunately for you, I have seen to it." Anderas's gaze widened with curiosity. "Come with me, captain."

Anderas followed him back along the path. Eamon delighted in the odd picture the captain's face made as they worked their way back to the study. Eamon pushed the door open and strode in.

The desk had been cleared for a long tray. The girl from the kitchen was setting a second tray down. As Hand and captain came in, she looked up and froze. Eamon imagined the long years she must have spent fleeing before the sound of footsteps. She had not heard them, her face betrayed her anxiety.

Anderas watched him as he walked forward. The girl curtseyed deeply.

"I am sorry, Lord Goodman," she began. "I –"

"I am not," Eamon answered with a smile. "Would you like to know why?" The girl looked at him with an expression torn between curiosity and terror. "When I see those that serve me, I can praise them. Thank you, Miss, for delivering what I am sure will be a fine breakfast."

The girl stared at him, then curtseyed again as a touch of embarrassment passed over her face. "Do you require anything else, Lord Goodman?"

"No, thank you."

The girl rose and withdrew quietly from the room, leaving the trays on the table. There were two large plates there, filled with warm bread, cheese, and a few slim slices of meat. The smile on Eamon's face grew broad as he looked at them, then he turned to Anderas. The captain watched him with a partially perplexed, partially delighted, expression.

"Where did you go this morning, Lord Goodman?"

"To ask for some breakfast," Eamon answered. He gestured to one of the extra chairs that stood in the room. "Care to join me, captain?"

"With pleasure, Lord Goodman," Anderas answered. He brought the chair across and set it at the table. Eamon sat down in his own chair and watched as Anderas paused by the seat he had brought. Looking at Eamon uncertainly, he hesitated to sit but at last took both seat and courage.

They each set to work at their generous plates.

"This is a little different to breakfast at Pinewood," Anderas mused. "Do you remember that *awful* broth?"

"The one that Lieutenant Dawes seemed so fond of?" Eamon pulled a face. "It must have been made with mouldy beans."

"Or worse," Anderas commented. "Apparently the recipe is a closely guarded Gauntlet secret. We may be thankful for that!"

They both laughed. Eamon took a bite of his bread and sat back with deep contentment as he ate it. After a moment he noticed Anderas watching him.

"Is there something on your mind, captain?"

"It is good, my lord, to see you eating," Anderas answered. "No more – and yet much more – than that."

Eamon smiled, marvelling again at the captain's regard for him. "Thank you, captain – for everything that you have said, and done, for me." He paused, and Anderas smiled. "I am afraid, however, that you shall now have to bear the terrifying consequences of my regained sight."

"Consequences?"

"Consequences." Eamon cast his eye briefly over some of the papers on his desk. "Captain, I have two tasks for you this morning."

"I will perform them, my lord."

"You don't know what they are yet," Eamon countered.

"Neither my heart nor my duty would permit me to refrain from performing what you allotted to me, whether allotted in wisdom or in malice," Anderas answered. They were true words, jovially and eloquently spoken. Eamon laughed.

"You comfort me, captain!"

"I am glad of that, my lord."

"But to return to this morning's business. First, captain, I would have you take me to college parade this morning, for which I wish to be fully furnished with a list naming every man who will be present."

"Yes, Lord Goodman."

"Then I would like you to escort me again through the East Quarter. I am afraid that I did not pay full attention the first time. I rue it heartily."

Anderas nodded. "You ask little, Lord Goodman."

"And you give much."

CHAPTER XIV

Eamon and Anderas finished breakfast together, then Anderas went to collect the papers detailing the name and rank of each man in the college. He advised Eamon that the men, including groups of drummers and trumpeters, would stand in strict order at the parade. Eamon set aside his heavy cloak, taking up instead one of the formal ones, hemmed in gold. The ring on his finger still felt heavy, but it did not burden him. Looking at it, he remembered Ashway. What would the Hand have made of the man who now held the East Quarter?

The Handquarters were springing to life as he left his study. Servants moved in the far corridors, and, as the sun rose higher, Gauntlet officers and ensigns made their appearance, collecting and bringing paperwork. Some of the junior Hands were also there and they bowed as Eamon passed. He greeted them cheerfully and felt their astonished stares on his back.

Anderas waited for him in the entry hall, where the timbers had been fashioned to resemble arching branches. Eamon gazed up as he walked beneath them.

"Lord Ashway told me that this building was once the home of a noble Easter family," Anderas said quietly, tracing the beams with his eyes. Eamon nodded; they looked too delicate for Dunthruik's architectural style. The whole of the Handquarters did, in fact. It was easy to imagine Ithel – or Anastasius – walking the halls.

"He said that was why they called this the East Quarter, even though it isn't quite *geographically* east. After the Master took the city," Anderas added, "the other quarters had their names based on the compass because of that; their original names were very different."

Eamon looked at Anderas. "Is your tour of the quarter going to be full of such ruminations?"

"I am no real authority on the matter, my lord," Anderas answered, "but I fear that I cannot always help myself."

"You are too modest, Captain Anderas," Eamon laughed. "Besides which," he added, "there is no shame in knowing where we came from or what the world was like before us. So much of what we are, and where we go, depends on that."

"So, for the benefit of those for whom we will constitute 'history', we must do rightly in our own days?" A look of mock concern passed over Anderas's face. "Does breakfast usually make you so philosophical, my lord?"

"Occasionally," Eamon confessed.

"Then I'm afraid that tomorrow's breakfast will be a meagre affair, if it is permitted at all."

Eamon laughed and invited Anderas to lead the way.

The East Quarter College had a wide gateway, similar in many ways to that of Waite's college. There was a long line of men outside the college wall, who either sat or stood, and who bore nervous looks. They were mostly young men, and as Eamon and Anderas passed they bowed hastily.

"Who are they?" Eamon asked.

"We're still short on quarter numbers. This afternoon there is a Gauntlet admittance. They will have come for that."

"But it is barely the second hour!"

"They are keen," Anderas replied, "and hope that standing there all day will show it."

"It does."

Two Gauntlet ensigns, their red jackets bright in the morning light, guarded the doorway into the college. Faint trees had been worked into the stonework at the door, their limbs reaching delicately up to a crown marked into the keystone. Eamon climbed the college steps and watched as the ensigns snapped to sharp attention. They raised their hands to their faces in a formal sword salute. Eamon greeted them cordially and passed through into the hall.

Anderas showed him the way through the wide passageways and out into the college parade yard. As he stepped out into that space, nostalgia overcame him. How many times – in Edesfield, and even in the West Quarter – had he marched into a college square for parade? As he looked, he yearned after the camaraderie of new cadets, the lessons in River Realm law and geography, and the weapons and formation practices. In that moment even the course held a peculiar, rose-tinted charm for him.

At the front of the parade square was a small wooden platform, with a few steps leading up to it. It was these steps that Anderas climbed, and Eamon followed him, his pace forgetting that he was a lord of Dunthruik – for a moment, he was just a simple Glove.

The speaking platform had a small podium on which Anderas laid the list of names. The square still empty, Eamon leaned against the stand and studied them. At the top of the list were the draybants and then the officers, some of whom he knew: Greenwood, Smith, Taine…

"Do you wish to speak to them, Lord Goodman?"

Eamon looked up. In his heart his thoughts had gone that far. Indeed, he knew that he needed to speak to the men to redress whatever damage he had done. But what could he say? The men who would fill the square were not kitchen servants or stablehands; they were Gauntlet, men of prowess and pride.

"Yes," he forced himself to answer before he could reconsider the matter. "I will speak to them."

Anderas nodded. A moment later the sound of men approached. The East Quarter College was coming to parade.

Eamon half expected to see Manners or Ford among the men who marched neatly into the parade ground, but soon enough remembered he was no longer in his old quarter. The men were resplendent in uniform, the officers and ensigns smartly polished.

Among them, Eamon caught sight of the lieutenant who had been drunk the previous evening – he seemed not much recovered. What was his name?

Eamon quietly turned to the list, scouring it for a name that seemed vaguely familiar. It only then occurred to him that most of the names would seem vaguely familiar. A quiet curse passed his lips. Either Anderas didn't hear it, or he chose to ignore it.

Eamon looked back up to survey the entering men. As the lines formed into ranks they saw him, and he saw their faces turning pale. Eamon watched them with interest but did not signal anything to them. His heart beat faster. What did he possibly think he could say to them?

The last men fell into their ranks, and all gave the formal salute. A breeze stirred the silent square.

Anderas turned to Eamon. "Would you inspect the lines, my lord?"

"Thank you, captain," Eamon answered, grateful that it was necessary – and would give him a much-needed chance to think.

He stepped down and made his way to the lines. He had seen Waite do it a hundred times and had sometimes dreamed he would do it himself. Now he did, but he was robed in black and the men did not know him – they knew only a broken shadow of who and what he was. Eamon understood that his task was immense; he saw it from the strange mix of fear and contempt in the eyes that watched him.

The lines were, as Eamon had expected, impeccable. Ashway and Anderas had crafted tight ranks.

After completing his circuit of the lines he returned to the head of the square. The men's eyes were on him, and he looked back at them. There was silence. Eamon knew that he had to speak. He had to do it before the silence grew too loud.

"East Quarter, I congratulate you. Rarely have I seen a smarter college," he said. "It speaks highly of you indeed. I have had but little opportunity to see you at your work, but I look forward to doing so."

He saw some of the cadets exchange glances. He had already spoken far more than they were accustomed to hearing. Eamon wondered whether he should continue. Had he not said enough? He had complimented them as befitted a Hand...

He was more than a Hand.

A seemingly interminable silence loomed over the courtyard. Eamon pressed himself to speak once more.

"I have been honoured in being named the lord of this quarter." As he spoke he felt the persona of Quarter Hand drop from him, leaving only himself behind. The men heard it in his changing voice, and watched him with bewilderment and anxiety as he continued. "It is an honour which, in the last week, I have been scarcely worthy of bearing. I dare say that you have all known such times. You will know also that a man's strength returns to him, as mine has to me."

He looked at them for a long moment, trying to gauge their reaction. Their faces were clouded. What had they spoken of him after Pinewood? What had they spoken of him in the past week?

Eamon could neither alter nor control what had been said about him – he feared even to imagine it. But he could show these men the shape of the hope that had been in him when he woke that morning.

What would he have them say of him that day?

"I have a vision for this quarter," he called. As he spoke, his whole heart came forth in his words. "I have a vision of the glory of Dunthruik, epitomized by the men and women who live and serve in these streets. They will be streets that do not fear the Serpent, streets running with devotion. In the way that we uphold the law; in the way that we speak; in the way that we trade and eat; in the way we lay ourselves down at night and rise in the morning; in all this we will bring honour and glory to the Master, and this city will speak of us with praise. This is my vision for this quarter." He said, more quietly: "I see it clearly now that my strength returns to me.

"Some men say that they have heard of me. I would rather have all men say that they have heard of *you*, and how you serve the Master."

He fell silent. He heard his heart beating rapidly in his breast. Now that he had spoken, he could barely remember the words that had left his lips. All he saw were the watching faces, unsure how to take the man before them.

He tried to steel himself against the discouragement welling in his thoughts.

Anderas stepped up and looked out across the gathered men. "Lord Goodman calls you on to service and glory."

Eamon's stomach churned as he looked at the myriad faces. They could either accept or reject him. How they spoke to him now would mark whether or not he could save himself and the quarter. He resisted the urge to close his eyes.

"How will you answer?" the captain called.

The college's swords, lowered during Eamon's inspection of the ranks, rose high.

"To his glory!"

The words came back as one voice. Eamon felt them wash over him and looked at the sea of faces. Some looked sceptical, others afraid. But some, not too few of them, looked at him with renewed eyes. It gave him cause to hope.

"Lord Goodman," Anderas said, "the East Quarter is for you. It will follow you."

Eamon looked at the captain and the assembled men. "No, captain," he answered. As he looked back to the long ranks of men he glimpsed a puzzled look on Anderas's face. "No," Eamon said again, loud enough for all to hear. "I am for the East Quarter. I will serve it."

The silence that followed was deafening.

Anderas turned to the men. "To your duties, gentlemen."

Eamon watched as the men filed out of the grounds, each to their different tasks. He wondered what they would do. He remembered walking in such lines, remembered Mathaiah walking by him, his smile. It pricked his heart, but he drew breath and steadied himself.

"Will they trust me?"

He had not intended to speak aloud and was surprised when Anderas answered him.

"If a manner such as yours could be bought, Lord Goodman, it would be the most highly sought commodity in all the River Realm," Anderas laughed, "and those who possessed it would go out of their way to boast of it at their feasts and banquets!"

"Are you going to speak of my particularity to me once again, captain?"

"You'll note that I carefully refrained from doing so." Anderas paused, then spoke more seriously. "They are good men, fiercely loyal. I have every confidence that they will see they can fiercely serve you. It will take some time to win them all, Lord Goodman, but I know them. I can already tell you that they have seen what I saw when I first met you."

Eamon hesitated. "Dare I ask?"

Anderas looked at him, and Eamon saw the captain searching for the right words. At length he shrugged, content to speak what came to mind.

"You are not like other men," he said simply. "There is something deeper to you than can be found in many – something truer. What the root of that might be, I do not know, but it is there."

Eamon looked at him. His whole being sang the King's name, but he held back; now was not the time to speak it out.

Anderas shook his head as his words failed him. "You are in Dunthruik, Lord Goodman, but you are not of it. And yet you love it."

Eamon gaped. The words humbled him and he could not answer.

The captain stepped down from the platform and gestured towards the college gates with a smile. "We will walk the quarter, my lord."

It was about the third hour when they stepped into the Ashen. The sunlight, strengthening both with the hour and the season, bathed the stones in gold. The line of men waiting outside the college had grown with the dawn.

The Ashen lay off Coronet Rise and was set back towards the heart of the quarter. Towards the North Gate were the Crown Offices, which dealt with a large amount of the city's paperwork and publicized any edicts made by the Lord of the East Quarter or the throned. Eamon remembered going to those offices when he had arrested Lorentide – the wayfarer who had been smuggling others out of the city with forged papers. Eamon had condemned both the man and his son to flames. He shuddered with the remembrance. He wondered whether any of the Lorentides' neighbours were still there. Would they recognize him? Had Lorentide's wife found safety, or had she also been captured in the months following her husband's death? It shamed him that he did not know.

Deeper in towards the city wall were large storehouses, intended to hold grain for the winter. They were under the charge of the quarter's logistics draybant and were mostly empty after a hard winter and a poor preceding harvest. There were small stalls near these well-guarded houses, selling some of the grain that was kept there. Eamon heard the sellers call out their prices – they were high.

The East Quarter had its fair share of inns and dozens of bakers and fishmongers. Now that the sea was becoming passable again, men from the city dared to seine the fickle waters to bring in as much as they could. Some fruits and vegetables were also available, drawn in from the mire of fields and farmland just outside the walls; some houses in the city had small plots of land where they also grew food, and those, at least, were faring well with the recent rains.

Many of the buildings in the East Quarter were in need of repair, the stonework bare, often falling away from rotting timbers. The roads leading into the deeper parts of the quarter were in desperate need of attention.

Wherever they walked, Eamon was aware of men and women watching him. It was not the open watching of people who marvelled at the man who had brought back an Easter's head; it was quiet, fearful, discreet – out of the corner of an eye or from a turned head.

They went on a little farther until a ragged building on Eamon's left caught his attention. A faded sign hung over its door. The place was an inn – or at least had been. Its windows were twisted and broken and the door was half-collapsed upon itself, while shattered chairs and broken, empty bottles lay outside it in the dust.

Eamon looked at the sign. The inn's name was no longer legible and there was no man to be seen. "What happened here?"

"The cull," Anderas answered. "Wayfarers were working for the keeper. They did not take kindly to arrest."

"And the keeper?"

The captain's eyes took in the reduced shell of the inn. "He will have to join the list awaiting building works."

"How long is the list?"

Anderas shook his head. "I am afraid that I couldn't rightly tell you, my lord. That would be a question for the Crown Office."

Eamon looked back at the building. As he watched it he felt other, hidden, eyes stare back at him.

"Then let us go to the Crown Office."

They returned through the quarter's streets to the small square that held the Crown Office – a broad building filled with diligently working men. They were received warmly and it wasn't long at all before Eamon met with the Crown official. It was as they went into the man's office that Eamon recognized him as the man who had spoken on the day of Lorentide's arrest. As they sat, they were brought drinks by a serving girl. Eamon wondered whether the official remembered him.

"May I say again what a pleasure it is to have you here, my lord," the man said. "How may we serve you?"

"I am, as you may imagine," Eamon told him, "still orienting myself in the quarter. I have come to see what work you do here, and how we may make best use of this office for the Master's glory."

The official – one Mr Rose – smiled ingratiatingly. "This office is a vital part in the mechanism of the quarter, my lord. We are responsible for a very wide spectrum of things," he continued, flicking through some of the papers on his desk, "such as exit and entry papers, a portion of which also go to yourself."

"Yes," Eamon nodded.

"We also keep records of quarter property; we are responsible for collecting taxes and for arbitrating in more petty matters of law – say, disputes between neighbours."

"And the office sees to the architectural upkeep of the quarter?"

"Indeed we do," Rose nodded. "We have a number of architects here in the office, and we deal directly with the guilds of workmen – masons, thatchers, carpenters, and the like – who work on the quarter's buildings."

"And how do you decide where and when to work?"

The official smiled. "There is a list, my lord."

"On average, how long would you say it takes this office to process the buildings on the list?"

The official pulled a pensive face. "Certainly no longer than any other quarter, my lord."

"For example," Eamon told him, "I passed a dilapidated inn this morning. I understand that it was only recently that it was reduced to its current state. How long will it be before the inn receives repairs?"

"That would depend. First, the work has to be requested," Rose answered.

"Who requests the work?"

"Usually a nominated representative from the place's inhabitants, or the proprietors." As Rose spoke, the serving girl passed through the office to offer them more wine to drink. With a slight shake of his head, Eamon declined. "Office architects then go to the site and make an initial assessment of the repairs required. A charge is levied for this, and an estimate given of the time and cost needed to effect the repairs. The proprietors pay both the assessment charge and a proportion of the estimated repair cost. Once these have been paid, the building is added to the list. Repairs are then carried out in proper course."

"And for those who cannot afford or fall short on payments?"

"This office is always willing to come to mutually beneficial agreements with such individuals," Rose answered. As he spoke his gaze flicked to the serving girl. His face swelled lecherously.

Eamon followed the man's gaze and reddened with the anger of sudden realization.

"It is a very efficient system, my lord."

"So I see."

They stayed a little longer in the office and Eamon was introduced to some of the staff and principal architects. The desks in that office were mostly covered with drawings of an expansive house belonging to one of the knights – Rose explained that a lot of restoration work was currently being carried out for the family in question. The Crown Office official saw them back to the square and bowed low as they left.

As they walked back along Coronet Rise towards the Ashen, Eamon felt heavy of heart.

"How many slaves are there in this quarter, captain?" he asked. He saw the logic of the system being run by the Crown Office, and hated it. He wondered if any of the servants in his own house had fallen foul of it.

The captain had remained silent while they were in the offices. His answer was restrained. "I do not know, my lord. Dunthruik has no law against forced labour."

Eamon nodded. He knew it – he had always known it – and yet now the idea disgusted him. He did not know if he could – or whether he dared – strike against it.

"What of the servants in the Handquarters?" he asked, already knowing the answer.

"They have their food and lodging, Lord Goodman," Anderas replied. "Nothing more."

"Slaves in all but name."

"Yes, Lord Goodman. But they are fed and housed, at least."

They continued walking and Eamon's thoughts wandered.

Dunthruik was full of slaves, prostitutes, beggars, prisoners, and families so poor and weak that they could barely raise the stolen food in their hands to their mouths. All the while, the Gauntlet and city militia ate and drank freely, and had sturdy roofs over their heads. He understood why there had been so many men waiting by the college that morning.

CHAPTER XV

They returned to the Ashen at about midday. Anderas had to prepare for his afternoon dealing with the Gauntlet admittance, and took his leave. Eamon stood for a while in the Ashen, watching the normal life of the quarter pass by him. He reflected on what he had seen that morning – broken buildings, moulding grains, starving mouths, staring faces. He had seen such things before but never had they beaten against his heart with their present force.

Dunthruik had once been a great city. The palace was great still, as was the noble West Quarter where theatre and palace stood and high-born dwelt. But in the deepest, darkest parts of the East Quarter, Dunthruik showed the dry veins of a destitute, crippled city, a city lacking hope and crushed by fear.

The East Quarter did not need a Hand; it needed a king.

Eamon drew breath and shivered. The King had not yet come.

The corruptive burdens and machinations of the city weighed on him. They were systems by which the Master was served and glorified – systems enshrined in his law and upheld by his Gauntlet. Eamon hated what he had seen – how it grieved him to see a place that he loved so trammelled by despair! As he gazed at the Ashen he was sickened by the thought that a Quarter Hand could never dare to strive against those parts of the city that grieved him – to do as much would be to strive against the throned.

He swallowed, feeling his hope of that morning becoming faint. If he was bound, if he could not do right in the city, if he could not challenge the wrong that he saw…

He remembered the Hidden Hall. He remembered Hughan's face and heard in his heart the King's words: "*Draw your sword to defend the helpless, lift your hands to raise up the needy, use your heart to love the people of the River and call your mind to challenge evil where you find it…*"

He breathed deep. He was the First Knight. Had it not always been a question of how much he dared to do?

He walked again into the college, the line of young men along its wall still anxiously waiting to be seen by the captain. None could join the Gauntlet unless they passed Anderas's inspection. As Eamon passed, the young men stared in awe.

Did they know that he had once stood in just such a line?

He remembered it well. After his father's death he had continued bookbinding for a number of years. Edesfield was not the best place to ply that trade, but Eamon managed to keep the business going.

He might have continued bookbinding all his days had it not been for the fire.

He had lost both home and trade that night. He remembered his despair when he saw the flames, and how Aeryn and Telo took him in and comforted him before he took lodgings with the smith. While he pumped the bellows and stoked the fires, he wondered whether he should try the Gauntlet, and watched the admittance lines outside the college. But he never had the courage to join them.

It was Ladomer who at last convinced him to try. In the evenings after his work for the smith, Eamon often went to Telo's inn and sat with his friends. One cold evening the inn was busy, and Aeryn was helping Telo, so Ladomer kept Eamon company, and they spoke of joining the Gauntlet. Eamon wanted to serve the people of Edesfield, the people who had looked after him ever since he and his father had arrived. He wanted to wear that red uniform, to be loved and respected – yet he feared to take the first step.

"Eamon," Ladomer admonished, "what have you to fear? The Gauntlet needs men just like you. There is surely no finer man in all of Edesfield!"

"But I'm not like you, Ladomer," Eamon answered. His friend already wore the red coat of a Gauntlet ensign, and was drawing great praise from the men he worked with. "I'm not strong, or skilled. I can't even ride a horse!"

"They *teach* you to do that, Eamon. That's why it's called a college."

"I don't think I would even pass the first inspection –"

"You won't unless you try." Ladomer pressed his arm in encouragement. "Come on, Eamon! You've always wanted this! I know you could do it. Why don't you prove me right?"

He joined the line the next day. Eamon stood in the grey cold of the chill, bitter, wintry Edesfield morning until Captain Belaal had seen him. The captain smiled and welcomed him. The following day Ladomer had welcomed him with jubilant and open arms into the college at Edesfield…

Eamon walked swiftly up the college steps and across the entry hall. He went through the shadowed corridors towards the officers' mess. He knew that most of them would be there at this hour, but even as he walked, he did not clearly know what he meant to do.

The hall bustled. Servants worked around the tables, bringing food to the officers and lieutenants. Eamon might have expected to hear laughter, but the atmosphere in the room was serious and reflective. Pausing just outside the door, he heard voices speaking at the nearest table.

"I didn't understand it," one said.

"I don't think anyone did."

"It was so at odds with what he was like at the dinner –"

"That's certain," agreed a third.

"Maybe Anderas drugged him with something," snorted a fourth, and Eamon recognized the voice: Mers, the man from the dinner who looked somewhat inebriated at the morning parade. Lieutenant Mers.

"That will do, lieutenant."

"You don't agree, sir?" Mers asked. Eamon guessed that he spoke to First Lieutenant Greenwood.

"With you speaking of the captain in such a way? No, I don't."

"Lord Ashway was bad enough," interrupted the first voice, adamant in its confusion, "but this Lord Goodman? I don't understand him."

"Has it occurred to any of you that he might just have been telling the truth this morning?" It was Greenwood who spoke now.

"Are you serious, sir?"

"Or is that what Anderas *told* you to say?"

"You feel me incapable of making up my own mind, Mr Mers?"

"No, sir," Mers retorted. "I think you want to make college draybant, and you'll do whatever sits well with the captain to do it."

"You would do well to mind your tongue, Mers," Greenwood told him.

"He's still drunk, sir," said the second voice. "From the dinner last night."

"It was the only good thing about the dinner. *Two crowns*, sir!" The first voice spun pitiably back into its tirade, and Eamon's heart fell deathly still. Had every man in the city realized his folly but him?

"But Lord Goodman was so different this morning."

"You're speaking in circles, both of you," the first lieutenant told them. "If this morning is any measure, we shall soon see what kind of a man Lord Goodman truly is."

"He's a contradiction!" Mers snorted.

"It would be interesting to ask him," the first voice observed.

"What?" The third voice laughed. "You? Scott! Talk about setting the snake among ravens! Are you insane? What exactly would you ask?"

"I don't know," Lieutenant Scott mused. Eamon imagined him tracing patterns on the table with an idle finger.

"Maybe he'd say you could ask three questions," the third voice said. "A friend of mine in the West Quarter told me that he likes literature."

"A true raven protégé, then," murmured Mers.

"Can't be," the second voice interrupted. "He doesn't have any dogs."

"Apart from the capt –"

"You will be held responsible for everything that you say, Mr Mers." Greenwood's voice cut firmly across the conversation, silencing it. "The more so," he added, "because you are drunk. Is that clear?"

There was no audible answer.

Eamon's heart pounded. He had wondered what men said about him; now he had heard it for himself. He was the lunatic who had served two crowns, the protégé of Lord Cathair who treated his captain like a dog... If that was what the officers in his own quarter said about him...

What would *the Master* say?

After a pause, the second voice piped up again. "So, Scott, suppose that things turn out as Taine suggested, and you have three questions for Lord Gooseman –"

"His name is Lord Goodman, lieutenant."

"*Goodman*," the voice corrected, recovering from a hiccup. "Sorry, sir. Your three questions?"

There was a pensive pause. Scott eventually drew breath. "I don't think I would want to ask him three. One would do."

"Really?" Taine sounded disappointed.

"Really. Lord Ashway was a formidable man, and it will need a formidable man to replace him. I think I'd ask Lord Goodman what kind of a man he is – and whether he meant what he said, about serving the quarter."

"That's two questions, ass!"

"But the answer to one answers the other," Scott told him. "I think he'd give a good one."

Mers scoffed quietly. "Already so endeared to him, Mr Scott?"

"Out of duty, yes," Scott answered. "That's what duty means. I followed Lord Ashway – we all did – and I will follow Lord

Goodman. My uniform demands that." The lieutenant paused. Eamon craned his neck, keen to hear every word.

"If," the lieutenant continued at last, "by your question you mean 'Does Lord Goodman have your unswerving loyalty and would you stand by him if the Serpent came?'…" Scott fell silent again. "If he gave a good answer – and proved it by what he did – then I think I might."

There was a long silence. In it, all Eamon heard was eating in the mess, and beating in his heart. There was still hope.

Courage, First Knight.

Taking a deep breath, Eamon stepped into the mess. The table seating the five officers was by the door. A man poured wine into their goblets, and, as he stepped out, Eamon saw the faces of half of the officers at the table. They didn't seem to see him immediately, but suddenly two of the speakers – one of them Mers – caught sight of him. They fell silent just as Taine, his back to the door, spoke again.

"So, Scott, when do you think you'll ask Lord Goodman your question?"

"He could ask it now if he wanted to," Eamon said quietly.

The whole table turned. The echo of scraping chairs filled the mess as every man there rose hastily and bowed low. One lieutenant was a short man with light brown hair who was much paler than his fellows. Eamon assumed him to be Lieutenant Scott.

"Lord Goodman," Greenwood said, "you honour us with your presence."

"And you this quarter with your loyalty, Mr Greenwood," Eamon answered, enjoying Greenwood's surprise at being correctly named.

Eamon looked to the other lieutenants at the table. Mers turned a particularly unhealthy shade of green – whether drawn on by fear or the excessive alcohol from the night before was difficult to tell – and the others merely watched him with fear.

"Mr Taine," Eamon added, "though you are well informed regarding my fondness for literature, I am afraid that I am far too ill-schooled to limit myself to three questions – even less to remember to answer them last first, as tradition dictates." He smiled. "I fear I would tell Mr Scott that he could ask as many questions as he liked, but that I would not be beholden to answer them all. In that, perhaps my approach would have had some advantages over the more classical model which you suggest."

Taine's face wrinkled, as though he was not sure whether to shy away and bow or burst into a grin.

"Yes, Lord Goodman."

Eamon turned to the palest of the lieutenants. "Mr Scott?"

"M-m-my lord."

"My offer stands. I will answer you your question if my own duties permit it." He smiled gently, and as the lieutenant drew himself up to meet that smile, Eamon thought he saw a little courage coming into his face.

"Lord Goodman," he said, his words spoken with a measure belied by his figure. "The Master chose you for this quarter, and so you must be a man of no little accomplishment. Captain Anderas trusts you – and the captain is a man with good eyes. Many of the ensigns who served with you at Pinewood speak well of you. This being the case, perhaps you would take my question amiss, but I hope you will forgive it."

Eamon admired the lieutenant's composure.

"Lord Goodman, may I ask what kind of a Hand you will be over this quarter?"

The man's voice shook as he reached the end of his question.

Eamon watched him for a moment. "You are a credit to yourself and to your captain, Lieutenant Scott."

"Thank you, Lord Goodman."

"I am the kind of Hand who believes that serving this quarter in a time of uncertainty is a great honour. I am the kind of Hand who holds service – the service of a willing heart – above all other things. I am the kind of Hand who would do all things well, so as to bring glory to whom I serve."

Scott gazed at him. "Thank you, Lord Goodman."

Eamon looked at the lieutenants with their varying expressions. More than one of them watched him now with an odd respect.

"Gentlemen," he said, "I'm afraid that I am keeping you from your meal." He gestured to the table and their cooling plates. "I bid you a good afternoon."

"Thank you, Lord Goodman," the first lieutenant replied.

Eamon returned to his study in the Handquarters, pensive. The light had shifted round so that it slanted through the tall window. He rested his hand against his chair.

His memory returned to the talk he had overheard between the officers, and as the light continued changing, his thoughts turned at last to one that he had sought to avoid.

Since he had been made Lord of the East he had maltreated more than house, college, and quarter. In miscarrying his duty, in allowing himself to be spoken of amiss, he had also tarnished the name of the one who had made him a Quarter Hand.

He had done what perhaps no man might do and live. He had brought dishonour to the throned.

You must go and speak with him, Eamon.

Eamon shivered. He knew that it was true. He had to go to the Master and plead his case such that he would be cleared – house, college, and quarter depended on it. He could do nothing, even if he acted for the King, without the throned's benevolence.

How he could go to the throned and beg clemency – and live to tell of it – he did not know.

The pile of papers on his desk had grown during the day. For a moment there was the temptation to leave them for Anderas – the captain would see to them. But he saw grief's claws before they sank into him, and veered out of its clutches.

He sat down at the desk and the papers. The ream was thick.

He took the first sheet and read it – a notice of the arrests made by the Gauntlet the previous day. Beneath it was a collection of exit papers from various people requesting permission to leave the quarter, either for another quarter or to leave the city entirely. As Eamon studied them, the enormity of responsibility touched him. He had the power that made these people stay or go.

He perused the papers into the early evening. Some – simpler ones, requesting building materials or a change in Gauntlet guard patterns – he signed. He had done similar work for Cathair, and knew what to do. But when it came to arrest warrants, exit papers, food distribution, and draybants' reports, he still did not quite know where to begin. He realized also that, until he had spoken to the throned and shown that he was in his right mind, he should not sign, seal, or mark them.

As the sun began to set, there was a knock at his door. He called to grant admittance. Anderas stepped in.

"You look tired, captain," Eamon noted, looking up from where he worked. Anderas glanced at him in surprise.

"My lord, you're –"

"Demonstrating that I am not as poor a student as you feared, I hope," Eamon answered with a smile, indicating the papers he had dealt with. "There are some that I still need to consider."

"Can I assist you in any way?"

"More than you have done?" Eamon laughed gently, and shook his head. "Thank you, captain, but all is well. Some of these cannot be seen to until tomorrow." He looked up. "How many new recruits did you get today?"

"Twenty-seven," Anderas answered quietly.

"Something the matter, captain? That seems a fair number."

"There are strict selection criteria for entry to the Gauntlet, as I am sure you remember, my lord." Anderas counted them off on his fingers. "No actual or putative involvement with the wayfarers, aged between sixteen and twenty-five at the time of admittance, good physical health, demonstrated devotion to the Master, strong personality, and potential to progress through the ranks." He paused. "For so many, joining the Gauntlet is no longer about service; it's about escape. The men are fed and watered every day, and there are wages, however scant, to send home. I imagine such considerations were not far from your mind when you joined. They were not always far from mine." He looked up with a sigh. "Twenty-seven is a good number of new recruits, Lord Goodman, a good number indeed. But it is only a fraction of those who came today. I could not take them all."

Eamon nodded. The captains – with the aid of their college draybants and lieutenants – were personally responsible for the selection of their men. It would have been a long and arduous task, especially as the East still did not have a college draybant.

Anderas sighed again. "Almost, but not quite, as many men as I accepted will be found dead in the streets of the East Quarter tomorrow. They will be men that I saw and turned away today." His voice caught. "Sometimes, Lord Goodman, you can tell when you meet them: you know that their names will be on a different list in the morning. The Gauntlet is their last hope – but it is no hope at all for them. They have already despaired."

They sat in silence. At length Anderas stirred and picked up some of the papers. Eamon reached out and stopped him.

"All is well, captain," he said to Anderas's surprise. "You can rest tonight. You have done enough."

"Yes, Lord Goodman." Anderas rose wearily and rubbed one hand across his eyes. The man was exhausted. "Will you be well this evening?"

A chill moved through Eamon, the quiet reminder of the grief and anger that would settle with falling darkness, when he was left alone.

"Yes, captain."

"Lord Goodman… will you retire to your quarters tonight?"

Eamon matched the captain's gaze and saw his concern. How long had it been since he had lain himself down in a bed to sleep? He stretched his shoulders self-consciously.

"Yes, captain," he said. "I think I shall."

Anderas nodded. "Send for me if you need anything, my lord."

Eamon smiled. "Despite your prior assertions as to the nature of a Gauntlet captaincy," he said, "it may surprise you to learn, Mr

Anderas, that you are not my butler. If I have need of a captain, I will send for you. If I have need of a butler, I will send for my major-domo…" he paused, trying to remember the name.

"Mr Slater," Anderas told him.

"Mr Slater," Eamon repeated.

"Of course, my lord." Anderas bowed, and turned to go, then he paused. "I met some of the lieutenants this evening, to discuss the allocation of the new recruits. I heard something about a question in the officers' mess?"

A smile flickered on Eamon's face. "I may have answered one," he said with a quiet laugh. "You have some very fine officers with you, captain. I am glad of it."

"So am I, my lord."

"There is one thing more you can tell me before you go," Eamon added. "I must see the Master tomorrow."

Confusion ran over Anderas's face. "Lord Goodman?"

"I must see him," Eamon repeated. "How did Lord Ashway arrange such meetings?"

"You are a lord of Dunthruik. You need simply go."

Eamon turned cold. "Then I will do so. Thank you, captain."

"Good night, Lord Goodman."

Eamon continued working for an hour or so at the pile of papers. One of the servants brought him supper in the latter part of the evening and he ate it slowly while he worked.

When he finished, darkness had fallen deeply outside, and the trees were dappled with starlight. Sitting back, he realized how tired he was. His whole back ached. Stretching his arms out high over his head, he winced as his old scars pulled and stung.

Quietly he rose and took up the lamp at his desk. He picked up his papers and made his way from the room.

There was a staircase in the corridor that led up to his quarters. He had gone there with Anderas on his first day, but he had not once set foot in the rooms beyond that. He was therefore surprised to hear footsteps at the head of the staircase as he ascended. A touch of light in the corridor soon explained this. Eamon stepped lightly into the hallway, shading his lamp.

He saw through the doorway into his chambers and bedroom. A small figure was hunched by the mantelpiece, setting a fire. The flames touched his face, picking out tiny beads of sweat. Eamon smiled; it was Callum. Behind the boy was the girl who had served breakfast that morning. She was straightening the sheets and covers on the great green bed.

How many times had they performed this work for him in vain over the last week? Surely they had seen that the bed had never been used? How they must resent him for it!

He stepped quietly through the outer room and on into the bedchamber. The girl looked up, saw him, and curtseyed – she did not flee.

"Lord Goodman," she said. The little boy rose to his feet, bowed, and went quickly to the girl's side.

Looking at the fire and the bed, Eamon smiled. Unexpected tears touched his eyes. "What's your name, Miss?" he asked.

"Cara, my lord."

"Well then, good evening, Callum and Cara," Eamon said.

The boy's head jerked up with a smile.

"You remembered my name!" Callum said. "Nobody ever remembers my name!"

"Callum!" the girl's voice was low with warning. Eamon looked at the boy with a smile.

"Your sister takes good care of you, doesn't she?"

Cara glanced at him, as if wondering how he had deduced their relationship. The boy nodded.

"Yes, Lord Goodman."

"I imagine that sometimes you think she is too careful, or fussy, or grown up," Eamon added, and the boy smiled again. "But I want you to remember something. When you are outside this house, or serving someone other than me, take all of her caution to heart. She is wise."

The boy pulled a curious face, but then nodded. "Yes, Lord Goodman."

A look that was part fear and part relief passed over the girl's face. She seemed no more than sixteen years old.

"That will be all," Eamon said.

"Thank you, Lord Goodman." Cara curtseyed, took her brother's hand, reminded him quietly to bow, and then led him from the room. The door closed behind them.

He was alone.

Eamon breathed slowly and deeply. The fears of the day began milling in his breast. What kind of Hand was he?

The fire cracked in the corner, casting strange shadows over the room. He drifted to the threshold of his wonted grief.

He shuddered. How easy it would be to give reign to his returning grief and horror, to permit them possession of the manor of his mind – to cast it down utterly. For Mathaiah was dead, and Alessia…

Eamon touched at his stinging eyes. Mathaiah was dead. Lillabeth was widowed. Her child was without a father, and its gift at birth would be grief.

You are to blame. The voice appeared at last, a familiar and bitter friend. *Remember his face, eyeless and bloody! That was your doing. His wife will hate you. His child will loathe you. There will never be peace between the house of Grahaven and you, Eben's son.*

"But we had peace." Eamon was filled with the song from the Pit, remembering it with startling clarity. He remembered Mathaiah and how they had spoken to each other and embraced.

They had been at peace. They had both known that their lives could be lost. Not lost – given. Mathaiah had given his life for his "awesome King alone", fearing nothing. Eamon was suddenly sure of it, and it brought him courage. Mathaiah was dead and there was sorrow in Eamon's heart, but he would no longer be in thrall to grief and rage.

"We had peace, voice of Edelred!" he spoke it out, more defiantly this time. "Peace! He has peace. The King's grace went before him. And while the King's grace holds, so will his name."

So you believe, Eben's son!

Shaking, Eamon sat heavily on the bed. It was soft. Alessia's face assailed him, twisted in treacherous glee. The wrenching stab of her betrayal tore him.

What of her, Eben's son? She warms another's bed while your ward burns. She said that she loved you, and you believed her! Remember her touch, son of Eben, and how you adored it!

Eamon cried out angrily as he forced the images from his mind. Each time he tried, the voice of Edelred pushed them back to him.

She betrayed you. She betrayed your ward. You may have peace with him, but you can never have peace with her. You may posture as you wish, and cover your wretched heart with lofty pretensions, but you are mine – and you will not have peace in this quarter, Eben's son.

Eamon's mind was awhirl, teeming with all the voices of the day – those that had disparaged him and loathed him – and every gaze that had gaped at him, the fool who had served *two* crowns.

You are my Hand, son of Eben.

Courage, Eamon. Peace.

Eamon mustered all his will to latch on to the quiet voice. With its encouragement, he pushed back the images of Alessia and the memory of Mathaiah's broken face.

"There is no place for you here, voice of Edelred," he breathed at last. "I am under the King's grace. Take your lies and leave."

Silence came, filling the room and Eamon's mind with calm. He sat still, drinking it in like a tonic. The fire crackled softly.

He took off his heavy cloak and ring, setting them on the table and chair by his bed. With them he set his sword belt and his black jacket. Slowly he laid himself back on the bed, allowing its covers to enfold him. There were leaves traced into the wooden posts, and, as he lay looking at them, the fire sounded like a wind-swayed wood.

He was the Lord of the East Quarter. He bore the mark of the throned but was given strength by the King's grace. By that grace Mathaiah had faced death, and, by it, Eamon meant to remember his promises to the King, and serve Dunthruik.

CHAPTER XVI

The eighteenth of March dawned warm, and the Coll was flushed with men and women going about their business. The winter waned and the first ships struck west across the sea from Dunthruik's port to Etraia and Anouria – two merchant states closely allied to the throned.

Many of those who walked the Coll that morning bore bags, baskets, or children. The cries of hopeful merchants echoed in the air, alongside the sounds of trotting horses and marching men, as Gauntlet patrols went about the city. The Four Quarters shone in the sunlight, glistening where the night's rain had touched its stones.

Eamon had never been terribly proficient at walking on wet cobbles, and much of the Coll was paved with slabs of stone made particularly slippery after rain. He carefully minded his footing as he worked his way up the bustling road. It was about the second hour. Though it would not appear so to any who looked at him, beneath his cloak and robes Eamon wore all of his courage. Streaks of sunlight passed over him as he wove his way across the Four Quarters. Green blades peeped up between the stones, daring the cold cobbles with as much courage as he did. Spring had arrived. The King would follow.

He walked with confidence and greeted all who passed him, regardless of whether or not they met his gaze. Many might have looked at him with contempt were it not for his black robes and the golden ring upon his hand.

"Lord Goodman!"

Eamon looked up and saw a group of young men come down

the Coll, no doubt returning to the West Quarter College from duty at the palace.

The cadets were his old group, the Third Banners. What must they think of him, now that ill was spoken of him? He was reluctant to meet their gazes.

"Good morning, gentlemen."

To his surprise, the Third Banners replied with an almost exultant "Good morning", in chorus.

"Congratulations on your quarter, Lord Goodman!" Manners called.

"Thank you, Mr Manners." The cadet's words bolstered Eamon's resolve to press his steps on to where they had to go. "Gentlemen, it is a pleasure to see you. Please give my warmest regards to Captain Waite."

The cadets affirmed his request with a round of smart bows, and they parted.

As he passed up the road, calls echoed from the port: vessels were docking, for the merchants had begun their perilous routes even earlier than usual. Soon Dunthruik would be flooded with wares from the south and west. Perhaps the ships would also bring much needed grain; he had heard that winter in the merchant west had not been as severe as in Dunthruik. Besides which, Etraia had always supplied the River Realm with grain.

As he approached the palace gates, his cloak snapping behind him in the sea-whipped wind, he remembered Captain Anderas's words at breakfast that morning:

"You're walking to the palace, my lord?"

"Yes."

"You should ride – you're a Quarter Hand."

"One who couldn't ride even if someone paid him half a crown –"

"You rode when you went to capture the Easter's head!"

" – and one whose horse is lost somewhere along the River."

"The latter can be remedied easily enough," Anderas laughed. "You have a whole stable *full* of horses! As for the former, you know how to ride."

"A feat better left to the knights." Even at the time he knew it was a poor excuse. "And I will walk."

"I will teach you."

"*I will walk.*"

"For today, maybe," Anderas smiled conspiratorially, "but not next time."

"My, you are insistent, captain!"

"Will you be taught?"

"Yes, captain."

"Good. And did you sleep well last night?"

"Yes," Eamon had answered. And he had.

Eamon stood at the palace gates, the sculptured archways yawning back at him, an imposing mass of stone and eagles and crowns. Beyond them he saw the Royal Plaza, the enormous square stretching back to the palace's main façade, to the Master's balcony. He kept walking.

The Gauntlet guards at the gate let him pass. Soon he trod the familiar stones across the Royal Plaza to the palace steps. Men led horses into the nearby stables. They were messengers from other parts of the River, the badges of distant Gauntlet colleges and regions marking their uniforms.

The shadow of the Master's balcony fell on him as he climbed the steps, and once again the guards at the doors saluted him. He had climbed those same steps with Alessia on the night of the masque; his footing faltered as a wash of memory soaked through him. He had been dressed in blue, with a sword and star at his breast, and he had walked freely in that attire. Maybe one day he would wear its like and climb these steps again. On that day, would the King walk with him? Would he, one day, look up to see pennants of the King's blue atop the palace towers?

His heart soared to think it. He stepped into the shade of the entrance hall, giddy with his imagining.

The cool air brought him back. He turned his steps from the jewelled hall and made his way along the corridor that led around to the throne room. The ring on his finger and the look on his face opened the way before him.

The corridor was long. The banners hung in the early light as dozens of woven witnesses to his bold stride; they shivered as he passed. Every step brought him closer to the throne room.

Do not be afraid, Eamon. You will know what to say.

Eamon walked on, the banners conducting him to the throne room.

A tall man stood at the door – the doorkeeper. For the first time Eamon saw him clearly – the man's hair was greying and he seemed to be in his late forties. He was robed all in red and his watchful eyes had a sharp glint. Red-tuniced and black-cloaked guards – guards from the Master's own house – and two Hands stood in the alcoves at the side of the corridor. The fanning banners shadowed them all.

"Lord Goodman," the doorkeeper inclined his head. "What would you, my lord?"

"I would see the Master, doorkeeper."

The doorkeeper bowed down low. "If you would wait a moment, Lord Goodman." He turned to enter the throne room. Eamon caught sight of a blade among the man's robes. From the way that the man moved – indeed, from his very look – Eamon imagined that the Master's doorkeeper knew well how to use it.

The Hands and other guards watched him as he waited. He kept his head aloft and did not look at them.

Perhaps he should go back. What if the Master's eyes seared right through him?

You will know what to say, Eamon.

The doors drew open and the doorkeeper bowed to him again.

"The Master will see you, Lord Goodman." Eamon felt the words slicing his resolve.

"Thank you, doorkeeper." Drawing breath, he stepped past the bowing man and into the throne room. The doors closed smoothly behind him.

Eamon stood upon the entry platform. The sun was high, and

the long room lit in every part. It threw back beams of gold, and arch-light from the high balconies flooded the ruddy floor with fire.

The Master was seated in his throne, the last jewel to deck that grisly artifice. A heavy crown sat in the red hair. Eamon met the grey eyes.

"Approach, son of Eben."

The Master, the throned, Edelred spoke, his voice dripping with indulgence. The traces of a smile played upon the man's face.

Eamon walked steadily across the long hall. His steps echoed. The throned's fearsome grey gaze bored into his brow until his whole face felt hollowed by it. It burnt at him as though with fire. The ring on his hand grew heavier. His heart snagged.

Courage, Eamon.

He reached the foot of the throne and there he bent his knee.

"Master," he said, bowing his head. "To your glory."

"The early bird strikes the Serpent." The Master's voice was cool and thunderous. "You are early indeed."

Eamon swallowed. What would he say? "I have not been early of late, Master," he answered at last.

"Speak."

The command struck Eamon's soul, and for a moment all his courage, so fickle in its staying power, vanished. His knee trembled where it touched the ground and his throat grew dry.

At once, Eamon thought that he should never have come. It was folly! The throned knew everything – the voice of Edelred knew what had sourced and succoured Eamon's grief. Surely the Master knew it, too? All he would reap was humiliation and death. He should rise and leave, begging forgiveness for his coming.

If the Master truly knew, would he not already have been killed?

As he struggled in his thought, his head stayed bowed. The Master's eyes always watched him. While they did he could never...

Eamon – speak fearlessly.

He raised his head. The grey eyes watched him indeed, piercing his own like daggers, but at last he met them.

"Master," Eamon said, and as he spoke his voice became clearer. "In your great glory and majesty you bestowed upon me an honour that I scarcely deserved; it is one that I have not repaid. I did not withhold my service willingly, but the fact remains that you have not been served by me. I have come, Master, to give account of myself, craving your clemency for the pardoning of my fault, your justice in the punishment which I must bear for it, and your grace to let me sow anew your will in me, that your glory would be shown indeed."

There was a long silence. Eamon's heart pounded. The words were his and yet came from somewhere deeper and stronger than his heart could bear. The piercing grey gaze filled his whole sight, daring him to flee, but Eamon held. He had just to hold that gaze. Though it might search him and try him and tempt him to treachery, he need only hold it.

A laugh touched the long room.

"They told me that you would not come, Eben's son. They told me that you would not, could not, and should not, be permitted to serve." The Master's voice rolled with pleasure. "They will not be pleased to learn that you have come to me with such words, at such a time, and in such a manner as you have done." The throned leaned forward, and though there was still distance between them, that face became Eamon's whole world. As it spoke, the Master's voice was soft and intimate. "But, Eben's son, it pleases *me*."

Fear thrilled through Eamon's every limb as he understood the words spoken against him by the other Quarter Hands. Had he not come to the Master his grief would have betrayed him. What Hand was sullen for the death of a wayfarer?

The horror of it struck him with force. As he mustered his courage, the Master laughed once more. "They speak against you much, Eben's son."

"Master, I know what they have spoken – of my ill-service to your glory."

The throned raised an amused eyebrow. Had he answered too swiftly? He froze.

"How is it that you know, Eben's son?" The Master's voice was deceptive in its gentleness. Eamon met the awful face before him.

"I would have spoken out the same things, Master, in my concern that you be served by men with an eagle's heart. No other service can render you that glory which you rightly claim."

The throned laughed – a deep, resounding laugh that filled the whole throne room, reaching up to the gilded rafters and dancing across the jewelled floor. Eamon nearly jumped in surprise.

"An eagle's heart! Have you an eagle's heart, Eben's son?" The steely eyes locked him. Eamon measured the gaze.

"You alone, Master, must judge my heart," he answered. "You must judge also what I bring before you." He paused. He could not turn back now. "I must speak to you of my ward."

The throned nodded indulgently. "Yes, Eben's son; that you must."

There was nothing in those words that should kindle fear in any man, and yet as they touched Eamon's ears, they terrified him. His knee ached where he knelt. Remembering his last visit to Mathaiah and the thrilling brilliance of the blue light in the Pit, Eamon steadied his tongue.

"I did not take well to his death, Master. Neither did I bear it well."

"When death falls upon ones that are loved, such is accounted natural."

"And I did love him, Master."

Eamon saw surprise pass over the Master's face. He knew that he trod dangerously – but his courage told him that the way had been cleared for him.

He knew what to say.

"I loved him, Master, because from the first moment I met him I saw what he would become in your service. I saw the youth and strength of his heart, and saw that it was for you.

"Master, the Serpent took that heart and poisoned it. He took it and worked it against you. I had hoped to see my ward healed of such a wound, and will not hide from you that I desired to be the agent of that cure. It grieved me that he was taken from your service, and I dreamed of a day when I might bring him before you and declare what work he had done, in your name and to your glory."

The throned watched him inscrutably. Eamon spoke again, more quietly. "When I saw him, Master, laid out as one of your enemies among your enemies, I grieved that he was taken from me because, at that time, he was taken from you also."

There was silence. Eamon's words fell in the long hall. He held his breath.

The throned did not speak. His hand rested lightly on the arm of the throne. Thick jewels lined it, colouring the Master's arm with hues of red and gold.

"In my grief, Master, I was laid open to folly," Eamon said quietly. "I alone am accountable for that. I have neglected my duties and brought disgrace upon myself. Grief is blinding and binding, but I kneel before you now to proclaim that I am no longer bound or blinded by it. I would repay to you all the honour you have bestowed on me, and I would bring back to you a harvest that is thrice tenfold of that."

"And you shall, son of Eben."

Eamon's heart trembled on a precipice. He did not know which was the greater terror – that he had dared to speak, or that he might be believed.

"Master," he breathed, "what is your will for the East Quarter?"

"It will serve me." The four words struck harsh, resonant in mastery. "It will glorify me. And it will crush any who stand against me." The throned smiled – a small, slow smile. "Where the Serpent dares to stand, you shall make the streets run with blood."

Eamon suppressed a shudder. "You will be glorified in my quarter, Master."

"That, son of Eben, son of mine, is why it is yours."

Eamon bowed his head. As he did so, the Master rose and lay his heavy hand upon Eamon's shoulder. His voice reverberated in every corner of Eamon's being: *"son of mine"*.

The grip on his shoulder was firm. Eamon's brow warmed as the words wound round him.

"You have the full authority of Crown and Eagle, son of Eben," the Master said. "Let none gainsay you."

Eamon looked up. The Master still smiled, his hand resting lightly at the side of Eamon's neck. Eamon realized that he had to respond to this renewed investing of authority and power. He had to answer in a way befitting one whom the throned would call his *son*.

He reached up and took hold of the palm and fingers that touched him. Slowly, he pressed Edelred's hand against his lips, and kissed it.

The Master laughed with pleasure. "Your fealty is received, Eben's son."

Eamon's face burned as he relinquished a hand that maybe no man before him had dared to kiss.

"To your glory, Master."

CHAPTER XVII

Lightheaded, Eamon emerged into the Royal Plaza in a daze. He felt unable to comprehend what had happened or what he had done.

He had sought an audience with the throned and been received. More than that: he had not betrayed himself. His weakness had been overlooked – or it had not been seen. He did not know which was more terrifying.

As that mix of fear and wonder flooded him, his thought turned to the papers that he had left on his desk that morning. Now he truly had the authority to deal with them as he chose: the throned had restored it to him. The East Quarter had once more been entrusted to him. Now he would set to work. Perhaps he could do only a little, perhaps he would be baited and struck, just as he had been since he came to the city, and perhaps he would be discovered and lose his life. But it was in serving the East Quarter of Dunthruik that he had to make his service to the King. He would render it with all his strength.

He went to the East Quarter College and bounded the steps two at a time. The guards' greeting could not keep up with him. He hurried along the passageways, seeking the Gauntlet exercise yard. The sound of lieutenants urging on their men rang in the air. He followed those calls.

A group of about twenty men ran around the yard. They did not wear red uniforms, although they had been issued with the Gauntlet's standard dark breeches and pale shirt. Some of the young men appeared to struggle with the exercises.

First Lieutenant Greenwood and Captain Anderas observed, while two other lieutenants called the running men on to the next lap. Had the East Quarter had a college draybant he would also have been present – but no one had yet been promoted to replace Anderas.

"Lord Goodman, good morning once again." Captain Anderas bowed as he spoke. Greenwood followed suit.

"I'll get the men to stop and greet you as you deserve, my lord," he said.

"By all means do let them stop," Eamon answered, looking at the backs of the men who ran along the length of the yard away from him. "They look as though they would appreciate that!"

"Yes, my lord." Greenwood bowed and made his way across the yard to stop the men.

There was a short pause. Anderas turned to him. "How was your audience, Lord Goodman?" he asked quietly.

"It went well, thank you." Eamon remembered the Master's hand beneath his lip, but now it did not seize him with horror. He had done it, and done it for the King.

"I am glad, my lord," said Anderas.

"How are your new recruits?"

"Unprepared for a long jog at this time of the morning," Anderas answered, smiling as he said it. "They will be terrified to see you, but cheered to stop, and," Anderas continued, his smile growing broader, "*most* disappointed to learn that, after they have stopped, I will make them run again – with a good, heavy pack."

Eamon glanced behind the captain to a pile of satchels. He knew that they were weighted. He remembered the cruelty of the exercise – at least, he imagined that all Gauntlet cadets found it cruel on their first day. It had certainly seemed so to him on his first morning in Belaal's college. But it was as necessary as the weapons practices, law and geography, and formation fighting training.

"I am sure that they will thank for it one day, captain."

"I suspect that they will have some rather unsavoury things to say about me first," Anderas answered lightly. "I certainly did for my captain."

"Did you ever say them to him?"

"No, Lord Goodman!" Anderas laughed. "I was given to complaining, like all young men, but unlike some of my fellows I found myself too intelligent to do it before my officers."

"Were you born wise, captain?" Eamon laughed.

"I cannot speak to that – but I hope, my lord, to die being it."

"An admirable goal." Eamon looked up to check on the cadets' progress. "Is this yard in use this afternoon?"

"Some of the ensigns are down for weapons," Anderas answered. "They can be moved to another yard if you have need of this one."

"I'd like the Hands of the Quarter summoned here then."

The Hands of the Quarter were the small number of Hands assigned to work in the quarter as auxiliaries to the Gauntlet college. Such Hands were not formally attached to the college but often worked there, answering to the Quarter Hand and doing as he asked. Such Hands were often protégés of the lord of their quarter. Eamon had been in such a position as a Hand in the West Quarter, and had served both Captain Waite and Lord Cathair as the latter directed.

The East Quarter College had fifteen of these Hands. Some had been present at his investiture as Lord of the East Quarter. Eamon had seen them not long after his formal instatement, and they had been present at the supper, but he had not seen them in person since then. If he wanted to win the respect of the quarter, he needed to win the Hands who served him.

"Of course," Anderas answered. "I will have them summoned."

"Thank you." The recruits reached the last corner. They turned and ran towards Eamon. "Captain," he added, "I want to arrange a dinner."

"A dinner, my lord?" Anderas repeated incredulously.

"I wish to invite those who attended my official banquet earlier in the week." The captain's eyes moved with thought as Anderas assessed Eamon's intentions. At last Anderas nodded.

"Of course, Lord Goodman," he said. "You need only speak to the head of the household. He will see to the invitations, and to organizing the kitchens. His name, as you might recall, is Slater."

Eamon's thoughts turned to the butler with whom he had discussed the menu. He wondered if that man was also the head of his household. He had the notion that, had he been paying attention over the last few days, he would have known the answer.

"Would you have me speak to him on your behalf?"

"No, I shall do it, thank you, captain," Eamon answered. "I will be sure to count the crowns this time."

Anderas smiled. "I am sure that you will do it admirably, my lord."

Greenwood walked over to them, followed by the two much younger looking lieutenants; the latter two dropped into low bows as soon as they saw Eamon. The new recruits at last jogged their way – for it was more of a jog than a run now – up the length of the yard to where they stood. Odd looks passed over the men's faces – looks that only grew more and more terrified as they bounded forward towards a Hand.

"How long have they been running, Mr Greenwood?" Eamon asked.

"Certainly less than an hour, my lord," Greenwood answered. He said little more, for at that moment the recruits staggered through the dust to where their lord and officers stood.

"Gentlemen, sign!" Anderas called.

The panting, blanched group of men mustered themselves into an ordered line and gasped out their names. Eamon reckoned that more than one of them were on the point of collapse. He remembered the way his own legs and lungs had burned the day when he had first barked (or rather, pitiably mewed) his name to his officer at Edesfield. Ladomer had found the spectacle deeply amusing.

The names ended and Anderas nodded, satisfied. Eamon stepped forward and looked at the new cadets with a smile.

"Gentlemen," he said, "I would like to take this opportunity to personally welcome you all to the East Quarter Gauntlet College.

Your officers and captain are fine men; they will make you more than worthy to wear the red that you came here to wear." He nodded once to Anderas, indicating that he had finished, and then took his leave. The men stared at his back as he went.

"Gentlemen, a pack each if you please." Anderas's irrefutable voice echoed in the yard air.

Eamon pitied the new cadets – they had a long morning ahead of them yet. The sight of the bedraggled men engaged courageously with their first steps in the Gauntlet somehow made him smile.

And yet he also knew that many of the young men running in the yard might, one day, fall in battle against the King. It was a thought that weighed on him as he left the college.

When he returned to the Handquarters, he sought out Slater, quizzing various servants until he found him. As Eamon had suspected, Slater was the man who had gone through the formal menu with him and was also the head of the household.

He found Slater allotting tasks to a group of servants in the garden. The man was taller and slimmer than Eamon remembered, but his mouse-like looks remained. Slater bowed low to him.

"My lord."

"I wish to arrange a dinner, Mr Slater."

To the servant's credit, his face showed no flicker of emotion. "Very good, my lord."

"I want you to invite all those who attended my formal reception."

"Yes, my lord."

"I entrust the menu entirely to your hands, Mr Slater," Eamon added. "No doubt that will relieve you!"

Slater did not reply. Eamon laughed.

"Are you a taciturn man by nature?"

"Yes, lord."

Eamon turned his head to one side as though to catch sight of the man's eyes. "It may surprise you, Mr Slater," he said, "but I would have the head of my household feel free to speak to me and meet my look."

"When would you have this meal, my lord?" Slater asked.

"The evening of the twentieth," Eamon answered. "Will that give you time enough?"

"Yes, my lord."

"Is that a truthful answer, Mr Slater, or lip service that will bind this household to two days' grinding until the chore is done, rather than gainsay my folly?"

Slowly, Slater raised his head. His eyes were touched with wariness and astonishment. "It is a truthful answer, lord," he said at last.

Eamon nodded. "Very well," he said. A new thought occurred to him. "How are we for wines, Mr Slater?"

"Ill-supplied, my lord," the servant answered. Eamon recognized the courage it took to utter the words. "We used many of them for your banquet."

"That doesn't matter," he said. Slater coloured with confusion. "I wish to procure some from Lord Cathair."

"I shall arrange it at once, my lord."

"No," Eamon interrupted. "I wish to see to that myself – if you feel I may be trusted with such a task," he added with a smile. "Have a word with the master cook, and let me know what wines I should get as soon as you can."

Slater looked a little embarrassed. "Of course, my lord."

"Please also do not concern yourself with extending an invitation to Captain Waite," Eamon added. "I wish to do so personally."

"Very well. Is that all, my lord?"

It was. Eamon thanked the man for his assistance and returned to his study.

Eamon went to see Captain Waite that afternoon. The sun had shifted round with the onward day, blinding him as he climbed the Coll. He wondered as to the wisdom of wanting to see Cathair and endear himself to him – for that was the motivation behind wanting to buy more wines. He was sure that word of his initial period in the East Quarter had travelled far by now. Cathair had always been suspicious of him, but that suspicion had borne bitterness since Eamon's failure at Pinewood. Eamon did not think that he could ever hope to obtain an ally in Cathair, but he had to do something to allay the Hand's acridity. If he could once more make himself the victim of Cathair's poetical tirades, he would have had a measure of success in the venture.

The West Quarter College had not changed since he had left it, and like the first day he had passed through its doors, none challenged him there. When he turned from the entry hall, towards Waite's office, he saw his own name glint on the Hand-board.

The captain was in his office with Farleigh, the West Quarter College draybant. They stood at the captain's desk, studying a group of papers. As Eamon knocked and entered both men looked up and bowed immediately.

"Lord Goodman," Waite said.

"Captain; Mr Farleigh," Eamon answered courteously. "A pleasure to see you both." The draybant looked at him uncomfortably. Eamon looked at Waite. "May I have a moment of your time, captain?"

"Of course."

Waite nodded to the draybant. The man set down the papers, bowed once more to Eamon, and then left, drawing the office doors closed.

"Please do sit, captain," Eamon said.

Waite gestured to the chair before his desk. Eamon sat, his cloak falling in thick folds around him. Waite carefully laid aside his papers.

"How may I serve you, my lord?"

"First, by accepting my apologies."

A measured look went over Waite's face. "I hardly feel it your place to apologize to me, Lord Goodman."

"I owe you many things, captain, this apology not least among them," Eamon answered sincerely. "My words to you when last we met were discourteous and unnecessary. More than this: they were spoken ill at a time when your care was, I believe, for me. Whatever my rank, it was not my place to treat you as I did. For this, Captain Waite, I apologize."

Waite nodded silently. For a moment, Eamon saw a touch of pride in the captain's eyes. Waite had always been proud of him. "Thank you, my lord."

"I wanted to come to you myself, to extend to you a personal invitation to an informal dinner in the East Quarter on the twentieth," Eamon added. "Though I do not wish to oblige you if your time must be spent elsewhere, it would please me greatly if you were to attend."

"Of course, Lord Goodman," Waite replied with a small smile. Eamon wondered how much of his intent in hosting a second meal the captain had understood – probably all of it. "It would be an honour."

"There is one more thing I have to ask of you."

Waite nodded obligingly.

"I need to see Lord Cathair, on the matter of wines, and I wish to bear him a gift." Waite's eyebrows lifted. "I suspect that you know Lord Cathair better than many men. In your opinion, captain, what should I take him?"

Waite sat pensive. Then he smiled.

"Lord Ashway had a large personal library," he said, and as he did so Eamon remembered the shelves that littered every available space in all of his rooms, each of them filled with book after book.

"I believe that Lord Cathair has long been envious of that library, for he is, as you know, a man of letters, and prides himself on that distinction. I imagine that a collection of volumes drawn from the shelves now in your possession would please him greatly."

Eamon knew at once that Waite was right. "An excellent thought, captain," he grinned.

"Lord Cathair has been out of the city this last week," Waite added, "though he has intention of returning tomorrow. He went to inspect the vineyards."

"Then my timing is good."

"As ever," Waite said with a smile. "Lord Cathair often stays at his Ravensill estate for almost a month at this time of the year. It puts some strain on the quarter," he added, "but we are accustomed to it, and prepared for such absences." Waite glanced at the papers on his desk. "The West Quarter is swearing in its new ensigns and lieutenants on the twenty-first and Lord Cathair, rightly, likes to be present at such times. Many of the Third Banners are to be formally appointed."

"Great news indeed," Eamon answered, forcing away the sudden thickness in his throat. His palm burned; he clenched it silently. Were the Third Banners to endure that, too? Were they to become marked and have the doors of their minds opened to the voice of Edelred?

"Perhaps you would also like to attend, Lord Goodman?" Waite said. "You would certainly do us great honour in doing so. One or two of the lads are particularly nervous about the swearing – though the Crown knows we've been through the ceremony a hundred times! I think that seeing you would encourage and inspire them."

"I should be delighted to attend. In fact," Eamon added, "you should bring some of them with you to the East Quarter." He smiled. "Let them see where their swearing-in may take them, if they work hard."

"Thank you, Lord Goodman. I think that will give them something to consider."

Eamon took his leave. Waite's clasp on his hand was friendly when they parted, and for that he was grateful. He admired the man and it would have grieved him greatly to cause – or not to heal – any rift between them.

But as he returned to the Coll his stomach churned. The Third Banner cadets – *his* cadets – were going to be sworn. They were going to be marked, burned and bound to the voice. Would Waite knowingly have them set their hands to that mark?

He thought suddenly of Mathaiah. Had he lived, Mathaiah would also have been due for formal swearing.

But Mathaiah Grahaven was beyond the grip of the throned's mark. Even had he lived, Eamon realized that the cadet would have found a way to absent himself from the ceremony – or to have himself barred from it.

With a shiver, he remembered the night he had spent seeking his dagger in the muddy woods around Edesfield. He had nearly lost his swearing that night. But he did not believe that any of the Third Banners would do anything as foolish as he has done – especially with Waite as their champion: every man in the West Quarter loved their captain. Waite's approval alone would be enough to press them on. And when they saw Lord Goodman sitting by at their hour of swearing...

They would not withdraw. And though he was a lord of Dunthruik, the appointed Lord of the East Quarter, he could not make them. Ford, Jenning, Brockhurst, Ostler, Manners, Smith, Barde... their faces passed before him. The Third Banner cadets would be made marked servants of the throned.

He was at the Four Quarters. He looked up, letting his eyes pass over the statues, the engravings, the crowns, and eagles. He could not stop them.

Turning his steps onto Coronet Rise, he returned to the East Quarter.

That afternoon he returned to the college grounds and found Anderas waiting for him. The captain greeted him warmly.

"Lord Goodman."

"Are the Hands of the Quarter coming?"

"They'll be here shortly." Anderas looked curiously at him. "What do you intend, my lord?"

"You think that I intend something?"

"No, my lord, I don't think it: I *know* it." Eamon laughed at the man's audacity. "You may laugh," Anderas told him, "but you are a man full of intention, made more fearsome by the fact that you have will brazen enough to act upon it."

"I shall take that as a compliment, captain, and thank you for it."

The evening breeze touched Eamon's hair. He looked back at Anderas. Like Waite, Anderas was responsible for selecting the men who would be branded, promoted, or Handed. In the following weeks, Anderas would arrange a swearing ceremony for the East Quarter College. It chilled him. The captain was a good man – an *exemplary* man – sharp of wit and compassionate, a dear friend, and yet…

There was no way that the Lord of the East Quarter could forbid a swearing. Eamon would be forced to watch more men swear and, when the King came, he feared he would have to give account for why he had not stopped it.

"Are you well, my lord?"

Eamon looked up. He was not surprised to find Anderas watching him.

"Thank you, yes."

"Your meeting with Captain Waite?"

"Went well," Eamon replied. After a moment he continued: "Have you any pressing duties upon the morrow, captain?"

"None that I cannot leave to Mr Greenwood, my lord."

"Perhaps, captain, we should formally appoint Mr Greenwood as the college draybant!"

"Lord Ashway and Captain Etchell had made note that Mr Greenwood might be considered for the Hands," Anderas replied quietly.

Eamon detected reservation. "Do you agree with their assessment?"

"It would be a great loss to us if Greenwood was Handed. But things in the East Quarter are settling. Perhaps we may now duly consider and appoint the best man to be college draybant."

"Rather than to act as it," Eamon nodded. "We will discuss it. I would like you to accompany me to Ravensill tomorrow, captain," he continued. "We shall also have need of a cart and driver. Will you see to that?"

"Of course, my lord."

At that moment the Hands of the Quarter arrived, grim-faced. The East Quarter had fifteen Hands. Eamon remembered some of their faces from his formal dinner and watched as the men fell into a long line and bowed to him. Familiar doubts assailed him; the men's faces were guarded and suspicious. No explanation would have been given to them of Lord Ashway's death, nor of Eamon's own appointment, and he had scarcely taken note of them in the days since he had been made their commander. These Hands would also be more than mindful of the fact that, until not so long ago, Lord Goodman had been but a Hand of the Quarter himself.

"Good afternoon, gentlemen," Eamon greeted them formally. "I will not keep you long from your duties, of which I know you have many." He regarded them each in turn. "Your names."

The Hands gave their names. Eamon recognized only the names of the three most accomplished: Lord Lonnam, Lord Brettal, and Lord Heathlode. Eamon matched each man's look evenly. Like every other man and woman in the whole of the East Quarter, the quarter's Hands had heard different and utterly conflicting stories about Eamon in recent days. He wanted – even needed – to give them a reason to obey him other than for duty's sake, but he could not address them the way he had his household or the college. If Lord Cathair had taught him anything, it was that Hands had to be treated with force.

He plunged straight in. "I read your looks, gentlemen: you served Lord Ashway well – and well you know it! You wonder whether in serving under me – the one who returned in disgrace from Pinewood and who served a two-crown dinner – your service will ever attain a great height. You wonder – jealously – whether you might have taken Lord Ashway's place better than I."

The Hands stared.

Eamon stepped forward to pace before them, meeting each of their gazes in turn.

"But when you think such things, my lords, you forget that I am the man who returned, from the Serpent's own camp, bearing the head of an Easter lord which to this day adorns the Blind Gate. I did so in less than seven days. You forget that the Master chose me himself, and that he gave me authority to rule over this quarter for his glory." Eamon's face grew hard.

"When you forget these things, gentlemen, you set yourselves against me. To set yourself against me is to do no less than set yourself against the Master himself, and against his glory. I counsel you to do so no more."

The Hands gaped.

"In recent days, I have not had the opportunity to assess your qualities," Eamon continued. "You have many duties here in the city, duties that have doubled with the orders for the culling, but such duties do not constitute an excuse for physical laxness. I want you to stay sharp. I have seen the Serpent, gentlemen, and how Hands that fall foul of him are treated – piled into open graves and left to wolves and crows. This day I would know if, seeing him, you would live to speak of it as I do. Captain Anderas."

"My lord?"

"Have Lieutenant Taine and the Crimsons bring practice infantry blades." Eamon knew that the quarter's Crimson ensigns were doing a weapons drill in a nearby training yard. "Invite them to come to this yard, to admire the skill of the quarter's Hands."

"Yes, my lord."

The line of Hands exchanged discreet glances.

"Lord Goodman," said one – Lord Lonnam – "what would you have us do?"

Eamon looked hard at Lonnam. "When the Master stretches out his Hands against the Serpent, they must be able to bend the bow and strike with steel. This quarter – and the whole of the River Realm – must know that the Master's Hands are a deadly and fearsome force. I will see evidence of it. Steel sharpens steel, so men do men. You will show your best, gentlemen, when you are observed."

The Hands looked grim.

Anderas returned, leading Lieutenant Taine, and behind him the Crimson Ensigns. The young men brought the wooden practice blades, and at Anderas's direction laid them together in a corner of the yard before drawing up into a neat group.

"The ensigns may stand at ease, captain," Eamon called.

Anderas nodded. The group of ensigns relaxed a little.

Eamon gestured for Anderas to bring him a couple of the wooden blades before looking back to the Hands.

"Lord Brettal, step forward," he commanded.

Gaze narrowed, Brettal hesitated for a fraction of a moment, then did so. Eamon took one of the weapons from Anderas and gave it to the Hand. The Hand stood and watched as Eamon took the second blade from the captain. He weighed it in his hand.

There was a long pause. The line of Hands watched expectantly. Brettal twitched his shoulders.

"Do you not mean to choose me an opponent, my lord?"

"I have done so," Eamon answered. He pulled off his cloak and handed it to Anderas.

Brettal stared. "You mean –?"

"Show me your strength, Lord Brettal," Eamon said, and struck at the Hand.

Lord Brettal was a Hand in good shape. Despite his surprise, he turned Eamon's initial strike with clean efficiency and stepped back. Eamon allowed Brettal this minor reprieve; it had been a long time since he had fought a duel. He had been good at it, back at college. But neither in Edesfield nor in the West Quarter had his opponent been a Hand, and in neither place had his own victory been so important. If, after all of his words, one of the quarter's Hands defeated him, it would only mire him in further tales of weakness.

Brettal returned to him with a strong, fast blow; Eamon was hard-pressed to parry in time. The blow jarred his limbs as the Hand drew back and swiped at him again. Brettal was well worthy of the black that he bore: he stepped lightly from his attack, and flexed his hilt-grip.

They fell apart again, circling about each other. Each assessed the other's guards. The ensigns called and cheered. The line of Hands remained silent.

Brettal came at Eamon again. Their blades met and locked. Eamon swung himself away from the bind and struck back. The Hand's guard was tight, but Eamon went through it, landing a blow across the man's arm.

"You have just lost the use of your arm, Lord Brettal," Eamon told him. His lungs worked hard but his voice was clear.

Brettal blinked hard. "Yes, Lord Goodman –"

Eamon turned his blade again and rested its point against the Hand's stomach.

"Now you've been run through," he added. "I understand, of course, that the shock of losing your arm may have contributed to that." He lowered his weapon and stepped back. "The Master has lost another loyal servant."

Brettal bowed low. "It would appear that I am in need of some practice, my lord." His face coloured.

"You shall be fearsome once you have it," Eamon told him. "You may return here at this hour tomorrow, if you wish, and attempt to decapitate me."

Brettal glanced up. A small smile passed over his face. "I will do so, my lord."

Brettal returned to the line and Eamon looked back to it, looking for another of the more senior Hands. "Lord Lonnam," he called, "let me see your mettle."

Lonnam took the wooden sword from Brettal and stepped boldly forward, jaw set. Delighted, the ensigns cheered.

Lonnam matched Eamon's gaze. "You shall not find me a simple foe, Lord Goodman," he said. He turned his blade to a whipping blow, aimed at Eamon's side.

By reflex, Eamon parried the blow and then pulled himself free in time to thwart a second strike. Lonnam was stronger than Brettal, probably stronger than Eamon himself, and he recognized it when their weapons jarred and bound a third and then a fourth time.

"You have a good arm, Lonnam."

"Thank you, my lord."

"It will avail you little when the Serpent takes your leg," Eamon answered, for at just that second the Hand left his right flank unguarded. Eamon swooped down hard.

"I appear to have been crippled, my lord," Lonnam chuckled nervously, and stepped back with a bow to join the line. The ensigns applauded him.

Eamon turned to Lord Heathlode. The blood rushed round his veins.

"Will you defeat me, Lord Heathlode?"

The third Hand was a lithe, diminuitive man. He laughed uncertainly.

"Lord Goodman, my fellows may be out of practice but I was never in practice; I was not made a Hand for martial prowess," he answered. "But as you ask it of me, I will attempt it."

The Hand stepped forward. Eamon saw at once that he was not a born swordsman. His grip on the weapon was poor, despite years of Gauntlet training. How long had it been since Heathlode had used a real weapon?

The Hand took but two steps forward. Eamon exploited the weakness in his grip – a single, sharp knock sent the weapon flying. Heathlode looked disappointed rather than surprised as his blade spun away and landed with a dull thud behind him.

Eamon touched his own weapon to the man's chest. "The Serpent takes your head home to adorn his wall."

"He has very poor taste, Lord Goodman," Heathlode replied with a bow.

Eamon looked at the three defeated Hands. They had seemed easy opponents. Perhaps they truly were out of practice – or perhaps some star had watched over him.

He looked firmly at them and lowered his voice so that only the Hands could hear him. "I expect that Lords Brettal, Heathlode, and Lonnam are representative of your skills," he said. "I am an infantryman by trade, gentlemen, sworn to the Gauntlet but seven months ago and yet, facing three of the East's own Hands, I stand here undefeated. Clearly this suits me as an exercise in vanity, but it does not suit any of you. You may be breachers, changers, dreamers, breakers, movers, or seers, or have a hundred other talents from when you first swore your oaths – but they will not save you against the skill of an armed and determined man. It did not save your fellows at Ashford, and it did not save many of the Hands who were with me at Pinewood." He surveyed them sternly. "Like the greenest Gauntlet recruits, you will each put in weapons practice every day. If I do not see substantial improvement I will pit you against the ensigns and cadets." A couple of faces grew wide. "You think this an unnecessary whim, gentlemen, designed for your discomfort?" he laughed. "It is not. To suffer defeat at the hands of ensigns and cadets would serve you better than the humiliation of being felled by a snake, and if by subjecting you to the former I saved you from the latter, I would count myself to have served the Master. To your duties, gentlemen," he finished. "Another day, I shall challenge others of you."

The Hands bowed low. Perhaps inspired by Eamon's threat, some of them made their way to the pile of blades that the ensigns had brought. Not long later these had split into pairs and threes and begun practising. To see so many Hands in action at once quieted the ensigns: they watched in awe.

Eamon watched too. Then he saw Lord Lonnam coming across to him.

"You have a good hand, my lord," said Lonnam, bowing.

"Thank you, Lord Lonnam."

The Hand looked at him curiously. "My lord," he said softly, "if you have such a hand for steel, why did you surrender your sword?"

The sounds of the other Hands caught in combat echoed in the yard, marked every now and then by the ensigns' voices. Eamon pressed his wooden blade into Lonnam's hands.

"Lord Lonnam," he said, "there are better things to live and die by."

Chapter XVIII

With each passing day, the winds that buffeted Dunthruik from the north-west grew less severe, and they brought with them touches of warmth. The great, trailing flowers in the Ashen bloomed.

Following his spar with the Hands of the Quarter Eamon had slept well, though his sleep was interrupted by odd dreams. As he sat at breakfast he struggled to remember anything of them but pale forms and flickering images.

Slater brought him his breakfast: the accustomed tray of breads, all of them fresh and accompanied by meats and cheeses. That morning Slater also brought a strange fruit that he did not – and could not – recognize. He had never seen its like before in his life. It was a little smaller than his fist, and was a ruddy golden colour.

"Good morning, my lord." Slater bowed as he laid the tray on the table, neatly avoiding Eamon's papers.

"Good morning," Eamon answered, eyeing the fruit suspiciously. He had not the courage to ask what it was, and if Slater observed the disconcerted fashion in which he stared at it, then the servant had the sense not to mention it.

Slater left, and Eamon ate. He had been left a knife and a small bowl of water. He presumed they were each for the fruit, though he was unsure how to cut it properly. Not long later there was a knock at his door. Eamon bade the knocker enter. Anderas stepped inside. The captain bowed.

"Good morning, Lord Goodman."

"Good morning, captain."

"I have a cart and driver waiting in the Ashen, and two horses ready at the stables. We will depart at your convenience, my lord."

"Good, thank you." Eamon rose from the table.

"You are sure that you have finished?" Anderas said, surprised. Eamon looked down at the untouched fruit on his otherwise empty plate.

"Yes?" he offered.

Anderas frowned at him.

"I couldn't ask Slater," Eamon explained. He gestured to the fruit in frustration. "I have little idea what that is, captain, and even less of an idea of how to eat it."

"You needn't eye it so, Lord Goodman!" Anderas said with a gentle laugh, and Eamon sighed, trying to relax the accusatory gaze with which he regarded the alien object.

"Is it even food?"

"Yes, lord, and very fine food, too," Anderas answered. "They're known as *lotti*, after some foreign word or other. My grandmother always used to call them 'western stars'." The captain stepped forward to the tray and picked up the fruit.

"Western stars?"

> *"When spring comes breathing over-seas,*
> *comes bringing word of lands afar;*
> *see there by port and river lea*
> *a shining haul of golden stars."*

Anderas smiled as the song spilled from his lips. He had a good voice.

"Of course, few call them 'stars' now," Anderas added quietly. "These come from Marboristia. I've heard it said that Dunthruik used to have whole orchards of these fruit – the city was full of them from spring until late autumn." He paused sadly. "I would have liked to have seen them; I'm told the trees are beautiful."

"What happened to them?" Eamon remembered the long entry into Dunthruik. The land running in to the Blind Gate was dotted with farmsteads, but none of the trees there bore these strange fruit.

"My grandmother used to tell me that the groves were felled and torched after the Serpent's last defenders were driven from the city. Now these fruit reach the city as the winter passes – the merchants bring them from the south." He smiled. "The first Marboristian vessel reached port yesterday evening."

Eamon watched as Anderas set the small knife against the side of the fruit and gently cut it in half. The sides came easily apart and Anderas gave one of them to him. Eamon took it and paused.

"I can see why they're called stars," he said. The fruit's core was ridged with fibres that struck out from the stone like the points of a bold star. The fibre marked out various segments of fruit.

"You have to take the segments out."

Eamon watched the captain ease a segment out of the half he held. "This is the part that you eat," Anderas added, proceeding to do just that. "It's easy, Lord Goodman!"

Eamon looked back to the fruit in his hand. "I suppose I have to try."

Anderas told him that this was indeed the case, and Eamon tried to get hold of one of the segments. Anderas made it look easy, but Eamon's half was uncooperative. Eventually he managed to extract a half-mauled segment. The juice was sticky and sweet.

"I trust that you find this amusing, captain," he said, glancing at the man's face.

"Not at all, my lord."

"You are a very poor liar," Eamon retorted.

Anderas gestured at another part of the fruit. "You can eat that part, my lord."

"Yes." Eamon looked at the partially mashed segment for a moment then eventually put the thing in his mouth. He had expected the fruit to be slimy and tasteless but it was sweet and succulent, full of vigour and flavour. Eamon looked up at Anderas with renewed surprise.

"Do you like it?"

"Who would burn orchards of these?" Eamon asked incredulously.

"Not I, lord."

"Nor I." Eamon ate another segment contentedly, then looked down at his sticky hands.

"That's what the water is for," Anderas told him.

It was about the second hour when they left the Handquarters. Eamon advised Slater that he hoped to return in time for supper and was pleased when the housekeeper told him that preparations for the following evening's meal were all well in hand.

"My lord, the master cook advises that you should seek a strong-bodied red wine," Slater told him, "especially one with fruity undertones."

"Thank you, Mr Slater," Eamon answered lightly. He went to the Ashen.

Anderas was as good as his word. Two saddled horses waited patiently with two servants. Nearby stood a broad cart, and a man sat at its front ready to drive it. All present bowed deeply as Eamon and Anderas approached.

Eamon bade them all a good morning, then turned to the servant standing by his horse. He could tell that the beast was to be ridden by him, for it had a black saddle showing an owl.

"Please would you stow this securely in the saddlebag," he said, handing the young man a parcel of books. Eamon had chosen them before retiring to bed the previous night, and hoped that they would go some way towards mollifying Cathair.

"Yes, Lord Goodman."

Eamon mounted. As he took the saddle he was suddenly in the abandoned dell, calling for Hughan's men to show themselves.

He laid his hand on the horse's neck.

Anderas mounted the second horse and brought it to his side.

"Where to, my lord?" he asked cheerfully. The captain was completely at home in the saddle. Eamon suspected that the man had not had a proper chance to ride since they had been to Pinewood.

"To Ravensill," Eamon answered, "and to Lord Cathair."

The land to the north-west of Dunthruik ran in long hills from the distant mountains to the sea. The hills – known as Ravensill – had for centuries been home to tall vines from which most of the city's wines were pressed. As they rode up through the North Gate and out onto the road, the hills sloped up and sunlight touched the long fields at their feet. Over to the east the trails led to the pyre; from that Eamon quickly drove his sight away.

The pace of the cart slowed them, but Eamon didn't mind. He and Anderas rode ahead, and as the city fell back behind them Eamon's heart grew lighter. He breathed deeply. It was a beautiful morning. Even the thought of mollifying Cathair did not trouble him.

"I assume that purchasing wine is not your only goal, my lord?" Anderas asked.

"No," Eamon answered. "Did I call you away from important work to do so?"

"I was only going to be drilling the new recruits today, lord. Mr Greenwood is perfectly capable of that. He's perfectly capable of everything," Anderas added, and his voice grew more serious. "I know that he was selected, both by your predecessor and by mine, but I would humbly recommend, my lord, that you not send Mr Greenwood forward for the Hand list."

"Not send him forward?" Eamon had seen the paperwork that morning, straight from the Right Hand's offices, advising that any man to be recommended by a quarter for Handing should have their name submitted – or withdrawn if such was felt necessary – by the end of the month. Eamon had been taken aback to see Ladomer's signature at the foot of that paper.

"On what grounds would you have me withhold him?"

"He's a good man," Anderas answered. "He will make a fine college draybant."

Eamon smiled. "So, you have finally decided on your draybant?" he said, delighted.

"Though you may have been speaking in jest at the time, my lord," Anderas answered, "it was none other than yourself who suggested Mr Greenwood. His promotion would, of course, bring another problem."

"You will need to choose another first lieutenant."

"Yes." Anderas paused a moment. "I am glad that choosing cadets and officers is the greater part of my lot," he added. "Black is a colour suited to too few men."

"Indeed it is!"

"It suits you well enough," Anderas told him, measuring his gaze. "In fact, it suits you more than any other man I have seen wearing it. And yet... it also doesn't." He shook his head with a small laugh. "Lord Goodman, I am forced to the conclusion that you are a living paradox, one beyond mere mortal comprehension."

Anderas could not know how near his words struck to the truth.

"You seem to understand me well, captain," Eamon replied. In that moment he wondered if the captain of the East Quarter would ever truly understand him.

It was not far to Ravensill, but the slopes slowed their approach. The road wound between the low hills, and Eamon marvelled at the vines that he saw. Servants were out among them, checking them and steadying them against wooden trellises. Up out of the city, the day was cooler. Eamon turned to look west to the sea. The waves reached far to the horizon, and on them ships and smaller craft readied for the time when the sea would fully relent its winter grief.

Cathair had a large residence nestled in the heart of the hills, protected from the wind. Eamon saw some Gauntlet soldiers about – but many more militiamen – and wondered how many men were detailed to protect the vineyards. It would certainly be a tempting target for thieves or bandits – or wayfarers. As they passed, servants bowed low and Gauntlet and militia paused to salute them.

They went up the road to the imposing building. It was framed by the hills and had a wide courtyard, stacked high with large barrels and busy with carts. Eamon saw a line of servants bringing a steady stream of casks up to them from a doorway. There were half a dozen tall wagons there also, and a group of men loading the casks and barrels onto them.

It was not until the last that Eamon caught sight of Cathair. The Hand stood on the steps of his immense estate, speaking to another Hand over a long list. Eamon imagined that these wines – and there were many of them – were destined to go back over the sea to the south or west, in exchange for western stars and sorely needed grain.

He told the driver to draw the cart to one side of the broad courtyard while he and Anderas halted. The captain dismounted easily, but Eamon managed to catch his cloak in the reins as he tried to descend and nearly crashed face first to the ground. Luckily Anderas was able to steady him, and with such grace that none apart from the captain noticed either his near error or his face burning red with embarrassment.

"It may seem uncouth of me, my lord," Anderas murmured, "but I do sometimes ask myself how you made it back with that head."

"You may recall that I wasn't on a horse when I came back."

"Some of the officers are beginning their riding practices next week." A smile filled Anderas's face. "Would you like to join us, my lord?"

"You wouldn't find it amusing if I did."

"The morning is a good time to ride, Lord Goodman. I can easily take you tomorrow. A few miles before breakfast every day and you'll soon find it much simpler."

"You're a cruel man, captain."

"Thank you, my lord."

Eamon drew himself up and looked towards the steps. The courtyard was filled with dust from the rolling casks. He did not think that Cathair could have seen him through the swathes of people. He neatened his cloak.

"I'll have the servants see to the horses," Anderas told him. Eamon thanked him and made his way across the courtyard to the steps of Cathair's estate.

The servants nearly didn't see him through the dust. The men and women breathed harshly with their fatigue and called to each other as they set the casks in place on the giant wagons. But as he drew closer, they fell back and bowed.

Cathair still stood on the steps, giving directions to the Hand with him. Eamon realized suddenly that the other Hand was Lord Febian. At about that moment Febian looked up. Their eyes met, and a look of surprise passed over Febian's face. Nearly at the foot of the steps, Eamon raised his voice.

"Good day, Lord Cathair!" He called it cheerfully. "I am not disturbing you, I trust?"

Cathair looked up as though thoroughly disturbed, then settled quickly into a long smile.

"Lord Goodman." Eamon remembered how much he hated the man's smooth, goading voice. "How good it is to see you. I've been hearing so much about your work in the East Quarter this last week." The green eyes flashed slyly. "How are you finding yourself there?"

"Well, thank you," Eamon answered. "The library is particularly rewarding."

An almost imperceptible sour look brushed Cathair's face.

"Lord Ashway was a great collector of books," the Hand answered. Eamon feigned surprise.

"Surely he was not better read than you, Lord Cathair?"

Febian shuffled uncomfortably. Eamon pitied him; he had done nothing to deserve being caught in the crossfire of civility.

"He was a great *collector*, Lord Goodman," Cathair repeated with a smile. "I hear that you also collect papers, after your own fashion?"

Eamon resisted the urge to cringe. "A long-held passion," he answered self-deprecatingly.

"Ah! The passions of a man! 'They drive unto sorrow and unto joy, until the senses that they serve do cloy.'" The verse poured slickly from Cathair's lips. "I am so sorry that I could not attend your official dinner. I hear from Waite that it was a crowning success to your first days in office."

Eamon matched his gaze boldly. "To my good fortune, the Master held a more temperate view of the matter."

Cathair faltered.

"The Master?"

"I went to him yesterday." Eamon offered Cathair an innocent smile. "He spoke very highly of you, Lord Cathair, and of the other lords of the city. I have much to attain if I wish to match you, but the Master gives me cause to hope that I may one day reach even your lofty height of service."

Febian broke into the long silence that ensued. "My lords, if you would excuse me, I must see to the wagons."

"Of course, Lord Febian," Cathair answered, his eyes fixed on Eamon. Febian descended the steps and walked away.

"You went to the Master?" Cathair's voice as he spoke was low and dangerous.

"Yes," Eamon replied, and he dropped a little of his pretence. "I went to excuse my folly. The Master was gracious to me."

"Of that I am glad, Lord Goodman," Cathair answered. "And were you able to discern the roots of your recent lapse?"

"Yes, Lord Cathair," Eamon answered, wondering at the smile that suddenly touched the Hand's face. "The Master was gracious to me in that also."

"Then tell me, Lord Goodman, to what do I owe the pleasure of your visit?" Cathair stepped down towards him and laid a welcoming hand on his shoulder. Eamon drove back a shiver. "I cannot think that you came to the Raven's Hill simply to speak to me!"

"For that alone, the journey would have been well made, but I have come with another purpose also. I wish," Eamon continued, meeting Cathair's gaze, "to buy some wine for a dinner being held tomorrow night in the East Quarter – to which you are most cordially invited."

"Most kind of you. I shall ruminate upon it," Cathair answered him. "Have you a scantling notion of the kind of wine that you would like?" he asked, his gaze patronizing. "Wines, like words, and more than deeds, are not a simple matter."

"My household advises me that a strong red with touches of fruit would be right," Eamon answered. "Some dessert wines are also required – sweet rather than dry."

The Hand smiled again. "Both fine choices."

"I have also brought a gift for you."

"A gift?" Cathair's brow furrowed with suspicion.

"Lord Cathair, you have been a mentor to me since before I entered this city. All that I do reflects that Hand who guided and guarded me in those early days, and to whom, even now, I come for counsel and for company." Eamon laughed. "My lord, if I hold the East Quarter then it is measure not just of my worth, but of yours also." He held out the package of books. "That is why I have brought these for you."

For a moment Cathair did nothing. At last he reached out and took the bound parcel, then slowly unwrapped it. Eamon watched the pale face as the hands moved. As the paper came away, the green eyes lit in surprise.

Eamon's time binding books had been enough to tell him that Lord Ashway's library was formidable indeed. Among the tall collections of tomes and dust-encrusted volumes, he had found three that he felt might be of interest to Cathair. One had been a beautifully bound, golden-leafed edition of the collected works of the River playwright, renowned for his great tragedies. The second was a slim collection of notes on the terrain around Dunthruik and its suitability for growing various crops. The third – of which he had chosen the finer of the two copies in the library – bore no title. As Cathair's eyes scanned the dark cover, Eamon spoke.

"'And in the tide of later days these words shall live, and rend him praise'," he recited. Cathair looked up, stunned, and Eamon smiled. "Alas, Lord Cathair! My taste for poetry is not of your doing, but my discovery of this poem is." He did not feel it necessary to mention that he had only read the opening page, or that he had made a special effort to memorize the couplet for Cathair's sake. "I thank you for that also."

Cathair nodded, seemingly torn between rage at Eamon's audacity in recital, and delight that he now held three volumes from Ashway's coveted library. Eamon waited. Given some of the doubts cast over its author, choosing the Edelred Cycle for the third book had been a bold move, but his luck seemed to have held.

Suddenly Cathair looked up. "Lord Goodman," he said, "these are very thoughtful gifts, for which I thank you. I will deposit them in my library right away, and I would relish the opportunity to show you my own Ravensill collection."

"Thank you, Lord Cathair," Eamon answered, with a touch of misgiving. "I would be delighted."

Cathair gestured for Eamon to follow him into the grand house.

The hallway was as grand as the house's brightly painted exterior would suggest. Paintings lined its walls and marble cases led off into bright stairwells.

Cathair stepped smartly across the hall. As he did so Eamon heard the bounding of clawed paws rattling over the floor. Cathair's dogs came charging into the hallway, yapping with delight. They leapt at their master, licking his hands and running round him endlessly, their tails striking at his legs. Cathair answered them with rough, but kindly, words.

Then the dogs spotted Eamon. They immediately charged at him, though they did not leap or jump. One of them began a low growl. As Eamon drew his hands close to himself so as to disabuse the dogs of any tempting targets, they followed the ring he bore with bright eyes. Cathair must have noted it too, for he laughed.

"Perhaps there is treacherous blood in you, Lord Goodman?"

Eamon's heart stopped. He glanced at the ring in alarm.

"Was Lord Ashway a traitor?" he breathed, his surprise genuine.

Cathair did not answer. Perhaps in his delight in baiting, he had spoken more than he meant to say. There was a long silence, broken when Cathair whistled softly. The dogs trotted obediently to his heels, though one still cast dark looks back at Eamon.

"Lord Ashway's mind was broken," Cathair said at last. "He

pressed too near, too hard." Eamon looked up; there seemed to be bitter and sorrowful notes in the Hand's voice.

"He did so against your wishes?"

"He was reckless and foolish," Cathair exploded wrathfully, "and he knew – *he knew* – the Master's will for the snake – Lord Arlaith was explicit on the matter. But no! Ashway was always too fond of his own vanity. He pressed too hard and it broke him. And when his mind was broken he displayed himself to the whole city, the gibbering mouthpiece of the Serpent's whoring brood!" Cathair spat the words out with utter hatred. When he paused he was breathing heavily, almost with grief.

Eamon blinked hard, barely comprehending what he heard.

Cathair spoke again, his voice quieter. "Ashway brought his madness on himself," he said. "He was removed – and you or I can be removed as easily, Goodman. Never forget that." Cathair suddenly fell silent and a smile returned to his lips. "Ah, here we are."

They stood before a tall door. Its handles were fashioned like ravens, their wings unfurled and talons outstretched. As Cathair opened the doors, Eamon felt a rush of moving air.

A long room met them. It was easily twice the size of the room where he worked in the East Quarter, and taller too. Every wall was filled with shelves and every wide shelf was crammed with books. The room was flooded with light, which emanated from the arched window that filled the opposite wall.

The dogs trotted in and settled on a large rug in the centre of the floor. The rug showed an enormous raven with a snake caught up in its beak.

"Welcome, Lord Goodman, to one of my many libraries!" Cathair's voice echoed. "This home being somewhat of a retreat, I keep material here that is more for my delectation than my edification. I am sure that you will understand that."

"Of course," Eamon answered, wondering with dread what kind of volumes were on the shelves. Even though the cloak of a

Hand lay on his shoulders and the signet of a quarter on his hand, Eamon's blood curdled before Cathair in all his chilling eloquence.

"On that side of the room I keep my collections of famous (and infamous) authors, in chronological order, of course," Cathair said, striding over to one of the bookcases. "I find it helpful to get inside the writer's thought, so to speak, to know what came before him, and what after." He leaned against one of the shelves and smiled broadly. "Tell me, Lord Goodman: do you know where the River Poet stands in the long string of his fellows?"

"He is contemporary with Terrol," Eamon answered quietly.

"Very good!" For a moment Eamon had a disturbing picture of Cathair as a master in a village schoolroom. He shuddered it away.

The Hand moved across the room and set the book into one of the shelves, between two much smaller ones. It seemed untidy to Eamon, but he supposed that was the fault of chronological order. Cathair moved back to his desk to pick up the other two books.

"This geographical volume will be a little harder to place," he said, stepping over to Eamon with a smile, "and I shall have to think on it. Its fellow proves easier to master. I wonder, Lord Goodman, if you would mind putting this up for me?" He held the Edelred Cycle out towards Eamon.

"Where would you have it, Lord Cathair?"

"The second case, Lord Goodman, eighth shelf up, on the left-hand side." Cathair busied himself with finding a place for the slimmest volume as Eamon stepped carefully over to the case, feeling oddly watched by both Cathair and his dogs.

Reaching the second case, he counted to the shelf in question. He had to make use of a nearby stool to reach it, and climbed up at the left-hand side. There, as he reached out to place the book, he stopped dead.

Cathair had been very literal in his description of where the book had to go: at the end of the long line of volumes, supporting them where they did not fill the shelf, was a tall, semi-cylindrical glass jar. Inside the jar was a stuffed, dismembered hand.

The limb had been set with its fingers stretched upwards, and its palm faced the books. Eamon glanced along the shelf and saw that a second hand stood at the other end. Grisly guardians of Cathair's library, the hands held the books steadily between them. Eamon stared.

Suddenly he became aware that Cathair stood below him. The Hand watched him.

"Ah yes! My latest amusements," Cathair said, his voice all smiles. "They're such lovely bookends, don't you think, Lord Goodman? Terribly *handy*."

Eamon steadied himself against the shelf.

"You know," Cathair mused, "it is most appropriate. Your ward was held for knowledge, and now he holds it for me."

The blood drained from Eamon's face. Horror and rage touched his heart.

Mathaiah's hands.

He moved the jar aside, making room so that he could place the book. His fingers touched the glass, just a tiny space away from the limb that was bound inside. How often had that hand strengthened him? How often had it expressed joy or grief or forgiveness?

The book was in place. He turned and stepped down. He met Cathair's gaze. The Hand watched him with a deceptive smile; Eamon knew he was being tested. He forced a smile of his own.

"I am glad that he is of some use at last, Lord Cathair," he said. "He always was a bit of a handful. You chose well in filling his."

"I am so glad that you approve," Cathair answered cheerfully. "He, of course, was not keen to part with them, but he had no further use for them." The nonchalant smile grew. "He screamed a good deal – seemed to think that his Serpent would save him!" Cathair laughed scornfully. "Mr Grahaven learnt well that night who is Master of the River Realm. I have other mementos of him, of course; he was a snake that rendered me particular satisfaction. But it would not do to keep all of him in the same place."

Eamon felt a dagger twist deep inside him. Mathaiah's eyes – what had Cathair done with them?

"He was shown great kindness if he did not see the end," Eamon answered quietly.

"He did not need to *see* it; his sense was sharp enough." Delight thrilled Cathair's voice. "But I am forgetting myself in all these pleasantries. You came for wine, Lord Goodman, and wine you shall have!"

Cathair led the way from the room. The dogs leapt instantly to his heels, snapping at each other. Eamon followed, steeling his heart. He had to bury his shock and grief. He *had* to.

They reached the steps. Sunlight touched Eamon's face. He drank it in, willing it to douse the grief that newly burned in him.

In the courtyard nothing had changed. Anderas waited patiently to the side and watched the doorway to Cathair's estate.

Cathair spread his arms wide and drew a deep breath. "Ah, the 'rolling hills and rolling winds that plough the furrows of the sea'!" He smiled. "You have brought a cart to take back your wines, I trust?"

"Yes," Eamon answered, and gestured to the edge of the courtyard where Anderas and the driver waited. His heart was heavy but he kept his nerve. "I will not rob you of an undue amount."

"I think four large casks would be sufficient for your needs."

"And would three hundred crowns be sufficient to cover your expense?" Eamon asked. Slater had previously advised him that a large cask would cost up to eighty crowns. It was more money that a Gauntlet officer would earn in six months.

"For you, Lord Goodman, a total of two hundred would be ample," Cathair replied genteelly. "I shall have them brought to you at once." The Hand called across to Febian. "Lord Febian, direct three casks of Raven Avol and one Passa to Lord Goodman's entourage."

Febian was in the midst of counting the number of casks on a wagon. To judge by the look on his face, the interruption made him lose count. "Yes, Lord Cathair."

At his command, several of the servants re-routed from the line to roll casks towards his cart. As one lifted the first cask onto the cart, he stumbled, partially losing his grip. Anderas stepped round and steadied the cask while the servant got his grip again.

"That is Captain Anderas, is it not?" Cathair asked.

A note of alarm ran through Eamon.

"Yes."

Anderas stepped back again, allowing the grateful servant to continue with his task.

"Does he often make a fool of himself, stooping to a servant's work?" Cathair's voice was filled with distaste. Eamon struggled to keep his own voice calm.

"He does not stoop, Lord Cathair. He is an exemplary and well-loved officer."

"He is dear to you, isn't he?" Cathair's voice was airy, light, insubstantial – but Eamon knew it signalled Cathair at his most dangerous.

"He is the captain of my quarter and a servant of the Master," Eamon answered.

"It is good to have men whom we are close to," Cathair continued smoothly. "They make our burdens the less. But when they are gone… Ah! We become men hewn by grief. Perhaps, Lord Goodman, you understand my meaning?"

Eamon's heart swelled with fear and rage. Would the Raven dare to strike at Anderas, a man sworn to the Master, just to injure him? *Courage and peace, Eamon.*

The Hand's pale face smiled, unperturbed. Eamon forced himself to return that smile.

"Of course, Lord Cathair."

"It has been a real pleasure to see you this morning, Lord Goodman. I would invite you to dine with me, but I am afraid that I have very few victuals to offer. I am, as you likely know, returning to the city later today."

"I have some business to attend to in any case," Eamon answered.

"I will send payment to you in the West Quarter this evening."

The Hand answered him with a mocking nod of his head. "Most kind. I trust that you will be present at tomorrow's swearing?"

"Yes. Captain Waite was kind enough to invite me."

"That rare man reads my every thought!" Cathair said, sounding pleased. "It will be a pleasure to see you again so soon, Lord Goodman. Have a very pleasant journey back to the city."

"Thank you, Lord Cathair."

With a steadiness that betrayed the rage burning inside him, Eamon returned to where Anderas and the driver awaited him. The captain bowed.

"Are we ready to depart, my lord?"

"Yes." Eamon strained to keep his composure.

He mounted quickly and led the way past the line of heaving servants and on through the gates. Anderas rode silently by him. The cart trundled heavily behind them. Eamon pushed his steed far ahead of it. He needed air, he needed to breathe – but every breath was laboured.

It wasn't until they reached the cover of the shallow hills, and Cathair and his mansion of horrors were far behind, that Eamon dared to draw breath. It shuddered out of him.

"Lord Goodman?"

Eamon was silent. He was glad that the driver was far behind. He covered his face with his hand.

Cathair had baited him: the green-eyed Hand was a master and knew how to torture without ever once setting an instrument against Eamon's body. All the Hand need do was bide his time and trade in suffering and treachery against those whom Eamon loved, knowing full well that the Hand over the East Quarter could do nothing but approve and bow to that will as though it were his own. It was for this that Cathair would be there to watch and gloat over the West Quarter cadets as they were sworn in, revelling as Eamon was forced to watch and take no action to stop it. It was to keep that grim hold over him that Cathair had threatened him, using Anderas. Eamon knew it, and knew that that, too, could betray him.

One thing more he knew.

A sob welled inside him. He did not hold it back. The city loomed ahead, great columns of smoke billowing high on his left – more had been fed to the pyres that morning. A cool sea wind drove through him and he shuddered. His horse made a disconcerted noise as he wept.

"Lord Goodman –"

"He killed Mathaiah."

"He cannot strike you, Lord Goodman."

"He would not withhold from killing men so as to strike at me." He was but a plaything in the raven's talons. His anger told him that a woman he had once loved had laid him in their reach.

Anderas matched his gaze. "Lord Goodman," he said, quietly and boldly, "call it folly if you will, but I do not fear for my life while it is in your service."

Eamon looked up. Anderas's face was calm and he spoke with earnest encouragement. "Have courage, my lord. Do not be afraid."

The words touched Eamon's heart – how often he had clung to them for comfort! Now it was not the calm, gentle voice that had tempered him in times of trouble and despair who spoke them to him; it was Anderas. It seemed to Eamon then that the kindly voice that had so often called him on to courage had but chosen another way to speak.

The captain nodded to him. Slowly, Eamon took better hold of his reins and turned his eyes back to the city.

CHAPTER XIX

Slater seemed pleased with the wine, greeting it with contented nodding. Eamon watched as servants from his household unloaded it from the cart and hauled it to the kitchens. Preparations for the following night's dinner were going well and Eamon knew that the servants worked hard towards it; their effort was etched across their faces in sweat and colour.

As he passed through the halls that evening, the men and women of his household still bowed to him, but they no longer fled. Some even spoke to him, and their quiet "good evenings" encouraged him.

He retired early to bed. As he lay among the blankets and covers, his mind returned to Cathair's words – to the man's library, to the eighth shelf…

He suppressed the grisly image as best he could. He had just been recovering himself and his ability to do what Hughan had entrusted to him to do. It angered and shamed him, but as he lay there, tears welled in his eyes once more.

What he must think of you, Eben's son! The voice swept uninvited through his thought, startling him in its ferocity. *What they must all think of you! They think you weak! They will not serve a man who cries like a child for a lost plaything.*

Eamon turned away. Though they ground at him relentlessly he knew that there was no truth to the words. Captain Anderas bore him fierce loyalty. Eamon knew that it was because of that loyalty that the captain served him. Indeed, Anderas had put his life in danger in that service, and would likely do so again. As Eamon pondered this the depth and trust of it terrified him: why would a man do such a thing? Yet Anderas was not the only one. Men throughout the quarter were beginning to show him warmth and respect. Why would they bind themselves in service to a weeping Hand?

Eamon, you are the King's Hand. The words passed gently through his heart. *Through you and what you do, they glimpse another.*

Eamon gazed across at the window and let the pale starlight fill all his thought. How terrifying it was to receive the service and devotion of another. Who was he to receive such love and loyalty from Anderas, from the college, from the servants in his household? For only love could describe what these men and women showed him. It encompassed everything that he had seen in Anderas's eyes while he had wept on the road from Ravensill, or in Mathaiah's when they had seen each other the final time. He had seen similar looks in the eyes of many. It was for that reason that Cathair's small smiles and deceptive words struck fear into him. It was so easy for a Hand to reach out and crush any one of them.

The starlight played through the casement. As he watched it he realized another in whom he had seen that loving look – he had seen it in the eyes of the King. He had seen it when they had first met and Hughan had welcomed him – a Gauntlet officer – into the Hidden Hall and into his service, despite the distrust of others. He had seen such a look fiercely stirred when he had been accused of treachery, and he had seen it when the King had been compassionate towards him in his suffering. He had never seen Hughan look on anyone without that same look.

How could he bear it? How could Hughan bear to love so many? How could he live without fearing for them?

Did Hughan fear for him?

The thought stilled him. The King might fear for him because he loved him, but with that love came trust. How many times had Hughan spoken encouragement to him and forgiven his faults, strengthened him and helped him back to face his own troubles? The King's love overcame Eamon's own fears: in loving Eamon fearlessly, Hughan strengthened him.

Anderas also loved him, fearlessly and unrepentantly. Eamon had recognized it from the first, and understood at last that that was how the captain reminded him of the King.

A breeze moved through the room. Eamon breathed deep of it. His tears diminished. Being fearless was rare in Dunthruik, but it was a powerful tool. If he could do rightly, as the King would do, and love with his whole heart, and do both fearlessly... what could withstand him?

Mathaiah had done just that.

Your ward was broken, Eben's son!

"No." Eamon shook his head with a quiet laugh. Mathaiah had not been broken – he had been fearless in his love and service. "He was a King's man and, to the hour of his death, the King's grace was with him."

He had not spoken loudly but the room filled with his voice. If so much as a mouse had heard him speak, then he was lost – a realization that stunned him to silence and demanded that he return in thrall to the halls of his grief.

Do not bandy words with me, Eben's son. Do not prattle witlessly on things that you do not and cannot ever understand.

"But I do understand them."

And the voice was gone.

In the silence that remained, Eamon listened to the rustle of branches in the night breeze. He watched the starlit window until he fell asleep.

"Will there be anything else, Lord Goodman?"

It was the morning of the twentieth. Eamon had risen early, refreshed, and stood by his window wrapped in his cloak. He watched the city awaken, the sun's palette painting the colours of a new day into the city's stones and streets. He saw the tall towers of the palace, and had almost heard the distant running of the waves and cries of the seafarers as another ship came to port. He imagined its mast like a spindle, woven round with a bright white sail, shuddering as the ship met its moorings. He had seen the first ensigns leave the college and the last return from their night patrols.

Eamon looked up from where he carefully halved a western star fruit. "No, thank you, Mr Slater. Is everything in order for this evening?"

"Yes, my lord."

"Good."

"My lord, Captain Anderas is waiting for you in the entrance hall. He asked me to let you know."

Eamon glanced up from the unruly fruit. "Did he say anything else?"

"That you had made arrangements for this meeting yesterday." Pallor touched Slater's face. "My lord, should I have sent him away –?"

"Of course not!" Eamon laughed gently. "Slater, you fear me too much. You are performing your duty, and so is he."

"Yes, my lord." Slater did not look overly convinced.

"You may tell Captain Anderas that he has missed breakfast, that he shall rue that heartily, and that I shall be with him shortly." Eamon set down his knife and began working segments out of the fruit. "Have you breakfasted this morning, Slater?"

"No, my lord."

"Be certain to do so: you have a long day ahead of you."

"Yes, my lord." Slater bowed low and left. Quietly, Eamon finished his breakfast.

Anderas was indeed waiting for him in the entrance hall. As Eamon entered he saw the captain standing in the centre of the circular space, his hands folded behind his back and his head tilted back as he admired the ceiling intently.

Eamon stepped beside the captain and looked up.

"Good morning, Lord Goodman."

"Good morning, captain."

"You see the style of work there, my lord?" Anderas pointed up at a trailing leaf motif that bordered the ceiling's rim – the painted vine that ran around the whole hallway, hemming in skies filled with flocking birds. "It's much later in style than the building itself; very much in keeping with early Dunthruik. I imagine that the original was painted over, whatever it was."

"Is that today's historical oddity?"

"Yes, my lord. And are you well?"

"Yes."

Anderas smiled. "I am glad. You have a little practice to do, my lord."

"I've already eaten breakfast," Eamon told him.

"Even fruit?"

"Even fruit."

"Then that was a foolish move on your part, my lord," Anderas told him, "for I cannot renege on my promise to teach you to ride."

"No?"

"No.

"I condone your nobility."

"And I your folly. You will have to ride on a full stomach."

"And you, captain, will have to endure the consequences of that sore trial."

"I consider myself well equal to the task."

Eamon laughed. "Very well, captain! We shall put your courage to the test."

Anderas led the way to the stables at the side of the Handquarters. They passed Lord Heathlode. The Hand bowed low.

"Good morning, Lord Goodman; Captain Anderas."

"Good morning," Eamon answered, offering him a smile. To his delight, the Hand returned it. He had never thought that he would love such a gesture, but the smile was not forced nor duplicitous – it was a smile of genuine greeting.

"Enjoy your ride, my lord," Heathlode added as he passed on.

"Thank you."

The Handquarters were provisioned with fine stables and plenty of horses to serve the household's every need. There were packhorses and palfreys, horses accustomed to swift riding and chargers for the thick of war. All were impeccably kept, and the stables sounded with the signs and calls of stablehands as they duly fed and served the beasts.

Two horses – saddled, bridled, and attended – awaited them. One was Anderas's own, given to him by Ashway on his promotion. Eamon did not think that the horse presented to him was the same as he had ridden to Ravensill. Many of the horses were tawny or greys, and as Eamon approached the well-tended grey that was offered to him, he thought of the handsome and intelligent beast that had carried him to Hughan. He wondered if this new horse would be as indulgent of his lack of skill.

He mounted swiftly, and took hold of the reins. The horse shuffled its weight, adjusting, then trotted forward a few steps. Eamon tugged it back a little as Anderas came up beside him.

"Are you set, Lord Goodman?"

"Yes," Eamon answered. He felt nervous in the saddle and wondered whether his own preoccupation with not being a terribly able rider was indeed the root of the problem. He saw the ease with which Anderas caught up the reins to urge his steed on, then glanced self-consciously at his own hands and reins. Setting gentle pressure to the horse's flanks, he obtained a few forward steps.

"You have to be confident, my lord," Anderas told him. "And you have to trust the horse."

"And it me, I don't doubt."

"You know more about this than you like to think."

The horse snorted heavily. Eamon looked at the captain. "I'm not so sure."

They went to the North Gate, the horses' hooves clattering crisply on the cobbles. There was some rideable ground beyond the North Gate, just before it reached the hills. It was towards this part of Dunthruik's plain that Anderas directed them.

"The knights use the fields nearby to exercise their chargers," Anderas explained, "and the college sometimes brings officers out this far. Often the riding field does as well, but there's nothing like real turf. How is your gallop, Lord Goodman?"

"More poor than middling," Eamon confessed.

"That would not serve you well on a field of battle."

"It has not hindered me thus far."

"Then you have not had to ride in a battle thus far. But if one day you do, you will be grateful that we had this conversation." Anderas grinned, and for a moment Eamon imagined how the cadets and ensigns must look up to this man; he was utterly at ease in service and authority. "Apart from that, Lord Goodman, there is nothing like riding this plain."

Anderas urged his horse forward – it seemed but a moment before the captain whirled away across the churning turf. Eamon laughed, delighted by the sight, and followed him.

It was the second hour when they re-entered the city. As they trotted through onto Coronet Rise, Eamon still felt the exhilaration of wind rushing through his hair and the powerful rhythm of the horse as it beat across the tumbled plain. Drawing the horse back into a canter and then a trot had been difficult, but Anderas had aided him by calling out instructions and bringing his own horse up beside and slowing it.

"What did you make of that, my lord?" Anderas asked. The guards at the gate bowed low as they passed.

"It is easier than I remembered it."

"That bodes well for tomorrow."

The sound of cobbles filled Eamon's hearing as they passed down the road, and the smell of fresh bread permeated the air. There were carts filled at last with grain, and while its price was not low, it was less than it had been of late. A group of soldiers from the college passed by, led by Lieutenant Scott. The group saluted.

"Good morning, Lord Goodman!" Scott called.

"And to you, gentlemen."

Eamon turned his horse towards the Ashen when a sudden noise reached him. It was like the sound of pelting rain or rushing water striking hard for about ten seconds, followed by a terrible silence.

He looked across at Anderas.

"I do not know, my lord –"

Then the screaming started.

Eamon did not pause to think. He dug his heels into his horse's flanks and commanded it forward. The horse leapt into action, charging down the streets of Dunthruik as easily as it had moved across the plain. He yelled at those in the streets to clear his way, and they did. Maybe they followed him, maybe they fled – he did not know, for he neither saw nor heard. All he saw was the quarter skyline littered with dust and debris; all he heard were the cries buried in the labyrinthine streets. He followed them both.

Suddenly he broke clear of the narrow roads and raced up a cobbled incline. A small courtyard opened up before him, the air choked with smoke and wails. Pulling back sharply on the reins he halted his horse and stared.

The yard was hemmed with tall buildings, each in various states of disrepair. Timbers showed through threadbare stonework, abandoned beams jutted out through walls to where other rooms had once been, and windows gazed down like eyeless faces, weeping fissures into the walls.

The ring of buildings round the courtyard was broken: one of them lay in a mass of crushing stone and splintered wood, its rocky entrails spilling out into the gorged, broken square. From within and without the screaming came. The building had collapsed and now its dying breaths filled the lungs of those who lived and died about it. Frail figures were caught among the wreckage, some at the edges trying to pull free, others lying still, their faces palled with dust.

"Captain!" Eamon yelled, for he knew that Anderas would be there. He had to shout to be heard over the terrible wails, and the deathly silence between them. "Get as many Gauntlet and militia as you can find. Bring them here."

Anderas wheeled his steed and careered through the narrow streets. Eamon dismounted, hastily threw the reins about a nearby post, and waded into the sea of dust.

He ran up to the nearest group of people – men and women wretchedly tugging their fellows from the edge. They did not see him at first.

"How many are in there?" he asked.

"We don't know – at least the Turrens," answered a young man. He turned. Recognizing to whom he spoke, his face grew paler than the ashen dust that covered him. "My lord –"

"You have strong arms?"

Trembling, the young man nodded. "Yes, my lord."

"Then come with me." Eamon turned to another man who stood nearby. "Captain Anderas is coming with aid. When he does, tell him to set them to recovering the wounded."

"Yes, lord." The man tried to bow, but coughed from the dust.

Eamon swept across to the rubble. Cries for help came from within the writhing beast of stone and its cutting jaws of wood. The man he had called to help hung back.

The voices that called for help were farther in, and Eamon knew that he was going to have to climb over the rubble to reach them. It looked as though the higher floors of the buildings had come down but that the lowest had mostly – and miraculously – withstood the impact.

Eamon laid his foot onto the nearest edge of stone and tested it with his weight: not entirely stable, but it held. He looked back at the young man – who gaped. There was no mistaking that the Hand who had served a two-crown dinner now meant to brave the rubble of a fallen building.

"Will you follow me?"

The young man looked once at the rocking stone, then back at Eamon. Their gazes met. A change came across the dark eyes.

"Yes, my lord."

Reaching out, Eamon stepped onto the stone, setting first one foot and then another on the treacherous floorway.

Picking a path across it was like choosing between a noose and high water: in places the ruins dropped into seemingly cavernous pits; in others what were once walls now made impassable barriers of stone. The debris shifted. The wooden beams were cracked and torn, jutting from their pools of stone like the snapped trunks of a desecrated forest.

Eamon made his way carefully around them, minding pitfalls and scrabbling over the collapsing paths, struggling with every step not to lose his balance and fall into one of the pits.

The cries grew louder, but as Eamon halted to take his bearings, they stopped. He froze; behind him his companion followed with uncertain steps. Back in the square, he heard slowing hooves. Anderas had returned, and with the captain he heard the crisp sound of Gauntlet officers giving orders. But he could no longer hear the voice that he had been following.

He searched the blasted landscape of stone, feeling its eerie quiet. His heart beat fast. He wiped at his face; his gloves were scuffed from where he had battled with the walls.

"Help is here," he shouted, "but you must keep calling." He was met with a disquieting silence. "Can you hear me?"

"Uncle?" The quailing voice was young. His heart went out to it.

"My name is Eamon," he answered, not caring for the panicked look that tore across the face of the young man by him. "I have come to help you. Are you alone?"

"No sir, m-my cousin is here. She's hurt…"

"Are you?"

The voice faltered. "I… I don't know."

"What's your name?"

"E-e-ellen."

"Ellen, I need you to keep speaking to me so that I can find you." Eamon steadied himself as stones slipped away from beneath his feet. "Can you describe where you are?"

"Yes," the girl answered, pausing now and then to cough. Eamon charted the stones, following her voice. "I'm in a kind of w-w-well, between two very t-t-tall walls. They fell in from the sides –" A touch of panic reached her voice.

"Ellen, are there any tall beams near you?" Eamon had followed her voice to where the stones and walls seemed to have formed a ditch marked by two heavy, jutting timbers. It was dark below and the shifting shafts of light were marred by dust as it struggled to settle.

"Y-y-yes; t-t-two of them."

"I think I am very near you, Ellen," Eamon spoke firmly but gently, and stepped carefully up to the ledge of the hollow fall, taking hold of one of the beams to steady himself. "Can you see light from where you are?"

"There's light in a hole above me, sir."

He leaned out over the hole before him. "Can you see me?"

There was a long pause. Eamon waited.

"Y-y-yes! I can s-s-ee you!"

Eamon looked over his shoulder to where the young man was picking his way across the stones and beams towards him. What seemed like miles away he saw Anderas, Lieutenant Scott, and a large group of Gauntlet and militia clearing away the initial rubble in the search for survivors. Some of the soldiers dealt with the dead while others moved the injured away from the clinging dust.

He looked back down the hole. "Ellen, can you stand where I can see you?"

He heard shuffling, and stones scrabbling and moving, and became painfully aware of how fragile the chamber had to be. It was a miracle that the walls had fallen as they did – it had saved the girl and her cousin, keeping the force of the rest of the collapse from them. "Do it carefully, Ellen!"

At last a figure came into view below. He realized that the hole was probably a little less than twice his height in depth.

"Can your cousin move, Ellen?"

The girl below him looked young, though she was so gaunt and straggly that he could not guess her age. She was plastered with dust and there was a long, deep cut along the side of her face.

"No sir," the girl stammered. "She isn't m-m-moving –"

"Ellen, I want you to stay there while I come down." Eamon

straightened up, found his balance, and quickly undid the cloak at his shoulders.

"Strong-arm!" he called. The young man struggled to his side.

"M-m-my lord?" he stammered.

"Hold on to this." Eamon drew the cloak out into a long, thick line and pressed one corner into the youth's hands. The other end he wrapped round his own hand, weaving it about his wrist and fingers.

The young man looked so surprised that it seemed a wonder he did not fall into the hole. "Yes, my lord."

"Take a firm footing, Strong-arm."

The young man broadened his stance. Eamon peered once more into the hole, then turned his back towards it and set his feet carefully against the stones. Then, entrusting his weight entirely to the young man, he edged his way into the pit. The stones scrabbled underfoot, darting from him almost as soon as he stepped on them, but he managed to work his way down.

His feet touched the ground. His breathing pounded in his ears. Stones fell in over him, and he sneezed in the dust as they struck his head and shoulders. When his eyes cleared, he turned to the girl. She darted forward and her frail, bleeding hands seized hold of his. She trembled.

"Ellen," he said, bowing to move beneath the debris, "where is your cousin?"

The girl jerked him towards the murky depths of the shallow cave. Eamon called towards the daylight. "Strong-arm!"

"My lord?" The young man's voice seemed faint, as though from a great distance.

"Stay there. And don't fall in."

Eamon looked back at the quivering girl. The stones and timbers around them boomed as though under strain.

He pressed her hand. "Show me to your cousin."

She tugged him on into the hole. Though it was early morning it seemed some strange and unnatural night within the building's entrails. Eamon made out the shapes of objects – perhaps a table, or what remained of one – under the dust. He had to duck to follow the girl.

At last she stopped and dropped down to her knees beside a figure in the dust. Eamon crouched down beside her.

The girl's cousin was a young woman. Her eyes were still. She was not moving.

The little girl pressed against Eamon's side. "Will she be –?"

"I don't know." It was too dark and he knew too little of the surgeon's trade to answer her.

He laid his face by the still woman's. The faintest trace of breath touched his cheek. He did not know what could be done, but knew that the little girl could not stay there.

"Ellen," he said, "you're going to go up." The child glanced nervously at her cousin and gripped his hand. "I'm going to see if I can help your cousin. Will you go?"

At last, the girl nodded silently.

Eamon took her back to the opening. She spluttered as they came to a stop at the dusty bottom.

"Strong-arm!"

"My lord?"

"Keep good hold of the cloak." Eamon turned to the girl. "You need to keep good hold, too."

"Why did he call you 'lord'?" the girl whispered. Eamon was grieved to hear new fear creep into her voice.

"Because he doesn't know my name," he answered gently. "Have courage, and hold on."

The girl nodded again and fixed the cloak in her hand. Eamon lifted her high above him, as though she were a feather, and supported her as she sought a foothold in the wall.

"Can you manage, Ellen?"

"Yes, sir."

He held her up as long as he could, stretching out his arms and fingers while the young man, his feet dug firmly into the broken walls, pulled hard on the cloak. Step by scrabbled step, the girl reached the lip of the hole and staggered against the young man's leg. He seemed to know her; he gathered her to him with words of encouragement.

"Tell Captain Anderas to send some men," Eamon called up. "There is another survivor, but she may be incapacitated. I will try to bring her to safety."

"Yes, my lord."

"See this girl safely back to the others."

The young man bound the cloak to a beam and then drew the girl up to her feet. As he led her away across the tumbled building, Eamon turned and worked his way back into the tunnel.

He reached the young woman's side and wondered just how he could help her. The girl's cousin was laid out as though she had been knocked to the ground, maybe by one of the beams that crossed the hole, and there was an ugly wound across the far side of her head. Eamon was grateful that Ellen had not seen it. The woman still drew breath faintly, but Eamon wondered if, as time passed, it grew fainter still. His eyes grew more and more accustomed to the dark and he saw that there was blood clogged in the dust about her. He took her hand, saw no reaction, and tried calling her. But the pale lids remained closed.

Overhead the beams boomed ominously. He heard the Gauntlet working their way through the debris. How many others were there, trapped or dead, in grottoes of mildewed stone? Looking back at the face before him, he decided that this woman would not remain among that number.

You are a Hand: the dead mean nothing to you. The voice was fierce but Eamon laughed when it reached him.

"I am the First Knight," he answered, "and I am the King's Hand; I tell you that this woman will live."

You cannot command it, son of Eben.

Eamon took the woman's hand and pressed the cold fingers in his.

"In the King's name I ask it," he said, "that this woman may live to see him walk these streets in triumph."

The flare of light was so great that he had to close his eyes. There was no burning in hand or brow as when the throned's mark spoke – just light, light, light, filling his hands and fingers and obliterating the grimy shadows of the fallen walls. It moved around the young woman. He watched it with amazement as it washed about her, and marvelled at the sense of peace that it brought with it.

The light slowly faded and the air hung still. Eamon was silent. Then he leaned down.

"Wake up," he said quietly.

He watched as she drew a deep breath and her eyes slowly opened. Like her cousin's, they were a deep, dark brown, and they searched the air before turning and seeing him.

"I'm alive?" she whispered.

"Yes," Eamon answered, "and you are going to live, and live long." She gazed at him in wonder. "Who are you?"

"My name is Eamon. I was passing when the building collapsed. I came to help." The woman nodded, and then suddenly she looked to her side. Seeing nothing there she sat up suddenly.

"Ellen!" she cried. Eamon reached out to keep her head from hitting the low beams as she started.

"She's already out, and safe," he told her, "and you will be too."

The woman ducked her head down, and as she did so saw the small pool of blood on the ground. She touched her head and hair, then looked at Eamon, completely bewildered. He pressed her hand.

"You weren't badly cut. Come with me."

Together they went from the hollow, half crawling and half standing, until they reached the lip of the deep well. Eamon looked up. He heard the noises of Gauntlet drawing near, and was sure that he heard Lieutenant Scott's voice among them.

"Lieutenant!"

The next moment a face appeared at the top of the ditch; it was Scott's.

"My cloak is tied there. Have your men take firm hold of it."

Scott nodded breathlessly and gestured to his men to take hold. Eamon turned to the young woman. "Hold on to the cloak. I'll help you to climb out." He pressed her hand against the black fabric, then formed a ledge for her feet with his hands. As he did so, she registered the cloak's colour. A startled look passed over her face.

"Ready, lieutenant?" Eamon called.

"Ready, my lord."

The woman gasped. "You're –"

"Climb up," Eamon said gently.

Timidly she set one foot in his hands and he lifted her. Scott reached down to help her from above. Eamon turned his head away as debris scuffed down the face of the ledge.

Soon the woman was out. Eamon paused to cough dust from his lungs. He sneezed ferociously, his eyes stinging.

"My lord!" Scott called down, and with his voice came the cloak again. Eamon took hold of it, set his foot against the crumbling stone, and began to climb.

It was much harder going up than it had been going down, and the creaking, shifting stones and wood sounded more ominous to him than before. He clawed his way back into the daylight. Scott seized his arm and pulled him onto the ledge, where they both staggered as the stones shifted.

"My lord, we should –"

"I am in complete agreement." A couple of ensigns were already escorting the young woman back across the mass of stones. Eamon took his torn, dusty cloak from Scott's cadets. Laughing at how ridiculous the thing looked, he drew it into a long sash over his back and shoulders and tied it firmly. Scott stared at him.

They worked their way back across the debris. Though Eamon called out regularly to check if there were any others trapped who could hear him, no answer came.

When he eventually reached the courtyard floor again he saw that dozens of people from the nearby buildings had flooded out, and were helping the Gauntlet to move the debris. A couple of carts had also appeared, and the rubble was being moved into some of them. Along the far side of the courtyard were two lines of people: in one they lay still and pale on the ground. Eamon counted the dead with a terrible weight in his stomach. Fifteen, probably all from the same, or related, families. In the other group were another dozen people – some shivering with fear, others crying and weeping, others staring into nothing. Anderas was by them and Eamon saw that a Gauntlet surgeon was present, too. It was highly unusual for such a man to treat any who did not belong to the Gauntlet, but Eamon thoroughly approved of what he expected was the captain's initiative.

He walked up to the group of survivors, shaking dust from his hair. None of them saw him at first. When Anderas greeted him, they gaped at him and his bedraggled dress.

"There are three more unaccounted for, my lord." Eamon saw the young man who had first helped him crouching by the woman he had rescued. They spoke together in low voices and stared at him. Ellen was at her cousin's side, holding her and crying. Near them were a couple of older women, both quaking and tearing at their hair in grief, and injured men.

Eamon drew the ragged cloak off his shoulders, shook it once, and stepped across to the trembling women. He wrapped it about them.

"I am sorry that it is so dusty," he apologized, "but I trust it will keep you warm."

The looks upon their faces expressed more than any words could.

Eamon returned to Anderas. "What is the name of this square, captain?"

"Tailor's Turn, my lord."

"I assume that these buildings are on the restoration list?"

Anderas looked at him strangely. "Yes, my lord."

"How long for?" Eamon persisted.

"Buildings in this area have been on the list for years, my lord."

Ferocious anger was building in Eamon's heart. "How many years?"

"At least three."

"And they pay to remain on the list?"

Anderas nodded.

"Continue with the clear-up," Eamon commanded. "See that these people are cared for." He turned for his horse. The beast still stood, unperturbed, among the Gauntlet soldiers who raced back and forth. As he went, Ellen looked up and called after him.

"Thank you, Eamon!"

Silence fell on the crowd, and the doctor, tending to one of the men, looked up in mortal alarm. Ellen seemed completely oblivious to the silence, tucking a tress of thick, matted hair behind one ear as she smiled at him.

The man Eamon called "Strong-arm" came to his feet. "Please, my lord –" he began, a pitiful look on his face.

"All is well, Strong-arm." Eamon looked at the girl and smiled. The faces around him waxed with bewilderment and fear. "You're welcome, Ellen," he said. "You take good care of your cousin."

CHAPTER XX

The doors to the Crown Office glistened in the mid-morning sun. Eamon dismounted at the ornate gates, throwing the reins to a nearby servant. The man at the door bowed low and Eamon, who had not stopped to change his dust-covered clothes, strode inside.

Everywhere he walked men leapt to their feet, struck dumb by his arrival. He spoke to none of them. He searched for one man and would not leave until he found him.

"You," he called to a passing servant.

"My lord," the woman answered, curtseying. As she rose, Eamon started in surprise.

It was Toriana, Alessia's maidservant.

He did not have the wit or time to ask how a servant of Alessia's house found herself there, but her face mollified his anger.

"Where is Mr Rose?"

"In his office, my lord."

Nodding once to her, Eamon surged towards the principal office. The Crown official was at his desk, reading some papers and sipping delicately at wine. Eamon swept into the room, leaving the doorman no time to announce him. In fact, the first that Mr Rose knew of his presence was his shadow as it passed over his desk.

"Mr Rose."

The official's head jerked up, spilling wine over the rim of his goblet.

"Lord Goodman!" he cried, bolting to his feet. "I am so very sorry. I did not know to expect you." As he took in the state of Eamon's dress, his mouth fell open. "My lord —"

"It is customary, Mr Rose, to bow to a Quarter Hand. In this, your servants are better schooled than you, it would appear."

Grey-faced, Rose bowed low. "What service can I offer you, my lord?"

"Offer me?" Eamon laughed sharply. "Offer *me* none. You will give me all the service which I, in the Master's name, command, Mr Rose." The official trembled before him. "Where is the list of building works for the East Quarter?" he demanded.

"Here, my lord." Rose gestured feebly to a tall pile of papers on his desk.

"Where are the quarter architects?"

"In their offices, my lord." Rose watched him nervously.

"Summon the head architect."

Rose edged round his table and leaned cautiously out of his door. The man's voice echoed down the corridors. Not long later he re-entered, followed by a tall man who seemed familiar. As the man entered, he bowed low.

"My lord," Rose told him, "this is Darren Lorentide. He was not here on your last visit. He is the East Quarter's chief architect."

Eamon took in the man and felt a long-forgotten grief rise in his heart. This man could be a brother, cousin, or an uncle to the Lorentide he himself had condemned to be delivered to Cathair for torment and death.

He tried hard to mask his surprise. "Mr Rose, give Mr Lorentide the list of building works."

Rose moved swiftly indeed. Lorentide looked bewildered as the list was given to him.

"Mr Lorentide, to the best of your knowledge, how urgent is reconstruction work in Tailor's Turn?"

Lorentide looked across at Rose, as though for guidance or support, but it was the look of a man whose better judgment had long been servant to another's will.

"Mr Lorentide," Eamon demanded sharply, "are you the head architect in my quarter?"

"Yes, Lord Goodman."

"Then why do you look to Mr Rose? I spoke to you."

Lorentide met his gaze. "The work is desperately urgent, my lord." Seeing the dust on Eamon's robes, he swallowed.

"Mr Lorentide, one of the buildings in the Turn collapsed this morning, taking with it the lives of at least fifteen citizens of this quarter."

Lorentide's face grew ashen, and Rose squirmed in discomfort.

"Yes, my lord," Lorentide said, his voice barely more than a whisper.

"You know of this, Mr Lorentide?"

"We heard of it an hour ago, my lord," Lorentide answered softly. "Mr Rose advised us that the Gauntlet were handling the situation, and that clean-up is not the preserve of the architects."

"What were you working on?"

"The Patagon estate, my lord."

Eamon's hackles rose. The Patagon estate belonged to one of the quarter's high-ranking families of knights. He angrily surmised how the quarter's building list was ordered. "How urgent is that work?"

Lorentide hesitated. "It was requested some time ago, my lord," he began, "and we have been working on it for a while."

"Is it life-threatening?"

"No, my lord. It is a matter of worn façades, and a new gateway."

Eamon glared at Rose. The official's jaw dropped.

"He speaks just to please you, my lord!" Rose blustered.

"No, Mr Rose," Eamon answered fiercely. "His honesty pleases me. His words do not, for they reflect the way that this office, bearing the Master's seal and authority, is managed." His voice grew harder. "What right have you, Mr Rose, to drain the resources of the city?"

Rose blinked hard. "My lord, I never –"

"By withholding the architects and founders and builders from the Turn this morning – as you have done every morning for the last three years since it was added to the list – and by leaving the

Gauntlet to deal with the consequences, you are responsible for a breach in city order. It is a very serious offence, Mr Rose." He looked back to Lorentide. "Mr Lorentide, from now on you will be the master of the reconstruction list. I want it reprioritized so that the buildings in most need of repair – whose damages represent a threat to lives and livelihood – appear at the head of the list. Residents of each building will contribute a percentage of their earnings to that work; the rest of the cost will be fronted by this office and by the city."

Lorentide stared at him, wide-eyed.

"My lord," Rose began, "you cannot –"

Eamon turned slowly to him. "*Cannot*, Mr Rose?"

Rose paled to a shade of yellowish-green. "I would strongly advise you not to go against the city's –" he began.

"I keep my counsel with the Master," Eamon replied. "When you act from this office, Mr Rose, you are a representative of the Master. How many people in this quarter do you think have cursed him because of what you have caused to happen today? The Master will hear about such rumours, and he will know that they spring from your ineptitude. I would be disquieted by such a thought, if I were you." Eamon looked again at Lorentide. "When you have prepared the new list, Mr Lorentide, take a copy of it to Captain Anderas," he said. "Any assistance that can be reasonably rendered by the Gauntlet shall be afforded to you."

"Thank you, Lord Goodman." Lorentide bowed low. Relief flooded his face.

Eamon looked at both men. "To his glory, gentlemen."

"To his glory," they replied.

As dusk fell that evening the Handquarters in the East Quarter filled with light from tall candelabrum, and groups of men decked out in full Gauntlet uniform arrived at the entrance. There, well-dressed servants met them, taking cloaks from those who wished to leave them and marking names on the list of expected attendees.

Eamon greeted each guest in turn, by name, for he had spent much of the afternoon studying the list and was at last finding himself capable of matching names to faces. Some faces he knew, and knew well – others not so well. Many of the lieutenants from the East Quarter came, though Greenwood, who was preparing for his formal installation as college draybant, remained behind. Some of the quarter's new cadets accompanied their more experienced peers. Their eyes were wide at the tall rooms filled with dark wood and brimming with officers. All of the East Quarter's Hands came, each of them refreshed after a late afternoon spar with Eamon in the practice yard. Waite was there, and with him a few of the West Quarter's cadets. Manners was among them.

"It is good to see you, captain." Eamon clasped Waite's hand as they met.

"And you, Lord Goodman." There was a smile to Waite's face and odd strength in his grip.

The guests waited in the main hall while the servants put the finishing touches to the dining room. Slater had been charging about with a very officious look all afternoon, and Eamon was sure that everything would be perfectly in order.

As they waited for the signal that the dining room was ready, Anderas crossed the hall and bowed to Eamon.

"Lord Goodman."

Eamon stepped to one side with him. "Is there any more news?"

The captain rose. "We found three more dead in the rubble this afternoon, my lord. There were some serious injuries among the survivors, but the surgeon was able to set the broken bones and bind the wounds. A detachment came from the Crown Office at about midday, under the head architect's orders to clear the debris and relocate the survivors to a temporary living space."

Eamon felt some relief. "Where were they sent?"

"There are a lot of tunnels and caves under the city, lord," Anderas answered, "made by old tributaries of the River. Some of the grottoes are used for storage, some were converted for the sewers,

315

but there are a couple held by the Crown Office for relocation purposes in times of need." Eamon looked at Anderas in surprise. He had known nothing about such caves.

"How big are they?"

"Ranging from room-size to the size of the Ashen."

"And the survivors have access to food and water?"

"A part of the River still runs through the office's cave."

Eamon nodded. He was about to speak again when a familiar voice assailed his ears:

"Ah, if it isn't the man himself!"

Eamon turned and, for a moment, was stunned by the man who swept across the hall towards him.

"Good evening, Lord Ratbag!"

"Mr Kentigern." Eamon smiled as Ladomer strolled up to him. "You are an unexpected surprise."

"An unpleasant one, to judge by your tone!" Ladomer laughed loudly and slapped Eamon's arm. "I am so sorry that I haven't been to see you since you were assigned here. I certainly meant to, but the Right Hand has kept me somewhat tied to my desk of late."

"Tied?"

"Indeed, one might almost say bound hand and foot. When you are told to send dispatches and orders to the colleges in every region of the River Realm, you have enough work to last you for some considerable time. By the throne! I forgot!" Ladomer grinned and then threw himself into a ridiculously elegant bow before Eamon. "Lord Goodman," he flattered, and rose. "How is it, being Lord of the East Quarter?"

"I hope I will learn to lord it well," Eamon answered.

"And this stony interlocutor is your captain?" Ladomer turned to Anderas, still smiling. "Your fame, Captain Anderas, precedes you," he said, saluting.

"Thank you, Mr Kentigern," Anderas replied. His brow was knit, but Eamon had no time to ponder it. Ladomer turned swiftly back to him.

"He serves you well, does he, Ratbag?"

"Yes," Eamon answered, "to a fault."

"The worth of a bird in the hand, as they say." Ladomer stepped back with a contented sigh. "I hope you've chosen a good menu this time, Lord Goodman – my fare has been rather poor of late!"

A wave of tension ran through Eamon. "I am sure that the choice will be exemplary."

"You didn't choose it?" Ladomer feigned surprise.

"Not in its entirety."

"The parts that make me ill, then, shall be blamed on the delicate tendencies of my stomach and not on your fair self," Ladomer answered with a small smile. "I like to indulge in a little altruism every now and then – as I hear you did this morning."

Eamon blinked hard at him, caught by the change in subject.

"I would hardly call it altruism, Mr Kentigern," he began, but Ladomer stopped him with a brusque wave of his hand.

"It had 'Goodman Altruism' branded all over it in incredibly, stupidly large letters," he answered, and an odd tone crept into his voice. "Half the city knows about it already. The Right Hand could talk of nothing else all day! Given the tally of your deeds of late, he asked me to come to inspect your sanity."

"Lord Goodman –" Anderas began. The captain bristled visibly at Ladomer's manner. Seeing it, Ladomer laughed down his words.

"Ah, captain! I jest, of course. Lord Arlaith actually told me to go and glut myself on some other lord's table this evening."

"I would highly recommend glutting yourself on food, in preference to the table," Eamon answered.

Ladomer's voice suddenly dropped. His face took on a peculiar expression. "And I highly recommend that you cease gorging your bastard idealism all over the city," he spat.

Eamon stared. "Idealism?"

"You're a Quarter Hand, Eamon! A lord of Dunthruik – and you were crawling in the mud and dust! What were you thinking?"

"Of the one I serve," Eamon replied.

There was a moment of silence.

Ladomer laughed acridly. "Ratbag, the Master doesn't care for the bloody faeces living in Tailor's Turn," he said. "Only you do that. What the Master *does* care about is the hierarchy in the Crown Office, which you appear to have rather perniciously abhorred this morning on one of your high-hearted, moral crusades."

Eamon stared at him, aghast. "Ladomer –"

Ladomer hissed: "You would have done better to offer a *ten*-crown dinner, and leave the office well alone. But no – discontent with being a laughing stock, you insisted upon making yourself an embarrassment. Embarrassments, Eamon – much like your idealism – cannot be excused."

Eamon felt the words like blows. How could Ladomer subject him to such an onslaught? His will steeled against the insult. He could not permit his friend to berate him further. "You overstep your bounds, Mr Kentigern. The Master gave me authority over this quarter," Eamon told him firmly. "I am exercising it."

"Exercise a little of your intellect in the process, Goodman!" Ladomer retorted.

There was the briefest pause in which Ladomer's eyes wandered to one side.

"Ah!" he said. "There's Captain Waite. If you'll excuse me, Lord Goodman, I have a message to carry to him."

Eamon felt speechless – but mustered the best response he could. "We shall continue this discourse in private."

Ladomer quirked an eyebrow. "Of course."

He turned and stalked away, arriving swiftly at Waite's side. Eamon watched him go.

"Lord Goodman," said a quiet voice beside him.

Eamon looked across to Anderas. The captain's face was grave. "Captain?"

"My lord, Mr Kentigern has no right to speak to you as he did." The captain's voice trembled with restrained fury.

Eamon frowned at him, barely able to comprehend what he

was saying. Released from Ladomer's attack, he reeled. "Ladomer Kentigern?"

"He treats you as though you were a cadet," Anderas said quietly; "treats you as though you were not the man who brought back an Easter's head from the Serpent's very camp. He treats you as little less than the dirt upon which he walks – and he does it publicly."

"Ladomer and I have known each other for a long time," Eamon answered gently. "He was my lieutenant in Edesfield, and my friend before then."

Anderas's resolve held. "Forgive me, Lord Goodman," he said, "but you are now the Lord of the East Quarter, appointed by the Master, and he is the Right Hand's lieutenant." He fixed Eamon with a deep gaze. "My lord, those days are past."

Eamon gazed at him. As the captain's words sank in he breathed deeply. He heard Ladomer laughing on the other side of the hall. Suddenly that laugh filled him with wariness.

"Lord Goodman."

Slater was at his side, bowing low. "Your table is ready, my lord."

"Thank you, Mr Slater," Eamon answered. "Please set an extra place at the high table for the Right Hand's lieutenant before summoning the guests to their places."

"Of course, my lord."

Not long later they were called to dinner. The broad hall was once again filled with beautifully laid places, each with a name delicately written by it. The cloth on the table was red, and the gold trimming rippled as guests brushed past, seeking their places. Eamon once again made his way to the high table, accompanied by Anderas. Waite was there also, and an extra place had been laid for Ladomer. Eamon made a note to thank Slater for his efficient discretion later.

He remained standing as the guests continued finding their places and filling the room with brilliant uniforms. Each man took his place behind the chair where he would sit. Their eyes turned towards Eamon. Only now he smiled at them, and for a moment, as they looked at him, the cloak on his shoulders did not feel heavy.

It was true that the men all about him served the throned, and true that they wore colours that stood against the King – but they were good men.

Silence fell over the hall. Given what Ladomer had said about how his latest deed was being interpreted in the city, Eamon wondered for a moment whether he should be wary with what he said. His reputation was a shy and slippery thing, and any good that he did seemed to mar it rather than make it brighter. But as he parted his lips to speak, he did not hesitate.

"Gentlemen," he said, "I wish to begin by welcoming you to the East Quarter, and by saying what a pleasure it is to see you all here this evening. Many of you will be wondering why I would ask you to a meal so soon after the one which inaugurated me as the lord of this quarter. It is a question well asked, and deserving of response, though you are intelligent men and I am sure that you will have reached an answer not far from my own.

"I could, of course, say that I enjoy good food, good company, and sharing the bounty of my household with those who serve the Master as unswervingly and faithfully as you each do. I could say that service such as that offered by each and every one of you must be feasted, for it glorifies the Master. I could say these things, and they would be true, but they would not be the whole truth of why we stand here this evening."

He looked across the hall. The men gathered there watched him with interest, caught up by his words, and he saw faces, so recently hostile towards him, now watching him with attention, and in more than a few cases, even with respect.

"The whole truth is in the fact that grace has been rendered to me to serve, even though I passed through a time of darkness. That grace was rendered to me by the Master, and to glorify him I would celebrate it, and this quarter, with you." Ladomer watched him as Eamon took his glass in his hand and raised it high.

"To your service, and his glory!" Eamon called, and the hall echoed it back to him.

As the call died down, the hall was filled with applause from every quarter until Eamon's ears rang with it. Eamon smiled. It wasn't until a bell rang that the gathered guests sat, and Eamon did likewise. As he did so Ladomer, who had been set near him, leaned across to him.

"It would appear that, despite your foibles, the East Quarter is truly for you, Ratbag," he muttered. His eyes were wide, and he shook his head with disbelief.

"You doubted it?"

"Yes, and I had good reason to." Ladomer paused as a servant passed and filled his goblet with wine. "Now I have reason to salute you. His glory, Lord Goodman," he said, raising his goblet.

Slater had made an excellent choice of dishes for the meal: a deep, ruddy soup was served first with warm bread, followed by red meat that was served with a large assortment of vegetables. With these came the warm, earthy wines that Eamon had bought from Cathair; they filled the palate and rested there, enhancing every flavour that passed. These courses were cleared away and followed by enormous platters of various fruits arranged in the shape of a crown. Beyond that there was cheese, veined with deep red-coloured creases, and then cakes laced with honey, accompanied by Cathair's Passa, a golden sweet wine.

Slater had outdone himself. Eamon saw how the household had worked to prepare every detail for him. It touched him deeply.

He spent much of the meal speaking with Waite and Anderas, who had once again been set at his right. Ladomer also joined in the conversation from Eamon's left, adding his observations, to each of which Anderas responded with stone-faced silence and a sip of wine. Eamon was glad when Ladomer was drawn into conversation with Tramist's captain.

When the meal had finished Eamon and his guests removed through to the main hallway, allowing the servants to clear the room unencumbered. Some of the guests gathered there and spoke together for a while.

It was as Eamon was emerging from the hall that he met Manners. The cadet was moving towards the archway that led out into the Ashen. When he saw Eamon, he smiled.

"Mr Manners," Eamon said.

"Lord Goodman." Manners bowed low, and as he rose, Eamon noticed something strange and uncertain about the young man, though he could not tell its nature. There was a short silence, in which the murmuring in the hall and the distant clattering sound of plates could be heard.

"You're being sworn in tomorrow."

Manners nodded. "Yes, my lord."

"Are you ready?" Eamon asked the question kindly, though in his heart he wished that he could deliver to Manners the warning that he had given to Mathaiah on the deck of a holk that had never reached the city, the same warning that Aeryn had given him too late. But the hall was full of watchers, and men stood on every side – he could do nothing. "From tomorrow you shall be Ensign Manners." Eamon offered the young man a smile and, by it, hoped to cover the emptiness in his own heart.

"No, my lord," Manners answered, and he laughed a little. Eamon raised an eyebrow.

"Of course," he said. "*Lieutenant* Manners."

"If the captain doesn't change his mind," Manners answered, and again Eamon saw a strange look to the young man's eye – a kind of steely glimmer. "I am ready, Lord Goodman."

"You're a good man," Eamon told him.

"I hope to be one, my lord," Manners said, and smiled.

Manners and the West Quarter men left early with Waite, who pleaded last-minute preparations for the following day's swearing. Eamon bade farewell to all of them, and as many of his other guests as he could, by name. They thanked him warmly. The only one he did not see leave was Ladomer. Anderas commented on it.

"Perhaps he had some business to attend to," Eamon said.

Anderas, who had remained with him until all others had left, allowed a sceptical look to pass over his face. "No man should leave your hall without your indulgence, nor without thanking you, my lord."

"He is the Right Hand's own lieutenant," Eamon answered, as though that might excuse the behaviour.

"Yes, Lord Goodman." Anderas's voice sounded restrained.

"You mistrust him?"

Anderas did not answer at once. He carefully weighed his reply. "I may not answer your question, my lord, without being frank."

"You may be frank with me, Anderas."

"But, in such matters, not without your leave," Anderas answered. "This is not a policy to which Mr Kentigern holds, and for that reason I mistrust him. My lord, I would urge you to be cautious. You may well have the Master's support, but you will have enemies at the palace; Mr Kentigern, and the Right Hand himself, may be among them."

Eamon looked at the captain in surprise. As much as he wanted to discount it, he knew that Anderas could be right. Ladomer worked for the Right Hand. Unwittingly, his friend could be being worked against him. Or perhaps his friend's words were warnings: warnings of how the other Hands – including Lord Arlaith – viewed him. He did not think that Ladomer would willingly work against him. They had been friends for so long; they had lived through Dunthruik together. It was Ladomer who had encouraged him in those days while he was estranged from Mathaiah, and Ladomer who had brought him to the Gauntlet. It was Ladomer who had always encouraged him not to despair of becoming Right Hand himself.

Eamon shuddered. That ambition had meant so much to him once. Now he reviled it.

Anderas looked at him and Eamon met the gaze. "I cannot know Mr Kentigern's heart, captain," he said, unable to suppress his sorrow. He had known it once.

"No, lord," Anderas replied. "And he cannot pretend familiarity with yours."

CHAPTER XXI

The twenty-first dawned clear and bright, with fading stars that glistened in the pale sky and air so crisp that the crying of the gulls at the port could be heard even in the East Quarter.

Eamon and Captain Anderas went out of the city to ride. Eamon once again envied both Anderas's horsemanship and his ability to cope with the early hours of the morning.

Upon their return to the East Quarter, Anderas announced that he had some Gauntlet business to attend to.

"You remember Lieutenant Greenwood?" he asked.

"Of course."

"He is being promoted to college draybant this morning – something I must oversee, though it will hardly be a trial! By your leave."

"It is a promotion he certainly deserves," Eamon nodded. "It pleases me greatly."

Anderas disappeared into the college. Eamon returned his horse to the stables and retired to his office, where Slater brought him breakfast as he studied the day's papers. The servant moved so silently that if Eamon had not seen him he might not have known the man was there at all. He watched his servant's movements with admiration. Just as the man was prepared to withdraw, Eamon spoke.

"Mr Slater."

"My lord?"

"You did well last night; the whole household did." It was true: everything had been perfectly performed. "It was a supreme effort, and much appreciated."

Slater bowed. "Thank you, my lord."

"Please pass my congratulations on to the whole household," Eamon added, "and let a glass of wine go to everyone with it."

Slater bowed, awkwardly this time, and left. Eamon thought he saw a trace of red on the man's face; whether it was from pride or embarrassment was difficult to tell.

About mid-morning, Anderas came to see him again. The captain bore a confused but pleased look on his face and a large collection of papers under his arm.

"Lord Goodman."

"Captain," Eamon answered, setting aside the pile of papers that he had finished dealing with – mostly regulations on how much could be traded and brought into the quarter. "You look bemused," he added.

"I am."

"Yet you seemed very lucid earlier this morning."

"I was very lucid this morning," Anderas told him.

"And what has bemused you, captain?"

"This," Anderas replied, setting the papers down. "A dispatch that Draybant Greenwood and I received this morning."

"After the ride?" Eamon asked.

"Most definitely. Indeed, these papers surprised me so much that I decided to come to you myself on the matter."

Eamon looked at the papers; they bore the symbol of the Crown Office and were marked with Rose's seal. Eamon flicked through the pages and then, seeing the signature that he expected at the end of the long document, he smiled.

"The chief architect, one Mr Lorentide, has been doing some work for me," he answered. He had not expected it to be done so swiftly.

"I understand Mr Kentigern's comments from last night a little more clearly now, my lord," Anderas told him, gesturing to the papers.

"Do you share his objections?" Eamon asked.

"Not at all," Anderas grinned.

Eamon took the papers in hand and looked again at the topmost sheet. He only needed to sign it to authorize the new pecking order for the reconstruction and renovation of the quarter.

He did so with a smile and a flourish, and then passed the papers across to his captain.

"Thank you, my lord."

"How are the people from Tailor's Turn?"

"Still in Crown Office care, but once the architects set to work – which should be today or tomorrow – we should be able to get them properly re-housed until repairs are complete."

"Good."

"There is another matter that needs your attention, my lord," Anderas said as he scooped the papers back into his arm. "Several arrests of suspected wayfarers were conducted yesterday on Mead Road."

Eamon's heart sank – more men and, more likely, entire families for the pyres.

"One of them insists that it is his right to plead his innocence before you."

Eamon looked at the captain in surprise. "That was bold of him!"

"It is a very unusual request," Anderas answered, "which is why I mention it. The law of appeal hasn't been invoked in living memory."

"Because it was abolished long before living memory." Eamon remembered reading about the law when he had been studying at the college in Edesfield. The law had given that any arrested man had the right to appeal before the highest authority available to him. Eamon suspected that the law had been abolished to enable and facilitate just the kind of cull that the Master was currently conducting.

He looked quietly at Anderas. "I cannot – and will not – see him under the law of appeal," he said. It would be an affront to the throned, and a dangerous one. "But I will see him. You may bring him to me."

"Yes, Lord Goodman."

Not long later, a servant arrived to announce that the quarter's draybant of law had come to see him. He was the man who dealt with the more problematic aspects of the Master's law in the quarter. Eamon granted him entrance and was not surprised to see that the draybant and several ensigns accompanied a man whose wrists were heavily bound. The prisoner was not young, but he did not seem old either. Though flanked by the ensigns, the man tried to hold his head high. As Eamon rose from the desk, the draybant bowed and the prisoner did also. The ensigns followed suit.

Eamon strode forward and stood before the prisoner. The man remained bowed low.

"My lord," he said, "may you show the Master's glory in all you do."

"Rise," Eamon told him. The man did so.

"My lord." The draybant handed a collection of papers across to him, and Eamon read them swiftly, enough to gain the man's name and the reasons for his arrest.

"Mr Fort," he said, addressing the prisoner, "there are some serious charges against you. You stand accused of plotting with wayfarers against the city and the Master. And I am told that you refute this charge." He paused seriously. "What have you to say?"

"Produce the plot, my lord," the man answered steadily.

"You are bold, Mr Fort," Eamon told him.

"If what I hear of you is true, my lord, and if my words are true, then I have nothing to fear in being so."

Eamon blinked hard. Had not Ladomer said that his stunt at Tailor's Turn had called his sanity into question?

The man before him did not seem to be of that opinion. Heartened by Eamon's attention, he spoke again. "My lord, my family has no part with the wayfarers. We are all loyal to the Master. Our taxes are paid, our work is done, my own son serves with the Gauntlet – he is posted to the south-western borders under Captain Iset. My daughter is married to Lieutenant Malter of the South Quarter. My wife, while she lived, was a woman who served the Master with her whole heart all the days of her life. *Now* I am told that I have a part in a wayfarer plot, but the truth is that I am envied!"

"According to these notes, Mr Fort, you were seen 'meeting at strange hours with wayfarers'."

"I work in fishing," Fort answered, exasperated. "I often meet men at dawn or dusk. These men were not wayfarers. If they had been, why weren't we all arrested whilst meeting? This is nothing more than an anonymous report delivered by an envious competitor, intended to harm me and my trade."

Eamon watched him for a moment. "Mr Wilson," he said, turning to the draybant of law, "what other evidences are there against Mr Fort?"

"Allegations of previous family involvement with wayfarers, my lord," Wilson replied.

Eamon looked back at the man before him. At the draybant's statement he rolled his eyes and flexed his hands in their bonds.

"I have been cleared of that!" he cried. "Lord Ashway investigated the matter years ago. Will you shame my children for that?"

"I would hear of this thing from you," Eamon told him. He did not make it a request.

The prisoner took a deep breath and closed his eyes, as though steeling himself against a bitter memory. "The alleged traitor was my cousin. She exhibited wayfarer sympathies from her youth. She held little respect for the Master; in that she disdained her name, and my family's generations-long tradition of service."

"And what did she do?" Eamon asked.

"She married a man from outside the city," Fort answered. "It was suspected that he was a wayfarer, though that was not known when she married him. My uncle would never have permitted their union, otherwise. He always wanted her to be loyal to the Master, as he was and I am still."

"To the point, Mr Fort."

"The Master began a purge of wayfarers in the city about fifteen years ago, when rumours of some 'Serpent's heir' started reaching

Dunthruik." His tone was derogatory. "During that cull, many suspected wayfarers disappeared from the city before they could be apprehended. My cousin and her husband were implicated. When the Gauntlet tried to apprehend them there was a skirmish and all three of them – wife, husband, and son – were killed and sent to the pyres, to the Master's glory. Lord Ashway cleared me of any connection to her and her filthy work," he continued, "and had my family change its name to avoid being tarnished. We dutifully did so, and we should not pay the price for her treachery now!"

"Calm yourself, Mr Fort," Eamon told him firmly. "You will not answer for what you have not done." Fort fell silent in surprise, and Eamon looked at the papers again. The thought crossed his mind that he might well be expected to breach the man to verify his story, but as it occurred to him he reviled it. Breaching was a tool of the throned's mark; he would not do it.

"Mr Wilson, is there any other evidence against this man?"

The draybant shook his head. "No, my lord, bar this single report."

Eamon paused for a moment. "In the absence of other evidence and of an accuser to bring this charge, Mr Wilson, please intercept the notices of arrest going to Mr Fort and to Mrs Malter."

"You will release me?" Fort gaped.

"Mr Fort, the Master has no delight in a falsely imprisoned man," Eamon answered, "just as he has no delight in being betrayed by a man to whom he has shown grace." Fort watched him carefully. Eamon gestured to the ensigns to unbind him. "You shall go free, Mr Fort – I will not even breach you – and no shame will fall on your family. But if it is found that you have been treacherous, then no mercy will be shown to you; less still will the Master show to your children."

Fort paled. "I am loyal to the Master."

"Then go free, Mr Fort."

The bindings fell away from the man's hands and he rubbed briskly at his wrists. Eamon wished that the man were loyal to the

King, as his cousin had been. He wondered what the woman's name had been.

Fort bowed low to him. "You truly glorify the Master, Lord Goodman."

"Do the same," Eamon answered. "You may go, Mr Fort."

Fort turned, and the ensigns left the room with him. Eamon looked across at the draybant before handing the papers to him. "Thank you, Mr Wilson. You may tell Captain Anderas that Mr Fort has been dealt with."

"Thank you, my lord," Wilson nodded. "I will make the necessary notes in quarter records."

"Thank you. Mr Wilson," Eamon added as the draybant prepared to leave, "who was this woman whom Mr Fort mentioned?"

"Her name is not known to me, my lord," Wilson replied. "It will be in the records. I can look for it. Captain Anderas might also know of it – he was close to Captain Etchell, who was serving under Lord Ashway at the time of the incident."

"Very well, I shall speak with Captain Anderas," Eamon answered. "If I have no luck there I shall send word to you. Thank you, Mr Wilson."

"My lord." Wilson bowed low and left. Feeling confused by something that he felt to be just beyond his reach, Eamon returned to work.

Later that morning messages came to remind him of the swearing to which he was invited that afternoon. He was grateful for the reminder, but the thought of Manners kneeling and setting his hand to the Master's pommel chilled him.

Anderas came to him again before lunch. The captain walked swiftly, and his face bore a similar look to the one it had borne that morning.

"Do you, or do you not, have a lieutenant with the express task of running messages to me?" Eamon asked as the captain rose from his bow.

"I do," Anderas replied. "'Lieutenant Lackey', the college fondly calls him. A traditional name, handed down from man to man, whatever his own might be."

Eamon laughed. All Gauntlet college captains were assisted by a lieutenant who was (after the captain) usually the next best source of college information. The man currently serving the East Quarter College in that capacity was called Lancer.

"Having such an aide, why didn't you send Mr Lancer to me?"

"Due to my perplexion," the captain answered. "There is a man at the stables," he continued, his brow increasingly furrowed. "Actually, there are two men. I left Mr Lancer with them. They say that they have asked all over the city for Lord Goodman, and that they were sent here. When they asked for you at the college they were sent to Lancer, and then to me."

"That isn't perplexing in the slightest."

"No," Anderas agreed, "but they have brought a very fine horse with them."

Eamon looked up in surprise, an enormous smile breaking on his face. "A horse?"

"They are asking to see you."

"Then I think we should go to the stables."

"Very good, Lord Goodman."

They went to the stables. Eamon went as swiftly as he could, barely able to contain the grin on his face. He knew who would be waiting for him.

As he arrived he saw three men and a few stablehands. One of them was Lancer, and the lieutenant looked only a little less confused than his captain. The second man was younger than Eamon, and had a crop of thick, black hair. At his side was a man whom Eamon recognized, and by him stood a beautiful black charger with a small, white pattern on its nose.

Eamon stopped before the group, still smiling. Seeing the ring on Eamon's hand the man who led the horse paled.

"Lord... Lord Goodman?"

"The very same," Eamon answered. "Perhaps I am difficult to recognize when I am not covered in rain and mud?"

"But you are a Quarter Hand –"

"I am one now, and a delighted one at that," Eamon interrupted, and laughed. "You have brought back to me a sorely missed friend of long adventures!"

"That was my promise, my lord."

"And you have kept it well, Mr Bellis."

The man gasped, amazed that his name should be remembered. Eamon stepped forward and set his hands to the horse's muzzle in contentment. To his delight, the horse pressed against him fondly.

"You remember me, don't you?" he said. The horse responded with a soft neigh. Perhaps, even for the horse, he had been difficult to forget.

Eamon looked back to Marilio Bellis. "How is he?"

"Well healed, my lord," Marilio answered, "for which my son is responsible. He has a doctor's skill in him."

Eamon looked across at the younger man, who threw himself at once into a hasty bow. "What's your name, young man?" Eamon asked.

"Wilhelm Bellis, my lord."

"Wilhelm, I am indebted to you," Eamon told him, "for this creature is a steed indeed, far more witting, I fear, than its master."

"Sahu is a bright one, my lord," Wilhelm replied.

"Sahu?"

"That is the name my son gave him, my lord," Marilio explained quickly. "If it does you offence –"

"It sounds a good name."

"It is an old name out of the south," Anderas mused with interest. "Something to do with the brightness of the stars, I believe. Or perhaps the Great Constellation?"

The captain's face creased with the effort of chasing after what eluded him, before the expression soon gave way to veiled annoyance. Eamon laughed heartily.

"A fine name indeed!" he cried, turning warmly to the father and son before him. "Wilhelm Bellis, you have succeeded in flummoxing a man who is both a recognized fount of knowledge and a very fine captain. It is a feat too little achieved, and I congratulate you!"

At his praise, a flash of delight lit Wilhelm's face. He bowed. "Thank you, my lord."

"Mr Bellis and Mr Bellis, you both have my thanks once again," Eamon continued. Such men as these, he thought, were few. "Is there anything that I might offer you in return?"

"Serving you, Lord Goodman, is reward enough," Marilio answered with a bow.

"Then that, if you wish it, is precisely what I shall grant you."

Marilio looked up, startled. "You mean that, my lord?"

"Yes," Eamon answered, and he looked at them both sincerely. "Marilio, if you wish it you may serve me in my household, and your son appears to have some skill in healing. If he desires it, he may join the Gauntlet." Marilio's eyes went wide. "If these things do not accord with you both, then you shall rest here some days, and then I will send you both home to Eastport."

He paused and looked at Anderas; the captain nodded to him. Eamon turned back to the two men before him. "What would you, Mr Bellis?"

Marilio and his son exchanged glances, and then the dark-haired man met Eamon's gaze. "There are many others who may see to the ferries, my lord," he said, "and the East Road is not as safe as once it was. If it is to be my choice, then I would serve you."

CHAPTER XXII

The afternoon came on swiftly, and Eamon felt as though no time at all had passed before another knock came at his door.

"You must find it very taxing, captain, coming through this office every few hours," he told Anderas as the man entered.

"I can hardly avoid it, my lord. I wanted to catch you before you went to the swearing."

"Yes."

"Had you forgotten it?"

"No." How could he?

"We received some entry papers that need signing," Anderas continued, laying them on Eamon's desk.

"*Entry* papers?" Eamon was so accustomed to denying exit papers that he sat up in surprise.

"Yes, Lord Goodman," Anderas answered. "I thought that you might enjoy the novelty. A few families from the South Quarter want permission to come into the East."

"I'll sign them," Eamon answered. "Have they got family here, or work?"

"I don't think so, my lord."

"Then why come?"

"I believe it may have something to do with the latest story about the Lord of the East Quarter," Anderas answered quietly.

Eamon looked up in astonishment. "Latest story?"

"My ensigns and patrols – who bring back to me the word from the city streets – have started reporting what is being told. They report it with pride. The people near Tailor's Turn have been

335

speaking to their neighbours. It goes about that the man who put his life on the line for the Gauntlet set it into a pit for the people of his quarter." Anderas met his gaze seriously. "They praise the Master in every part of this quarter, my lord, because he made you lord over it."

Eamon was utterly stunned.

"What does Lord Tramist have to say about this?" he asked. He could not imagine the Lord of the South Quarter taking kindly to the family's movements.

"I am not sure," Anderas replied. "The South is often hard pressed for space. Lord Tramist has granted the families permission to leave."

Eamon set his quill to the papers and signed them. They were only two families, looking to go into one of the poorest parts of the East Quarter. He hoped that they would find themselves well there.

"Perhaps, as it is only two families, he will forgive me." Eamon rose from his seat. "I suppose I shall have to dress very formally for this afternoon's ceremony."

"I expect that Mr Slater has already laid out the appropriate attire for you," Anderas answered. "He is very particular about such things. Marilio Bellis is being inducted into the household and Draybant Greenwood is testing his son for the cadets," he added.

"Will he do?" Eamon asked.

"He is a little nervous, my lord – but that is not unusual."

"Indeed." Eamon smiled. "Thank you, captain."

"Is there anything else, my lord?" Anderas gathered all the day's papers from Eamon's desk, ready to dispatch them to the appropriate quarters.

"One thing more," Eamon told him. "When I interviewed Mr Fort this morning, he mentioned an incident with his cousin during the cull some fifteen years ago. Draybant Wilson advised me that you might know something about it."

The captain paused pensively. "I was just shy of joining the Gauntlet during the cull," he answered, "so know near nothing of the matter personally. Lord Ashway mentioned something of the case to me once, I believe, just after my appointment. Smuggling wayfarers from the city?"

"So Mr Fort said," Eamon nodded. "Is the woman's name known to you at all?"

Anderas thought for a moment, then nodded. "Yes, my lord," he said. "Her family name was Forthay but she is down in the official account by her husband's name, as Alleana Tiller."

Eamon felt a terrible chill seize him. How could he not have guessed it sooner?

"Alleana Tiller?" he whispered.

"Yes. Distinctive names, both of them. As I recall, that was why Fort had to change his. Are you well, my lord?"

"Yes," Eamon answered, though shaken.

Mr Fort maintained that Alleana, her husband, and her son had been killed by the Gauntlet. Perhaps he believed it. But Eamon knew Alleana had escaped the Gauntlet. He had seen her bloodied hands. He had sat with her through her gasps of pain and had been there to receive her final kiss on his forehead. He had been there when his father had knelt down and wept beside her cold, still body. He had been told that thieves, trying to take her purse, had attacked her. At last he knew the truth.

Alleana Forthay. How could he have forgotten that name? It had been so long since he had heard it; she had told it to him only once. In Dunthruik, she went by the name of Tiller – the name of her husband's mother, used because he had trade connections in the city by that name. But when they had travelled beyond Dunthruik and returned to Edesfield, his hometown, she was Alleana Goodman.

Fort's words ran through Eamon again: "*My family has no part with wayfarers…*"

It was not true – there was at least one. Fort could never have known – and could not know – that the man who had granted him his freedom that morning was First Knight to the Serpent's heir.

Nor could he know that the Lord of the East Quarter was the son of the woman who had smuggled wayfarers from the city at the cost of her own life.

"Lord Goodman?"

Eamon looked up. There was a thin veil of tears over his eyes. He blinked it back. "I, too, was a boy during the cull."

"I understand," Anderas said quietly.

They watched each other in silence for a moment.

"If I may, my lord," Anderas said, "I have to inspect the new First Pennants this afternoon."

"Of course," Eamon replied – and he had to be witness to the swearing of the Third Banners.

CHAPTER XXIII

Jubilant red and gold attired the West Quarter College courtyard. Banners bearing eagles, ravens, and crowns snapped over the doorposts and blazed in the sun. It was a beautiful morning, and far hotter than was normal for the time of year.

The courtyard was lined with seats, behind which was space for those visitors whose lot it was to stand. This space, as much as there was, was filled with people dressed in their finest: families and friends of the young men who were to swear that morning. Added to these witnesses were officers, ensigns, and cadets, resplendent in their uniforms, who alone among the observers stood in silence, their faces marked with smiles. It was to be a great day.

Eamon was seated apart from the other onlookers. A raised seating area had been prepared opposite the platform where Captain Waite was to conduct the swearing-in of the cadets. From where he sat, shaded by a long red awning, Eamon would have a clear view of the ceremony.

He restrained a sigh and shuffled his robes. Before leaving the Ashen he had donned the most formal of his rather large collection of Quarter Hand attire, and the owl and ash sat heavily on him. He fiddled with the ring on his finger. There was nothing he could do but wait.

Suddenly the two Gauntlet soldiers by the seating platform snapped sharply to attention. Eamon glanced up and saw Cathair stepping up the stairs to the platform. The Hand was thickly attired but bore it better than Eamon did. Approaching, he cast Eamon a smile so pleasant that Eamon had to suppress the urge to screw up his face in disgust.

"Lord Cathair."

"Ah, Lord Goodman! Isn't it a fine day?" Cathair drew a deep breath of the still air as he took the seat next to Eamon's. The smile on the Hand's pale face terrified Eamon.

"It is."

"You have never been in Dunthruik in high summer, I take it?" Cathair laughed. Eamon did not answer. He knew Dunthruik's summers from his childhood, and as Cathair continued, he distinctly remembered the choking humidity that would fall like a shroud on the worst days.

"Ah, Lord Goodman, the sea becomes as a balm to the city, and the sun! 'Jewel of the sceptred skies'…" Eamon realized that Cathair was probably reciting poetry, though he did not know what. It was terrible evidence of how jovial a mood the Hand was in.

Cathair turned to him again. "I regret that I could not attend last night. Your dinner was a success, I trust?"

"Indeed, Lord Cathair," Eamon replied. "Your wine was very greatly appreciated. The Raven's Avol was a particularly finely balanced vintage."

"You know a little of wines, Lord Goodman?"

"Nothing at all," Eamon replied truthfully "By which I mean I know nothing about grapes or soils or barrels or styles of wine. I can about distinguish a red from a white," he added with a smile, "and so the fact that my uncultured tongue was struck so keenly by your wines only goes to prove how excellent they were."

"The veil of your ignorance was pierced by their exceeding quality?" Cathair asked.

"As ever, Lord Cathair, you are more poetic a man than I," Eamon answered. "Yes, that is what I mean. I was so strongly struck that I may even be able to name the grape when next I taste it."

Cathair laughed. For a moment, the tension and distrust between them almost evaporated.

"Ah, Lord Goodman, I am glad indeed that you enjoyed what poor things my little hills have to offer."

In that moment a trumpet sounded and silence arrested the gathered onlookers. Eamon turned his eyes to the courtyard gateway and watched as Captain Waite, followed by Draybant Farleigh and the college's first lieutenant, walked steadily through the yard. Waite struck a truly imposing figure. The young man who followed him carried the small pommelled sceptre on which the cadets would make their oaths. The pommel glistened in the light. It froze Eamon's blood.

Waite reached the platform where the ceremony would take place – draybant and first lieutenant close by him. Both turned to look to the gateway, and the watching officers, ensigns, and cadets turned as a single body towards it, raising their swords in a formal salute. The yard became awash with reflected light as some of the college's third-year cadets – the Banner, Longsword, Raven, and Quiver groups – marched in impeccable order into the yard. It was an impressive sight.

"Ah! The fortunate number." Cathair leaned across slightly to speak into Eamon's ear. "The Third Banners were your own cadets, were they not?" he asked, gesturing to some of the marching men with a slight incline of his head.

"Yes, Lord Cathair." Cathair knew full well that they had been his. As the long line drew up before Waite's platform, Eamon saw the faces of men he knew and loved. Pity churned in his stomach, for he knew what they were to endure and he felt guilty, for he had not stopped them.

"You must be very pleased to be here today," Cathair continued, still smiling. "Have you seen the final list?"

"No, Lord Cathair."

"Such a pity! I am sure that you will find it absolutely delightful. Some of the lieutenantcies will, I believe, be especially pleasing to you."

The knot in Eamon's stomach grew tighter. He looked back to the young men who stood but a few feet before him, their faces radiant in the sun as they looked up to the captain who had brought them to that day. The young men had likely anticipated this day with eagerness their whole lives; Eamon knew that he had been the same. He remembered the feverish anticipation that had flowed relentlessly through his veins, the barely contained excitement with which he had watched his colleagues kneeling to lay their hands on the pommel that he longed to touch for himself. He closed his eyes briefly.

Could he not stop them, even now?

You will not dare, Eben's son.

That day, he had redefined the building list, acquitted a falsely arrested man, and drawn a father and son into his household. All those things he had done thinking, not of the Master's glory, but of what the King would have had him do. But he did not dare to stop the swearing.

As he looked back down the lines and scanned the rows of familiar faces, the voice mocked his cowardice. But he could do nothing. To act would be to betray himself and to betray Hughan. By helping Hughan he might yet hope to help these men.

The line came to a halt. The number gathered was about sixty in total, twelve of them Third Banners. As one, the cadets formally saluted their captain.

"His glory!"

"Wonderful, isn't it?" Cathair spoke even more quietly now, affecting awe at the beauty of the sight.

"Yes." Eamon's heart was heavy. "I remember it well."

"Most," Cathair answered, a slight barb to his tone, "never forget it."

Eamon looked to the lines again, then stopped suddenly. He had counted the men, examining their faces, and knew that, though he rued that any of them should be bound to the throned that day, he had been seeking one face over all the others. Waite stepped forward to the front of the platform with a proud smile on his face, to look out across the gathered watchers.

"Today, these young men formally make known their allegiance to the Master." Waite's voice, tremulous with pride, carried effortlessly across the yard. "Each man here has earned this distinction through his skill, honour, and loyalty. May it be for all of you the first step of many in a life of glorious service."

Waite stepped back slightly and the first lieutenant laid the staff into the captain's hands. Eamon's palm tingled inside his glove. He held his breath as Waite called the first cadet forward by name.

"Farrow Ostler of the West Quarter."

The young man stepped up to the platform and knelt. The courtyard was utterly silent as Waite, the staff now in his hand, turned to the young man. "What do you seek?"

"Service with the Gauntlet, captain."

"And what is your pledge?"

The words pounded in Eamon's head. He saw Captain Belaal's face before his own as he had answered that question what seemed a lifetime ago: "*I, Eamon Goodman, do hereby pledge…*"

"I, Farrow Ostler, do hereby pledge my allegiance to the Master. My blood, my blade, my body are all given in his service."

Your blood is mine, Eben's son. Did you not swear it then even as he does now?

Eamon drew breath as the words cut through him. He *had* sworn it…

Waite smiled at the cadet. "And do you swear this most solemnly to the Master, such an oath as may not be broken?"

"*Do not swear!*" The words rose up in Eamon's heart. His lungs filled to cry them out, but his voice was bound just as he was; for Cathair watched him, and he knew he had to smile.

The kneeling cadet looked up to Waite, his eyes shining with emotion. "I do swear it."

"Ah!" Cathair gave out a satisfied sigh. A shudder ran down Eamon's spine.

"Then receive the mark of your allegiance." As Waite brought forward the staff, Eamon's hand curled in memory of what had touched his own skin. If only Ostler could be stopped, and Ford and Smith and all the others who stood behind him… He searched the line again, saw the eager faces.

Manners. Where was Manners?

Ostler's hand was on the pommel, and the curious silence grew deeper. Eamon's heart sank as he saw Waite's solemn face. Did the captain not remember what happened when the oath was sworn? How could he so benignly give that to men whom he loved? Had Waite not been tormented by the voice of Edelred all the days of his service?

Perhaps he had not.

Waite withdrew the staff and Ostler looked up, a contented look on his face. Waite smiled at him. "Thus are you sworn," he said. "Rise, Ensign Farrow Ostler: you belong to the Master."

Ostler rose. He saluted Waite and descended from the platform to applause from the onlookers. It died away as Waite called forward the next cadet. "Luther Ford of the West Quarter."

Eamon was aware of Cathair leaning close by him. "A ceremony as delicate as it is beautiful – would you not agree, Lord Goodman?"

Eamon could not answer. He watched as Ford knelt and laid his hand to the staff, and closed his eyes.

It took over an hour for all the cadets to be sworn. Most were made ensigns and were to remain, at least for the present, stationed in Dunthruik. Some were assigned to external divisions that worked in nearby towns or to special Dunthruik detachments that would prowl the East Road looking for wayfarer activity. One or two were promoted directly to lieutenant, some in the college and others to other garrisons. But Manners was not there.

As the ceremony ended, Cathair rose. Eamon followed him and watched as the whole courtyard bowed down before them. They left the yard and returned to the entry hall.

"I think that all went delightfully well," Cathair mused. "Waite has run a hundred other ceremonies like it and has a singularly special talent for it, I believe."

"Indeed," Eamon answered. With that, at least, he agreed.

"Your captain at Edesfield had not such a talent?"

Eamon looked up, surprised. It had been so long since he had heard the name of Edesfield spoken.

Cathair smiled at him and laughed encouragingly. "Come now, Lord Goodman, you can speak to me of such things! You are a Quarter Hand, are you not, and perhaps you have your old captain to thank in part for that."

"Captain Belaal did little to teach me devotion to the Master," Eamon replied, surprised at the anger in his own voice. It was true that Belaal had honed him, helping to make him worthy of the Gauntlet, but it was also Belaal who had tortured Aeryn and made him breach for the first time. Belaal had not made him worthy of being a Hand. "Belaal sent me to Dunthruik, Lord Cathair, for which I am grateful."

"It was not his choice."

Eamon blanched. If Belaal had not assigned him to Dunthruik...?

Cathair smiled. "Surely you know, Lord Goodman, that it is rare for regional ensigns – and more so for lieutenants! – to be drawn to the city for service? As you can see," he laughed, "we have so many of our own!"

"I am not sure that I follow you, Lord Cathair," Eamon almost stammered.

"I wonder little at that, Lord Goodman," Cathair replied. "But perhaps you can ask your erstwhile captain when he arrives."

"Belaal is coming here?" The thought chilled him.

"Indeed he is," Cathair replied, and his tone grew more sour. "Perhaps you have not yet heard the news? Edesfield, and much of its province, has been lost."

Eamon gaped. "What?"

"I see you had not heard it," Cathair murmured. "It does not surprise me. Some of us, Lord Goodman, know better than to gallivant on the plains early in the morning."

"You learned of this only this morning?"

"The movers brought news," Cathair supplied airily.

"What happened?"

Cathair raised an unpleasant, condescending eyebrow. "You need not sound so troubled, Lord Goodman! It means but little."

345

But Eamon continued to stare at him, for it was not true. Edesfield, despite a somewhat maligned and ornamental reputation, lay at the very heart of the northern reaches of the River Realm, and was the last bridgeable point on the River before the mouth. It was not so very distant from Dunthruik itself. If the wayfarers had taken Edesfield then the war was turning badly against the throned. If the wayfarers had taken Edesfield it meant that they were once again connected to their allies coming out of the Land of the Seven Sons. It meant that the wayfarers could now control the long southern stretch of the River, and that would greatly increase their ability to hinder and hamper the regional Gauntlet units, which were already severely harrowed. If Hughan – and Eamon was sure that Hughan would have led the attack – had taken Edesfield, then he would soon turn to Dunthruik.

"You worry that your little town has fallen?" Cathair asked snidely, seeing his face. "Do not. It will not aid the Serpent. The Master is well prepared for him."

It was then that Eamon's heart froze. With a start, Eamon's thought turned to the Nightholt, the inscrutable tome that he had delivered to the Master long months before. He did not know what it was, and could not guess at it, but Eamon felt with a chilling surety that, with the war against the wayfarers worsening in every region, the only feasible explanation for Edelred's confidence was in the power of the book. It could only be that the book held some terrible peril for Hughan.

"Captain Belaal and his men are on their way to the city," Cathair continued. "He is not the only one. A lot of regional captains are being summoned here over the next few weeks. Perhaps you and your starry-eyed captain missed the dispatches that I sent today?" Eamon frowned – no, Anderas would have brought such news straight away. It was more likely, he realized, that Cathair had sent the dispatches to him last of all. "Well, if you will occupy yourself with the work of architects, and not of a Quarter Hand, I suppose being uninformed is the consequence. Let me save you some embarrassment by telling you that the dispatches advise that the regional captains will each give reports on their own regions and bring forces to bolster the Gauntlet here in Dunthruik."

Eamon looked at him. Bolster the Gauntlet in Dunthruik? His mind began to whirl. If the throned was beginning to centralize all his forces in Dunthruik...

"The Serpent plans something?"

"Well, my own suggestion was that we ask *you* about that, Lord Goodman."

Eamon's blood ran cold. Cathair's green eyes danced with delight as the net of words fell.

Eamon shook his head and then laughed uproariously.

"Ask me?" he cried, aware that others now moved in the hallway and that some stared at him as he laughed. "Lord Cathair, your reputation for wit is well deserved!" He drew a couple more breaths, then met Cathair's gaze again. He thought he detected disappointment in it, but there was a sly smile on the Hand's face. "In all seriousness, Lord Cathair, I must ask my question again, and press you to answer it, if I may."

"I have no answer to it," Cathair replied. "You would have to speak to the Right Hand, or wait to be summoned by the Master. Should such a threat against this city arise, we will hear of it."

"Of course."

There was a brief silence. "I must speak with Captain Waite," Cathair told him, and smiled. "Good day to you, Lord Goodman."

"And to you, Lord Cathair."

Eamon watched the Hand as he left the hall and made his way towards the captain. With Cathair no longer at his side, his breath returned to him and his mind churned through what he had heard.

The place where Ede had fallen had been reclaimed for the house of Brenuin. Surely the throned, and his Hands, had been shaken by the symbolic significance of that loss? Surely they could not overlook the strategic loss that the fall of Edesfield signalled for Dunthruik? Hughan would, even now, be making his final plans to come against the city. Eamon shivered. When the Master made his plans against the King, Eamon would be present to hear them.

When the King came, and the Master met him with the Nightholt…

Eamon realized with a horrifying lurch that he had never once mentioned the book to Hughan. He had held it in his own hands, he had delivered it to the throned's closest… and, when speaking to Hughan at his camp, he had never once thought to speak of it. Perhaps he had been too ashamed.

Mathaiah spoke of it, Eamon.

The thought ran through him and calmed him. Of course Mathaiah had sent word of the book. But Mathaiah had known no more about it than Eamon, and the King had no way of knowing that Mathaiah had lost his life because of the Master's book. If he was to send news to Hughan, Eamon realized, then he had to send word of the Nightholt. And yet, what good would it be for him to send word, if he had no word other than "Nightholt" to send?

He looked up and saw Cathair finishing his conversation with Waite. The captain bowed and Cathair turned to move away. As he strode on, Cathair sang. The tune was that of a popular ballad, but Eamon did not recognize the words. He imagined at once that they were some extracts from one of Cathair's favourite, and long-studied, volumes of poetry.

With the force of lightning the thought pierced him. *Poetry.* Eamon had an entire library – and one that Cathair envied – at his disposal. Surely he could find something, one single thing, in that library that would help him to understand the book that so emboldened the throned and threatened the King?

It was then that he heard footsteps approach.

"Ratbag!"

The name forced all thoughts of King, Nightholt, and library from his mind.

Ladomer stood by him, a thick collection of papers in his hands. His friend smiled broadly and Eamon wondered from where he had come.

"It was a great ceremony, wasn't it?" Ladomer enthused, laughing, then lowered his voice somewhat conspiratorially and continued: "I was checking the list of markees against the list of expected cadets. Did you know that two of them didn't get sworn in? Apparently the bloody idiots got themselves into a fight last night after your do." Eamon's blood chilled. He stared at Ladomer. "Quite your style, you'll be pleased to hear; I'm told it was over some woman. Didn't even manage to leave the East Quarter! Must have been the wine – evidently it was too good for their kind." Ladomer shook his head as though he found the whole thing deeply amusing. "Anyway, they made absolute idiots of themselves and Waite has remanded them. They've been thrown into the college brig and had black marks set against their records. There'll be no swearing-in for either of them until they're old and grey, unless they break the Serpent's neck themselves!" Ladomer laughed again. "Can you imagine it, Ratbag? Over a woman! Glad you weren't privy to such fits of hot-blooded rage when you were a cadet, otherwise where would we be now? Slaving in Backwater. As it stands, your own womanizing streak seems to have served you well enough."

"Mr Kentigern."

Ladomer looked up in surprise. Eamon surprised himself, for his tone was impeccably formal. As Ladomer met his gaze, his eyes narrowed. Eamon drew a deep breath.

"When you address me, Mr Kentigern, you will remember that I am the Lord of the East Quarter, and favoured by the Master. You will remember that this station is above your own. There is no glory for the Master in the despicable behaviour of cadets and there is nothing amusing in bandying round stories of their dishonour. If you wish to speak to me frankly you will do so in private, and even there you will treat me with deference befitting the position that I, by the Master's grace and glory, have attained."

Ladomer gaped. It grieved Eamon to speak such words: Ladomer was, first and foremost, his friend. But Dunthruik was too dangerous a place for Ladomer to speak as he did. Surely his friend knew that?

The Right Hand's lieutenant rounded on him balefully.

"I understand," he snapped, his voice thick with injury and betrayal. "You're the Hand, and I'm the worm unworthy of you. Give me a moment to hurl myself down in the mud so that I can writhe and grovel before you, since that's what you want."

"It's not what I want."

Ladomer laughed bitterly. "That's right, take the moral high ground. You're better than me, after all – we've established that. And our years together in Edesfield – well, they can just be brushed away, can't they?"

"Ladomer," Eamon breathed, "this isn't Edesfield. And we've changed."

"Maybe you have, Goodman."

Eamon regained himself. "You will henceforth be mindful to address me by my title, Mr Kentigern," he said firmly, "and you will not speak of these cadets as you have done. Their dishonour brings dishonour to Captain Waite, Lord Cathair, and to the Master."

Ladomer bowed low, his hands shaking slightly. "Yes, Lord Goodman."

"Convey my warmest regards to Lord Arlaith," Eamon said.

"I will do so, *Lord Goodman*," Ladomer answered stiffly. Rising, but not once meeting Eamon's gaze, he left the hall.

When Eamon returned to the East Quarter it was to find a pale-faced Anderas, a collection of dispatches clutched in his hand. They were from Lord Cathair.

Eamon ate little and alone that evening, making his study his dining room and the sound of the trees beyond his window his company.

Once he had finished he went through the papers on his desk, sorting them into small piles to wait for him in the morning. The rustling of the parchment filled his hearing, though not his thought. That was filled, over and again, with the fall of Edesfield, the faces of the cadets who had sworn, the bitter look on Ladomer's face – the look of a wounded heart. Eamon rued what he had had to do. For years uncounted, Ladomer had been a man with whom Eamon had divided his hopes and fears. Now, Dunthruik had divided them. Ladomer was wrong: the city had changed them both.

Tears stung his eyes and he tried to press them away. He had lost Mathaiah. Was he to lose Ladomer, too?

He looked up, forcing his eyes to focus instead on the dimmed forms in his study. The long bookshelves, filled with parchment and closely bound volumes, looked back at him. The flicker of the lamplight made him remember the tracts of darkness in the tunnels of Ellenswell.

Startled by the memory, he reached to where he had once borne the heart of the King, but it resided there no longer. Instead he touched the clasp of his cloak. It was cold.

He remembered the feeling of the papers in his hands the last time he saw Mathaiah. Some of them had borne the same writing as marked the Hands' Hall and the Nightholt itself. He felt sure that Mathaiah had been kept to read and interpret those symbols. But why should the Hands force him to do such? Why should they need to make Mathaiah read it?

Was it possible that they – Cathair and Ashway, Dehelt and Tramist, Lord Arlaith and the Master himself – could *not* read it? Why would the Hands have needed Mathaiah if they could read the Nightholt? What could be written in that book that they could not read and yet desired so ardently to know? What power would the throned have once he gained what he desired?

But the throned already had the Nightholt. Eamon had himself delivered it to Cathair and Ashway's hands. The Nightholt had gone to the Master. Surely that was why Hughan's increasing strength did not concern him.

But what *was* the Nightholt?

Shaking, Eamon looked back to the shelves, to the spines and scrolls. Each intimidated him in the odd light. At least one of them had to hold something about the Nightholt – some reference, however veiled. He swallowed as he stared at the volumes. The tomes would hold their secrets, and would hold them well. Even a bookbinder's son would struggle to go through as many books as were there – especially when that same man was also the Lord of the East Quarter, weighed down with the duties of his office.

Where could he begin? Eamon knew that several years would not suffice to read every book – but he also knew that he likely did not need to read every book – one well-placed one would do. But which one? Perhaps, if he had thought to ask it, Lord Ashway might have answered him his question. But he could not turn to Ashway. The best-read man in Dunthruik appeared to be Lord Cathair – and Eamon could not go to him.

Thought of the Lord of the West Quarter brought to Eamon's mind a memory of one of the many occasions on which Cathair had spoken in verse. He had challenged Eamon to place the citation, and Eamon had been unable to. He remembered the amused and mocking expression that had passed over the Hand's face:

"*You are a man of little learning, Mr Goodman! Perhaps you should ask Cadet Overbrook; he has the look of a scholar to him.*"

Eamon drew a deep breath. He had asked Overbrook. He had given the quotation to the young man – ill with the winter fever – hoping that the search for the words would help to stave off his grim illness. It had done so – and Overbrook had found the quotation's source.

Suddenly, Eamon laughed. Cathair would never know it, but by his baiting of so long ago, Dunthruik's Raven had inadvertently brought to Eamon the answer to a question that he could never have dared to ask.

Eamon set down his papers and approached Ashway's shelves. Slowly, he scanned the titles, looking for one in particular. He knew that it was there; in fact, he had seen several copies in varying editions when he had scoured the shelves, seeking gifts to mollify his erstwhile mentor. Finding the shelves dim he brought his lamp across, setting it on a nearby stool as he continued in his search. He pulled one or two books out to glance through their dusty pages before setting them back and gazing back up at the numerous shelves. Where had he seen it? He sighed with frustration.

He knew nothing that the other Hands knew, and he knew nothing of what had driven Edelred to take the throne from Ede. He knew nothing of the fall of the city that had become Dunthruik except those things that the strange, unpredictable – and uncontrollable – visions had sometimes shown him.

His eyes fell on several thick, fraily bound volumes. He drew the most sturdy-looking one out and flicked through its pages.

It was what he sought.

Relieved, he tucked the book under his arm and settled matters at his desk before leaving his office and climbing the lit stairwell to his room. A small fire had been set for him and there was a lamp at his bedside. The lamp was already lit, and Eamon set the book down on his bed while he changed, putting aside the trappings of his office and drawing on a comfortable night-shirt. Climbing carefully between his covers, he settled back on the cushions and drew up his knees. Against them he rested the back of the book. As he opened it, the book's bindings cracked ominously. He persevered. After all, if the bindings broke he could mend them. He turned to the first page.

If there was any book in the whole of Dunthruik's canon that would speak of the Nightholt, then it had to be this one.

Setting his head comfortably on the pillows and arranging the lamp so that it shed as much light as was possible over the delicate pages, Eamon drew a deep breath and read:

> *And in the tide of later days*
> *These words shall live, and rend him praise.*

The book he had taken from Ashway's library was a copy of the Edelred Cycle.

Two weeks passed. As March closed and April began, the very last heavy rains pelted across the city from the coast, moving north and inland. Eamon wondered whether the same dark clouds and rains would cover the towers of Istanaria, far away in the Land of the

Seven Sons, or wash over the men who served the King in Edesfield, or in whatever hidden valley Hughan now made his home. The thought was a strange one. The city became fretted with incoming Gauntlet groups, each one looking harried, and regional Hands came with them. The war was worsening.

As Eamon's reputation in the East Quarter grew and grew, he found that his own love for the place did also. He was greeted with smiles wherever he went, and, as with the servants in his own household, the smiles of the people in the streets where he walked grew less fearful. Perhaps the people were growing to love him, too.

He inspected the work done by the architects on the most derelict buildings and watched proudly as the families from Tailor's Turn were put into new homes. The little girl, Ellen, had thanked him, almost flinging her arms about him as she bubbled about what it had been like to live in the caves and how delighted she was with where she was going to live. Where once Eamon imagined that the onlookers would have feared for her safety, now, as he crouched down to speak to her, they smiled.

The little girl at last paused to draw breath.

"So, you like your new home?" Eamon asked her.

The little girl laughed. "Yes! The caves were comfortable, but there were some really *horrid* spiders in the dark corner."

"You don't like spiders?"

"No, but it was all right – Strong-arm scared them all away."

"I am glad of it," Eamon answered with a smile. He had learned that, since the collapse of the building in Tailor's Turn, the young man who had helped him to cross the fallen stones had kept the name that Eamon had given him. It touched him deeply.

Ellen paused thoughtfully, then looked up. "Now that we have somewhere to live, do you want me to bring your cloak back?"

"Has it been put to good use?"

"Mrs Turrell used it as a blanket most nights. It was cold in the caves, but she said it kept her warm!"

"Well then, tell Mrs Turrell that she may keep it, and I hope that it will keep her warm for many a night to come. When it gets too threadbare for that, it will make fine curtain patches."

Ellen grinned. "I'll tell her, sir!"

As the days went by, Eamon grew increasingly accustomed to his duties. In the evenings he made slow progress with his reading. Often he fell asleep before he could read more than two or three pages, but each night, despite the heaviness of his eyes, he pressed himself to read on.

Despite Cathair's jibes he continued to ride early every morning with Anderas. The captain assured him that the sore muscles that burned the length of his entire legs were sure evidence that the extended practice was doing him good. Indeed, Eamon soon found that his legs stopped aching quite so much, and he was occasionally able to match his captain's speed – though never his grace – as they rode on the city plains. When he had a spare hour in the afternoons he often practised swordplay with the Hands of the Quarter, and was pleased to see them improving. He was especially pleased when Heathlode was able to parry several quick blows in succession.

"Your hand is improving, Lord Heathlode," Eamon told him.

"Thanks no doubt only to your own patience, Lord Goodman," a panting Heathlode replied.

"I am sure you are a skilled man of your own accord."

"Not really, Lord Goodman."

"Lord Heathlode is incurably modest, Lord Goodman," Lord Brettal interjected. "What he hasn't told you is that he is a fearsome dreamer, and Lord Ashway thought that he might have traces of a seer in him."

"Skills of great importance, Lord Heathlode," Eamon said. The Hand beamed to receive his praise while Eamon buried the wince of a burdened heart.

Eamon came to see more of the servants in his household. Even Slater grew more open with him. The man was sometimes drawn into conversation, and when Eamon had to be consulted on household matters Slater no longer looked terrified to discuss them with him. After hearing that several of the younger servants, Callum included, longed to see the stables, Eamon arranged for them to spend a few days with the stablehands, learning their trades. He often saw Cara in the evenings, for she had charge of his room, clothes, and linens. He made sure to thank her for that, for they were all in excellent condition.

Marilio Bellis was assigned to the kitchens, and Slater, when asked, reported that the chief cook came from a village very near to Marilio's own. The two men often spent whole days discussing the best way of preparing various dishes and, in the days after Marilio's arrival, Eamon found that his meals became steadily more varied and adventurous. Sometimes he went down to the kitchens himself to ask a few questions as to how the food was prepared. Though both Cook and Marilio were nervous to start, they soon warmed to the idea, and Eamon was able to spend some time hearing the two men trade ideas on the best ways to balance flavours and prepare different dishes. He especially enjoyed learning how to fillet fish and cook snails, and was ridiculously pleased when the two cooks encouraged him to try his hand at the preparations for both. He discovered then that he was far better at eating food than cooking it.

Wilhelm Bellis proved a very able cadet and integrated swiftly into life with the other new recruits. According to Greenwood, the young man expressed an interest in being considered for transfer to one of the surgeon-training units after he completed his cadet training. Sometimes Eamon caught the cadets drilling or studying at the college; when he did, he often made the time to encourage them as they ran the course.

As far as Eamon could tell, the East Quarter was quietly flourishing. Eamon saw people with bread on their tables and roofs under which to set them. There was still crime and corruption, and every night the Gauntlet brought in more suspected wayfarers, and every morning heavily laden carts ran along the stony road to the North Gate and the steady pyres. But the requests for exit papers from the quarter shrank and Eamon found himself with several entry papers from other quarters during the course of a week. He could not sanction them all – the city was filling with captains, officers, and men from other regions, and the East was housing its fair share of them.

One evening Eamon watched the latest column of arriving soldiers pass down Coronet Rise. Anderas was with him. The captain shook his head.

"The war does not go well, Lord Goodman."

"Such is indeed the case, if we can judge it by the men," Eamon told him. News of the loss of Edesfield had gone out, and Eamon had seen some of the ensigns and officers who came from more distant regions. Many bore grim or haunted looks, and tales of bitter skirmishes and battles were to be heard, whispered in the quarter colleges.

"I do not judge it from the men, my lord," Anderas answered. "I judge it from their colours."

Eamon looked at him curiously. "Their colours?"

"Apart from the men withdrawing here because they must, during the last two weeks, the city has received additional men from only twenty-five regions," Anderas explained.

Eamon raised an eyebrow. "You've counted?" he asked incredulously. The River Realm had thirty-one provinces, in which number the city of Dunthruik was counted as one.

"Yes. Even *Larkbury* Province managed to send one hundred men. But from the Tallendor, Tungol, Escherbruck, Waldeburg, and Arudia regions?" He shook his head as he numbered the provinces off on his hand. "From them we have not received a man."

Eamon breathed deeply and looked back to the lines. Most of the men arriving in the city had, notwithstanding the loss of Edesfield, managed to reach it by River. It had kept them more or less out of the clutches of the wayfarer and Easter forces, all of which still seemed land-bound. The five missing provinces were the southernmost regions of the River Realm, with little or difficult access to the River and its tributaries. Eamon suspected that, if the regions had not sent men, it was because Hughan and his allies had impeded them.

"Things would be bad enough if our losses were restricted to the south. But it isn't just the southern regions. Since the Easter incursion over the borders before the winter, the east has been hard-pressed, and the provinces of the West Bank fare little better. The north has been ill-secured for some time – we saw that at Pinewood. I fear, my lord," he added quietly, "that, for all our valour, Dunthruik is swift becoming our last outpost. Trouble has been brewing all the winter long – now, it nears our gates."

Eamon agreed. But if the city of Dunthruik knew how near to its own walls danger pressed, such knowledge did not dampen the mood of the majesty celebration which was held that week. The Master appeared at the balcony and the crowds hailed him uproariously, ravenously.

He could not read that night.

After the incident which led to Cadet Manners missing his swearing, he was sentenced to fifteen days in the West Quarter brig. Upon conclusion of this punishment he was assigned, at Cathair's insistence, to heavy manual labour in the port. So as not to draw undue attention to himself, Eamon waited until Manners' release to have Greenwood arrange a meeting with Manners for him. This request was still somewhat unconventional, but not entirely without precedent, for though Manners no longer served under Eamon's authority, the incident in question occurred in the East Quarter under Eamon's jurisdiction. Eamon therefore held the legal right to question Manners on his conduct.

Greenwood arranged for Manners to be brought to the East Quarter to give account. Eamon noted that the cadet's arms and face looked red from the sun, while his arms seemed more muscular than before. But he looked content.

"I know that you have told your story before, Mr Manners, but I would hear it for my own quarter's records," Eamon told him. A scribe sat with them to make notes of the interview.

"There is little to tell, Lord Goodman. My judgment was

somewhat impeded by the excellent wine in which I had overindulged that evening. When Cadet Plier and I passed the Crown Inn, we became involved in a brawl over a woman."

Eamon found that difficult to believe. "You did not seem terribly drunken when I spoke with you."

"I fear that I hid it well enough from you, my lord," Manners answered. "Beyond your presence, I lost any restraining sense. I understand that when I was arrested in my altered state, I spoke in a shameful and disrespecting manner of the Gauntlet, struck the lieutenant who sought to restrain me, and spoke exceedingly ill, I believe, of Lord Cathair." Manners kept his face quite calm as he spoke. Eamon wondered at it.

"What exactly did you say, Mr Manners?" he pressed.

"I am afraid I have very little memory of that, Lord Goodman."

Eamon thought this a touch too convenient. "Speaking ill of a Hand carries hefty penalties. It seems that you were fortunate to be assigned to the port."

"Work on the sewers finished early this year," Manners answered, with the slightest trace of a smile.

Their gazes met. "I am very sorry that you were not sworn in, Mr Manners," Eamon said quietly, "and will not hide from you that you are unlikely to receive that honour for the foreseeable future, unless you distinguish yourself."

Manners nodded. "Yes, Lord Goodman," he replied steadily.

Eamon thanked him for the interview and then dismissed him back to his work.

During the second week of April, Slater bustled busily into his office. Eamon was surprised by the man's unwonted forwardness.

"Mr Slater?" he asked.

"My lord," Slater answered, bowing low, "Mr Montano is here."

"Mr Montano?" Eamon repeated the name, feeling sure that he had heard it before, and that he should show some familiarity with it. At a loss, he met the servant's gaze. "I am sorry, Mr Slater, this is an appointment which I appear to have forgotten…"

"We spoke of him yesterday, my lord," Slater answered. Eamon shook his head blankly. "The Master's painter. He has come for your inaugural *portrait*, my lord."

"Oh."

Eamon proceeded to spend much of that morning (and of several other mornings that week) sitting in an august chair in front of a deep red curtain, dressed in his finest robes and doing his best to hold still while the greatest painter in Dunthruik took his details and set them on canvas. It was an agonizing experience, and Eamon felt uncomfortable beneath the painter's scrutinizing gaze, which drilled into every part of him. As the brush and oils moved on the thick material, Eamon's skin tingled.

Slater often popped in to judge the progress, and Eamon was able to chart the success of the painting in the servant's face as it lit and fell during Montano's work.

"Are you fond of art, Mr Slater?" Eamon asked.

"Yes, my lord." The man's enthusiasm was wonderful to hear, and though Eamon was forbidden to see the painting between sittings, Slater assured him that it would be worth the wait.

One morning Anderas came by to update Eamon on a couple of developments in the college. His report was crisply delivered, and once he had finished, he stayed for a few moments to watch the artist work. Eamon caught the occasional glimpse of him as he stood, just beyond the easel, with a broad smile on his face.

"It's a good likeness, my lord," he said. "He has your eyes just right."

Eamon would have answered, but felt that too much movement would not be helpful. He could not even frown. Anderas noted his expression and grinned. "Would you like me to go and smirk elsewhere, my lord?"

"If you wouldn't mind, captain."

"You must be *still*, Lord Goodman!" cried the paint-smeared artist in frustration.

Chapter XXIII

Eamon apologized, but it made the situation worse. Laughing, Anderas absented himself.

It took some time before the painting was done, though even Eamon had to agree with Anderas's assessment when he finally saw it officially hung in his hall. It seemed strange to him, to see himself robed in black and bearing the marks of the throned's favour. It seemed strangest of all because it no longer frightened him: the Hand in the painting was not the Master's, but the King's.

CHAPTER XXIV

It was mid-April. Having finished his morning's work, Eamon decided to leave the Handquarters behind him and take a stroll through the quarter. It was a habit to which he was more and more accustomed, and the people of the East Quarter no longer looked at him in surprise or alarm when they saw him in the streets.

He took one of the smaller roads that ran parallel with Coronet Rise. At one end it curved and struck across to the North Quarter, but Eamon did not follow it that far. Instead, he followed it round into some of the quieter roads, pausing every now and then to look at the wares that were on sale. He never lingered too long, for it made some shopkeepers uncomfortable. When he paused to look at the rich fabrics on display in Draper's Way, he remembered the small shop where he and Mathaiah had bought the colours of the King. He looked again at the myriad colours that decked the whole road. Blue cloth could be found almost nowhere in the streets of Dunthruik.

"Does it please you, my lord?"

Eamon looked up to see a seamstress watching him as he held a fabric pensively in his hand.

"It is beautiful," he answered truthfully.

"Please do take it," she told him, beginning to unwind the fabric from its reel. "A gift for you, my lord –"

"No, good lady," Eamon replied with a laugh. "I need no gifts. This quarter's livelihood depends on the services of those who work in it. Sell this fine cloth, and feed your family."

"Yes, my lord," she replied, and Eamon smiled. He had also grown accustomed to refusing gifts from enthusiastic shopkeepers. At first, trembling hands and fearful, furtive eyes had offered such things to him. Now, gifts were offered to him because the people delighted in him, and when he passed they would call to the Master's glory. Sometimes he wondered – and dreaded to think – what Cathair and the other Hands made of the way the East Quarter received him. His comfort lay in the fact that, by all accounts, the Master himself was pleased.

Eamon continued on his way along the small streets, halting every now and then to greet and be greeted. At about midday he came to the road that he had seen with Anderas on his second tour of the quarter, where they had seen the desecrated inn. As he looked at it, he smiled, for he saw that men worked there to reset windows and stone, and clean and repaint wood. One man set a clumsy ladder to the wall, preparing to climb up and take down the sign that bore the inn's name.

Eamon quietly watched as the man tested the first rung of the ladder before looking up at the signpost with a frown.

"Terribly high, it is," the man murmured to himself. None of the others, busily painting and scrubbing wood, seemed to hear him, and he shook his head then drew breath as though steeling himself to a task not much to his liking.

Eamon stepped forward. "Perhaps I can help you?" he offered.

"Thank you, sir," the man began, and then saw the black cloak. "Lord Goodman!" he cried, nearly tripping on the rung of the ladder as he hurried to bow. The other men working nearby turned at his exclamation and bowed as well.

"I have not the pleasure of knowing your name, I'm afraid," Eamon answered, "but I see that you know mine."

"My name is Miles, my lord."

"Then I repeat my offer to you, Mr Miles," Eamon replied, and gestured at the sign. "I can have that down for you in a moment, and it would give me great pleasure to help you."

"Of course, my lord," Miles answered, stepping away from the ladder and bowing again.

Eamon undid his cloak where it was clasped at his neck, folded it, and set it carefully to one side. It was hot, and so he wore only a shirt beneath his cloak that day, rather than shirt and black jacket.

"Climbing ladders is complicated enough," he told the surprised innkeeper. "No need to make it more so."

"Indeed, my lord."

Eamon took the ladder and tested it against the sign-beam. He reckoned that it would hold. "Would you steady the ladder for me?"

"Certainly, my lord."

Eamon climbed the ladder, and as he reached the beam he examined the holding. The sign had been mostly ratcheted off, and long, rusted nails hung half out of the wood. With a tool he could wedge it out completely.

"A hammer, Mr Miles?" he called.

The man handed one up to him swiftly. Eamon thanked him and then set to work. It was neither difficult nor time-consuming, and as he worked he hummed quietly. It was a liberty he rarely afforded himself, and after a moment the humming became quiet singing.

"You've a fine voice, Lord Goodman," Miles called up cautiously. Eamon laughed; he had forgotten that he was watched.

"My schoolmaster held a different opinion," he replied, touched by the compliment, "though I believe that may have been because I was supposed to be studying grammar at the time – a burdensome task, and one that I did not enjoy." He carefully drew out the last nail, supporting the sign with his hand as it came loose.

Balancing the hammer over the ladder rung he climbed down, the sign clasped in one hand. The paint was faded and cracked beyond recognition. "Mr Miles, what is this inn called?" Eamon asked as he reached the ground.

"It was called the Horse and Cart, Lord Goodman," Miles replied, "though perhaps I may change it."

Eamon steadied the faded sign on a tabletop. "Make it a good name."

"I will that, my lord. Please don't trouble yourself," he added, as Eamon examined the torn gashes in the wood where the nails had held it firm. Eamon smiled.

"It is no trouble at all, Mr Miles." He straightened up from the table, about to take his leave when he looked across to the other side of the road.

In the shadow of the tall building was a fruit vendor, his wide crates at last well stocked with produce. But it was not this that had caught Eamon's attention; it was the raised voices.

The vendor was at the front of his store, his face pale as he spoke to another, much taller, man. The man wore the bright red uniform of the Gauntlet. Though Eamon could not make out which division the man belonged to, he imagined, from the man's bearing, that he was not an ensign. As Eamon watched, the man in uniform gestured to the three younger ensigns with him. One took up a large bag of apples; the other two cast down a crate and, despite the vendor's cries, stomped the fruit into the ground.

"Please!" the vendor cried. The Gauntlet officer laughed.

Eamon carefully set down the sign he held.

"If you will excuse me, Mr Miles," he said. There was anger in his heart. But it did not drive him on to rage or violence; it merely drove him quietly across the road to where the four Gauntlet men laughed as the vendor stared at what had been done, and his other customers watched in horror, unable either to intervene or to leave.

"Get on your knees and lick it off the ground, you bastard!" It was the Gauntlet officer who spoke, and as Eamon approached he saw the flames that marked a first lieutenant and the emblem that marked his province: Edesfield. Indeed, the gaunt face was familiar to him: First Lieutenant Curtis. Although Curtis had been stationed in one of the towns near Edesfield, Eamon had met him while training at the college and on active service at the borders.

As Eamon stepped quietly across the street, the lieutenant raised his fist to strike the vendor who slowly bent to his knees in the mulch.

"Lick it!" the first lieutenant cried again, and with the toe of his boot he scuffed the sodden mess up towards the man's face.

"Good afternoon, First Lieutenant Curtis," Eamon said. He set his own boot firmly before the lieutenant's, blocking the kick he was sure was about to be delivered to the kneeling man's face, then crouched down for a moment beside the vendor. "You can get up," he said quietly, and took the man's arm to help him to his feet.

As they both rose, the silence was thick enough to cut with a knife. Eamon faced the first lieutenant. Curtis stared at him, his expression something between indignance and amusement. The vendor stepped to one side, and his wife gathered him into her arms before wiping the thick mess from her husband's face.

Eamon met the first lieutenant's gaze, then looked meaningfully at the fruit held by the three cadets. "Have you paid for this fruit, First Lieutenant Curtis?"

The man stared at him, and suddenly he laughed. "I remember you," he sneered. "Goodman. Yes – Goodman."

The silence in the street grew tenser. "You have a good memory," Eamon answered calmly, "though apparently you are incapable of answering questions."

The man bristled. "What was that?"

"I asked you a question and I would have you answer it."

"Oh you would, would you?" The man laughed again. "That's rich, very rich indeed! You, Belaal's jumped-up lieutenant!" Eamon looked at Curtis as he laughed louder. The first lieutenant stopped suddenly and smiled cruelly. "If you don't want him to lick the ground, Goodman, perhaps you should do it," he said. One big hand reached forward to grab Eamon by his shirt.

"Do not lay your hands on me." Eamon's voice was quiet, but stayed the man's hand. "The charges against you are high enough as they stand. Do not add to them."

"Charges?" The man spat at Eamon's feet. The other faces nearby – faces that knew more than Curtis – went pale. "Prithee, *dear* Lieutenant Goodman, what would they be?"

"Theft. Violence and intimidation, actual and intended against a citizen of Dunthruik. Wasting of city resources." Eamon met his gaze. "Disrespecting the Lord of the East Quarter."

Curtis rolled his eyes. "I'm sure the Lord of the East Quarter would take my part if he were here! These peasants deserve everything that's coming to them."

"He is here," Eamon answered. "And you would do well to address him as befits his station."

Curtis stared at him. "You?" he cried, and threw back his head. "You! Oh, but of course, *Lord* Goodman!" He threw himself into a mocking bow. "Do let me introduce myself. Perhaps you know me? I am the Right Hand."

The silence became deathly.

"It is treasonous, First Lieutenant Curtis, to take Lord Arlaith's name in vain – more so than it is to take my own. Yet you have done both." Eamon gestured towards the man, and the movement caught light on the ring on his hand. Curtis's face paled, and his eyes went wide with growing horror.

"What's that?" he whispered, pointing at the ring.

"Now you would ask a question of me? That seems foolish indeed." Eamon's tone hardened. "You stand in very real peril, First Lieutenant Curtis. For to take in vain the Right Hand's name is to take in vain the name of the Master. To take my name in vain is to do the same. And to treat with disrespect the men and women of the East Quarter, wherein you are but a guest, violates the glory of the one you claim to serve."

Curtis grew ashen. "Lord Goodman," he began, "I ask for clemency –"

"And I asked you a question a long time ago," Eamon replied, "to which you gave no answer. You will forgive me, then, if I do not answer you."

"It was not paid for." The words tumbled out of the man's mouth.

"What right had you not to pay for it?" Eamon demanded. "What right have you to wear that uniform, when you comport yourself in a way that befits no man? What right have you to trammel the lives of people for whom you should give your body and blood in service? That is your oath: body, blade, and blood to the Master. To serve the Master is to protect his people. What right have you, First Lieutenant Curtis, to my clemency?" he asked at last, more quietly. "What right have I to grant it, when the offence is not against me, but against the Lord of Dunthruik?"

Shaking, the first lieutenant sank to his knees. Eamon shook his head.

"Do not kneel to me," he said. "You will pay this man for everything that you have destroyed, and you will pay for the goods that your ensigns hold, whether you take them or not. You will conduct yourself to the East Quarter College, where you will report to the brig." Stepping forward to the kneeling man, Eamon briskly removed the pins from his collar. The man winced. "The Master will hear of how you have disgraced him. That is all, Ensign Curtis."

"Yes, Lord Goodman."

Eamon saw that the fruit vendor was paid and that Curtis was escorted into the brig before returning to the Handquarters. He wrote a report of the altercation and dispatched it that afternoon. Anderas advised him that Belaal was stationed in the South Quarter. Eamon sent a copy of the report there. Another he sent to the palace, for the attention of Lord Arlaith's lieutenant. It would come to the Master's attention soon enough.

By early evening he felt strangely tired. Quietly setting aside all the papers on his desk, he made his way to his own rooms. He heard singing as he climbed the stairs, and when he peered about the doorway he saw Cara. The girl was folding in the edges of the freshly changed linens for his bed, and singing as she pulled the thick green cover over them. The rest of his room was in startling order.

She curtseyed as he entered, bid him a good night, and then left, pulling the door gently closed behind her. He smiled. The evening breeze drew in from the window.

It was still light outside. Drawing off his cloak, he laid it over the back of a chair and set his boots carefully to one side. Eamon set himself down on his bed, letting the thick green cover mould about him as he did so. He read for as long as he could, but it was not long before he felt waves of tiredness wash over him. He was soon asleep.

A shrill howling ripped through the air and a wind whipped in from far away. He staggered forward, not knowing where he was going, and he followed the howling along the banks of the River that flowed by him. It led down through blasted valleys to the plains around Dunthruik. The city gates creaked and shattered in the strange wind. No guards stood by them. Eamon followed the road in through the Blind Gate and made his way into the East Quarter, calling out as he went. There was nobody there.

He reached the Ashen and there he stopped in horror. The square was filled with ragged corpses. Pale faces stared at him, their eyes vacant. Children lay among them, shrunken and shrivelled.

Retching, Eamon tore himself away and ran through roads that he knew and loved. Suddenly, they were filled with people who raised their hands and mouths towards him, crying out his name, and he covered his ears and ran, ran as fast as he could from the gate and back onto the plain, through fires that raged in plagued streets.

There he stopped, for grim-faced men, dressed in blue, filled the plain. At their head rode a silent man and Eamon recognized him: Hughan. And yet his face seemed strange, as though cast in iron.

Eamon fell down before the King. "Hughan!" he cried. "The city is dying!"

"First they shall be put to hunger, and then to the sword," the distant face replied, and as the words crushed him, Eamon felt something strange on his hands. He looked down and saw that they were covered in rotting food and clotting blood. With a cry of alarm he tried to wipe the stuff from himself, but as he did it only grew. He looked up at the King once more.

"They are your people!" he screamed.

Chapter XXIV

"They are not fit to live, Eben's son," the cruel face replied, and it smiled at him.

It was dark. Eamon felt sweat on his hands and brow and he clutched at the covers, searching for proof that he was awake. The Edelred Cycle lay at his side, its pages crumpled where he had crushed them in his sleep. His heart pounded in his breast as he struggled to bring his mind back to the bed, the window, the evening breeze, the shape of the book by him – to anything but the nightmarish plain.

It had not been Hughan. He repeated it to himself again and again. It had not been Hughan.

Hunger before the sword, Eben's son. The voice was there and his pulse quickened in panic. *Hunger before the sword. It is no less than they deserve, and when they die their blood will be on you, their beloved Hand. For when the Serpent comes and takes their wretched lives, they will see that you betrayed them to him.*

Eamon sat upright on the bed and shook his head. His stomach was knotted. It was not true.

And yet there was truth to it. Hughan would come soon. The King would have little choice but to lay siege to the city, and then the people of the East Quarter would starve and die. Then the ensigns and cadets, his own men, would be sent out of the city gates to face the claws of the King's men.

Eamon. The terrible vision faded away as the gentle word touched his heart. *Eamon, your heart is for the people of this city. So is the King's. Keep hold of your heart and use your courage, First Knight.*

He breathed deeply. He would only have betrayed the people he loved if he did nothing. He had done much in the quarter – but not yet enough.

A short while later, as he set his cloak about his shoulders once more, there was a knock at the door.

"Come," he called. The door opened and Eamon looked up to see Slater. "Mr Slater."

"I am very sorry to disturb you, Lord Goodman. Cara told me

that you were resting. I would not have come if it had not been important."

"I know. Thank you, Mr Slater."

"A messenger has come for you, Lord Goodman," Slater continued. "He comes from the Right Hand."

Eamon looked at him for a moment in surprise. "Please let him know that I shall be there directly," he answered. Slater bowed in acknowledgment and quietly left the room. After taking a few moments more to compose himself, Eamon followed him.

A pale-faced messenger waited for him in his hall. Eamon was not surprised to learn that the Quarter Hands had been summoned to see the Master.

The palace seemed strange to him as he followed through its halls, walking ever towards the throne room. His mind whirled.

He met Dehelt in the corridor. The Lord of the North Quarter greeted him cordially.

"Lord Goodman."

"Lord Dehelt," Eamon replied, and took a moment to take the man in a little better. He was a tall, broad-shouldered man who reminded Eamon a little of Giles. His hair was tawny and he wore his black robes with an easy grace. It occurred to Eamon that he knew surprisingly little about the two Hands who had charge of the quarters bordering his own, and even less about what they knew or thought of him.

"You are well?" he asked.

"Thank you, yes," Dehelt replied. He seemed a quiet man, but it was a daunting kind of quiet. "Your riding improves, I trust?"

"Yes," Eamon replied, feeling a little discomfort. Though he had not realized it, it now seemed perfectly logical to him that he would be visible to the Lord of the North Quarter when he rode out of the North Gate. He would be sure to remember it. "Considerably."

"I am pleased to hear it."

They reached the passage near the throne room, where Cathair and Tramist already waited. They spoke quietly together, and as they approached, Tramist shot Eamon a scathing look. He steeled himself against it, and instead presented both Hands with a warm smile.

"My lords," he said, though he did not bow.

"Ah, Lord Goodman! I am so glad to see that your habit of appearing without your due attire is dispensed with for such occasions," Cathair said jovially, though Eamon detected stark disapproval.

"I am Lord of the East Quarter, Lord Cathair," Eamon replied, "and I retain that position whether I am recognizable by robe or not."

"It seems *Ensign* Curtis learned that to his own cost this afternoon," Dehelt commented.

"Gentlemen," said a voice: the Right Hand's. They had not seen him approach. Eamon at once joined the other Hands in bowing before him. "Let us go in."

The Master waited for them – no less resplendent or imposing in his robes than ever – and Eamon at once felt the power of the grey stare on him. He matched pace with the other Hands and bowed low with them before the Master.

"Your glory, Master," the Right Hand said.

"Rise," the throned commanded. They did so, and the Master spoke.

"The Serpent has taken much of the River Realm," he said, "and he comes here." The grey gaze followed Eamon. "But we will be ready. His house will be crushed, and you, my Hands, will be there to see me put it to the sword."

A horrified shiver ran down Eamon's spine as he thought of Hughan coming within this man's grasp. Surely the King would be torn, disembowelled, and set in grisly triumph upon the Blind Gate, where his broken body would be exulted over by these men…

Eamon met the Master's gaze, and saw him smile. What other outcome could there be? He was foolish to question the matter. What was the house of Brenuin before the Lord of Dunthruik?

Courage, Eamon.

The other Hands watched him from the corners of their eyes. His vivid thoughts faded and he drew his mind back to the Master's words.

As he had thought, the presence of more and more Gauntlet in the city was preparative against an expected strike. The throned knew that Hughan would come and knew that Dunthruik would be the place where the last battle was fought. The quarter colleges were to be set to harsher drills and the thresholders were to be named so that, should a final defence of the city become necessary, they would know their places. Any man suspected of aiding, abetting, or sympathizing with the Serpent was to be sent to the pyre without question.

The Master looked at Eamon with peculiar emphasis. "There will be no more acquittals."

Eamon felt the eyes heavy on him. The Master knew about Fort: the words were for him. He bowed his head, giving his assent to the command along with the other Hands.

"This is my will," the throned said at last. "See it done."

"To your glory," the Hands answered, and rose to their feet. Eamon rose with them and bowed, preparing to leave with the others. Then he heard the terrifying voice speak his name.

"Son of Eben, you will stay."

Eamon looked up, then almost laughed to see that the other Hands seemed more alarmed by this prospect than he was. The Right Hand drew breath as though to speak, but the Master smiled and stole it from him.

"You will go, Lord Arlaith."

"Your will and glory, Master," the Right Hand answered, and bowed.

Eamon stood before the throned, matching his gaze as the sound of the other Hands receded behind them. The Master smiled at him wryly, as though enjoying the awkwardness of the situation he had created – perhaps, Eamon mused, because he had created it and he would undo it, or not, as it suited him.

He swallowed in a dry throat, heard the throne room's doors closing behind him, and bowed down to one knee before the Master.

"How may I serve you, Master?"

"You serve me, Eben's son, with a boldness that my Hands envy," the throned answered. An indulgent smile played about his lips.

"Is it to your glory and pleasure?" Eamon dared.

"Yes, Eben's son. It is."

It was terrifying praise to receive.

"Then until you deem otherwise, I shall continue as I have begun, Master. My quarter sings your praise and that is how I would have it."

"Continue as you do, Eben's son," the throned told him, "and the East Quarter shall not be all that you will hold for me."

Eamon looked up agog. The Master's face seemed immense before him, and his eyes held him with inescapable intimacy. It chilled him to his core, diminishing him to a vulnerable child to be praised or beaten as his deeds dictated. He was subjected to the whim of those terrible eyes…

"*To your awesome King alone.*" Memory of Mathaiah's song washed through him.

Drawing a deep breath he bowed his head down to his breast. "May I serve your glory, Master," he said.

The following dawn he rode with Anderas as was routine. He had spent much of the night awake, unable to shake a deep sense of unease. He feared that Dunthruik would be besieged and that people who did not serve the throned, people who served the throned through fear, even those who served by choice, would never know the King because they would not live to see him come.

A siege would kill many, but as he lay gathered in his sheets he thought of a way that he could lessen what was to come to the people of the East Quarter.

As they went along the road that led back into the city, Eamon turned to his captain. He wondered how he might speak without arousing suspicion. And yet, was he not simply taking the simplest of precautions? Were they not the sort of precautions that only a lord of Dunthruik could lay in place?

"How many caves are there beneath the quarter?" he asked.

Anderas looked at him and was silent for a moment. Eamon marvelled that the man rarely seemed surprised by anything he said.

"Maybe a dozen," the captain answered.

"Is there one near the Handquarters?"

"There is one beneath one of the college outbuildings," Anderas told him.

"Is it large?"

"Reasonably so."

"Is it well known?"

"Not beyond the officers of the quarter, though wild rumours of lost treasure in hidden caves predictably abound among the cadets from time to time."

"The next grain ship comes in tomorrow." Eamon knew he was thinking out loud, but in part he wanted Anderas to hear it.

"Yes. From the state of Etraia, I believe."

Eamon nodded. It was one of the merchant states most loyal to the throned. A portion of the grain that the ship bore would already have been allocated by palace officials to go to the East Quarter, to be sold at the grain market.

"Mr Greenwood is on logistics duty tomorrow?" he asked. The quarter's logistics draybant had been having difficulty in keeping the college and quarter in order that week, and Greenwood had offered to assist by organizing the groups of ensigns that would collect the grain from the port when it came in.

"Mr Greenwood shall be marshalling our granarians, yes."

"Captain," Eamon said quietly, "have him acquire as close to all of it as he can for my private use."

Anderas glanced at him and Eamon saw the reservation on the man's face. It would drive up the cost of grain in the quarter, and it would be known that Eamon had bought it. Eamon swallowed. The throned had congratulated him because the quarter praised him. Would they praise the work of Lord Goodman when it took food from their plates and money from their purses? Would the Master cast scorn on him? Would the people jeer and scowl…?

"Lord Goodman?"

"Have Draybant Greenwood go across to the port early tomorrow," Eamon answered. "Let him take some trusted men. I want as much of the quarter's portion as can be feasibly taken removed and stored securely in the college cavern. I want the cavern guarded."

Eamon matched Anderas's gaze. He saw the captain assess what he had said, piecing it together, and almost wanted Anderas to ask him why he commanded such things, so that he could explain it.

But Captain Anderas was no fool, and as the captain nodded Eamon knew that the man understood. "Yes, Lord Goodman."

So it was that Eamon met Anderas, Greenwood, and several other ensigns and officers in the college grounds early the following morning. Greenwood and Anderas chose a small contingent of men to guard the cavern in watches. When Eamon arrived it was to find the last few sacks of grain being moved from a large wagon down into the cavern. The entrance lay behind a normal-looking door in what was the college storehouse.

Eamon gestured to Anderas, and the captain called a brief halt in the unloading, gathering the draybant, a lieutenant, and a unit of ensigns. As they assembled, Eamon turned quietly to Anderas.

"Did Mr Greenwood encounter any trouble?"

"No, my lord," Anderas answered. "He took two-fifths of the quarter's allotment. The rest he sent on to logistics, as normal. This is the last of it."

"Thank you." Eamon waited for the men to be gathered before him. Some panted from the exertion of heaving the sacks, but the men were alert and attentive as he spoke.

"Gentlemen," he said, "the first thing I must make absolutely clear to you all is how vital it is that this store is kept secret and safe.

I want no word of it to be passed to your colleagues or families. It will go out, I am sure, that Lord Goodman is taking what is not his to take."

He looked at them each in turn. He had thought very carefully about what he needed to say. "I asked Captain Anderas and Draybant Greenwood to choose the most trustworthy men in this college for this task. You are those men, and so I want you to know why this is being done. Not so that you can speak it out, nor so that you can indulge in fears and gossips that have no place in the Gauntlet, but so that you may perform your duties with stronger hearts."

He surveyed the men before him and saw a row of faces that followed him utterly. He imagined that few of them would have dared to question him, and knew that the bond of silence he was asking them to keep would be kept.

"Gentlemen, a time may be coming when this city is besieged by the Serpent." He saw a couple of the ensigns look at him uneasily and he understood why. The Gauntlet had always been taught that the Serpent was a scattered enemy, but recent news had given the whole city reason to believe otherwise. "If that day comes, the Gauntlet will be provisioned but the people of this quarter will not. If that day comes, I want the people of this quarter to live.

"Rumours may go abroad that this grain is being kept for private use – let it. Speak no word in my defence if you hear words against me. This quarter is already on its knees from months of hunger, from the cull, from fear of the snakes that skirmish in the fields. I do not want the fear of a siege, and an even keener hunger, to take hold of the people here. Every time a grain ship comes in, Mr Greenwood will take a group of you to the port to take as much of the grain as can reasonably be taken. It will be brought here; this door will be guarded. Both of these orders will stand until I countermand them."

Silence fell. The faces watched him still, but they were men who understood what they had been asked to do. They were loyal to him.

"Yes, Lord Goodman," they answered.

Eamon nodded once to Greenwood, who urged the young men back to their work. As Eamon left the courtyard, Anderas joined him.

"They're good men, captain."

"They have a good lord."

The grain prices rose, but it did not stop the growing number of requests for entry into the East Quarter, and over the next week Eamon was pleased to see a good amount of grain stored in the cavern. The guards were diligent young men, and although some rumours as to the location of the missing grain abounded, and the East Quarter's logistics draybant decided to bring in some extra supplies at an exorbitant price from the minuscule South Quarter surplus, there was no widespread civil unrest. Eamon, for one, was glad of it, and hoped that his precaution would go a long way to helping the people whom he was coming to view as his own.

The Crown Office, spearheaded by Lorentide's new list, continued their work, and Eamon was delighted to see construction and renovation taking place throughout the quarter. That week he also received a deliriously eloquent letter of apology from Ensign Curtis. It was inscrutably worded, and Eamon imagined that it had been forced unwillingly from the man's hand, probably under Belaal's watchful eye, for the captain's reputation would have been damaged by the event.

That week he took another walk through the quarter and again inspected the streets. It had grown hot and his cloak was more troublesome than usual. He had begun routinely forgoing his black jacket when he dressed.

He walked past the Horse and Cart inn and was brought up short, for it had been completely reworked. The windows glistened and people moved about inside. Perhaps, more than this, it was the inn's new name that caught his eye: The Good Man. It was written in bold red, and emblems of the quarter stood beneath it.

He stood there in astonishment, then movement caught his eye:

the innkeeper opened the door for a leaving guest. He caught sight of Eamon and fell into a deep bow.

"Good day, my lord!"

"And to you, good keeper," Eamon replied. He did not know what else to say. It was then that he recognized the person leaving the inn – the wife of the vendor from across the road.

"Lord Goodman!" she breathed, and curtseyed.

"Good day to you," he said.

"Lord Goodman," she began, before her words vanished in a stammer as she nervously lowered her eyes.

"Do speak," Eamon encouraged her.

She raised her eyes again. "I wanted to thank you for helping my husband," she said quietly. "How may I?"

"Serve the lord of the city," Eamon answered her. "Serve him with all your heart." The woman and the innkeeper gazed at him, and he nodded carefully at them. "To his glory," he said.

"To his glory."

The streets were quiet as the heat of the sun rolled past. Eamon took refuge in the shade on Coronet Rise, near one of the reconstruction works. Workmen rested there, some of them sipping water from thick flasks, but they were some of the few who braved the unusual heat.

As Eamon approached they leapt to their feet one by one, but Eamon gestured to them to sit again. They did so, reluctantly, and as they returned to their water Eamon examined the stonework. It was being well set, and he drew off one glove and gently laid his hand to the stone to inspect the joins. He gasped as a piece of stone snagged against his hand, and a thin line of blood marked his palm. Instinctively he set it to his mouth.

"Did you hurt yourself?" a young voice said.

Eamon looked down in surprise to see a small boy looking up at him. He did not know from where the child had come.

"Did you?" the boy insisted again.

Eamon nodded. "Yes, I did, but not badly –"

Barely had the words left his mouth when the little boy reached up with a determined hand and took hold of Eamon's own. The child began an interested inspection of the wound, shuffling Eamon's fingers out flat so as to look at his palm more clearly. His fingers fumbled over Eamon's ring for a moment. "I like your ring. There's an owl on it."

"Yes, there is," Eamon replied. The boy didn't seem to understand what the owl tokened – either that or he was too busy looking at the cut.

"I like owls."

Eamon crouched down beside the child as the boy's fingers tapped lightly at his cut.

"Does it hurt a lot?" the boy asked.

"Only a little," Eamon told him. "I'm sure it will be –"

He fell silent as the boy set his fingers against the cut and faintly, so faintly that he almost could not see it – so faintly that he hoped he alone could see it – Eamon saw the tiniest flicker of light. Blue light.

The little boy handed Eamon's palm back to him and smiled. "There," he pronounced. The cut was gone.

"Thank you," Eamon answered. He tried not to look alarmed. "What's your name, young man?"

"Damien."

"Damien," Eamon repeated. This child was kind but in grave danger; if anyone saw him, he and his family would go straight to the pyre. "Damien, where do you live?"

The child pulled a confused face. "Stone Way," he answered, looking up at the road where he was. His face creased into a frown. "But I'm not sure…"

"Let me take you," Eamon told him. He rose quietly to his feet. "Follow me, Damien."

Stone Way was a road that ran from the East Quarter down towards the South Quarter. Eamon encouraged the boy to walk by him and spoke quietly with him as they went. He was grateful that the heat of the sun was such that many were indoors, and the time of day meant that they ate or slept. Few saw them as they passed.

"Damien," he asked, "what you did for me, do you do it often?"

"Sometimes."

"And your parents – do they know about it?"

Damien looked at him as though this were a silly question. "Yes."

"What do they say about it?"

"That I shouldn't." The boy pulled a face. "But I don't understand why not –"

"Damien," Eamon told him, "there's something you need to know –"

"My brother says that there are lots of things I need to know!"

"What you can do is a good thing," Eamon told him gently, "and one day it will be recognized as a good thing, and on that day you will be able to do it freely."

"When?"

"I don't know exactly what day it will be, but I know that you will know it when it comes, and so will your parents." Eamon paused as they passed a small group of shops, then spoke again as they stepped into the shadows of Stone Way. "But until that day, Damien, what you can do frightens people."

"It makes them better!" the boy protested.

"Sometimes the things that are best for us are frightening," Eamon answered. "Sometimes, when people are frightened, they do terrible things to whatever frightens them. That is why you must listen to your parents. What you did for me was kind, and I thank you for it. At the same time, Damien, I charge you not to do it again, unless the time and place is truly desperate, until the right day comes." He fixed the little boy with a firm gaze and saw that the child's face had grown very serious.

"Are you an important person, sir?" The young brown eyes assessed Eamon with renewed interest.

"Some people say so," Eamon answered. "But whether I am or

not does not change what I have said. You must promise me that you will do as I have asked, and that you will tell no one of what I have said. Your parents don't want to see you hurt, and neither do I."

Damien looked down at his small hands, and chewed at his lip. Flexing his fingers he looked up again. "I suppose I could wait until that day you told me about," he said.

Eamon nodded and smiled. "I think you could."

They had come a few hundred yards down Stone Way and Eamon looked at the child again. "Which house is yours?" he asked. Damien looked across the street with narrowed eyes, shielding them against a glint of sun, then grinned and pointed wildly across the cobbles.

"That one!" he cried. "Come and see!"

He seized Eamon's hand and tugged him across the road to a building nestled by a gnarled tree. Damien led him past the front entrance and round the side of the building towards the back. As they approached the back door, Eamon heard anxious voices inside, though he could not make out what they said.

"Is that your mother?" he asked. Damien paused on the path, listening, then nodded, his face a little distressed.

"Yes," he said, then looked up in concern. "She's crying."

"She's probably worried about you," Eamon told him. Damien looked at him as though this was a strange idea and slowly his face grew more anxious.

"She'll be angry with me," he said, twisting the bottom of his shirt in his hands.

Eamon crouched down by him. "She'll be angry because she loves you and she doesn't want you to come to harm. My own mother was the same."

"She got cross with you?"

"Very often. I was a very naughty boy."

The boy didn't look convinced. Eamon touched his arm in encouragement. "Damien, it's very warm," he said. "Let me take this heavy cloak off, and we'll go inside. Then we can see your mother together."

Damien nodded his approval, and Eamon carefully removed his cloak. Immensely grateful that there was nobody else on the street, he folded it and laid it between two barrels that stood by the door, then slipped the ring from his finger and tucked it into the pouch at his waist. He held his hand out to the boy.

"Shall we go in?" he asked. Taking his hand, Damien moved towards the door, and pushed it open.

They entered a small kitchen area with a table and a couple of chairs stacked to one side. The walls were whitewashed and bore some shelves with various utensils, while a fire burned low in a corner grate. A boy, probably no older than fourteen, opened tall cupboards in the manner of a searcher. Hearing the door latch, he looked up.

"Hello," Damien offered cheerfully.

The boy stared at him, then at Eamon, and then called into the next room. "Ma!" he shouted. "Damien's here." Eamon heard a pause.

"Damien," called a woman's voice, "we've told you a hundred times that hiding and making us worried is not a good game!"

"Ma —"

"Don't defend your brother, Neithan," the woman called crossly as she approached. "You know perfectly well —"

"Ma, there's someone with him."

The woman reached the kitchen doorway and stopped there, her face caught in surprise. Damien gripped Eamon's hand.

"Hello, Ma," the boy whispered. The child ducked behind Eamon a little, but his mother's attention was focused not on the boy but on Eamon. Her eyes fell on his sword; it marked him as a Gauntlet officer, for he had never exchanged it for the more distinctive blades borne by the Hands.

"Good afternoon, madam," Eamon said kindly.

"Good afternoon, Mr...?"

"Tiller," he answered after a moment's hesitation. "Madam, I was passing by and came across this young man. His exploratory spirit is highly commendable, though he seems to have left home without his map today. Fortunately, I was able to help him chart a course back."

"Thank you, Mr Tiller."

"I'm sorry if I worried you, Ma," Damien said quietly. "Truly I am." He edged forward from his hiding place. His mother came from the doorway and dropped to one knee before him, throwing her arms wide. Damien ran to them and his mother caught him into a warm embrace.

"I am so sorry if he caused you any trouble, Mr Tiller," she said.

"None at all, madam," Eamon answered. "He is a very amicable young man, and I am sure he is a credit to your family."

"Yes," the woman answered. She rose to her feet with Damien gathered in her arms. "Mr Tiller, how can we thank you for bringing him home?"

"No thanks are necessary," Eamon replied kindly.

"Please, let us give you something," the woman insisted.

"Please allow me to decline," Eamon told her. "I would not take anything from you when your need is doubtless more than my own."

"Then will you let us do something?" the woman asked. "Will you be our guest to dinner?"

Eamon looked at her. It was unheard of for a Hand to dine with a family in his quarter. But this woman could not know that he was a Hand and he could not tell her now. Apart from that, the woman's earnest desire to thank him touched his heart. He delighted in the thought of setting aside all the trappings of his office to enjoy a meal with ordinary people... It had been so long since he had done so.

He met the woman's gaze again. "Madam –"

"Mrs Grennil," the woman answered. Eamon smiled.

"Mrs Grennil," he said, "I would be deeply honoured to take a seat at your table."

"Tonight?"

"I'm afraid that my duties prevent me from joining you this evening. But I could sup with you…" He paused, considering his appointments over the next day or two. "In two days' time, I believe."

Mrs Grennil curtsied. "Then we shall welcome you then, Mr Tiller!"

Chapter XXV

"Your style, Lord Goodman, will become the stuff of legend."

"If you have anything to do with the writing of it I dare say it will, captain."

Two days after his meeting with the Grennils, he prepared to join them for supper. He had let it be known among his servants that he would be absent that evening, but he had entrusted the nature of his engagement to Anderas alone. He did not think that the idea of the lord of the quarter dining out among his people would go down well at the palace, and Anderas had agreed with his assessment – and hadn't been convinced that the visit was prudent. However, he had agreed to cover Eamon's duties for an hour or two, and knew where Eamon would be, so would be able to reach him at need. Eamon decided to go without his cloak and ring. As he set them discreetly aside in his bedchamber, he marvelled at how free he felt without them. He breathed deep and smiled.

"Have a very pleasant evening, Lord Goodman," Anderas told him.

"Thank you, captain. You know where to find me if you need me."

It was dark when he left the Handquarters, slipping quietly out through one of the side gates, mostly unnoticed and certainly unrecognized. He wove his way through the streets until he came again to Stone Way and to the small house by the tree. The front door was open and lights twinkled in the windows, masked by thin curtains.

Cats prowled on the steps, and as he approached the gate, a small figure leapt up from the doorstep and ran excitedly inside. A voice called:

"Ma, Ma! He's here!"

Eamon smiled as Mrs Grennil advised her son to go and meet their guest rather than run about like a headless chicken. The small boy tumbled out of the door again. Damien ran happily down the steps to where Eamon stood and took him by the hand.

"Come inside – we've been waiting for you! It's nearly ready!"

"Thank you," Eamon replied, allowing the small boy to tug him into the house.

The front room had been set with a large table, or rather three much smaller tables of slightly mismatched height set closely together, with a broad cloth over them. A group of chairs had been set to it – some of whole wood, some more like stools than chairs, some with straw seats woven into their wooden frames. About ten places had been set at the table, and Eamon wondered who else would be joining them. He soon learned, for as he cleared the doorway he saw a collection of people in the room speaking together. They rose to their feet as they saw him.

"Mr Tiller?" asked one, a tall man who seemed at least a decade his senior. Eamon nodded.

"Yes."

"I'm Mr Grennil. My wife told me about what happened with Damien the other day. Please, let me offer my own thanks once again –"

"It really was no trouble."

"Thank you nonetheless. And welcome!" Mr Grennil took his hand and clasped it warmly.

One by one, he introduced Eamon to the others. Present were the man's elder son, whom Eamon had met in the kitchen, and Mr Grennil's sister, who had come with her own husband and three children, two young girls and a boy of similar age to the Grennils' eldest. The smaller children greeted him politely and returned to their play, involving some small wooden toys in a corner of the room, while the men and older boys invited Eamon to sit with them. The two young cousins watched him with interest, and the sound of the two women working filtered in from the kitchen.

Mr Grennil rose and brought across a small tray of grey mugs filled with ale, and offered the first to Eamon.

"Mr Tiller?"

"Thank you," Eamon replied, and took the heavy mug. It rested comfortably in his hand and he smiled as memories of the inn at Edesfield filled him. It felt closer than it had for a long time. He listened as Mr Grennil and his brother-in-law, Jehim, spoke a little of their trades. Jehim was a carpenter and one of the many men who worked for Lorentide.

Food was swiftly brought to the table, and Eamon was invited to sit at its head. He greeted the two wives kindly and watched in admiration as they set down a bowl of thick soup, along with large slices of bread. As they took their places, and the children were encouraged to sit still, Mrs Grennil turned to him.

"Would you like to say the majesty?" she asked quietly. He felt the eyes of the whole family turn to him.

"Yes," Eamon answered, and as he drew breath to speak they bowed their heads. "To the Master of the River and defender of the city; to his glory."

"To his glory," came the hearty reply. Eamon couldn't help but glance at Damien's parents as they replied. He wondered if they too were wayfarers, as their son was. If so, did they direct the words meant for the throned's glory towards the King as he did?

"Thank you, Mr Tiller," Mrs Grennil said, smiling. She gestured to the soup. "Please, do help yourself."

"You shan't have to ask me twice, Mrs Grennil," Eamon replied.

"So, your name's Tiller?" It was one of the older boys, Damien's cousin, who spoke. He gazed at Eamon with deep curiosity. He was older than Neithan, perhaps sixteen.

"Joel," said his mother quietly, as though warding him from rudeness.

"Yes, my name is Tiller," Eamon answered, giving the woman an encouraging smile. An odd silence touched the table. Eamon glanced surreptitiously to check that he was not wearing his cloak. He was not – just his standard, Gauntlet-issue, white shirt.

"It's just that there haven't been any Tillers in the city for years – they left long ago. Chased out. Where did you say you were from?"

"Neithan! Mr Tiller, please allow me to apologize for my son," said the boy's mother, leaning forward. "He asks too many questions."

"I never asked enough when I was his age," Eamon replied with a laugh. "I came from Edesfield, originally. I've been in Dunthruik almost a year."

"Edesfield? Did that just fall to the Serpent?" said Joel.

Mrs Grennil gave him a withering stare. "That is a conversation better left for when we are not entertaining company."

"Do you know who else is from Edesfield?" interjected Neithan. "They say that Lord Goodman is from there."

"And we don't discuss the Lord of the East Quarter either!" Mrs Grennil warned.

"I don't think there's anything wrong with talking about Lord Goodman," Mr Grennil added, and his son smiled at him thankfully, for the words saved him from his mother's wrath.

"It's difficult not to," Jehim added grimly, pausing to help himself to some bread.

"He's done some real good in this quarter," Mr Grennil continued, with a strange look at his brother-in-law. "I was talking to some of the folk who saw him down at Tailor's Turn a month back, when the building caved in. Said they'd never seen anything like it. I mean, how many Hands – and *Quarter* Hands at that – go crawling through wreckage to pull the likes of us from danger?"

"And he brought back the Easter lord's head," said Joel enthusiastically. His eyes were wide – Eamon wondered if the young man had been down to the Blind Gate to see it. "They say that he struck it clean off himself!"

"And that he saved the men who served under him at Pinewood doing it," Jehim's wife added.

"Did you hear what he did the other day by the Good Man?" Neithan asked.

Feeling more than a little awkward, Eamon dipped his spoon into his soup and blew over it.

"Mrs Grennil, please allow me to compliment you on what is a very fine soup indeed," he said. Mrs Grennil smiled at him across the table.

"I'm glad you like it, Mr Tiller."

"Hush, Ma! Nei was going to tell me the story!" Damien hissed, tapping his mother's wrist gently. The small boy looked pleadingly across at his brother. "Tell me the story!" he cried. "I want to hear it!"

Neithan grinned at him and began to tell the tale. As he did so he affected voices and manners to go with it such that the whole table was caught up in the words he wove together.

"They say that there was nobody else there in the street that day, except this great big mountain of a Gauntlet officer. Now, the officer wanted fruit without paying for it, and the seller refused him. 'Well, *nobody* refuses a Gauntlet officer', cried the man, and he threatened the seller, but still the seller refused. So the officer began taking the fruit anyway. When the man protested, he knocked him down hard to the ground. The cadets with him crushed the seller's fruit into the mud, and the officer demanded that the seller lick it all up. The seller didn't do it."

"Oh no!" Damien breathed, his tiny hands clutching at his spoon. "What happened?"

Smiling, Neithan took an enormous piece of bread and put it into his mouth. He chewed it slowly. Damien gaped at his brother.

"That's not fair!" he cried. "Ma, ma! He's doing it *on purpose!*"

"You'll have to be patient and wait for him to finish," Joel answered. Damien huffed and folded his arms. He drummed his fingers impatiently – and loudly – on the table.

His brother made a show of swallowing his bread, took up his mug, drained it, refilled it from the jug on the table, sat back for a moment as though trying to remember what he had been doing, then reached for more bread. Damien pointed at him.

"You promised to tell me the story!" he cried.

"So I did," Neithan answered, grinning.

"Well?"

"I may just not finish…"

Damien gasped and looked around for support. "Somebody tell him –"

"Neithan, stop torturing your brother," Mr Grennil said.

Neithan turned back to the little boy. "Where was I?"

"The fruit seller was on the ground," Damien answered, leaning forward with deep, barely restrained excitement. He began bouncing up and down in his seat. "Come on!" he cried.

"Ah yes! So the fruit seller was on the ground, and the officer was going to beat him and humiliate him. But what the officer *didn't* know was that Lord Goodman was there, and Lord Goodman had seen it all. He wasn't wearing his cloak or jacket, and as he strode across the silent street to meet the officer, nobody recognized him."

Eamon shuffled in his chair.

"Lord Goodman brought the seller up from the ground and demanded that the officer pay for what he had done. 'Why should I?' the officer asked him. 'You're nobody important. If it matters that much to you, you can take his place and lick the fruit off the ground yourself.'"

Damien gasped. "What did he do?"

"Lord Goodman looked the officer straight in the eye and said: 'You add crimes to your crime, lieutenant!'" The young man imitated the voice of the infamous Lord of the East Quarter – not a bad approximation, if a little theatrical. Eamon smiled. "'How dare you torment the people of this quarter, and ridicule the lord of it, to his very face? Now you will pay for everything that this good man has lost, and you shall be arrested, and right now I take away your rank, for speaking as you have done dishonours you and dishonours the Master.' And Lord Goodman made him pay back to the fruit seller the worth of everything that had been lost, and demoted him on the spot."

Damien laughed in delight and clapped his hands. "It's just like in that story you told me last night –"

"Lord Goodman has certainly done a lot of good," Mr Grennil interrupted, and Damien fell quiet, deflated. "A great deal of good. Particularly to the Renovation and Repair lists."

"They're certainly keeping Jehim busy at the Crown Office just now," the carpenter's wife said with a smile.

"The problem is that his capabilities are not solely good," Jehim replied harshly. Eamon, and the whole table, looked across at him. The man was older than his brother-in-law, and his voice grew harsher as he spoke. "The Lord of the East is not a man with a stable head."

"Jehim –" Mr Grennil interjected.

"That's what happens when your head is fixed to a pike, Pa," Joel told his father, grinning. "Tends to wobble a little bit." He wobbled his own back and forth wildly. Damien and the two little girls burst into furious laughter.

"Do it again!" one of them cried, and Joel obliged.

"You'll be sick," his mother warned, as her son stilled his gyrating head.

"I might just," he answered, and reached across for one of his sisters' plates as though to do just that. When she squealed, he grinned and handed it back to her.

"You can say what you like about the good he's done, but it won't last," Jehim continued, and the mood at the table grew uncomfortable. "Have you all forgotten that he served two crowns, and for weeks his captain did all his work while he did nothing at all?"

Eamon swallowed. It had not been weeks. He supposed that, just as stories of what good he had done were exaggerated, so were those of his mistakes.

"Jehim, this is not a conversation for –"

"When he brought in more grain and the prices went down, the whole quarter rejoiced," Jehim continued. "Now what has he done? He's buying up over half of every load that comes in, and we're paying for his indulgence. We're paying it out of our own pockets, and most are so infatuated with him that they won't say a word."

"What's there to say, Jehim?" his wife asked quietly, as though trying to encourage him to drop the matter, but he laughed bitterly.

"What's there to say? He's a Hand, just like any other – this is proof of it. And he'll soon be like all the others."

Eamon sat back in his chair uncomfortably, hoping that the men might somehow forget that he was there, and hoping that he would have the wisdom not to speak out of turn. After all the good that he had done, did people in the quarter still eye him with suspicion? Had he achieved nothing?

"You cannot judge that," Mr Grennil said at last.

"You cannot be defending –"

"Jehim," Mr Grennil said firmly.

His brother-in-law shrugged his shoulders. "We suffered under Lord Ashway, and we'll suffer under this one just the same," he said viciously. "They don't care at all for the likes of us."

"What do you think, Mr Tiller?" It was Neithan who asked it, and as he did, all eyes turned to Eamon. He set aside his bowl of soup, and looked carefully at those who watched him.

"Of the Lord of the East Quarter?" he asked.

"Yes," Neithan nodded.

There was no way of avoiding the subject. Eamon paused for a moment, measuring his words carefully. "I think he's young," he said.

A stunned silence fell on the room. Jehim and Mr Grennil stared openly at him.

"What do you mean?" Neithan asked.

"Just what I say," Eamon replied.

"H-h-how old is he?" Neithan stammered.

"About my age," Eamon answered him, "and so about ten years older than you. Not only is he young, but he has been promoted very swiftly indeed. That's to his credit, I'm sure," he added, "just as I am sure that he would not have gone so far so fast if he were not skilled. But with that promotion goes responsibility that his shoulders are perhaps too young to fully bear."

Neithan frowned and leaned forward as Eamon spoke.

"Your father, Neithan, is responsible for the safety of this family, for its care and well-being, for getting food to your table every night." He paused and his voice grew passionate as he went on. "Lord Goodman is responsible for the entire East Quarter and a college full of cadets about your cousin's age. He is also responsible for many other ensigns, lieutenants, militia, and the Hands of the Quarter.

"Suppose for a moment that this city is attacked by the Serpent. What will happen then? The people of the East Quarter will go to Lord Goodman for leadership and support. But what if he has not made adequate preparations for the safety of this quarter?"

"People will die."

"Yes," Eamon answered. "People will die, and if he has not carried out his responsibilities as he must, Lord Goodman will bear their innocent blood on his hands."

"Innocent blood never seemed to bother Lord Ashway," Jehim sniffed. Eamon looked firmly at him.

"Lord Goodman is not like Lord Ashway."

There was an odd, shocked silence.

Jehim looked at him strangely. His son leaned across the table.

"Do you know Lord Goodman?" Joel asked.

"I do," Eamon replied.

"You are very bold, Mr Tiller," Mrs Grennil said at last.

"You're not the first to tell me so," Eamon answered. Seeing their shocked faces, he laughed and tried to relax a little. "I am sorry – I have worried you by speaking frankly," he said. "I have said nothing to you that I have not said to Lord Goodman himself. He knows what I think of him, and he is content."

"Well, all things considered," Jehim said at last, "things are better under Lord Goodman than they were under Lord Ashway." Eamon wondered if the man didn't look at him oddly as he spoke.

"So, he's a good man!" Neithan grinned at his joke, but Joel rolled his eyes.

"Well then, tell us a little about yourself, Mr Tiller," Mrs Grennil added with a smile.

Eamon paused. "I am afraid there is little to tell, Mrs Grennil, but that I serve in this city and in this quarter. I count myself very fortunate in that."

"Were you at Tailor's Turn when it collapsed?" Mr Grennil added.

"Yes, I was."

"The Gauntlet did a fine job in rescuing the survivors."

"My friend Ellen was there," Damien said, "and she says that Lord Goodman was there, and she said that he rescued her!"

Mrs Grennil offered Eamon an apologetic smile. "Ellen is a very sweet girl," she said. "She has a bit of an imagination."

"We play together," Damien added, "when Neithan doesn't get in the way."

"I make them study," Neithan interrupted, eager to rescue his sullied reputation. "They'd never do it otherwise."

"They spend a lot of time building small shelters for the cats that live round here," Joel added.

"Yesterday Joel helped us build a new one!" Damien enthused, his little eyes shining brightly. "He found some old wood and we fixed it all together and the cat even went in!"

"An aspiring carpenter, perhaps?" Eamon said with a smile.

"Like his father," said Jehim's wife.

"Don't know if I want to be a carpenter," Joel added. "Uncle has a better job, I think."

"I work at the port," Mr Grennil explained. "A big merchant ship came in two days ago, carrying a lot of grain, and wood too. Both bought up pretty quick. Loaded the same ship full of wines from the Raven estate. The captain was a strange man!" he laughed. "All dressed in these ridiculous purple breeches and in a shirt that was so thick you might think he'd come to port in December. Had a very self-important air – was from Calatia," he added, as though that explained everything. "All a bit theatrical."

"Do you like the theatre, Mr Tiller?" Mrs Grennil asked.

"My father took me sometimes, when I was about Damien's age," Eamon answered. "I always enjoyed it very much."

"You must go to the Crown Theatre," said Mr Grennil. "It's an absolute masterpiece. Sometimes the Right Hand lets the theatre give performances for free. They're called 'commoners' – I imagine because folk like us can go."

"They're not a common occurrence," his brother-in-law added wryly.

"It has been a while since we've had one," Mr Grennil agreed.

Mrs Grennil had the two older boys collect up the empty bowls and brought a dish of fruit in their place, while the little girls and Damien fought over the last scraps of bread. In the end Neithan gathered all the remains together and divided them equally between the three. When the fruit was brought, the smallest girl sat back and declared that there was no room for it in her stomach. She was granted permission to leave the table and scurried off to the floor where the wooden toys – a collection of horses, dogs, and bears – lay discarded. Her sister and Damien soon followed her.

"I must congratulate you both on very lovely children," Eamon said, looking to the two mothers at the table. Both women blushed a little, and thanked him.

Suddenly there was a knock on the door. Mrs Grennil rose to answer it.

"G-good evening," she stammered with the breathless air of one startled and struggling to regain her composure.

"I'm terribly sorry to disturb you, madam," said a voice. Eamon recognized it at once. Everyone in the room stood as the newcomer spoke again. "I understand that one Mr Tiller is your guest this evening?"

"Mr Tiller?" the woman offered. "He is here, sir."

Eamon looked up as Anderas stepped across the threshold. Eamon detected traces of anxiety beneath Anderas's polite exterior.

"Is something the matter, captain?" he asked.

"You are required at the Ashen, Mr Tiller. It is a matter of some urgency."

"I shall come at once."

Eamon turned to his hosts. "I'm sorry I can't stay," he said. "You've been most gracious."

A sudden draught pushed into the house through the open door. Damien shivered, then looked at Eamon with eyes wide with concern. "You'll want your cloak!" he cried. "Mother always says that if you don't wear your cloak when it's cold then you'll catch your death."

"Mothers are very wise things," Eamon returned. "But my mother would be most displeased, as I did not think to bring mine this evening. But it isn't far to the Ashen – I am sure I will be all right."

Mrs Grennil smiled. "We can easily lend you one."

"That's very kind –"

"But he has one," Damien interrupted. "A great big black one! He was wearing it when he brought me home."

Confusion and then alarm passed over Mrs Grennil's face.

Anderas raised his hand to his mouth and cleared his throat. "We should be on our way, Tiller."

"Yes, captain." Eamon bowed to his hosts. "Thank you for a splendid evening. I bid you farewell."

"The pleasure was ours," Jehim replied curtly. His eyes narrowed as he studied Eamon intently. "Think nothing of it."

At that moment Eamon and Anderas would have made good their parting but for the impetuousness of a small boy. Without warning, Damien ran across the floor and threw his arms around Eamon in a hearty embrace.

"Goodbye, Mr Tiller. I hope your hand feels better, and – Oh! What happened to your ring?"

"I left it at the college," Eamon said quickly. He glanced towards Anderas.

"Let us go, Mr Tiller," said Anderas.

But Damien was not so easily distracted. "Ma, you should have seen it! It had an owl on it!"

This time the boy's mother paled visibly. "An owl...?" she whispered.

Damien beamed. "That's right, an owl!"

The silence that followed was stunned and terrified. Only the little boy seemed not to notice it. The men and women with whom Eamon had been eating and drinking only moments earlier lowered their gazes and bowed their heads. "Please, do not be so before me," Eamon said quietly.

"My lord, if any of us have spoken rashly in your presence, I beg you, have mercy. We are poor folk with coarse tongues, who give little thought to our words," Mrs Grennil began, her voice trembling.

Eamon laughed gently. He stepped forward to press her hands between his own.

"My dear, foolish woman!" he told her, surprised by the passion in his own voice. He tempered it, and smiled at them. "You have been the best of company to me this evening," he continued. "Forgive me my deception, for I only meant to spare you from undue distress. You have my thanks, both for your 'coarse words' and your wonderful meal."

"But it was nothing!" Mrs Grennil quaked – she seemed close to tears. "It was but dust and mildew! We laid insult to you by daring to host you at this table –"

"There are few honours in the world so great," Eamon replied. He pressed her cold hands again and looked at the gathered family. They stared at him. "There are things more wholesome in this city than fine meat and wine, or bright clothes. There are many honourable and whole things in this house, and at this table. You have delighted me and honoured me in every way, and in that you have glorified the Master also." He looked at Mrs Grennil and smiled again. "Thank you."

"I am very sorry, my lord," said Anderas. "This matter at the Ashen will not wait."

Eamon looked back at the family. "I must take my leave. But before I do so, there is one thing more I wish to say." He looked at Jehim Grennil. The man stood awkwardly at one side of the room, a worried look on his gruff face.

"I apologize for my harsh words, Lord Goodman," he said, bowing.

"Some of what you spoke was based on truth," Eamon told him. "I will not hold you at fault for it. I accept your apology, and would have you know that you need not fear me. I hope," he said, more quietly, "that you will be able to believe me when I say that my heart is for the people of this quarter. I hope also that, as I serve the quarter, I will be able to give you reason to believe me."

Jehim nodded, and bowed again. "Thank you, Lord Goodman," he said.

"You will always be welcome at this table, Lord Goodman." Mrs Grennil curtsied as she spoke.

Tears welled in Eamon's eyes. "Thank you," he answered.

He left with Anderas at once. When they were out of earshot of the Grennil household, Eamon asked, "What has happened?"

"But little – yet," Anderas replied, but his face was grim. "Lord Arlaith waits for you."

The words brought crushing dread to Eamon's stomach. Why should the Right Hand be waiting for him, and at that time of night?

Anderas spoke again: "I took the liberty of arranging for Mr Slater to wait for you in the hall with your formal attire so you will be able to present yourself properly to Lord Arlaith."

Eamon nodded, grateful again for the captain's provision. "Thank you."

In the halls of the Ashen, Slater waited nervously in the shadows. As Eamon entered through the doors, the servant crossed the floor to greet him. Eamon felt absurdly conscious of his own portrait gazing down at him.

"Please come with me, my lord," Slater said, leading Eamon into one of the small reception rooms off the main hall. One of Eamon's cloaks was laid carefully on a chair inside. Slater picked it up and laid it across Eamon's shoulders.

"Thank you, Slater," Eamon said. As his servant fiddled to do up the brooch, his hands shook.

"I am sorry, my lord. I'll have this done in a moment," Slater told him. Carefully Eamon eased the brooch from Slater's hands, fastened it, then turned to look at him. In the scant light he saw that the servant's face was pale.

"Mr Slater," he said quietly, "what is the matter?"

The servant did not reply, but lowered his eyes. "I apologize for my manner," he murmured, folding his trembling hands together.

"Yet you do not answer my question."

"Lord Arlaith waits for you, my lord." Slater paused and then looked up. "My lord, the Right Hand went first to your quarters seeking you, and then to your rooms… He asked Cara regarding your whereabouts."

Eamon's blood ran cold.

"He…" Slater's voice broke and he struggled to bring it back under control. "My lord, he struck her –"

"He did what?"

" – and breached her."

Eamon stared at him. He knew that the Right Hand would have found nothing in Cara's mind, but that did not matter. What mattered to him was that Arlaith had breached her and wronged his household.

Anger filled Eamon's veins. "Where is he?" he demanded.

Slater quailed. "Your office, my lord."

Eamon did not wait for a further word. With his cloak thick on his shoulders, he turned and made his way down the halls to his office. His blood pounded through him. He felt none of the fear that he knew he should feel in going to an unexpected meeting with the Right Hand.

The door to his office was closed. Eamon boldly cast it back.

The tall lamps in his room had been lit, casting a steady light that rebounded from windows and shelves.

Lord Arlaith was there. He sat, with his hands folded on Eamon's desk and his dark cloak draped tenebrously about him. As Eamon entered, the Right Hand looked up and the light shadowed forth a terrifyingly pale, quiet face.

"Close the door, Goodman."

Eamon matched his gaze.

"I have a title but little less than your own," he replied. "You will use it when you address me, Lord Arlaith."

"I came here as a courtesy to you," Arlaith replied. "You will answer to me by whatever name I give you." As he spoke, he rose to his feet and surged forward like a dark tide until he stood before Eamon, his thunderous eyes flashing. In that moment, Eamon felt the first tremor of fear run through him – but his anger was still the greater.

"Close the door, *boy*." Arlaith's voice was grim and terrible, but Eamon did not shrink back from him.

"What kind of courtesy is it, Lord Arlaith, that brings you into my household to strike and breach my servants?" he demanded.

Arlaith gave a clipped laugh. "Your serving wench may count herself lucky that my business precluded rendering to her the punishment that she deserved for her reticence," he spat.

"My household deserves no punishment."

"Do not contradict me." the Right Hand appeared hideously tall; the sight stole Eamon's breath. He knew that he should keep silent, but he could not still his tongue.

"If you spoke truth, Lord Arlaith," he retorted, "you would not find it a contradiction."

"Did you enjoy your dinner, Lord Goodman?" the Right Hand asked.

Eamon was chilled to the very bone. The Right Hand's face was an impenetrable mask that betrayed nothing. It was that total absence that struck deep into Eamon's heart. How had Lord Arlaith known where he had been?

"What did you eat?" Arlaith continued genteelly. "Stewed rat? Wilted cabbage? Was there wine, or did the Grennils have only vinegar to offer you?"

Eamon floundered. "I –"

"Yes, you are none other than Eamon Goodman, the helping Hand who eats in the charnel houses of his quarter, places fit only for the breeding of vermin," the Right Hand said. As he spoke, Arlaith's talon-like fingers held Eamon's ring, thieved from his bedchamber. Noting Eamon's gaze, Arlaith closed his fist around it and stared down at him. "Do you truly see no peril in your defiance?"

"It is not defiance," Eamon replied, tearing his eyes from the caged ring. "Who are you to cry defiance at me? My allegiance is not to you."

"Do you know what you are?" Arlaith replied, his voice so quiet that it was more terrifying than the most thunderous rage. "You are nothing but an insolent, blood-licking cur from mud-sodden streets – streets which served only to bear witness to the Serpent's screeching howls as he went down in the dust and died."

Eamon's breath grew short with fear as the Right Hand held him in his black gaze. Arlaith had not laid a single finger on him, and yet Eamon felt contained within an iron grip. It was a grip that hated him, that would brook no more of him, and could crush him at a single thought.

Eamon steeled himself against it. "I am sworn to the Master," he said.

"There is an inn in your quarter that bears your name," Arlaith told him. "There are ensigns in the West Quarter, and men in the East, who arrogantly call themselves by it – the 'Good Men'! They would do well to fear for their lives. There are men and women in this city who tell tales of 'the people's Hand'."

"I do nothing but what I have been charged to do," Eamon

replied hotly. "I am the Master's servant, and if you would take fault with me you will take it to him."

"My bane is with you, Goodman," Arlaith answered him. "You dare to abase yourself before these people? Very well! They shall be repaid according to your errors." Turning to stare out of the open door into the corridor, the Right Hand raised his voice. "Slater!"

Slowly, trembling such that he could barely stand, Slater appeared in the shadows of the passage. He bowed and did not rise. Eamon wondered how much the man had heard.

"Yes, Lord Arlaith?"

"Take the serving wench out into the Ashen, and have her flogged," Arlaith commanded.

Slater paled, but did not dare to look to Eamon.

"She will take twenty lashes."

"You cannot!" Eamon yelled.

Slowly, Arlaith rounded on him. "*Cannot*, Lord Goodman?" he repeated, his words deathly quiet.

Eamon heard the warning tone in the Right Hand's voice, but in his anger he did not heed it. "You do not have the right to –"

"She will take fifty lashes."

Eamon stared at him and fell back a pace, aghast. "The law permits no more than –"

"One hundred lashes, Slater," Arlaith told the shaking servant, "and make sure 'Miss Cara' knows who she has to thank for them."

Eamon gaped at him in horror. With wild eyes he looked up again at the Right Hand. "Lord Arlaith –"

"Is one hundred lashes not enough, Lord Goodman?" Arlaith asked. "Very well; we shall make it one hundred and thirty. Perhaps you would have me flog her young brother, too?" Eamon was staggered. There was nothing he could do to stop it. Nothing at all. The Right Hand knew it, and smiled.

Slowly, not caring that Slater stood there watching him, not caring that the door to his chamber stood wide open and that any number of people might see him, not caring that he was the Lord of the East Quarter, he lowered himself down to his knees. He shook as he knelt upon the hard ground.

"Please, Lord Arlaith," he whispered. Arlaith looked at him with crooked and perverse delight. "Please, be merciful."

"You make a pitiful and wretched display, Goodman," Arlaith sneered. "You would beg for the back of a servant? Do you bed her after she makes your bed?"

Eamon closed his burning eyes against the temptation to further rage. "Be merciful, Lord Arlaith."

"Mercy ill befits a Hand, Lord Goodman." Arlaith's voice was chilling.

"Please." Eamon could do no other: he prostrated himself utterly before the Right Hand. "I beg it of you."

There was a clatter on the stones by his ear. Looking up, Eamon saw his ring glinting at him. He did not dare to meet Arlaith's gaze.

"Mr Slater," the Right Hand said at last, "the wench will take twenty-five lashes, and will count me gracious. Go and prepare her for it."

"Yes, Lord Arlaith," Slater answered.

Eamon heard footsteps retreating as his servant returned down the hallway. This latest news would be of sore comfort to her.

As he lay on the ground, the Right Hand moved by him, sending a quiver of fear in his wake.

"This is the nature of my courtesy, Lord Goodman," he said, "and that – among the dirt and the stones – is your place. Be mindful of it."

Eamon bit the inside of his cheek as the Right Hand spoke. "Yes, Lord Arlaith."

The Right Hand turned from him and left. Eamon knew that the man went out into the Ashen where, in moments, his whole household would be gathered to witness the flogging of an undeserving girl.

What a grand trophy you shall have this day, Eben's son! A girl's blood upon the stones of your hall. It is your doing.

Eamon lay on the ground. Grief and anger churned together in his breast. As the voice tormented him, he laid his forehead against the cold stone floor; salty tears passed down his face. The owl gazed up at him from between the paving slabs. For a long moment he wanted nothing but to remain there. How could he stand and watch? And yet if he did not go, he knew that Arlaith's grace would grow the less.

Rise, Eamon. Be not afraid.

Choking back a sob, he brought himself to his feet. Taking the fallen ring in his hand, he staggered to the doorway, forcing himself down the passageway and out into the Ashen.

CHAPTER XXVI

The Ashen felt unusually bright to Eamon's burning eyes. Extra torches lit the edges and centre of the square, casting twisted shadows up into the overhanging trees as they swayed in the night breeze.

Eamon's whole household tumbled out of the Handquarters into the alleviated darkness. The servants looked pale and frightened. Some of them were half-asleep, but they knew at whose command they had been summoned and so they formed a silent and orderly line near the Handquarter steps.

Several Gauntlet officers, no doubt commanded from their watch duties by the Right Hand, set up the flogging frame near the steps to the Handquarters. They raised and fixed the beams and hanging ropes to hold Cara's arms spread-eagled. As Eamon watched them, his heart and back wrenched with remembered pain and fresh horror.

Slowly he descended the steps. The whole household watched him as he walked towards the frame, near to Arlaith. Did the servants think he had ordered this flogging himself? Would they expect him to stop it? But they knew as well as he that before Lord Arlaith, he was powerless. Eamon felt sure that it was that same knowledge that gave the Right Hand his long, glinting smile.

As he halted, the sound of feet scraped the steps behind him. Eamon turned to see Slater. The head of his household led Cara, pale and trembling, by the arm. As she came forward into the torchlight at the foot of the steps, Eamon saw that her eyes were red and swollen while half her face was bruised. He felt rage swelling anew in his breast. But rage quickly turned to grief as the murmurs of alarm ran through the gathered household – many of them did not know what had happened that night – and among those voices he heard the cry of Cara's brother.

Guilt swept through him like wildfire. Callum would be made to watch his own sister punished for serving a Hand. What would it teach him?

Cara walked towards the frame where one of the stablehands, a strong, tall man, stood with the lash in his hand. His face was grim. The lash was his duty; he was no more able to defy Arlaith than Eamon.

Eamon looked wildly across at the lines of serving men and women. He was horrified to see Callum pushing his way to the front of them. Once there, the small boy stopped to stare, aghast, at the grisly procession that held his quivering sibling as its centrepiece.

Why had he not thought sooner? Why had he not removed Callum to some other duty to spare him from watching his sister's torture? He could have tried. Or perhaps that small defiance would also have been laid against the serving girl.

Eamon looked back to the line, trying to calm himself. Callum stared at his sister. Then Marilio laid a hand on the boy's shoulder. The man met Eamon's gaze and nodded slightly. It was but small comfort.

Slater led Cara before them. She did not raise her head. Perhaps she could not look up. Indeed, Eamon wondered that she could stand at all. She shuddered and wept quietly.

Arlaith stepped forward and took harsh hold of her face, forcing it up towards his own. She shied back, but could not resist the Hand's grasp.

"See where disobedience leads you?" Arlaith told her quietly.

"Y-yes, my lord," Cara stammered. The grip on her jaw was tight. Her reddened skin went pale beneath it. Eamon yearned to speak, but he could not.

Arlaith threw the girl's head aside in vague disgust and then turned to the household.

"This servant has been arrogant and disobedient," he called. "Let this be a lesson to you all as to how such manners are received in Dunthruik." He turned to Slater. "Bind her to the frame."

The household could only watch as Slater led Cara to the frame's posts. The girl's arms were spread wide over her head and bound to the beams while Slater, with a shamed and downcast look, tore open the back of Cara's work smock to reveal her trembling back. She wept. The stablehand prepared his lash. Eamon suddenly realized that no protection had been bound round her. It was customary to weave thick cloth about the lower back to keep the ropes from damaging the victim's internal organs. He looked to Arlaith in alarm.

"Lord Arlaith —" he began, his voice shaking.

"Offer to take her place," Arlaith answered quietly, his voice full of disdain, "and I will have her killed."

Eamon drew a deep breath. Arlaith knew that he had taken the cadets' place on board the holk. For a moment the thought froze him, but as the stablehand prepared the coil for the first strike, Eamon shook the spell of silence and spoke again.

"They will not count you gracious, my lord, if the cloths are not wound round her," he said, desperately hoping that his words would not go amiss.

A deathly silence descended. All was still for a moment as Arlaith thought. "Slater," the Right Hand called, "apply the appropriate bindings."

A shudder of relief ran through Eamon as the stablehand halted. Slater diligently and willingly took up some thick lengths of leather. He bound the material about Cara's lower back and then took a second length.

Eamon clenched his lips closed and choked back the torrent of abuse that he wanted to hurl indiscriminately at the Right Hand. Arlaith had known full well about the bindings and had fully intended to have them forgotten.

Slater finished his work and then withdrew to solemnly take his place in the servants' line near Marilio, where he spoke quiet words to the trembling Callum.

"Commence," Arlaith called.

Eamon watched as the stablehand stepped up behind Cara, his lash heavy in his hand. Across the Ashen stood a group of Gauntlet soldiers and their officer. Perhaps beyond the firelight there were other onlookers.

The stablehand drew his arm back for the first blow. With horrid vividness, Eamon remembered the feeling of the sour bit in his mouth, the tension in his every muscle. He had held them firm with the notion of warding off the feared blow, but it had availed him nothing. He remembered the way the men had stared at him, remembered the snarling bite of the ropes as they drove and snagged into his back with hellish intensity. His back burned and his eyes welled with tears.

"One," barked the Right Hand.

The first blow landed with a horrendous crack. Cara gave a muffled scream, for she too had a bit to bite. Eamon saw her hands gripping feverishly at the ropes about her wrists, for support and for release.

"Two."

A spasm of pain ran down his back as the second blow snapped through the air. His knees threatened to give way. There were gasps of horror among the servants, cries of fear for their fellow.

"Three."

Cara shrieked again, pleas for mercy caught up in her sobs. Her brother flinched in horror.

It is your doing, Eben's son.

"Four."

Eamon clenched his eyes shut. He wished that he could grant Cara strength. He wished that he could know that she would live. But he could do neither.

The fifth blow landed. Blow after blow followed it. Blood streamed on the servant's back, caught and trammelled in the cords that returned to strike her again and again. Slater tried to turn Callum's sobbing eyes from the scene. The pale faces of Eamon's household simply endured what had to be endured. And all the while, the Right Hand counted and smiled.

"Eleven."

Eamon drove his fingers into his palm as he closed his fists at his side. Cara's cries grew less, not because the blows hurt any the less but rather because she was losing consciousness. The girl's head lolled forward senselessly against the apex of the frame between the heavy blows. She was young – her body had already endured too much.

Eamon glanced up at the Right Hand. "Lord Arlaith –"

"Fourteen."

Cara's head rested against the board and Eamon saw her hands losing their grip as her whole body sagged downwards. Her brother cried wildly.

"My lord –" Eamon tried again.

"*Fifteen.*"

The blow was struck.

"My lord, she will hardly speak of your grace if she is dead!" Eamon cried.

The commanded sixteenth blow struck across the unconscious girl's raw flesh. Tears burned Eamon's eyes and he looked up to seek the Right Hand's gaze. He held it as the seventeenth blow was called and struck.

Suddenly Arlaith raised a hand. "Cease," he called.

There was a stunned silence as the flogger fell back from his task, his arms splattered with blood. The Right Hand turned to the silent household. "Behold the nature of my grace," he said. "To his glory."

"His glory," came the reply, and the household bowed low before him.

Arlaith turned for a moment to Eamon. "Good night, Lord Goodman," he said, then turned and strode past the prostrate household into the dark streets.

For a moment Eamon stood there, shaking, waiting for his sense to return to him. Blinking back his tears, he looked back to the men and women who served him.

"Cut her down at once," he called. The words had barely left his mouth when Marilio darted from the line to the stricken body. The man's big hands carefully undid the holds and lowered Cara from the frame.

"Mr Slater!" Eamon yelled.

"My lord?"

"Find the lieutenant-surgeon. Have him tend her wounds." It was an unorthodox request, but Slater left at such speed that Eamon barely saw him acknowledge the command.

A couple of other servants, including Callum, left the line and ran to Marilio as he heaved the bloodied girl in his arms. Callum, his face crushed with tears, ran up to his sister but then held back in fear. Marilio spoke gently to him, and at last the boy came slowly forward and touched Cara's hands.

Eamon turned to the other servants who, rooted to their places with horror, still watched.

"Return to your duties," he told them.

As the servants disappeared Eamon hurried over to Marilio. He reached his side just as Slater reappeared with the lieutenant-surgeon. The doctor took in the situation at once.

"Your permission to take her to the college infirmary, my lord?"

"Do whatever is necessary, lieutenant," Eamon replied.

He slept little that night and, when he lay still, his back arched with the agony of blows. It had been a long time since they, or their memory, had tormented him.

He tried to read, but he could not focus on the words before him. As his lamp burned out, he rose, dressed, and then strolled across to the college. It was silent in the Ashen and the frame – still bearing testimony to its grisly work – stood, unmoved, by the steps.

Eamon tore his eyes from it and passed the college gates into the entry hall. There, he turned his steps towards the inner parts of the building and the infirmary. He found it well lit and was glad to see that a doctor attended to those who were ill. The winter and constant skirmishes against the wayfarers had left their marks.

He passed through several small wards to a darker room at the back of the infirmary. There he found Cara, lying still on her front in a bed. The girl was covered by thin linen sheets that were, in places, marked with blood. Her face was ragged and pale but, in the stillness of the room, he heard her shallow breathing. Nobody was with her. An empty chair stood by the head of the bed, and by it a small candle burned.

For a long time Eamon stood just inside the doorway, watching her. His mind was numb, but he knew that just as the Right Hand had struck at Cara, so he would strike at any others with whom he felt the Lord of the East Quarter had been too familiar. The thought filled him with mounting terror.

After a while he heard footsteps, and then someone entered the room. As the figure crouched down over Cara's bed, he smoothed the tangled hair back from her face. The visitor was a young man. He eased himself into the chair beside the bed, keeping his movement slow in case it should wake the sleeping girl.

"Shouldn't you be in bed, cadet?" Eamon asked quietly.

The young man at the bedside rose hurriedly to his feet to salute. "I have the permission of the lieutenant-surgeon," he said. As he spoke, Eamon recognized him: Wilhelm Bellis. At the same moment the cadet recognized him in return and bowed. "My lord," he said.

"At ease, Mr Bellis," Eamon answered with a gentle gesture of his hand. The young man nodded.

"I saw my father bring her in," he explained quietly. "I wanted to stay with her, my lord, to make sure she was well."

"I understand," Eamon answered. "You need not leave."

"Thank you, my lord." Wilhelm looked back at the resting girl with deep concern on his face.

"What was the lieutenant-surgeon's opinion?" Eamon asked.

"It was too early for him to say," Wilhelm answered. "He said we'd have to wait until the morning."

"Are you on duty in the morning, cadet?"

"Yes, my lord."

"Do you intend to rest before then?"

Wilhelm looked at him. "No, my lord," he answered quietly.

"Do you think that wise, Mr Bellis?"

The young man didn't answer but dropped his gaze to the floor. Eamon stepped forward.

"Mr Bellis," he said.

The cadet looked up. "My lord?"

"Tomorrow, when you are not on duty, you may attend Miss Cara, but you should rest now."

The cadet looked up at him and nodded resolutely. "Yes, my lord."

Eamon bade him a good night. As he left, the cadet reached out across the bed to take Cara's still hand and cradle it in his own.

When the dawn came at last, Eamon took to his horse and spurred down Coronet Rise to the Four Quarters. It was early still, and not many people were about. The dawn chill caught in his lungs and rested there. As he rode, he glanced along each street in case the Right Hand should be there. The ring felt heavy on his finger as he held the reins.

He made his way towards the port, and the ships' rigging rattled in the breeze as he came down the cobbled streets. Parts of the way he took were pieces of road he had helped to lay. The thought felt curious to him as he tethered his horse in the care of a local innkeeper. The keeper recognized him and greeted him warmly.

"Lord Goodman!" he cried. "A pleasure to see you!"

The man's joy reached Eamon's ears, and under the shadow of the Right Hand's smile, mutated into a crushing fear. Would this man also pay for rendering him service?

"I am looking for the cargo contingent," he said, not returning the man's warm greeting. The man nodded, seemingly unoffended.

"I saw them making their way up the north quay, my lord," the man answered. Eamon thanked him and hurried along the seafront.

Sure enough, the contingent was there – dozens of men lifting broad crates and barrels onto a merchant ship. As he approached, the smell of fish – no doubt the night's catch – passed his nostrils. For a moment he thought of Edesfield.

The men were busy working but soon noted him, calling to each other to halt so that they could pay him the respect that the badge of his office merited.

"Lord Goodman," said one, bowing low. Eamon assumed the man to be the head of the contingent.

"Where is Cadet Manners?" he asked.

"He's here somewhere, my lord," the man answered. "I'll fetch him for you." After a brief pause he turned and called over his shoulder. "Rory!"

Eamon blinked. He knew it to be Manners' first name – he had known it ever since he had become the young man's lieutenant – but had never heard anyone address him by it. Gauntlet protocol used surnames as a mode of address, and the fact that, in this place, the cadet had been stripped of even that title was witness to just how much damage he had done to his Gauntlet record.

Manners appeared from behind a large cart of barrels, his hands and arms tanned now rather than burnt, and the young man seemed relaxed despite looking somewhat dishevelled from the salty sea breeze that caught and wrenched his hair every which way.

"Sir?" he called.

"Lord Goodman asks for you."

Manners came forward and then halted, dropping into a low bow before Eamon. "My lord."

Eamon looked across at the head of the gang. "I will not keep him from you long," he said, and then turned back to Manners. "Come with me a moment."

"Yes, my lord."

Manners followed him to a quiet part of the dock. There, Eamon turned to look at the harbour. The cries of the men and sailors were behind them; before them was the rush of the sea. The stones of the quay were slippery beneath Eamon's feet and when the wind picked up, it carried the spray into his face.

"Stop," he said, and Manners did so immediately. He turned his face towards Eamon, and for a brief moment Eamon felt a stab run through his heart. Something about the way the young man looked at him reminded him of Mathaiah.

"How may I serve you, my lord?" Manners asked.

"By keeping my name from being used."

Manners' brow furrowed into a deep frown. "My lord, I don't understand what –"

"I mean the 'Good Men'." Eamon said it fast, and then bit his lip. It was the name that the survivors of Pinewood, and the Third Banners in particular, had given themselves. In the short silence that followed, broken only by the rushing waters, the cadet's face ran pale.

"My lord, no harm was meant –"

"Manners," Eamon told him softly, "I will speak frankly for a moment."

Manners matched his gaze and nodded. "Yes, my lord."

"I am sure that you have done nothing but good under my name, and I am deeply honoured by the loyalty that you, and others, have shown to me by doing so."

"We're men who have served you," Manners answered, "who owe you our lives, and who want to do in this city what we see and hear you do."

A wave broke against the stones like the crack of a whip. Eamon stared hard at the young man. "Don't you see how dangerous that is?" The words exploded from Eamon's mouth.

Manners shrank back in surprise. "My lord –"

"I'm sorry," Eamon said, and drew a deep breath. The waves fell back from the stones, and for a moment there was a strange quiet.

Eamon matched the cadet's gaze again. "I have enemies, Mr Manners," he said quietly; "enemies who do not like the idea of men who bear my name. These same enemies have threatened death against those who call themselves by it. You are one of them."

Manners seemed undaunted. "Yes, my lord."

"You must not be one henceforth. Do you understand?" A tremor crept into his voice. Eamon resisted the urge to glance over his shoulder. "None of you must."

"My lord, are you well –?"

"*Do* you understand?" His tone was harsh.

Manners fell back with a nod.

"Yes, Lord Goodman." The young man looked back at him, unafraid.

Eamon sighed. For a moment, he was not the Lord of the East Quarter; he might have been the lieutenant of the Third Banners once more. "I'm sorry, Manners," he said.

"May I speak frankly, my lord?"

Eamon looked at him. The cadet's eyes pierced like midnight stars. He nodded.

"There are men at the college," Manners said, "who put themselves through the course every morning because you assured them that they could."

Manners paused as another breaker crashed against the quay. The sea rushed up at their faces. When he spoke again, his voice was quiet. "I know that the men who went to Pinewood still serve because they saw you serve. Every quarter of this city saw you bring back the Easter's head to save your men. There are men who never thought once about the people of this city. Now they think of those they meet, because they know that you do."

Eamon stared at him, not believing what he heard, and did not know whether to rejoice or weep.

Manners looked up at him again, a little warily, but he continued. "There are men in the Gauntlet, my lord, who never knew what it meant to be a loyal man until they served under you."

"Men cannot serve me," Eamon answered at last. "They must serve the Master."

The cadet looked him straight in the eye. "I have seen and heard what you do," the young man told him. "For myself, Lord Goodman, I will serve whom you serve."

Eamon stared at him. The cadet's face was firm and unchanging.

"Do you understand what you're saying, Cadet Manners?"

The young man matched his gaze. In a moment both terrifying and astonishing, he nodded.

"Yes, Lord Goodman," Manners replied. "I understand it." He paused. "I promise you that you will hear no more of the 'Good Men'."

"Thank you, Mr Manners."

He dismissed Manners back to his work, but could not help but stare at him as the young man returned to the ropes that were his lot. He could scarcely comprehend what Manners had said, and dared not think on it too long.

He returned to the inn and reclaimed his horse, leaving several coins with the keeper for his trouble.

On his way back to the Handquarters, he stopped at the Good Man and spoke swiftly and softly with the grey-faced innkeeper. It was a short meeting that grieved them both, but the keeper understood the request that Eamon made of him. He promised to effect the Hand's command as soon as he could.

Later that day, word came to Eamon that a new inn called the Horse and Cart had opened where once the Good Man had stood.

CHAPTER XXVII

Two days after Cara's flogging, Eamon sat at his desk in his office, staring at the papers he had to sign. As usual, he had received a small number of requests for transfers into the East Quarter, but that morning he could not bring himself to sign them. With quill in hand and ink at his side he looked at them, fear and doubt hovering near him. Alone with his thoughts, all he could think of was Arlaith's face, his harsh words. If Eamon stepped out of line, more would die, just like Mathaiah had, and more would be flogged and beaten for their love of him.

He stared at the papers until he heard a knock on his door. Anderas entered the room, looking warm in his thick jacket. The weather persisted in being hotter than usual. The previous day Eamon had seen people lining up at the wells. It boded ill for the summer to come.

Would the city still be under the hand of the throned in high summer?

"Good morning, captain."

"Good morning." The captain laid the day's reports down on Eamon's desk and then stood in silence for a moment. "Are you well, my lord?"

"What?" Eamon looked up, distracted.

"Are you well?"

"Yes."

"It's two days since you've ridden, my lord."

"Do you think my well-being depends on whether or not I choose to ride at a time when most normal people prefer to sleep?" Eamon snapped. Anderas did not flinch.

"No, my lord. I would be short-sighted if I did. But it may be that whether or not you ride indicates your well-being."

Eamon tried to ignore the captain's gaze. In the end, he sighed and looked up.

"How is Cara?" he asked.

"Your servant? I believe she is faring better, my lord."

"Is she well enough for me to see her?"

"The lieutenant-surgeon believes so, yes."

"Then have her come here this morning. I need to make some notes about what happened, for the quarter records."

"Of course, my lord." Anderas remained watching him for another moment. "Lord Goodman?"

Eamon pressed at his eyes. "Captain."

"I am a man with men under my command, and so I understand why this incident has disquieted you – for your house is also under you." He paused. "Lamentable as it may seem to you, my lord, I do not believe you could have done better than you did."

"It does seem lamentable to me," Eamon replied, "but I must endure it."

"Yes, Lord Goodman," Anderas replied. "You have endured many other things, and you shall endure this also. You must not fear for us." Eamon glanced up in surprise, but the captain only offered him an encouraging smile. "I will send Mr Slater with Cara."

"I would like you and the lieutenant-surgeon to be present also, captain," Eamon told him. "Choose a time that fits with your various duties."

"Thank you, my lord. I shall."

Eamon watched the door for a long time after Anderas left before turning back to his papers. He could not sign them. To do so would grant them his favour – and the Right Hand's grace. He could not condemn them to that.

And should the Right Hand go after the Grennils, or Ellen's cousin, or the "Good Men", what then? Did he really believe that in hushing a name or removing a sign he could save them?

Eamon's blood curdled. If Lord Arlaith struck and breached such men and women, then the Right Hand would learn that the Lord of the East Quarter was a lord who knew the blue light and did not report it – indeed, that the Lord of the East Quarter was a lord who used it. Lord Arlaith would learn that the man who had begged his clemency was none other than First Knight to the Serpent. Eamon would be discovered, he would be tortured and killed… and many of the quarter would be sent to the pyres with him.

Eamon. The quiet voice came suddenly and gently to him. *Be encouraged.*

Eamon drew a deep breath. "That's easy for you to say," he murmured, knowing not to whom or what he spoke, only that it was a whisper that moved in his heart. He had no other to turn to.

Eamon, the voice answered him, and somehow Eamon realized that it was deeper and broader and keener than he could understand; that from this, from something beyond it, the King drew the very nature of his kingliness. It was the kindness, unflinching justice, and grace of this true voice that the voice of Edelred mocked and perverted when it spoke to him. As knowledge of that settled over him he felt both ashamed and awed.

Peace, Eamon. See with better eyes!

Eamon sighed and looked again at his woeful thoughts. Supposing that he was discovered? Supposing that they found him to be a wayfarer after all this time? What would they do to him? They could torture him, but he did not fear that. Perhaps they would kill him, but Eamon realized even that did not frighten him greatly. At the very least, death would release him from his fears.

But while he was alive they could use him against the King. As the thought struck through him he shook. *That* he feared more than any other thing – that his will and his blood would be wrought in treachery against Hughan.

Fear it not.

The words ran through Eamon's heart and he recoiled in anguish.

Did the voice not know of Eben? Did it not know how the throned called him in Eben's name?

"But I am the traitor's heir!" he cried. "Treachery is in my blood!"

Your blood is your own; your heart you have given to the King.

Eamon sighed. It was true; he had given his heart and service to the King. In that service he served the East Quarter. If they found him to be a wayfarer, and defamed him as such; if they brought him out of the Pit – tortured and scarred, bloodied and torn – to parade him before the people…

Suddenly Eamon laughed. They could not; not now. For if the Lord of the East Quarter – the lord whose ways caused the quarter to sing the throned's praises more than any other – were shown to be a King's man… What recourse would the Master have, or his Right Hand? All the praise that had been given to the throned would rebound and return to Hughan, to whom it was rightly owed. Hughan would be served, whether Eamon was revealed or not. The thought was of comfort to him.

It was not long later that Anderas returned. With him came Slater and a notary who would make a record of what was said. The lieutenant-surgeon and Cara came behind. The girl walked slowly and stiffly, her face creased with pain. Another servant escorted her; he held her arm as she went and had one of his own looped lightly about her lower back to help her stand.

Eamon rose as the group entered. A shiver ran down his spine when he looked at Cara. He offered the notary a chair, and then turned to her.

"Would you like a chair, Miss Cara?"

She did not look at him.

"I'll get one, my lord."

Slater stepped quickly to one side and chose one of the many chairs in Eamon's office. It had a tall, straight back, but Slater stepped from the room and returned a moment later with a cushion tucked under his arm. As the servant helped the girl to sit, Slater tucked the cushion gently behind her back. The lieutenant-surgeon looked nervous that the servants moved so freely before a Hand, but Eamon did not say a word, for he thoroughly approved.

"Thank you, Mr Slater."

"My pleasure, my lord."

"Notary, please begin your work," Eamon said. "Note that those present are myself, Captain Anderas, Mr Slater, Mr Hill, and Miss…" He faltered. "Miss Tenent," he remembered at last.

"Yes, my lord."

Drawing a breath, Eamon looked at each of them. "I am sure that this whole affair has been an unpleasant experience for all of you, but I must ask: what happened when Lord Arlaith came here, seeking me?"

Cara flinched and began to shiver. Eamon stepped up to her – she tensed as he moved. The side of her face was still swollen from where she had been struck.

"Miss Tenent," Eamon tried again, "are you able to tell me what happened?"

She did not answer him. Slowly, Eamon crouched down beside the girl so that he could peer up into her hidden face.

"Will you not speak?" he asked quietly.

At his words she turned her face into her hands and wept. The other men in the room looked at each other. The lieutenant-surgeon seemed sympathetic though distant, as though he had seen such before. The notary merely wrote.

Eamon tried to catch a glimpse of the girl's eyes. "Cara," he said gently. "Why are you afraid of me?"

The girl did not answer, her voice choked with sobs. Eamon looked across to Anderas, who drew a large handkerchief from the pouch at his side. Without a word he extended it to Eamon, and Eamon gently touched it against Cara's hands. But she did not take it; instead, she turned her face farther from his. He thought he heard her try to speak.

"I can't hear you, Cara," he said softly.

"You must be angry with me, Lord Goodman," she whispered, then struggled to continue as sobs pressed her throat. "I have brought dishonour and shame – on this house and on you. You won't believe anything that I can say. You'll breach me and you'll –"

"Did he tell you that?"

The girl shuddered with another violent sob. Rage against Arlaith grew in his heart, but he knew that this was not the place to speak it.

When he spoke again his voice was gentle. "Know this, and believe it: if I am angry, Cara, it is not with you. Neither have I any cause to disbelieve what you say, and I have not been shamed by you." He laid the handkerchief in her palm again and was encouraged when her fingers closed around it. "Tell me what happened."

At last, and after a long pause, Cara spoke.

"Lord Arlaith came late, my lord. I was tidying in your room when he asked me where you were. I told him that I did not know. Lord Arlaith became angry and demanded to speak with you, but it did not change what I knew. He… he breached me." Her breath grew short and she cried out as she remembered it. Slater laid a hand on her arm. "My lord," she cried, "he-he hurt me…"

"I know," Eamon answered. "I am sorry."

"I did not know where you were. I told him that I did not know… he saw that I did not know, but he would not let me go…" Her voice faded as she was caught in the horrific memory.

"I heard her screaming, my lord." Slater spoke warily. "I was passing by the stair. When I heard, I went up to your rooms. I saw Lord Arlaith breaching her, and then he took his hand from her face and struck her. Then he asked me where you were. I did not know, but I invited him to retire to your study to wait while I sent for you." Eamon nodded, impressed by Slater's quick thinking given the circumstance. "I accompanied him there, then went to find Captain Anderas."

"Slater explained to me what had happened," Anderas added quietly, "and while he went to tend to Cara I came to find you, my lord."

Eamon nodded; it made sense to him. He could see the notary in the corner looking up as he finished his notes.

"Please note that this servant was flogged for displeasing Lord Arlaith," Eamon said. He saw a shadow pass over Cara's face. "Thank you," he added, rising to his feet.

The notary rose and bowed before leaving. Eamon looked to the others. "You may return to your duties," he said. "Mr Slater, you may take Miss Tenent to the servants' rooms in a moment. Please wait outside."

"Yes, my lord."

Eamon gestured to Anderas to remain. Quietly the other men cleared the room until Eamon and Anderas were left alone with Cara.

"Miss Tenent?" Eamon said. The girl looked up at him. "Miss Tenent, how is your back?"

"Sore, my lord." Cara did her best to put a brave face on it.

"Have you seen your brother since you were beaten?"

"Yes, lord. Mr Bellis brought him to see me this morning."

"I'm glad to hear it," Eamon answered with a smile. "And how is he?"

"Shaken, my lord."

"As are you. Do you feel able to return to your duties?"

Cara nodded firmly. "Yes, lord."

"Then you will do so after you have taken a further three days' rest."

Cara looked at him in surprise. "My lord –"

"That is my will, Cara."

She fell silent, then looked up at him. "Yes, my lord."

Eamon dismissed her with his best wishes for her continuing improvement, and asked Slater to escort her back to the servants' quarters to rest. As the servants left, Anderas stepped to Eamon's side.

"She's making a good recovery," he said.

"Good." Eamon wondered whether the girl held him responsible for what she had received, or if she knew how many lashes the Right Hand had planned to give her. His own back burned in discomfort and he involuntarily drew a sharp breath.

"Are you well, my lord?"

"Yes," Eamon answered. He wondered whether Anderas knew that the Lord of the East Quarter had also once been flogged. "Thank you, captain."

"Will you ride tomorrow?"

Eamon nodded.

That evening Eamon sat once again at his desk. Many of his papers had not moved, although he had at least dealt with the most important of them. He watched the first beams of moonlight touch the wooden bookshelves. They shifted between the branches of the trees beyond his window.

After a short while there was a knock at his door. He called to grant admittance and was surprised to see Marilio framed in the doorway.

"Mr Bellis," he said. The man bowed, showing traces of white in his dark hair. He bore a broad tray.

"Good evening, my lord. Mr Slater was attending to another matter and asked me to see to your supper."

"So I shall now have the chance to thank at least one of my cooks personally for what I am sure is a very fine meal indeed," Eamon told him.

"Yes, my lord," Marilio answered with a laugh, and laid the platter carefully down on the table. Eamon met his gaze again.

"Tell me, Marilio, how are you finding yourself in this household?"

The man smiled. "Well," he answered, "you are a kind and noble master." The use of the word chilled Eamon to his core, but it was true: he was the master of the household.

"I suspect that not everyone will hold so kind a view of me as that."

"You worry much about what men think of you, my lord – too much!" Marilio told him. "I have heard no cause for such worry."

"Would you tell me if you had?" Eamon challenged with a laugh of his own. He didn't leave the man time to reply. "That was an unfair question – I apologize for asking it."

"You are very free with your apologies, my lord."

"I err often enough to warrant it." Eamon caught a glimpse of the ring on his finger and sighed. Lord Arlaith was right: he behaved so little like a lord of Dunthruik…

Marilio stood while he was silent. Eventually the man spoke again. "Can I be of further service to you, my lord?"

"No, I am well," Eamon answered. "How is Miss Tenent this evening?"

"She is getting stronger," Marilio answered. "She would not have admitted it herself, but she sorely needs the days of rest you granted her." He paused for a moment. "My son visits her: he said that you had granted him permission to stay with her when he was not on duty."

"He tells the truth in that," Eamon answered, catching the tiniest flicker of concern on Marilio's face. "I found him sitting by her the night she was flogged. There was no harm in him to my mind, and he seems a very able guardian."

"There is a great deal of good in it, my lord."

Eamon looked at him with a questioning gaze. "How is that, Marilio?"

"My son met Cara about two weeks ago, my lord. He was not on duty and came to visit me. She was helping me to prepare a terribly unruly beast for your table."

"Ah!" Eamon smiled. He understood.

"My lord, her recovery is much the greater for him being there – and for your grace."

"Of that I am well content."

"And I am more than well content with the honour that I have found serving in this house, my lord."

An odd shot of grief ran through his heart. Could Marilio mean that? Could he mean that he was content to serve a bastard Hand, one belittled and humiliated by the Right Hand? Did he truly mean that he was happy to serve such a man when that service could so easily turn and strike him like a snake? Yet Marilio's face was unconcerned by such things, and every word seemed his true and very thought.

"You are an honour to this household and to me, Mr Bellis," Eamon said quietly. Marilio beamed from ear to ear.

"I hope that you enjoy your supper. Mr Cook and I had some healthy debate as to how it should best be done."

"And is the resulting dish predominantly of your hand, or his?"

"I bow always to the superior palate of Mr Cook," Marilio replied, "but, should you find it lacking in herbs, that will not be for a want of trying on my part."

"Mr Cook is resistant to herbs?"

"Yes, and a great pity it is, too; there are a great many traditions of cooking that make ample use of them in our province." Marilio smiled and bowed. "Good evening, my lord."

"Thank you, Mr Bellis. Please thank Mr Cook also."

Nodding, Marilio bowed and left. Eamon applied himself to his meal – a slim cut of meat accompanied by various vegetables and an impeccably presented fruit.

Eamon ate, slowly at first, but soon the feel of the food and his memory of Marilio's words encouraged him. His appetite grew, and he ate heartily.

When he went to bed he read, with clear eyes and an astute sense, until long into the night.

CHAPTER XXVIII

He woke slowly with the coming dawn, the emerging light gently touching his eyelids and summoning him back from the realms of his sleep. As his senses slowly returned, he felt the weight of the Edelred Cycle on the bed beside him, still gathered in the curve of his hand. Blinking sleep from his eyes, he sat up and held it in front of him, bringing into focus the neatly scribed words. He had read a good deal of the poem now, scrutinizing every page, but he still had not found what he sought – not a single reference to the Nightholt. Just as it had been in Ellenswell, the Master's book was well hidden.

Would he find reference to it at all?

Eamon sighed. He could not allow himself to become discouraged. He looked down at the book again. More pages had been irrevocably creased and folded while he slept. For a moment he pitied the torment to which Ashway's volume was subject. At least the book would not have to endure it much longer.

Knowing that he was up earlier than was usual, he went down to the kitchens, seeking breakfast. As he moved through the corridors, footsteps approached him from behind. Turning, he saw a sleepy and pale-looking Callum stumbling down the hall with wood in his hands. The little boy rubbed at one eye; the child seemed not to have seen Eamon.

"Good morning, Callum," Eamon said.

The boy jumped and looked up before bowing hastily. "Good morning, my lord."

"How are you, Callum?"

"She's getting better, my lord –"

"I asked how *you* were faring."

The boy looked up with round eyes. "Me, my lord?"

"Is your name still Callum?" Eamon asked with a small laugh.

"Yes…"

"Then I think I was asking you."

"I am well, my lord," Callum told him.

"Are you sure?"

"I'm upset about what happened to Cara," the boy added. Eamon watched him.

"And angry?"

"Yes." The confession took an enormous amount of restraint. The boy struggled to keep back the tears in his eyes.

"I'm sorry," Eamon said. "She will get better."

Callum nodded quietly. In silence they went together to the kitchens, arriving just as Cook and Marilio broke a collection of eggs on the side of a wide pan.

"Good morning, Lord Goodman!" Marilio called, as cheerful as ever.

"You're up early, my lord," Cook added. "Mr Slater didn't tell me that you were to be up early, else I would have brought you something."

"Contrary to popular belief, Mr Slater is unable to control the hours of my waking and sleeping," Eamon answered with a smile. Callum took the wood across to the grate where the fire burned. Cook stepped to one side to let him feed the fire and then looked at Eamon again.

"I've heard no such superstition, my lord," he answered.

"You should grow larger ears, dear cook," Eamon replied, and sat down at the table. There were no other servants in the kitchens – Eamon realized that they had likely already been and gone on to their daily tasks. Not long later the cook brought a plate of cooked eggs and a thick slice of bread across to him on a tray.

"Your breakfast, my lord," he said.

"I'll take it here," Eamon answered.

"At the servants' table?" Cook asked.

"I also am a servant." Eamon took the plate from the astonished cook and set it by the boy. "Come and eat, Callum," he called as the child was about to leave the kitchens. Reluctantly, Callum came and stood by him. Eamon pushed the plate to him. "When you've eaten you can take some to your sister."

"Will you be wanting some more eggs, my lord?" Cook asked uncertainly. Eamon watched as Callum ate, and smiled.

"I believe I will," he answered.

When Eamon had finished eating, and Callum was well equipped with food for his sister, Eamon made his way to the main hall.

For once, he had to wait for Anderas. Eventually the captain appeared, and Eamon watched him climb the steps.

"Good morning," he called.

Anderas looked up in surprise and then smiled. "Good morning."

They took horses from the stables and rode as usual. Eamon noted wryly that after a few days without practice his muscles ached far more than was usual when they clattered back in through the North Gate.

"You rode well this morning, my lord."

"Really?" Eamon groaned, while trying to stretch his sore limbs. Anderas laughed. "Truly."

They walked back through the streets that began to teem with Dunthruik's daily business. Passing Gauntlet watches greeted them.

They continued together into the Ashen, where a large group of men were gathered in one of its corners. Some were Gauntlet officers, and they stood about a person. Eamon heard raised voices and looked up at the group. He could not make out what was said, but as he watched, one of the ensigns moved as though to strike someone.

"Come with me, captain." He tugged at the reins and moved his horse closer to the disturbance. Anderas followed.

"Good day, gentlemen. I trust all is well?"

"Lord Goodman! Captain Anderas!" The men of the Gauntlet jumped to attention. As the men drew back, Eamon saw a man on horseback, whom he recognized as one of the quarter's knights.

Near him the ensigns surrounded a young man, bound by ropes. A woman wept beside him.

"Lord Goodman!" The woman, her greying hair pulled back in streaks about her head, called to him. She ran to his horse.

Two ensigns grabbed her arms to keep her back from him. "How dare you address the Lord of the East Quarter?" demanded the knight. "Back to your hovel, peasant!"

"Lord Goodman, please!" she called again. The ensigns pulled her away from Eamon.

"Wait," Eamon commanded. "Let her speak." The two ensigns stopped dragging her away, but kept their heavy hands upon her shoulders. "What is the matter, madam?"

"My lord, they have arrested my son!" The woman gestured to the young man, who was bound hand and foot. One of the ensigns struck him. Another spoke:

"My lord, he is guilty of theft. He was taken at Sir Patagon's manor this morning."

"Madam," Eamon said, meeting her distraught gaze, "if your son is guilty of theft then he must face the consequences of that action."

"He is not guilty!" the woman cried. One of the ensigns tried to silence her but she carried on. "He is not guilty! Lord Goodman, they will not let him speak for himself, they will not listen! He has done no wrong. Lord Goodman, please!"

"I have heard you, madam," Eamon told her, "and I will hear these men also." He turned to the ensigns, and nodded.

"We have the testimony of Sir Patagon, my lord. He saw the servant fleeing his halls. He demands the death penalty."

"Does the law not require at least two witnesses?" Eamon asked quietly.

The ensign before him drew breath. "Sir Patagon expects a full confession, my lord."

Eamon turned his steed and drove it forward to the group of ensigns that guarded the woman's son.

The knight – Sir Patagon – gestured in disgust at the prisoner. "A servant from my own house, thieving and scheming against me!" he cried. "Surely you would deal severely with such a one in your own house, Lord Goodman!"

"He would receive the proper penalty should his offence be proven," Eamon replied. "What has your servant to say about the charge against him?" The knight's face puffed with indignation.

"I have the witness of my own eyes, Lord Goodman!"

"On that basis alone you would so swiftly condemn a man? Eyes can be deceived."

"The miserable wretch deserves no less than death!" the knight persisted. "His word cannot stand against mine."

"If such is the case, then why require him to make a confession?" Eamon asked quietly.

"His kind are born with lies on their tongue. Only the pain of torture extracts the truth."

"Nevertheless, would it not be prudent to hear him first and perhaps save us all some hassle?" Eamon asked.

Patagon glared at him, but dared not gainsay the Lord of the East Quarter. Eamon looked across at the young man. "Are you guilty of that with which Sir Patagon charges you?"

"No, Lord Goodman."

Eamon looked back at the knight. "Already the situation is more complex, Sir Patagon."

"Meaning no disrespect to you, my lord, but what else did you expect him to say?" Patagon erupted. "He is guilty, and he will confess to what he has done before he dies."

"Have you a second witness?" Eamon asked.

"I do not need one," Patagon answered coldly. "A confession will suffice."

"And the man's present assertion of his innocence does not disconcert you?"

"I am well within my rights, Lord Goodman," Patagon answered.

"Lord Goodman, I did not do it." The young man spoke up from his captivity. Patagon cried in rage and struck him.

433

"Miserable wretch! You'll soon change your tongue!"

"Under torture?" Anger seeped into Eamon's voice. Patagon looked at Eamon haughtily. "Then what would you do, Sir Patagon, if you find more things stolen from your care? How would you repay this woman for the son she lost? Or perhaps you would not care so long as you sate the bite of your anger in this man's flesh."

"I am sure that I need not remind you of the law, Lord Goodman," Patagon told him. "In the absence of a second witness, a confession –"

"I know the law," Eamon retorted. He turned to Anderas. "Captain!"

"My lord."

"See to it that this young man is imprisoned, but he will under no circumstances be questioned until my return."

"Your return?" Patagon laughed irately. "If you go seeking his innocence, you may never return. As to his guilt, it is before you; you need do no more than breach him."

Eamon rounded on him. "Do not presume to tell me when to breach a man, Sir Patagon, unless you are willing to undergo the same."

The man paled. Eamon ignored it. He turned his horse and tore out of the Ashen.

His anger carried him swiftly to the palace, through its broad corridors and to the door of the throne room itself. He did not know what he would say, but knew that the words would come to him. He was known and greeted as he passed, but was so intent on his purpose that he gave no return. Part of him knew that his passion moved him on to folly, but he did not heed the salient warnings of his thought: his heart was aflame.

At the throne room door, the Master's doorkeeper greeted him cordially.

"Lord Goodman."

"I must see the Master."

The doorkeeper bowed.

"The Master is in a meeting at this time –"

"This will not wait."

"I am afraid that the Master –"

"I will see him now," Eamon thundered.

The doorkeeper was silent for a moment. "My lord," he said, "if I might offer you counsel –"

"You may not."

The doorkeeper paused. After a moment, he nodded.

"Very well, Lord Goodman; the Master will see you."

Stepping to one side, the doorkeeper pushed the door quietly open, and Eamon stepped through.

The Master was there, his crown glinting in its nest of flaming hair. Eamon felt the throned's eyes bore into him coolly. Before the throned stood another, dressed in black. Eamon recognized him at once: Lord Arlaith.

A gasp escaped Eamon's lips as he gagged for breath. The sound magnified tenfold in the cavernous room, and echoed back to him from every wall. He could not interrupt a meeting between the Master and the Right Hand! Yet there he stood. They watched him. In terror, he realized that he could not now leave.

"Come forward, Eben's son." The Master's voice carried effortlessly to his ears. "Let us hear what ails you such that it will not wait."

Eamon felt as though a hand pressed down on him. The words that invited him forward both disdained and diminished him. Crippled, he stumbled his way across the hall.

At last he reached the foot of the throne. There he bowed low to one knee.

"Your glory, Master," he said. The throned smiled at him.

"Rise, Eben's son."

Eamon rose, painfully aware of the Right Hand's ire. "Master," he began, "I had no desire to interrupt –"

"If that were true, Eben's son, then you would not have disturbed us."

A chill cracked down his spine. He could not tell whether the words signalled approval or chastisement. "Being here," the Master told him, "you would now prove yourself unwise not to press your suit."

Eamon's chest heaved with barely restrained alarm as he looked up and met the Master's eyes. He saw the flicker of dying embers in his ash-grey stare, and understood the fragility of the ground on which he trod. Of a sudden, Cathair's words returned to him: "*you or I can be removed as easily…*"

Carefully, Eamon bowed his head low. "I thank you for your gracious manner towards my folly, Master," he said. "I come to speak to you about the law."

The throned raised his eyebrows in unfettered joy. "The law, Eben's son?" It was the kind of surprise that delighted in the unexpected foibles of a child.

"Yes, Master." Eamon swallowed. "If it would please you, Master, I would discuss the use of confession."

"Surely, Eben's son, you mean that you would discuss the changing of it?" The Master's voice was very quiet. "You would change a law laid by my own hand?"

Eamon looked again at the deep pools of grey that held and toyed with him. He could give only one answer.

"Yes, Master. I would."

A terrible silence fell. The Right Hand's acerbic indignation struck at Eamon as the man's eyes rested on him, but he kept his gaze fixed firmly on the Master. The throned watched him. Then a curious smile curved on his lip.

"You are bold and presumptuous, Eben's son." Eamon tried to keep himself from trembling. "But, where you are such, you will see that I am gracious. You will return here tomorrow morning, and you will lay your case before me and before my Hands."

"Yes, Master," Eamon answered. The idea terrified him. "To your glory."

"Leave, Eben's son."

Eamon bowed again and turned. As he walked back to the

throne room door he felt eyes piercing the back of his skull. The doorkeeper opened it before him. He did not look back.

"I'm a fool, Anderas."

"Would you prefer me to confirm or refute the statement?"

"I honestly don't know," Eamon answered, and shivered.

They walked the evening together in the gardens of the East Quarter Handquarters. Eamon had been nervous all day, unable to concentrate on anything. Always his mind returned to the terrifying thought of going before the Hands and the Master, of laying before them an argument that would be ridiculed and a case that could only be denied. Worse, Lord Arlaith would be there, and the Right Hand would avenge any slight… And yet, Eamon knew that to not speak out against the law of confession in the city was worse than a disservice to the throned: it was a disservice to Hughan. He knew that what he proposed to do – what he had so often sought to do in the East Quarter – was what the King would have him do, and he desperately feared that the Master would see it, too.

He looked back to Anderas, who watched him quietly. "How is the young man in question?"

"In holding," Anderas replied. "Sir Patagon was somewhat irritated by the fact that you returned and nobody is torturing his servant yet, but he was reminded that, as you have taken a personal interest in the case, only your command could now initiate such a process."

Eamon looked down at his hands. "I don't want him tortured. Confessions under torture are not born in truth. There must be better ways to determine a man's guilt or innocence."

"When charges are pressed and in the absence of a second witness, my lord, the law requires a confession."

"Forgive me, captain," Eamon said angrily, "I am clearly not as expert in the law as you. What provision does it make for when a man has nothing to confess?"

"It affords the power to effect a second attempt to acquire a confession," Anderas replied. They both knew it.

"And if a man has a witness who can prove his inability to have committed the crime?"

"Said witness can also be questioned for the purpose of drawing out a confession."

"So the proportion of parties found guilty…?"

"Is high indeed, my lord."

Eamon grimaced. If nothing else, the law was a powerful deterrent, but it afforded no hope to a man like the one who even now sat in the college brig. If Patagon had his way, the man's mother could be questioned as well, and both would finish on the pyres.

"Anderas," he said quietly, "does this law seem crooked only to me?"

"Lord Goodman, it is not my place to judge the law; it comes from the hands of men nobler than myself. My duty is to execute it."

"And those that break it."

There was a long silence. Eamon turned his head back and gazed up at the stars. He knew that if he were to breach the servant, he would know without a doubt whether or not the man was guilty.

You cannot breach every man trusting in his innocence, Eben's son.

The voice stirred his thought. He could not breach every man, and he did not want to breach even one. Breaching was a tool of the throned, designed to break minds and torment them. He knew it well.

But could he not breach one man without injuring him? Would it not be worth a try, if the man's life could be saved?

You are foolish to think it, Eben's son. He will burn beneath your hand, just as your ward did beneath mine.

He drew a deep breath. "Will you summon Sir Patagon, captain?" The captain nodded, brow furrowed.

"Yes, my lord. What shall I tell him?"

"That I wish to see him and resolve this matter."

Anderas bowed. "Of course, Lord Goodman."

Eamon returned to his office and waited. He paced quietly among the shelves, his hands clasped behind his back. His thoughts turned to Hughan: what would the King do in the city, in the quarter, or in that room that very night, in his place? Would he try to breach the man? Would he go to the throned in the morning and speak against the law the Master had inaugurated? Would he have gone to supper with the Grennils, or given Cara leave? Would he have stored grain in a secret cave beneath the quarter?

The questions baited him. For weeks, he had sought to do the work of a King's man – to be the King's Hand in Dunthruik. Sometimes he had even managed to. How long would it be before he was discovered, and how much would he have left undone?

His thoughts raced until at last they were shattered by a knock at the door. He faced the door as it opened. Anderas entered, escorting Sir Patagon.

"You asked for me, Lord Goodman?" Patagon bowed. Though his tone was impeccable, his face twitched.

"Yes. I apologize if I disturbed you." Eamon looked to Anderas. "Captain, would you be so kind as to lead the way to the brig?"

"Of course." The captain's face betrayed nothing of his own thoughts.

Eamon gestured for Patagon to leave the office. They followed Anderas into the Ashen and across to the college. There the captain took them into the college building, down several long passages, and then to a small set of rooms at the far end of one wing. The brig was a small and temporary holding area. Any prisoners to be held at length would be taken to the palace and likely confined to the Pit or its vicinities, dependent upon the seriousness of their crimes.

In one of the college cells the young man accused by Patagon was held. He sat quietly in a corner of the cell, staring up at the small window high in the wall above him. The moonlight fell on his face, showing an odd pensiveness. As they approached, he started and looked up, then rose and bowed.

"Lord Goodman," he said. "Sir Patagon; Captain."

"Good evening," Eamon replied, suspicious of a nerve that allowed the man to be so composed.

"Captain Anderas told me that you meant to resolve this matter," Patagon said. "May I presume upon you and ask how?"

Eamon looked back to the knight. "I intend to breach him."

The young man stiffened in alarm. Eamon fixed his eyes on the knight.

"Before I do, however, I want your word that, should such a thing prove his innocence, you will take this man back into your service should he wish it, without reproach, and with an apology." The knight snickered. Eamon looked hard at him. "Do not agree to this blithely," he warned, "for I will hold you to your word."

"I agree to your terms, my lord," the knight answered.

Eamon looked back to the young man: he was white.

"You will get what you deserve, wretch!" the knight said.

"Captain, open the cell," Eamon commanded.

Anderas complied immediately. The young man's eyes followed the keys as they turned in the lock and flicked up to Eamon as he stepped into the small cell.

"My lord," the servant said, and bowed again. He trembled. Eamon felt a touch of fear himself.

What if he could not do it? What if he had no choice but to hurt the man?

"Sit down," he said.

The man obeyed instantly. The servant looked at him again. "This will be easier if you afford me no resistance," Eamon added. He knew he stalled for time, but he was driven on by a need to know whether the man was innocent. Somehow, his ability to go before the throned in the morning relied upon it.

"Yes, my lord." The man nodded, though the look on his face implied that he had no idea how he might resist a Hand intent on breaching him. As Eamon approached, he flinched back. "I am innocent, lord!" he yelped.

Eamon laid his hand on the man's shoulder – the servant shook raggedly.

"If you are innocent," Eamon told him, "you have no reason to fear me. But I must see."

He kept his hand on the man's shoulder until his breathing calmed. The fear in the servant's eyes reminded Eamon of Slater on their first few meetings – it was fear of Eamon's power and reputation.

For a moment he felt a swell of pride, pride in himself and at what he had accomplished that men should fear him. The voice exulted in it, and as he laid his hand against the man's face, he saw a trace of red by his fingers.

Eamon.

He closed his eyes. What he did, he did for Hughan. Though his own skills and wits had been used, he was proud that they had been tools for the King, and he did not want his pride to become arrogance. The humility and grace that he had seen in Hughan had to be like a cloak, one that he could draw about himself to become ever a truer servant of the King.

You cannot breach this man as a snake, Eben's son. The voice was there and laughed at him. *There is no such thing! You breach, you breach for me. If you would save him, you should let him make his confession. Breach him and he will be destroyed; I will destroy him through you.*

Doubt assailed him. For a moment, he staggered on the point of believing what he was told. His hand faltered short of touching the man's face.

You cannot withdraw now, Eben's son. Do so and they will know – both knight and your precious captain. They will see you for what you really are. You must breach. This man's blood is the coin with which you must pay for your own.

Was it true? Eamon searched his heart. He knew that the voice of Edelred had always been that of a liar…

He does not speak the truth to you, Eamon. The other voice ran through him with a force that was both fierce and loving. *Have courage, and serve the King.*

Eamon looked back to the man's eyes – they were wide with fear. He smiled gently at him.

"Courage," he whispered, and laid his fingers against the man's brow.

It had been a long time since he had seen the plain, and the strangeness of it struck him again as it had done that first time, when he had breached Aeryn. He saw the strange half dark, heard the roaring of a distant wind as of a crashing sea, and saw before him the figure of the man who sat before him in the cell in Dunthruik. As he watched, the young man leapt up in alarm and stared, before giving a cry of terror.

"Where am I?" he shrieked.

Eamon reached out and touched his shoulder. "Do not be afraid," he said. As he touched the man he felt the deep calm of the King's grace within him, just as he had felt it when he had healed by it. It was the light of the King's grace that he saw gently resting on Patagon's servant, though the servant seemed not to see it.

Slowly the howling winds resided, leaving calm. The young man looked at him in surprise. Eamon spoke again:

"Show me what happened."

"How?" It was a fair question.

Eamon laughed good-naturedly. "Remember it!" he said, and laughed again. It could be done: the throned's mark and power had not made him a breacher, it had merely twisted a gift already in him. Now it was that gift that he would use to save one of the King's people. "Just remember."

The man thought. Images and shapes – fragments of his memory – appeared about them. At first they shocked the servant, and became faint, but then the man concentrated and Eamon saw his memories of the last few hours of imprisonment in the college. Then the servant cast his mind back further, and Eamon saw what he presumed to be the sumptuous hall of the Patagon manor, decked in dark woods and furniture with gilded feet. Great banners hung from the walls, crowns woven into them.

The young man remembered going into the great hallway early that morning. He heard retreating feet. The sound of something falling. The servant followed the noise. He found another man – swarthy, broad, with weathered skin – in the hall, clutching a small wooden box. The servant gave a cry and leapt at the stranger. He wrenched the box away from the thief's hands; the thief struck him, hard, in the ribs. The servant crumpled. The box fell to the ground and cracked apart, scattering a necklace of gold and pearls across the floor. The servant tried to grab them but the thief kicked him, seized the jewels, and fled towards an open window. The servant staggered to his feet, pieces of the jewel box in his hand. A lady cried out. The servant turned, broken box in hand. Sir Patagon stared at him in a rage. He proclaimed his innocence. The Gauntlet was summoned. His mother begged clemency.

Eamon took his hand from the man's shoulders. Relief flooded through him.

"Thank you," he said. The young man, still dazed by what he had seen, looked back at Eamon.

"I'd heard that being breached hurts; that it destroys parts of your mind." He looked confused. "It doesn't seem to…"

"It depends very much on the talent and will of the breacher," Eamon replied.

He opened his eyes. His fingers still rested against the man's face. As he withdrew them, he was aware of the stillness and calm in the cell. For a moment, the familiar panic that blue light might have been seen and betrayed him clamoured at him, but at the same moment he knew with certainty that it had not. It would not betray him. How could the King's grace betray him?

He stepped silently back from the man and turned to look at Patagon and Anderas. Both stared at him, the former with terror and the latter in awe. Eamon looked at Patagon.

"Your hall is finely decked, Sir Patagon," he said. "I particularly like the gilt-footed table there."

Patagon blinked in surprise. "Thank you, my lord," he managed.

"Your wife lost a necklace made of pearls linked together with gold," Eamon continued. "Is that correct?"

"Yes, my lord."

"And you found this man in your hall, with the shattered remains of the jewel case."

"That is so," Patagon answered.

"Does it not seem strange to you, Sir Patagon, that your servant would keep fervent hold of a broken case and not its contents?"

Patagon looked at him oddly. "Lord Goodman –"

"This man is innocent," Eamon said, "and witnessed the flight of the thief – a man that was dark-haired and weather-beaten – whom he tried to stop. He garnered very sore ribs in the process," Eamon added, reaching across to the servant's shirt. He lifted it up to show Patagon the enormous black bruise beneath.

Patagon looked stunned and turned an odd shade. "But I saw him –"

"I believe that your rage blinded you, Sir Patagon," Eamon told him, "and I might have felt similarly had such a necklace been stolen from a wife of mine. I am sure that you hold her in high esteem."

"Yes, my lord. I do."

Eamon drew a deep breath. "Sir Patagon, I will happily lend you the Gauntlet's assistance in tracking down the man who took your wife's possession. The crime is not lessened by the fact that your servant did not commit it. We will have a sketch made of the thief, and post it around the quarter. But you will take this man back into your service, and leash your anger in future."

"Of course, Lord Goodman." The pale knight bowed to him.

"You will also apologize to him."

Patagon stared uncomprehendingly at Eamon for a moment, then turned to his servant. He blinked hard a couple of times. "I apologize for rashly seeking your life."

The servant bowed awkwardly to him. "Yes, sir."

There was a moment of quiet. "Captain," Eamon said, "release this man."

Anderas moved forward at once. The servant stepped out of the cell as though in a daze.

"You truly show the Master's glory," the servant said as he bowed. "Thank you, Lord Goodman."

Eamon smiled. "May all your service to this noble man be to the Master's glory also," he said.

He dismissed both knight and servant. The two men left together.

Feeling suddenly tired, Eamon leaned against the cell door. Anderas watched him.

"One of my men was breached by Lord Tramist once," the captain murmured.

"I was breached by Lord Tramist once," Eamon answered, with a small laugh.

The captain looked surprised. "What I mean to say, my lord, is that I have seen breaching done before." Anderas paused uncertainly. "I have never seen it done like that."

Eamon looked up. The captain met his gaze, a furrow on his brow. "The man whom I saw breached screamed in agony for every second that it was done. When Lord Tramist let him go he could not talk, and could scarcely breathe. He must have come within inches of his life." Anderas looked back to the empty cell. "This man… This man did not make a sound."

Bewilderment filled the captain's eyes. Eamon smiled and touched his shoulder.

"You'll forgive me if I am not there to ride in the morning," he said. "I must go and see the Master."

"Of course, my lord," Anderas nodded. "Good luck."

CHAPTER XXIX

The following morning dawned overcast and grim with a strong, chill wind that scythed through the city. Resolved not to take it as an omen, Eamon rose and dressed.

He took breakfast in his office while he glanced through the reports that had already come in, and was pleased to see a note from Greenwood about the latest grain shipment to have been divided. Eamon was surprised the ships had managed to dock in the wind, and marvelled at the skill that feat attributed to the merchant mariners.

He rode to the palace, Sahu tossing his mane gleefully in the wind. When Eamon steered him towards the Four Quarters rather than the North Gate, the horse initially resisted the tug on the reins.

"Not this morning, Sahu," he told him. The creature snorted indignantly, though it seemed to allow itself to be consoled with kind words and the promise of a hearty breakfast on their return.

Eamon left the horse at the stables to one side of the Royal Plaza and made his way up the steps into the great edifice of the palace. He barely noticed the corridors as he strode down them. He came at last to the throne room.

The doorkeeper smiled as he bowed. "Lord Goodman," he said. "I beg your patience."

"Of course," Eamon answered. He wondered whether the other Quarter Hands had already arrived.

His question was soon answered by the sound of footsteps echoing down the hallway. Cathair, his green eyes curiously lucid, soon followed. He did not acknowledge Eamon as he passed, but was immediately admitted into the room. Beyond the doorway

Eamon caught a glimpse of the other Hands before the throne – they were all there. Only he was absent. He realized that the doorkeeper watched him. He drew breath to steel his nerve, and waited.

He did not know how long it was before they called him in. He was aware of the doorkeeper throwing back the door for him, of the other Hands gathered before the throned, and of his own thunderous footsteps sounding down the length of the room until he reached the dais, and knelt.

"Your glory, Master."

"Welcome, son of Eben," the throned answered, and at his command Eamon rose. He was grimly cogent of the other Hands watching him, the Right Hand chief among them. He dared not think what had been said in his absence.

"The ways to the city are being harrowed by the Serpent and his allies," the throned said. A shudder ran through Eamon; the topic threw him. He struggled to stay calm. "Those Gauntlet already withdrawn to here have been adequately placed, but more come. Each of you will look to your quarters to find places to put these men."

"Great Master, whose glory flames forever," spoke Tramist, his voice slick and bitter in the stillness of the room, "it is not fitting that such men as those who serve you squat in the ditches and hollows afforded by so many of the remaining buildings in this city. I would suggest, Master, that these men be sent to the East. Its renovation programme has become renowned of late, and I am sure that it would please Lord Goodman no end to serve you in such a way."

Eamon started, and stared at the Hand. The man's narrow eyes watched him balefully. Eamon knew that he was being baited.

"I would gladly offer the East for such a service," Eamon said. "It is true that the renovation has been going well, but only the most urgent work has been done and it is not work that gives the East any significant extra capacity for holding men. I cannot hold men in the numbers –"

"But so many have been moving to your quarter, Lord Goodman!" Cathair interrupted. "Surely you cannot now say that you have not the space to house a handful of men? Such a response would seem unbecoming of you." Eamon stared at him. It was not that simple, and Cathair knew it.

"Lord Cathair –"

"Some of the families in the quarter could be removed," Dehelt suggested. "I am sure that any citizen of Dunthruik would gladly vacate their home for the city's good and the Master's glory. You may serve them with compulsory exit orders where necessary," he added. "The city needs this service."

"Then remove them," Tramist pronounced with a dismissive wave of his hand. "If the Serpent's men glut themselves on their corpses, so be it."

There was a brief silence. Eamon's mind whirled; he was sure that the whole affair had been engineered to his discomfort. The throned watched him.

At last he nodded. "Let it be to your glory, Master," he said. "The East will serve."

"So shall it be." The throned smiled. "Lord Goodman, have you not a suit to play before us?" Those words chilled Eamon to his very core.

"Yes," he answered. "Glorious Master and noble lords, I would have you consider the law of confession."

"In what way would you have us consider it?" Cathair asked. Surprise was written on the Hand's face. He had not been told of Eamon's request. Eamon allowed himself some small satisfaction in knowing that it was not only him who knew not everything.

"Rather, I would have you reconsider it," Eamon answered. The throned leaned in his seat, his fiery hair rimming his smiling face, as though to observe an enjoyable spectacle. Eamon felt the tension in the air. He realized too late he had become the beast to be torn by the Master's hounds.

He drew a deep breath and spoke again. "My lords, from my experience of this law in practice yesterday, I feel it my duty to express my heartfelt opinion that it is flawed."

"You would not have men pay for their crimes?" Dehelt asked.

"No," Eamon corrected hastily, "it is right that a man who has committed a crime against a citizen of this city or this land, and has thus transgressed against the Master himself, receives punishment according to the law."

"Then what fault is there?" Cathair asked icily.

"That in the absence of two witnesses confession is deemed a suitable means of assessing guilt."

There was a moment of silence. Suddenly, Tramist laughed.

"Master, this Lord Goodman grows more and more deranged!" He rounded on Eamon with unprecedented fierceness. "How else is guilt to be established?"

"A confession drawn under torture cannot be counted as a valid admission of guilt," Eamon retorted.

"Perhaps Lord Goodman would have every criminal breached and set free?" Arlaith commented. His tone was deathly quiet, and cut across the words of the other Hands like a scythe through grass. Fear laid hold of Eamon: how did Arlaith know about Patagon's servant? "Perhaps Lord Goodman would have every criminal set free."

"When a man is innocent, what reason is there to punish him?"

"But, Lord Goodman, every man you pardon and release back into the city has a purpose to which his guilt or innocence is indifferent," Arlaith replied. He stepped forward. The Right Hand's eyes flashed with fire. "Every man that you set free goes out to sing your praises. They do not go to glorify the Master; they glorify *you*."

Silence rent the air.

Eamon gaped at Arlaith in horror. He could not bring words to his lips with which to reply to so serious a charge.

The Right Hand laughed. "See, Master? He does not refute it. Such is the nature of his confession, though with that he need not have bothered. There are witnesses enough here to see that he betrays you."

"I do not deem this charge worthy of a rebuttal, but I will give it!" Eamon cried, his tongue freed at last. He felt his peril keenly but knew that in this deadly game, the only piece that mattered was the Master's. The throned watched him with a smile.

"All my service, Master," he cried, "every stone and post reset, every man aided and saved, every paper signed, every word spoken, do they not bring you glory? Is not all my thought and deed for you?"

"How dare you speak thus before the Lord of Dunthruik?" the Right Hand snarled. "He sees you for what you are, Goodman!"

"And what am I?" Eamon demanded. Suddenly he was filled with boldness that feared neither the Right Hand nor the fearful hall in which he stood. "Am I not as faithful to him as you? The one who dares too much before the Lord of Dunthruik is not I. Had I your place, Lord Arlaith, I would think more carefully before assailing one, chosen by the Master for his service, with such words."

"You dare to speak of service and faithfulness?" The Right Hand surged towards Eamon; even the other Hands shied from his fury. "The Master's glory is never in your mind!"

"Never in my mind? No day goes by when I do not think of it!" Eamon answered. "But I will tell you what never is, and has never once been, in my mind, Lord Arlaith. I am to the Master less than a single feather to an eagle. Tell me, then, how I could ever hope – or dare – to rise against him who has graced me with service and made me a symbol of his glory? What I am this day, I am because I have served him and used every deed of my hands to work for his glory. How could I ever eke out any portion of greatness, or make his glory my own, when without him all that I do is nothing? His glory is both life and breath to me, and I have never striven against it, for when I do, I die.

"Master," Eamon said, turning fearlessly to the throned. "The people of this city live in fear. They fear that at any moment the Serpent will erupt through the gates; that he will drive through your streets and steal their children and homes; that his followers will destroy this city and cast you down from the very throne upon which you sit.

"Why should they be so fearful? Lord Arlaith cannot answer that, because the Right Hand knows nothing of the hearts of these

451

people; he is sapient only of the arts of fear, not the quelling of it, and it is the quelling of fear that brings glory to you."

"You will learn to hold your tongue, Goodman!" Arlaith cried, but Eamon ignored him.

"The fear of the people does not glorify you, Master; it shows their belief that your power is insufficient to save them from the Serpent. That fear, so easy to eradicate, is graven indelibly into the people's hearts by laws, such as this law of confession. It is a law that grinds the innocent into the ground at the whim of those more powerful than they. This law binds the people to you in fear, increasing their fear that you may yourself be bound by one greater than you. Their fear brings your name down into the dust where they walk and weep day by day. They weep because an unjust law shows weakness; it tarnishes the glory that your name should rightly hold. A law made for fear is no law at all.

"Show these men and women a law that fills them with fear, and they can no longer glorify you. But show them a law that shows your confidence, Master, and their confidence in you grows. When they fear you," he cried at last, "let it be because they are overawed by your greatness; let them glorify you for that."

Eamon's blood pulsed through his veins and he fell back in silence. His words hung in the air and his limbs trembled.

Everything now rested with the throned.

The Master leaned forward. "What change would you have made to this law, Eben's son?" They were words that neither promised nor threatened, but the Master bore in his eyes a glance of terrifying, and intimate, indulgence.

"Master," Eamon breathed, "I would have men give their accounts without fear of proclaiming themselves innocent."

Edelred smiled at him. "You would restrict the law of confession, and by extension the application of torture."

He bowed his head. "Yes, Master," he said, "and I would see men proclaim your glory in our courts, knowing that your law upholds the innocent and rightly condemns the guilty."

"It shall be so, Eben's son."

The words shattered the silence. Eamon stared, jaw agape. The other Hands shared in his amazement. The Right Hand's face fell in irate horror.

"Master –"

"You would gainsay my glory, Lord Arlaith?" the throned asked, and Eamon caught a glimpse of a terrible power in the cold gaze that turned to the Right Hand. Arlaith visibly paled, but could not answer. "That disappoints me."

The words were crushing. The Right Hand gasped for breath. The throned turned to the others. "Go, and do the work of my Hands," he said. "Bring me glory as Lord Goodman brings me glory."

The Hands, Eamon dizzy among them, bowed in unison. "Your glory, Master," they said.

As they departed, the Master spoke one more time:

"You will remain, Lord Arlaith." It was a terrifying pronouncement.

"Yes, Master."

Eamon left the hall with the other Quarter Hands. As he stepped into the corridor, his blood thinned in his veins, as though it could not reach every part of him swiftly enough. He felt lightheaded, jubilant.

It might seem only a small change to the law, but the Master had heard him.

Cathair and Tramist disappeared swiftly, their heads lowered together. Eamon walked after them, still in a daze. As he turned a corner in the empty corridor, he heard a voice by him.

"Beware Lord Arlaith's ire, Lord Goodman," it said. "In peril it is second only to the Master's favour."

Eamon turned to see Lord Dehelt. The North Quarter Hand inclined his head slightly towards him, and then, without a further word, followed in the wake of the others.

Eamon was still dazed with his success as he clattered back into the Ashen. He must have had a ridiculous smile on his face, for people stared at him as though he were a madman. Perhaps he was; he had stood before the throned and the throned had listened to him. Hughan would be proud.

Marilio was in the stables as he rode his horse in through the gates. The big man laughed to see him.

"You look as though you have had a productive morning, my lord!"

Eamon threw the reins to him and dismounted with a grace and agility that he had learned from Anderas, enhanced by his exultant mood.

"I have, Mr Bellis!"

On his way into the Handquarters he met Greenwood. The draybant was deeply involved in some papers that he carried, but looked up as Eamon passed. "Mr Greenwood!" Eamon called.

"My lord?" Greenwood bowed.

"I would like you to send to Stone Way to seek out a certain Mr Grennil and bring him to me as soon as you can," he said. He had had one triumph that morning; he would seek to work another from the ruin that the other Hands planned for him.

"Yes, my lord."

"And please ask Captain Anderas to come and see me this evening, when he has dispensed with his duties."

"Yes, Lord Goodman."

Greenwood bowed and hurried away, and Eamon returned to his office.

About midday there was a knock at his door. Eamon looked up from his papers – reams of exit papers to make room in the quarter for the Gauntlet that would be sent to him – and called to grant admittance. Slater entered and bowed.

"My lord, I have a Mr Grennil for you?" Slater sounded unconvinced, but Eamon's smile reassured him.

"Yes," he replied. "Please show him in."

Slater escorted Mr Grennil into the room, then left, closing the door behind him. Grennil bowed deeply.

"You wanted to see me, my lord?" Eamon thought that there was an odd tone to the man's voice.

"Yes," Eamon replied. Slowly he rose from his seat and came across to the man. "All is well, Mr Grennil," he said, and held out a piece of paper to him. The man took it and looked at it.

"An exit order?" he said, and looked up. Their eyes met. Grennil searched his face.

"My lord, I don't understand –"

"Mr Grennil, has Damien told you how we met?"

Tension drew Grennil's jaws together. The man's knuckles grew tight on the exit papers.

Eamon carefully kept his manner neutral. "It was a curious thing, Mr Grennil. He came to help me with a small injury to my hand. I may have mis-seen – it was a very hot, bright day – but when he looked at my hurt, it was as if there was a strange blue light in his hand."

Grennil's knuckles had gone white.

"What would you say to that, Mr Grennil?"

Grennil was silent. Shaking touched his knees. Eamon waited. If he was to trust this man, he needed to know that he was a King's man, like his son. He could not justify the risk he meant to take without that knowledge.

"My son is only a child, my lord. Please, let him go free."

"He will go free, and he will not be harmed," Eamon promised. "He has learned well from his father."

Grennil's trembling became outright quaking. "You know what we are, my lord," he said. " I… I will not deny it."

"You are a brave man." Eamon drew a deep breath. Now, he also had to have courage. He lowered his voice to an audible whisper. "You have one lord, Mr Grennil, and you know as well as I it is not the throned," Eamon continued quietly. "Just as this same lord sent me, now I must send you."

Grennil gaped. "S-s-sent you?"

"I serve the same lord as you, Mr Grennil."

Grennil staggered – he grabbed a nearby chair for support. "Who are you?" he whispered.

"Exactly what you see," Eamon answered with a smile. "I am the Lord of the East Quarter, appointed by the Master. But I am not that alone. Like an actor on the stage, my parts are many."

Mr Grennil looked bewildered. "I do not understand, my lord."

"I am the First Knight, Mr Grennil."

Mr Grennil's eyes widened in utter awe. "The First Knight?"

Now shaking a little himself, Eamon nodded.

A deep silence fell between them. Grennil stared at him in astonishment. Tears glistened suddenly in his eyes.

"When my son told me what had happened, Lord Goodman, I thought you had simply spared him for his youth. I never thought that you might be –"

"My name is Eamon," Eamon told him. "I am no greater a man than you."

Grennil watched him for a moment, and then looked down at the paper again. "What would you have me do?" he asked earnestly.

"I have been charged with making space in the quarter to house further Gauntlet reinforcements," Eamon explained. "There simply isn't enough room. I am having to empty a large number of residential areas, yours among them. To this end, I need you to recommend the names of families to me that it would be… shall we say *convenient* to evict. I will serve them their eviction notices."

Grennil's eyes were touched with wariness. There was a silence as he considered.

"I am entirely in earnest, Mr Grennil," Eamon continued. "Dunthruik will soon be under siege, and is already no place for those that serve the King. Assist me in this, and we can give those who love the King the chance to flee to safety under the auspices of the law. I would have you lead these families to the King. He will protect them."

Grennil breathed deeply, then met Eamon's gaze with resolve. "You told me before that you are not like Lord Ashway," he said.

"Now I understand why. I will do as you ask, First Knight."

"Then go, Mr Grennil. Bring back the names of as many as you can as soon as you can, and I will evict as many as I can."

Grennil nodded, and swayed against the chair. "I will."

"I know it is obvious, but I must stress that my true nature is not known," Eamon added quietly. "Please take care that you speak of it to no one, and please do not let your own family fall into the clutches of the Hands. I ask this as much for your sake as for mine."

"I will do my utmost."

"I am sure that you will."

Grennil looked at the papers in his hands again, then back to Eamon with a confused glance. "What about the head over the Blind Gate?" he whispered. "Did you really…?"

Eamon smiled broadly. "If you encounter the King on your journey, Mr Grennil, give him my greetings and ask him to teach your son the real story. I am sure that young Neithan would tell it well."

Grennil nodded with delight.

"I will." There was another long pause, and he looked at Eamon with a deep respect. "You are a courageous man, Eamon Goodman," he said. Eamon looked at him in surprise. "Perhaps you would say to me that we must each serve the King in different ways, and with that I would agree. Perhaps you would say that each man is fitted to the service that is asked of him."

"The King asks no man for more than he can do," Eamon replied.

"You have sacrificed much in your service, Eamon," Grennil told him. "I can see it written on your face. And yet you serve still, and you serve in a way that I am not sure any other man could."

"This was the service chosen for me," Eamon answered. "It is the King's grace, and his faith in me, that has brought me here."

"And you hold to that. Thus I say that you are a courageous man," Grennil replied. "It is one thing being shown what service you can perform; it is another to choose to perform it."

"Thank you," Eamon breathed.

"No," Grennil answered; "thank *you*."

Eamon reached out and clasped Grennil's hand. "May the King's grace go with you."

"And with you, First Knight."

CHAPTER XXX

Grennil was true to his word: a list of names, scribed in a variety of hands, discreetly arrived later in the day. Now being expert in handling the city's papers, Eamon was swiftly able to draw up the exit orders required.

Late that evening Eamon went across to the college to find Anderas. On the way he delivered the exit papers to Greenwood, asking for them to be dispatched as soon as possible. The draybant looked surprised, but nodded and took the stack away.

Eamon met the captain on the stairs into the college. Anderas was obviously deep in thought and had not seen him, for he made as though to hurry past the arches where Eamon waited. Eamon laughed and called out after him.

"I see my cloak is more effective than ever this evening, captain!" he said.

Anderas jumped, and came back to where Eamon stood.

"Good evening, Lord Goodman," he said, bowing.

"Yes, captain," Eamon answered, "it is."

Anderas frowned at him. The frown quickly turned to a look of astonished surprise. "Your meeting with the Master –"

Eamon grinned from ear to ear. "My meeting with the Master was a great success, Anderas," he said, and laughed again. "It was a triumph, for his glory and for the people of this city."

"Nobody but you, my lord, could have concocted and conducted such a reckless scheme." Anderas shook his head. "I don't believe it."

"Perhaps once you have shared a glass of something with me to celebrate, you will find the believing of it a little easier," Eamon replied. "As to the charge of recklessness: that, I fear, will remain untouched."

"May I make rash comments about the particularity of your style?"

"I think you may just have done so," Eamon replied.

"My lord, I fear that were I to live a thousand years I would never find another able to lay claim to such spectacular folly as yourself."

"That, I am told, is all due to my particularity," Eamon answered with a smile.

Eamon requested a fine bottle to be brought to his office. He and Anderas drank some of it together. The captain asked to hear the details of the meeting. Eamon was as honest in the telling of what had happened as he could be. Anderas was fascinated by his glimpse into the world of the Hands, and singularly delighted with the change in the law.

"It will save lives, my lord," he said.

"I know," Eamon answered. "And perhaps it might just result in more effort being spent on catching actual thieves rather than the easiest available culprit."

After the captain had left, Eamon retired to bed. Again he took up the Edelred Cycle and tried reading another part of it, but his mind was restless, and it was difficult to concentrate.

He fell swiftly asleep, and awoke only briefly during the night at the sound of an owl screeching beyond his window. But in sleep, something just beyond hearing nagged at him, demanding his attention. His sleepy mind ignored it, but the premonition grew with the passing minutes till it filled his whole mind.

He opened his eyes. He heard nothing now, but the work was done: he was awake. As he gained consciousness, he realized that it was not yet fully light outside. The first birdsong cautiously touched the air, as though even the birds wondered if they woke too soon.

Eamon rose and drew on his breeches and boots, then crossed the floor to the wash basin. He cast his arms out wide, and stretched his back. His shirt and cloak were set carefully over a chair. He looked between them and the basin. He knew that he ought to throw some of the cold water over his face, knew it would help him wake up, but there was also the undeniable fact that it would be *cold*…

He heard a timid knock at his door. He paused, wondering if he had imagined it, but it was soon followed by a voice.

"Lord Goodman?"

"You can come in," he called. He splashed some water on his face. The door opened behind him.

"I'm so sorry to disturb you, Lord Goodman," the voice continued. Cara's voice. A great smile broke across his face. "There is a…" Cara trailed off into a gasp.

Eamon rose, rubbing his face against a cloth to dry it, then turned towards her. "Good morning to you, Miss Tenent," he said. "I'm glad to see you back on duty. How are you feeling?"

"Well, my lord," Cara answered, though her face was pale and she clenched one of her hands. Concern washed over him. He furrowed his brow and walked over to her.

"Forgive me, but your words and manner do not match. Are you sure everything is well, Miss Cara?" he said.

"Yes, my lord," Cara breathed. She looked at him with wide eyes. "Your back…"

Suddenly, Eamon understood.

"Is it the scars?" he asked, and slowly turned his back to her. She nodded. One of her hands reached towards the scars on his back as though to ward off the disbelief that consumed her. It sent a chill down his spine.

With a gasp she withdrew. "My lord, I'm sorry –"

"Be at peace," Eamon answered, and turned to look at her again. The girl froze in terror. As he looked at her, he was overwhelmed by how young and fragile, and in her own way beautiful, she was. He stared at her.

In that one, terrifyingly vivid, moment he saw himself seize her and claim that hitherto unclaimed innocence for himself.

It is the work of but a moment, Eben's son, and your due. She cannot refuse you. She will subject herself to you, and count herself as honoured. How many others could lay claim to such an honour?

With a shudder, he tore himself away from his thoughts. The voice's suggestion revolted him. Not only would such a thing be an abuse of her, it would also be an abuse of him and a betrayal of them both. It would betray the King, and in betraying Hughan, Eamon would dishonour him.

It would betray Alessia.

That this last thought should enter his mind surprised him. For a moment he longed for her face and the touch of her hand in his own.

Answer her betrayal, Eben's son! It is widely thought that this wench is your whore. What shame is there in making her so?

Eamon repulsed the voice and turned his heart from it.

He realized that he had been quiet for a long time. Cara watched him with concern.

"Are you well, my lord?"

Take her now.

Eamon met her gaze. He felt deeply ashamed of his thoughts, but still he answered her.

"Yes," he said at last. With a final effort he forced the last traces of the voice from his mind. When he looked at her again, he saw that he loved the servant because she, just like Slater and Marilio and Callum and Cook and so many others, served him. "Yes, I am well."

"When were you flogged?" Cara asked quietly. She suddenly drew breath as though to apologize for her boldness. Eamon smiled and interrupted her.

"Seven months ago," he answered. Tears welled in Cara's eyes.

"I never knew…"

"Not many people do," Eamon answered gently. "I am not sure what people would think if they realized that the Lord of the East Quarter was once a lieutenant who was flogged for miscarrying his duty."

Cara looked at him in surprise. "That cannot be true."

"You're right," Eamon answered. "I suppose it is only partially true."

"What happened?"

"Three cadets under my command were guarding a prisoner we were transporting from Edesfield to Dunthruik."

"Edesfield?" Cara repeated uncertainly.

"Not the province," Eamon answered, "the town. It is some way from Dunthruik." Cara nodded and he continued. "The prisoner was my charge. One day the cadets were careless and she attempted to escape. She was caught, but three of them were held responsible for her attempt to escape. They were young, Cara, as most cadets are. Younger than Cadet Bellis." She blushed a little. "They were to be flogged." It seemed so long ago. "I took the flogging in their place," he finished simply.

There was a long silence. Cara watched him, as though unsure what to make of what she had heard.

"That is not a story that they tell about you."

"Most of the men who would tell it are dead," Eamon replied. "They were killed when the holk was boarded."

"Even though you surrendered?"

"Yes."

"I'm sorry," she whispered. Eamon offered her another smile.

"I'm not sorry for what I did," he told her. "There is no shame in bearing scars like these, Cara. You took them well, and they are a testament to your courage."

"And to yours, my lord," Cara answered quietly. "You bore near to a flogging from Lord Arlaith for my sake."

Eamon's face flooded with momentary embarrassment as he remembered how he had grovelled before the Right Hand.

"Slater told you?" he guessed.

"Please don't be angry with him," Cara said anxiously.

"I'm not, Cara."

"He felt that I should know what happened. When he explained to me what you had done I couldn't understand it," Cara said quietly. "Now perhaps I do a little better."

"Miss Tenent, I did not try to stop Arlaith because I was once flogged myself," Eamon told her. "I tried to stop him because…" He faltered. He could not say it was because she did not deserve it; if he did, it would be to gainsay the Right Hand, and that was dangerous for them both. He looked up at her again. "I had to try."

"Thank you."

"You deserved nothing less, and much more, than what I was able to do."

There was a long and slightly awkward silence. Quietly Eamon stepped away from her and went to the chair where his shirt and cloak lay. He drew them on. As he did so, Cara came forward to help him. He laughed quietly.

"I am sure that you often assisted Lord Ashway when he dressed," he said, "but you need not do the same for me. I am well able to dress myself."

Cara fell back a pace. "Yes, my lord."

Eamon quickly settled his robes and cloak over his shoulders.

"My apologies, my lord, but I nearly forgot. A messenger came for you," Cara said.

"From whom?"

"From the Master," Cara replied quietly. "You're to go to him at once."

Eamon frowned as he straightened the cloak on his shoulders, and at last pushed his ring onto his finger.

"Then to the Master I shall go," he said.

CHAPTER XXXI

The doorkeeper awaited him. He lurked in the shadows that surrounded the door to the throne room. As Eamon approached, the man bowed deeply – far more deeply than Eamon had ever been bowed to before. It surprised and alarmed him.

"My lord," the doorkeeper said. "You are expected."

"Thank you, doorkeeper," Eamon answered. The man remained folded before him. For a moment Eamon didn't know what to do.

"Rise," he tried at last, and the man did so before slowly drawing open the doors. Eamon stared at him.

"My lord," the doorkeeper said again.

Flummoxed, Eamon stepped into the throne room. The doors closed behind him.

The grey dawn's first touch loaned the grand hall a ghostly quality, almost as though the place were wreathed in mist.

Eamon stepped down from the door and crossed the hall. It was only as he reached the halfway point that he saw the throne. The Master stood before it, his eyes fixed on Eamon. The grey stare cut through the twilight shades, making a breach straight in his heart.

Eamon reached the foot of the dais and bowed down to one knee as he had done so many other times.

"Your glory, Master." His voice came as a threadbare whisper.

"Rise, Eben's son," the throned replied. Eamon did so and looked up at the Master's deep, dark eyes. The throned smiled. Eamon realized – with a mix of awe, delight, and utter dread – that it was a smile given to no other.

As the Master descended the steps of the throne and approached him, another realization dawned: he was alone with the Master.

The Master stood before him. His towering height made Eamon cower, and a searing thrill ran through his flesh as the Master reached down and touched his face. He could not move and could not breathe, even as his palm and forehead burned at the flare of the throned's mark.

"You will be the youngest, Eben's son." The throned's voice was quiet, and Eamon wondered if it was not also a little wistful. The words chilled him to his very core. "And yet, none will have been as you will be."

"How may I serve you, Master?" Eamon asked.

The throned smiled. "Son of Eben," he said, "you will become my Right Hand."

Eamon's breath was torn viciously from his lungs as at a blow. He reeled. With startling suddenness Waite's words, spoken at their first meeting, came back to him: *Right Hand is not beyond you.*

Eamon remembered how much he had longed for it, how he had hankered after it when he had lain awake night after night in Alessia's bed; how Ladomer had encouraged him to yearn after it, though it had seemed far beyond him…

Now, it was freely given to him from the hand of the Master himself. The hand that gave it lay on his cheek in a dreadful tenderness that he could scarcely endure.

"You have shown yourself trustworthy with little; now you will be entrusted with much." The Master's voice seeped into him through every pore.

Shaking from head to foot, Eamon sank down to his knees before the kindly smile of the throned.

"Master," he breathed, "I cannot of my own merit accept what you offer me. Only if it is your will shall I dare set my hand to such a thing."

There was a moment of silence, broken at the last by a laugh. It was a rich, round, deep-chested laugh, and it shook Eamon through his very bones.

"Few have been offered this task, Eben's son; none have taken it with such words." He laughed again. "You show promise, my son."

"I hope to make good on it, Master," Eamon replied. "But Lord Arlaith –?"

"In seven days, Eben's son, you shall take his place," the Master answered, and as he finished Eamon's heart sunk into a petrifying mire. "And, on that day, he shall take yours."

When he left the palace, Eamon could barely walk; he was glad that he needed only mount his horse. The creature proved cooperative and went slowly, not minding that the reins trembled in his fingers. Dunthruik passed by him in a daze. The Master's last words ran through his mind again. *One week*: a single week, and Arlaith would take the East Quarter. The thought cut at his heart like a deathblow. His servants, his college, the streets and people that he had come to know and love… they would be taken from him.

And the work that he had done? Arlaith would undo it. He would do so out of spite against Eamon. His hatred would do nothing but grow more terrible. Eamon did not know if he would be able to stop it, even if he was the Right Hand. And what of the servants? They could not be as free as they had been with him. They had to be retrained to be as they had been under Lord Ashway, trained again to tread in silence and in fear.

He came into the Ashen. "Lord Goodman!" called a voice. The earnestness of that voice dealt him a further blow.

"Good morning, captain," he answered.

In seven days he would lose Captain Anderas, his dearest friend in the entire city. Eamon was sure that Arlaith knew it too.

"I see you have been riding already," Anderas commented cheerfully.

Eamon could not answer. He felt as though he restrained tears by a thread. The captain looked at him in concern. "Are you well, my lord?"

"Yes," Eamon answered.

"You're lying," Anderas told him quietly. It was too bold a statement for a captain to make to a Hand, and to say as much to a *Right* Hand…

"Yes," Eamon replied. "I am."

"You're very bad at it. It's as well that you never thought about becoming a spy; they'd have rooted you out in seconds."

"Yes," Eamon answered, his throat terribly dry. "They would have."

But they had not.

He decided to go to bed early that night. He tucked his papers away into neat piles and stood at the window in his office, letting his hand rest on the wooden frame. There was a knock on his door.

"I beg your pardon, my lord," said a voice – Slater's. "Mr Bellis asks whether you will take supper in your office this evening?"

Eamon sighed. Cook had fallen ill that morning and so Marilio had taken charge of the kitchen in his stead, and seemed determined to run it in a manner of which the cook would approve.

"I do not think that I will sup tonight," he answered.

"He'll make you take an enormous breakfast in the morning," the servant warned with a smile. Even Slater had become relaxed in his role. Eamon swallowed nervously. How was he to tell these people that they would, for all their kindness and service, reap Lord Arlaith in place of Lord Goodman?

"I know," he answered with a tiny smile. "Tell him that I look forward to it."

"Very good, my lord," Slater replied, and disappeared.

Eamon made his way wearily upstairs to bed. He had told no one of the news he had received that morning, and it weighed on him. Whom could he tell? He knew that they all had to know, but he would first need to have a hold of himself. It was something that he very much lacked.

He climbed into bed. The sheets trembled about his shaking limbs as he tried to read. It was a lost cause, and he soon doused the lamp and lay staring at the dark window. He stared for a long time before slipping into a troubled sleep.

He did not know how long he had been asleep when a loud banging at his door woke him. Someone called his name.

"Lord Goodman! Lord Goodman!"

Eamon stirred and then bolted awake. The voice was Slater's and it sounded terrified.

"*Lord Goodman!*"

"I'm coming, Slater." He got quickly out of bed and pulled his thick cloak on over his night-shirt; there was not the time for any further attempts at decency.

He pulled open the door. Pale and trembling, Slater fell back a pace. He held a slender candle in his hand. It was still pitch dark outside.

"Mr Slater, what is the matter?"

His servant could not answer him, but gestured for Eamon to follow him and led the way back down the stairway into the corridors of the Handquarters. Eamon followed, growing increasingly nervous. The candle threw their shadows in arches over the walls. They approached the kitchens. As they neared the doorway, traces of firelight struck up the walls from the kitchen fires burning low in the grates. With the smell of smoke mingled something else; something which made his flesh crawl.

Blood.

"What has happened?" he asked.

Slater stepped, trembling, through the kitchen doorway and then shrank back against the wall and pointed. A ghastly cry left his lips. Eamon followed the direction of the gesture and then felt his heart stop.

Slumped in the corner of the kitchen was a figure. It was crumpled in a pool of its own blood and glistened hellishly in the firelight. There was no sound other than Slater's cry.

"No," he breathed, but then even his breath was taken from him.

It was Marilio Bellis.

CHAPTER XXXII

The dawn came grey and mournful to the city, bringing with it gritty drizzle that struck the stones like so many beating hands.

Eamon stood in the courtyard of the Handquarters with his cloak drawn thickly about him against the rain. The drops slid down over his face and through his hair, rendering his cloak futile, but still he held it about his dripping throat.

In a line behind him stood his household. Several cadets were with them. Wilhelm Bellis's ravaged face was clear among them. Cara stood by him, her fingers knotted tightly through his own as he tried to keep back his tears. Many of the household wept. A cart had been brought into the yard where they stood. Two ensigns guarded it like graven images.

The beat of the rain was broken by the sound of footsteps coming down from the doors, from which four servants emerged solemnly. They stepped out into the rain, bearing a stretcher between them.

The stretcher bore Marilio's body; it had been swathed in a funerary pall, hiding the devastating violence of what had been done to him. Tears burned the back of Eamon's eyes. His mind was filled with Slater's anguished howls. When he blinked, he still saw the bloody kitchen.

Silently, he stepped forward to face the household. The stretcher and its bound load were set down before him. He could not look down at the body upon it; the swaddled mass bore no resemblance to the man he knew. Eamon lamented that it was the last sight Wilhelm would have of his father.

He looked up at the servants and their pale faces, blurred by the

471

rain. The words he spoke came haltingly and the sound of pounding rain vied with his quavering voice.

"In life and in death Marilio Bellis served the Master. As was his coming, so is his going to the Master's glory. Let ours be also."

"To his glory," the household answered. He barely heard them.

Eamon nodded once to the pallbearers. The stretcher was raised from the wet ground and delivered safely onto the cart. Eamon trembled as he watched. Tears streaked his face. There would be no noble resting-place for Wilhelm's father; all the city could offer to a servant was a place in the pyres.

The cadet in charge of the cart urged the horse on, and it stepped into a slow pace. The whole household watched as the cart ran out of the yard, into the Ashen and the rain.

Eamon looked back to the servants. "Return to your duties," he told them. They obeyed him.

Turning, he stepped quietly across to Wilhelm. Cara pressed the young man's hand in encouragement before she followed the other servants into the house. The cadet stared in anguish through the empty door to the Ashen, no doubt seeing his father's last journey over and over again in his mind.

"Mr Bellis," Eamon said softly.

The cadet looked up, his eyes red with tears. "My lord," he answered. He had to force himself to speak, and his voice shook as he tried to make it sound stronger than he felt.

"I am deeply sorry for your loss, Mr Bellis. Your father was dear to me."

In his memory, Eamon felt Marilio's blood thick on his hands as he checked the body for signs of life; felt the grief that lodged in his breast as he realized that he had come late – too late to do anything but weep…

"Who did it, my lord?" Wilhelm's voice trembled with anger. Vengeful grief filled the young man's eyes. "Who did it?"

"I don't know," Eamon answered.

But it was not true. He believed that it had not been just any hand that had slaughtered his servant. He believed it to have been the Right Hand, or at least someone in his service. Arlaith had every reason to loathe Eamon, and Eamon knew all too clearly that the Right Hand would come back against those near to the Lord of the East Quarter.

He looked back to Wilhelm. "Mr Bellis," he said gently.

"My lord?"

"I need you to promise me that you will not take this matter into your own hands."

Wilhelm shook, whether with rage or the surfeit of some other emotion Eamon did not know.

"You have been violated and I appreciate your desire for justice, even for vengeance. But when a man strikes against my servants he strikes against me. It is therefore right that I deal with this matter. For a man to strike against me he must be powerful indeed, and I would not have you pit yourself against such a man."

"With all due respect, my lord, I couldn't care how powerful the villain is." Wilhelm's eyes flamed as he spoke. "I wouldn't care if he were the Right Hand himself –"

"Mr Bellis," Eamon spoke firmly and the cadet quieted before his tone. "You have lost much this day, but by pursuing vengeance you stand to lose even more." The young man's eyes glanced up to the household where the last of the servants entered the building. "You must think of those who love you."

Wilhelm drew a shuddering breath. "Yes, my lord."

"Your father was indisputably faithful to me, and he was a good man. I see his heart in you, Mr Bellis. I will do everything in my power to bring whoever did this to justice," Eamon told him. "Promise me that you will let me do that. I will not lose your life as I have lost your father's."

The cadet was silent for a long moment. Then he nodded, giving his tacit agreement. "Yes, my lord," he said.

Relief coursed through Eamon's veins. "Do you want to take some time off duty?"

"No, my lord."

"Very well, Mr Bellis," Eamon replied. "You can return to the college. Report as normal."

"Thank you, my lord."

Wilhelm bowed low and left by the doorway through which his father had lately gone.

Eamon stood for a long time, thinking, until the rain penetrated through his cloak to his skin.

It had been Arlaith. He was certain of it. As he shivered in the cold, Eamon wondered whether it was a strike of vengeance or a warning, and whether Marilio would be the last to die.

Later that day, the rain still falling in sheets, Eamon visited the kitchens to see how the servants fared. The place where Marilio's body had been discovered was impeccably clean and fearfully avoided.

Despite still being unwell, Mr Cook returned to duty. He stood over the fire, fixed on his task with concentration that betrayed fraught nerves. Eamon joined him, watching as Cook's hands steadily plied the pots and pans of his trade.

"Mr Cook?" he said at last.

"My lord."

"Do not bear something beyond what is yours to carry."

The cook set down his ladle with trembling hands, and closed his eyes. "If I hadn't been ill…"

There was a long pause.

"What happened isn't your fault," Eamon said gently.

"How will his son ever forgive me?"

"He does not blame you. Neither do I. Do not blame yourself."

The cook looked over at the corner where the body had lain; tears filmed his eyes. "He was such a good man, my lord. There is no justice in it."

"I know." Eamon laid a hand on the man's shoulder. The cook shuddered beneath his fingers. "You are also a good man, Mr Cook."

The cook nodded wordlessly.

Eamon also made a point of seeking out Slater. He found the head of the household in the dining room. The man had laid out all the Handquarters' cutlery on the table and was in the process of cleaning it. As Eamon walked in, the servant set aside his cloth with a tremulous sigh.

"Mr Slater."

Slater looked up with a start, trying rapidly to compose himself. "My lord, I –"

"Be at peace, Mr Slater." The man looked back at the knives and forks on the table, and Eamon smiled at him. "You've been doing some good work here," he said kindly.

"Thank you, my lord."

"Be sure you take some rest."

"Yes, my lord." He breathed deeply and looked up at Eamon. "Lord Goodman…" He paused. "I've served in Dunthruik for a long time, Lord Goodman," he said. "I've served Hands for a long time."

"I am sure that you have been a great boon in every household that you have served," Eamon told him.

"My lord, I've never seen…"

"I wish you had never seen its like, Mr Slater," Eamon said quietly, "but, having seen it, do not fear it."

Slater was silent for a moment. "Perhaps," he said at last, "a Hand is more accustomed to the realities of war against the wayfarers…"

Eamon carefully hid his surprise. "Wayfarers?" Was that the rumour that went with Marilio's body as it trundled out of the city to the pyres – that wayfarers had done it?

Slater nodded. "Perhaps they meant some harm against you, my lord…"

Much as Eamon desperately desired to tell the man that the wayfarers would not do such a thing, and certainly not to someone in Eamon's house, he could not.

Slater breathed deeply and then looked at him with a quivering lip. "Where do you find such strength, my lord?" Eamon looked at him enquiringly. "I mean, the strength to look at such things, yet still carry on?"

"In the one I serve," Eamon replied.

Slater looked at him and nodded. "So shall this house, my lord."

Eamon retired early to bed, his mind in a trance-like state. In a strange way, his house had never been closer to him than it was now in grief. How could he tell them he was to leave them? They were so vulnerable.

He lay still for a long time, his thoughts moving heavily. Already a day had passed, and he had made no preparations. He had spoken to no one and he knew that he must. Perhaps it was fear that made him delay. He feared to see the disappointed faces, feared to speak from his own lips words that would seal him to the Master's will, and draw him away from a part of the city that he loved. He had not liked the idea of being a Quarter Hand at first, and yet it was in the East Quarter that he had found companionship and strength to do the King's work better than in any other place. Now, that all had to change: he had to leave all the people he loved behind him to walk unfamiliar new halls, to become once again the stranger who learned the ropes. It terrified him, but to whom could a Right Hand turn for guidance? Eamon knew that as the Right Hand he would be reliant only on the Master and on that smile, which looked on him as though he were a son...

He shook the thought from himself with a shudder of revulsion. How could he exchange his household and his college for that? He did not want to become Right Hand. Yet he had no choice. Would he be able to work for the King, even there?

He did not know. He could only hope that he could.

There were things in the quarter that he had to safeguard against Arlaith's arrival. He had to speak to Anderas.

As his thought turned to the captain, his stomach churned. Anderas needed to know. More than that: Eamon realized suddenly that he had to tell the captain everything, the whole truth.

Why? The voice's question was cold. *You will earn nothing from that, Eben's son, except loss.*

Eamon sighed. Surely having Anderas alive – and having his friendship – was more important than the truth? Was it not the captain's friendship that he wanted to preserve, even though they would be driven apart? If he told Anderas the truth, then the captain's life, and even his own, would be in danger.

Eamon, how can he know you if he does not know who you are? The words spoke deeply into his heart. *Would not knowing the truth save his life? How can he be a true friend to you if he does not know whom you serve?*

The grim voice laughed. *If you value his friendship, son of Eben, then you will say nothing to him. He will not love you for what you are. He will reject you, totally and utterly. He will betray you, even as she did.*

Eamon did not answer but set his resolve sternly against the voice of Edelred. He had to speak to Anderas, and not just because of his friendship with the man. Did the captain not also deserve the chance to serve the King?

And if he rejects you, Eben's son? The voice relished the thought. *If he rejects you, you cannot then let him live.*

Eamon's blood ran cold. If Anderas, despite the weeks and months that they had spent working together, despite the fact that they had saved each other from death and despair… if Anderas were to turn against him, what other choice would he have but to take the captain's life?

The idea haunted him. He could not sleep.

Take heart, Eamon.

At last he sat up. Stacking the cushions up behind his back he set himself upright in his bed and reached across to his table for the Edelred Cycle.

Have you not yet understood? You will learn nothing of value there, Eben's son, the voice of Edelred told him.

"I certainly won't if I don't read it," Eamon answered, somewhat petulantly. Carefully flicking the book open, he leaned it against his legs, drew a deep breath to drive the voice away, and continued reading.

He had already read a large amount of the work, which went to great lengths to describe the Master's skill, cunning, and greatness against his enemies. From what Eamon had understood from the poem, Edelred's aim was that of liberating the River Realm from a deluded king, although Eamon could not see how Ede might have fit such a description. The king he had seen in his visions had seemed noble, though troubled.

He had read how Edelred had gone as a diplomatic envoy to Ede's court and wooed a lady, Liana. This lady was sister to the King's closest counsellor, and Eamon's skin had crawled when he had realized that this lady had been the sister of Eben, and of his own blood.

In the poem the King (who disapproved of her love for Edelred) had struck down Liana – this was framed by the poem as proof of the King's wickedness. Eben was drawn, reluctantly but steadily, to Edelred's cause until he became the man's staunchest supporter – a shift of loyalties that filled Eamon with anguish and revulsion. The poem's words opened up the way to the battle at the watchtower wherein Edelred asked the King to relinquish his tyrannical hold over the River Realm, and Ede had rashly and arrogantly refused. The battle was joined and then Eben, in a moment of brazen courage, landed a blow against Ede's steed, allowing Edelred to take the King's life.

Eamon read the text carefully, knowing that the words did not tell the truth, or at least not the whole of it. He wondered what had truly happened.

He set his eyes to the text once again as he found his place. Edelred defeated the King, and went on to make a lengthy speech which lasted a number of pages and – in the manner of the best poetry – said little that was truly relevant. It took every part of Eamon's resolve to read, rather than skip over, the words. It was as well that he had nearly finished the book. Had he spent much longer reading it, he would not be overly surprised to hear himself speaking in the poet's eight-syllable verse.

At last the speech concluded. Eamon drew a deep breath, hoping that the end of the speech might signal a return to something of note. His eyes were blurred. He rubbed his hand across them before quietly counting the scant number of remaining pages.

Perhaps the voice of Edelred was right: perhaps there was nothing for him to find. Perhaps he wasted his time.

With a great effort of will he turned his eyes back to the verse. While there were still pages left to read, he would not abandon his hope.

An odd chill crept down his spine. The words on the page before him crystallized. As he read them they painted vivid pictures in his trembling thought:

> *Cracked was the Serpent's helm and shield.*
> *His blood; bleak on the ground it spread*
> *And there, where sword and shield lay strewn*
> *Beneath the watchtower's gaze, and hewn*
> *From flesh and breath of men was all*
> *The road to Allera's last hall*
> *Stood Edelred, whole wreathed in flame*
> *While dark skies echoed back his name.*
> *And in his hand aloft – Dark Tome!*
> *Great covenant to claim the throne!*
> *Its witness were those shattered fields*
> *Where Serpent's right was made to yield.*

Eamon's pulse raced. His thoughts fell back in on themselves in wonder and dismay. A *dark tome*.

All at once he felt the weight of the Nightholt in his fingers. He saw the grim, angled writing on its pages, smelled the scent of death erupt from them, and remembered his vision of Eben, weeping as he hid it deep in Ellenswell.

He drew a deep breath. Surely, by a "dark tome", the poet could mean nothing but the Nightholt?

Eamon stared at the words again, scanning them, re-reading them, trying to interpret them in as many different ways as possible, but he came again and again to the same terrifying conclusion:

the Nightholt had been at the battle of Edesfield. More than that, somehow it seemed to validate Edelred's rule. Why else should it make the Serpent's "right" yield? What other right had a king, other than that of governance?

He sat back in dismay. What, then, could be written in the Nightholt? And why was it so vital to the throned to have it? Having it, what danger did it pose to Hughan?

He did not know, but in one matter alone he was left in no doubt. Eamon again read the line about Edelred being wreathed in flame. His flesh crawled – *the red light*. Eamon's palm burned.

The throned's mark had begun there, at that moment. Eamon remembered Hughan say that at Ede's death the King's grace had also shown itself. Lights, tome, King, and throned... somehow all things met in that moment at Edesfield.

Eamon read a little more but his eyes grew heavy, and at last he set the book aside. Then he slipped into a deep sleep where armies clashed on a darkened plain.

He woke long before morning came. Reluctantly sense returned to his limbs, and thought to his mind. The first traces of the dawn touched the distant sky. All in the house was silent.

He had to speak to Anderas.

He rose and dressed himself with care. Much as he tried to distract his thoughts from what he was about to do, he could not halt their hawk-like circling.

In silence he slung his sword to his belt.

You shall have need of that, Eben's son, the voice told him. *He will deny you.*

Eamon saw Anderas in his mind, the captain's face wrenched with horror and rage. His hand flew to his weapon as a cry erupted from his lips: "*Traitor!*"

His pulse quickened. What if what he saw in the fearful cracks of his mind happened before his eyes? He had struck and killed men, but could he truly turn a blade to strike Captain Anderas?

What other choice would he have?

Shaking, he took up his cloak. It seemed heavy as he set it over his shoulders and fastened it. He tried to marshal his thoughts.

He would speak to Anderas during their ride. He would make sure they went far from the city that morning – somewhere where the spies in Lord Dehelt's towers could not watch them. Maybe they would go up into the first curves of Ravensill; there were some wooded copses there. Then he could speak to Anderas fearlessly.

That you will never do, Eben's son.

He left his rooms and went swiftly down to the stables, where the stablehands were already at work. One of them brought his horse for him while he waited. Servants passed and greeted him. The early light grew stronger, and still he waited. Every now and then he glanced up at the doorway through which he knew the captain had to come.

What if he did not come? A shudder ran down his spine as he looked at the doorway again with horror. What if Anderas had been called away by other business?

The cruel torment of his thoughts began again. He had left it too late; he should have spoken to the captain weeks ago. Now the chance had been taken from him. Captain Anderas would die in battle against the King. His lifeless face would fall, pale and bloodied, in the tangled mud of Dunthruik because Eamon had not spoken. It tore at his heart. Why had he done nothing?

You glutted yourself on him, Eben's son, and fed on him for your selfish gain. Such is your friendship! Go back to your rooms and reap what you have sown. It is too late: he will not come.

A rustling sound by his face stirred him. Startled from his dark thoughts, he looked up. Suddenly a warm face was by his own and he smiled: Sahu. The beast, as always, seemed ridiculously content to see him. Eamon laid his hand on the charger's broad nose, tracing the white, star-like pattern there, and seeking encouragement in the horse's intelligent eyes.

"Do you think it will turn out well, Sahu?"

"Will what turn out well, my lord?" asked a voice.

Eamon started in surprise and turned to see the captain staring at him. The captain nodded to one of the stablehands to fetch his horse. Then he looked back to Eamon and smiled.

"Are you well, Lord Goodman?"

"Yes," Eamon answered with a relieved laugh. "I thought for some reason that you would not come today."

Anderas frowned seriously. "I would have advised you, my lord, if that were the case."

"I know, captain." He had known it well.

They rode from the city gates as normal, and followed the path towards the plains and the East Road. Eamon was terribly aware of the breeze in his face and the sound of the earth and stones beneath their horses' hooves. Every noise, every sensation, was tenfold itself, such was his fear. Yet the captain was disturbingly distant, as though he were a league away. Eamon knew that it was a figment of his own imagining. Anderas spoke confidently with him, and advised him on the latest news from the college and its cadets.

"Another month or so and we shall be due a swearing-in of our own, my lord," he said. "Some of the third cadets are coming along very nicely indeed. If battle is imminent, perhaps we should consider bringing the swearing forward. It certainly aids morale on the battlefield."

"Yes," Eamon replied distractedly. They reached the crossroads that branched both across the plains and towards the hills. The paths stretched in various directions. His heart faltered.

Take your usual road, Eben's son. You will gain nothing by your folly.

"Captain," Eamon said suddenly, and Anderas looked at him. Eamon straightened in his saddle. "Captain, I would ride by a different way today – I would go up across the foot of the hills into the woodland."

For a terrible moment he was afraid that the captain would not answer. But Anderas smiled.

"A change is, they say, as good as a rest, my lord."

They rode north, and the treeline grew closer. With the arrival of spring the leaves were full, and the boughs weighed down with foliage that rustled in the wind like the waves of the distant sea. As they rode beneath the wooded canopy, the branches moved, and the turf changed beneath the horses' hooves. The temperature dropped slightly as they entered the shade. Anderas followed Eamon. There was no sound about them other than what they brought, the morning birds, and the moving leaves.

The trees soon opened out into a clearing that was cool and shaded. Eamon paused as they reached it, stunned for a moment by the beauty of the trees themselves as their barks and arms were lit by the sunlight. The place felt at peace. This was where Eamon would confide.

Gently, he tugged back on the reins, bringing his horse to a slow stop. Anderas's horse went on a few paces. The captain's eyes turned towards the leaves in quiet wonder.

"There were once many trees on this plain and gathered in these hills," he breathed. A smile spread over his face. "I am told that there were even birches once."

"Silver ones?" Eamon asked. The trees were rare in the valleys and plains of the River Realm – no sooner did they spring up but they were torn down, at the Master's orders.

Anderas laughed. "I do not know, my lord," he confessed, "but I rather like the idea." Eamon did not answer, and the captain turned to him with a concerned frown. "Is everything well, my lord?"

It was the question Eamon had known would come. He trembled. Now – he knew it had to be now.

Anderas watched him dismount. His hands shook as he tethered Sahu to one of the trees. He did not believe that the horse would bolt, but he needed the security of the gesture.

At last he looked back to the captain. The man's swift eyes assessed him, and he wondered what thoughts were passing through his mind.

"Captain, I must speak with you."

"Of course, my lord."

Anderas dismounted and tied his own horse. He came and stood before Eamon. The first rays of sunlight were now high enough to pass through the eaves. Anderas blinked to clear them from his sight.

"How may I serve you?" he asked.

Eamon watched him for a long moment, his heart pounding. Could he really trust himself to this man? Anderas was a Gauntlet captain, sworn to the throned, while Eamon was the First Knight, sworn to the King. Grief filled his heart. What trust – or peace – could there ever be between them?

"Anderas," he said at last, "I am going away."

He saw the captain frown. "Going?"

"Yes."

"Where are you going, my lord?" Anderas's voice was scarcely more than a whisper.

"It is the Master's will to draw me away from the East Quarter," Eamon answered slowly. "He has another purpose for me, and I must perform it."

"What must you do?"

Eamon matched his gaze as steadily as he could. "I am to become his Right Hand."

Silence fell between them. Anderas exhaled deeply. When the captain next spoke, his eyes were veiled, and his voice dulled.

"Congratulations, my lord."

"The news grieves you?" Eamon asked.

Anderas closed his eyes and drew breath before answering. "I cannot, nor will not, lie to you, my lord. Yes, it grieves me." He looked up at last. "It is as doleful a blow as I have taken in a long time."

"Neither can I lie to you," Eamon replied. "It grieves me also."

The captain looked at him as though this surprised him. Then he laughed quietly.

"I still remember, my lord, your uncertainty when they first gave you black to wear. It never really seemed your colour, and yet you have worn it well. I do not doubt that you will bear your new office as well as you have this." He held out his hand to clasp Eamon's. "I must again offer you my most sincere congratulations."

Eamon's heartbeat picked up again. This was it – this was the moment. He had to take it or lose it.

The captain's hand extended towards him and the smile on the man's face was genuine, if bittersweet. How easy it would be to accept that hand, how easy to take that praise, mount his horse, and leave.

A look of confusion ran across the captain's face as Eamon set his hands to his belt and unslung his sword from it. The blade and scabbard seemed heavy, but he held them out and set the sheathed blade in the captain's outstretched hand. The captain took it with both his hands, not daring to speak as Eamon also drew his dagger and laid it with the sword.

Anderas stared at him. "My lord," he said, looking up in alarm from the blades, "what do you mean to –?"

"Anderas."

The captain's face paled to hear his name passing so solemnly from Eamon's lips. Eamon held the breath that he had drawn, as though it would somehow steel him against what he had to do. He could not now go back. But how could he say what he had to say? The captain stared at him in bewilderment, and he knew that he had to speak.

Courage, Eamon!

"Anderas," he said, and his words came haltingly. "I have found no truer friend in the whole of Dunthruik than you. You have made my way – a way blighted at times with grief and fear – easier to bear. I could not have borne it up to now without you."

"Thank you, my lord," Anderas now looked doubly uncertain. Eamon met his gaze again and smiled despite his fear.

"Anderas! You are gracious and noble in more ways than you understand, and you have been true to me when I little deserved that. You are true to me even now, though you cannot fathom what I do, why I have brought you here, or what I try to say. The truth of it is that I do not know how to speak what I must, but I must do it nonetheless."

"I will bear with you, my lord."

Eamon paused. If Anderas only knew what he had said. Would the captain really bear with Eamon the burden of being a King's man?

"The news that I must become Right Hand grieved me," Eamon continued, "for the fact that I will no longer be in the East Quarter, in the college, in the Handquarters, nor have the company of those there whom I love." He looked up again. The captain's face was grave. "You know that I love you, Anderas," Eamon told him quietly, "yet I am drawn and commanded by a higher loyalty."

"I understand," Anderas answered.

"It is of that loyalty that I must speak." Eamon drew another breath. "Do you love me, Anderas?"

"My lord," Anderas answered quietly, "you know that I do."

"It is because I love you that I would have you know me for what I am." Anderas stared at him. "Let me tell you a story, Anderas," Eamon continued. "It is not a story about Lord Goodman – it is not a story about Pinewood or a dinner with two crowns, nor a story about a head set upon a city gate. It is a story about Eamon Goodman."

Anderas watched him nervously. The captain swallowed.

"When Eamon surrendered his sword, the man who captured his ship threatened death to all on board. He intended to kill Eamon first, and would indeed have done so," Eamon said quietly. "But a young cadet threw himself in the way and took the blow. The cadet's name was Mathaiah Grahaven, and he received his death in that blow. But he was saved."

Anderas shook his head slightly. "I do not understand."

"Mathaiah was saved by blue light – the grace of the King in the hands of a King's man."

A worried look passed over the captain's face.

"B-b-blue light?"

Eamon saw the fear in his eyes, and knew it. His heart was filled with courage, and when he met Anderas's gaze again, his voice was clear.

"You are right: black is not a colour that I bear well, though I have tried. You had the right of it, long ago, when you observed that I bore red better than I do the black. But, Captain Anderas, there is another colour that I wear better than either red or black. I wear it in my heart, and through it and for it, I have borne all the others. It is to that which I give my highest loyalty – to that colour, and the one to whom it pertains."

A look of utter amazement ran across Anderas's face.

"You're a wayfarer," he gasped.

Eamon's blood raced in his veins. "I am a King's man."

Anderas gaped at him. "A King's man?"

"Yes."

Anderas's eyes fell to the blades in his hands. The shaking palms tensed. The fingers tightened about the hilt of the sword. Anderas looked up at him again.

"Why have you told me this?" he cried at last, his voice full of rage. "*Why?*"

"Because I want you to know the truth, Andreas Anderas," Eamon answered. The captain blinked tears from his eyes as the name echoed in the air. How long, Eamon wondered, had it been since any man had called the captain by his full name? "Now you do."

Silence fell between them, broken only by the captain's ragged breath. Eamon stood still, and silent, and waited.

At last, the captain looked up. "After Pinewood," he said quietly, "I was convinced that I was going to die. I knew that nothing the surgeons could do would save me from the wound; death circled round me. The only one who saw how close it stood to me was you, and I sought to convince you otherwise." He paused and swallowed. There were tears on his face and he brushed them aside.

"On the night that I was meant to die, I had a dream. I dreamt that I was to go down into a dark land alone, set on the path into some strange darkness by a man who seemed all of fire. He encouraged me to go, and I would have done so – all my hope was spent and the wound could not be healed – it festered and rotted within me. The dark path was all that was left, though I did not want it."

A deep breath shuddered out of the captain with the closeness of the memory. Eamon wanted to offer him comfort but knew that he could not, not at that moment. Anderas looked up again.

"I would have taken it, Eamon Goodman, but for one thing. At the moment of my choice a voice reached me. I could not hear its words, but there was light behind me, and the fire that showed me the path fled before it, leaving me at the crossroads, alone." He met Eamon's gaze. "The voice was yours," he whispered, "and in the dimness of my mind, the light seemed blue."

Eamon's heart jumped. He remembered well how he had knelt by Anderas that night, how he had begged and implored that the captain's life be saved...

Anderas looked back down to the sword in his hands. "I did not speak of my dream to anyone," he said. "How could I? And I could not believe it. I could not let myself interpret it as anything other than what I convinced myself it was: the figment of a mind tormented by impending death, by fever, and by whatever medicines the surgeons had me take." He looked up again. "You have been a King's man since the very first day I met you?"

"Yes," Eamon replied. "Since long before that."

A glint appeared in Anderas's eyes. "Is that why the outer provinces fell so swiftly? Because you were here, spying for the Serpent!"

"No one has witnessed my actions as closely as you these last few months," Eamon told him. "When have I acted unjustly? Have I ever wronged the people of Dunthruik? Have I ever failed to protect them, or act for their betterment?"

Anderas's face softened. "No," he managed. "No, you... you've acted more rightly and justly than any Hand that I, or anyone in the city, have ever known."

"My task in this city was once to spy for the King; now, it is to act as his messenger, to herald his coming, to uphold his laws, his goodness, and his righteousness before he comes," Eamon told him.

"No one can say that you have failed in that." Anderas fell silent. A tempest of thought raged across his face. He looked up. "Now what would you have me do?" he demanded angrily. "What would you have me do, Lord Goodman? I cannot return to that city as I left it this morning!"

"No," Eamon answered. "You cannot."

His sword dangled in Anderas's trembling hands. Eamon drew breath once again and met Anderas's gaze. The captain shook, as though he knew or guessed what words Eamon meant to speak.

"Andreas," he said, "I am on a journey. I know full well that the road I take is perilous and burdensome; I may be called to lay down my very life upon it. I know that treachery lurks at the wayside, and that I am not the only one who lies open to it. I expose all those whom I love to that same treachery by what I do. But I know this also – that where the road leads is good, and that those who walk in the King's name, and with his grace, need not travel in fear.

"You have seen me taking halting steps, and bold strides, along this path. I have been honoured by the companionship that you have offered me. I will not command you, Andreas, and I will not tell you what you must choose. That choice only you can make, and you must make it in your own heart, regardless of what regard you hold for me. But, as I have done, you must now make a choice." He fell silent for a moment. "Andreas, will you fare along this way with me?"

Once again Anderas's hands tensed on the blade, steel crept from its sheath, tension creased the captain's brow.

"You speak much of grace, but say nothing of the atrocities committed by the Serpent and his allies," Anderas rejoined. "Have you not heard what the men retreating into the city are saying? Devastation, blood, murder? Their lips are full of it. How can you forget the road to Pinewood? Bloated corpses of sworn men hanging from trees, food for carrion birds? How can you forget the way they murdered our men?"

"I do not forget the men we lost in that battle," Eamon replied. "I do not claim that every wayfarer always does right. I speak about the King, the true King, whom the throned calls Serpent, about whom he lies and scaremongers to legitimize his stolen throne. The true King is the one by whose grace you were saved on the battlefield at Pinewood. This true King loves and serves his people. This true King desires to save his people from bloodshed and oppression. He does not work for it alone – I am but one of those who work with him. If I have been in any way better or truer than another man, it is only by the King's grace that I have done so."

Anderas's eyes darted across his face. "My hands could never serve such a man as you describe," he breathed. "What do you think a Gauntlet captain does in Dunthruik during a time of culling? *He culls*. How many men and women, *children* even, have gone to those pyres because of me? My hands sent them. The King cannot release me from that. I am his known enemy!"

"So was I when first I met him. Know this: the King is gracious and merciful. I have performed deeds far more vile than yours, Anderas – knowingly, despite my avowed fealty, I acted against the King's own people. Yet he did not despise me, imprison me, or take my life – though I deserved all these things. He forgave me." Eamon looked at Anderas, filled anew with the wonder of Hughan's love. "His grace has sustained me. Andreas, what I ask, I do not ask lightly – I know what it is to be torn between two oaths. But I could not ask it of a truer man. Andreas Anderas, would you be a King's man?"

Anderas trembled. "I am a sworn man, Eamon Goodman. I would… but… but I can't."

"I understand. I am a sworn man, too. That is how I can say to you that whatever you have done can be and is forgiven, even if it cannot be undone, and you can serve him."

The dawn's chorus skittered through the trees around them. Anderas chewed at his lip, clenched and unclenched his hands about the sword they held.

"A man like me needs a lot of grace," he whispered.

"So does a man like me," Eamon returned. "I have not found it wanting."

There was a hiss as the sword returned to its sheath. Anderas blinked tears fiercely from his eyes and looked up.

"I will follow the King," the captain whispered.

A deep silence fell. Eamon gazed at the man before him with awe. Anderas breathed deeply, and choked back a sob, laughing as he did so. Somehow, in that moment when he was caught between strength and weakness, the captain seemed to be more than Eamon had ever seen in him.

"If the King is anything like you," Anderas managed at the last, "then it is him whom I have sought to serve all my life."

"Then a King's man you shall be." Quietly, Eamon stepped forward and set his hand to the captain's shoulder. "Andreas Anderas, may the King's grace be with you and may you stay true to the King. May you find joy and life and good in his service."

As Eamon spoke, a faint blue light flitted about his fingers. He realized with joy that it was not just about him but also in Anderas. He laughed with delight and stepped back as the light faded away.

His eyes met Anderas's. The captain's smile was broad and free.

"At last, Lord Goodman," Anderas said, "I know you."

"And I see that, in knowing you, I have much left to learn," Eamon replied.

They rode back to the city together. Though their conversation turned to other things as soon as they left the woods, Eamon's nerves tingled, and every now and then as he watched Anderas, he felt a wave of delighted astonishment.

The captain had chosen the King. Eamon had scarcely dared to hope it, and had feared their meeting terribly. Inside he trembled, seeing clearly at last how perilous his decision to speak to Anderas had been, seeing that the motivations behind it would seem strange to perhaps any other man. He had wanted Anderas to understand him better. Now there were few others who did, and in many ways, the captain understood him best of all. How many other Gauntlet officers had pledged themselves to the King while still bearing the throned's mark?

They rode back into the Ashen and the stable yard. Servants came to take their horses. Eamon's heart sank as the weights of the world fell back upon him. He still had to speak to the servants, and he could not speak to them as he had to Anderas. What comfort could he offer them?

He dismounted and Anderas did the same. He turned to the captain. "I must speak to my household about the Master's decision," he said.

"Of course, my lord." Anderas nodded. The captain's first quiet sorrow returned to his eyes. "I am sure that you will find the best words to say."

"Thank you."

"Would you have me make an announcement of your impending departure to the college?" Anderas asked.

Eamon closed his eyes for a moment. "Yes," he said, "I would."

"Very well."

Eamon looked at him, wondering how he should now bid the captain farewell. Everything had changed, and yet all that had been remained.

Seeing his indecision Anderas smiled, and laughed quietly. "Good day, my lord," he said.

"And to you, captain," Eamon replied.

CHAPTER XXXIII

He went slowly into the household, his mind agog with thoughts. He had to find Slater. It was already the second day; within five more he must set the whole household back into its old habits. He wondered if he had been a fool to leave it so long.

He summoned Slater to his office, and not long afterwards, the man appeared. He seemed calmer than when Eamon had last seen him, although still pale. His eyes were darkly rimmed.

"Good morning, my lord."

"Good morning," Eamon replied. "How are you faring?"

"Better, my lord," Slater answered with a small nod.

"And the rest of the household?"

"Mr Bellis was with us but a short time, my lord, but well regarded nonetheless," Slater answered. "He is missed."

Eamon nodded. "Mr Slater, I must speak with the entire household," he said. "I want to do it this morning."

"I will arrange it, my lord," Slater replied.

Slater was good to his word. Barely an hour had passed before Eamon was informed that the whole household was gathered in the dining room, the one place inside the Handquarters large enough to hold them all. Laying aside the quill with which he signed the very last exit orders, Eamon rose from his desk and made his way slowly through the corridors. His cloak seemed heavy to him, his ring cumbersome and clumsy on his hand.

He entered the dining room. Gathered there were stablehands and scullery servants, cooks, seamstresses, and laundry maids. They all bowed, almost as a unit. Eamon walked past them to climb the small dais where the high table was set. A great banner, bearing an owl and ash, hung on the wall behind him. As he turned to look out across the faces, his heart grew heavy.

He knew these men and women, and he loved them. Yet he had to deliver to them a blow that he could scarcely bear himself. Their upturned faces reminded him of how much he wanted to shun what he could not renounce.

"Good morning," he said, and it sounded awkward on his lips. He swallowed. For a terrible moment he realized that he did not know what to say. The servants' eyes were fixed on him, though if they saw his hesitation, none of them minded it.

Drawing a deep breath, he looked up. He set his courage to his task and spoke again. "First of all, I wish to congratulate you all on the exceptionally fine service you have all rendered me since I came to this hall. I daresay that only the Master enjoys a household that is more dedicated than you are to me. For that I thank you."

Some of them smiled. Some almost clapped. Eamon's courage nearly melted.

"It is not only to be thanked that you are here this morning," he said. "In a few days, I will no longer have the honour of being served by you."

The smiling faces quickly turned to alarm.

"The Master has reassigned me," Eamon said heavily. "To his glory, and at his bidding, I must leave this quarter to become Right Hand."

An audible gasp ran through the room, one as much riddled by awe as by horror. Eamon drew another breath, knowing that the worst blow was yet to come.

"Another comes to take my place," he said. "In five days, you will serve Lord Arlaith." He swallowed to keep his voice from catching. "You have seen what kind of a man Lord Arlaith is. He is strong, and bold, and faithful to the Master in every way. But you cannot serve him in the way that you serve me. This you all know. From this very day," he continued, an odd fierceness in his voice, "you will serve me as though I were Lord Ashway, for that is how you must serve Lord Arlaith. You will be discreet in your service and you will keep from my path. I would have this be such a household that even Lord Arlaith shall find no fault with it; thus will none of you fall foul of him, or his zealous anger." The words cut him as he spoke them, but not as much as the shocked faces tore at his heart.

"Return to your duties," he finished quietly.

The household obeyed.

Over the course of that day Eamon saw none of the servants. His meals appeared, silently and mysteriously, at his table. When Eamon strolled that afternoon in the Handquarter gardens, he saw no man tending the trees and plants, and when he passed by the kitchens he heard no singing. All he saw were linens hung over a long cord by the scullery to dry.

The silence grieved him.

That evening there was a knock at his door. He called to grant admittance and saw Draybant Greenwood there.

"Good evening, my lord," the man said, bowing smartly. "May I offer you my congratulations on your new appointment?"

"Very kind of you, Mr Greenwood," Eamon answered. So Anderas had spoken to them.

"If I may be so bold, my lord," Greenwood added, "I feel that no man would serve Dunthruik better as Right Hand than you."

"Thank you." Eamon smiled at him. It was then that he noted that the draybant carried the day's Gauntlet papers. "Is something the matter with the captain?" Eamon asked. The delivery of the papers, though not obliged to be Anderas's duty, was one that he had always performed.

"He was at the mess, my lord, but left without finishing his meal," Greenwood answered. "He told me that he felt unwell, and asked me to cover his duties for this evening." Greenwood set the papers gently and neatly down on the desk.

Eamon followed the draybant's words with mild unease, but set it gently aside. A Gauntlet captain had as much right as any man to feel unwell from time to time. "Thank you, Mr Greenwood."

The draybant nodded and Eamon spoke again. "There is another grain shipment coming in tomorrow."

"Yes, my lord. I shall take men to curtail the quarter's share, as you ordered."

"Good." Eamon paused, then looked up. "Mr Greenwood," he said quietly, "Lord Arlaith does not know about the grain store in the college. I would not like him to be informed. Please leave it out of any official reports that you give to him."

"Yes, Lord Goodman," Greenwood answered faultlessly; the idea of deceiving Lord Arlaith did not seem to faze him. "Your command as Right Hand will be no less than when you served in this house. If your desire is to withhold this information from him, it will be done."

"Once Lord Arlaith is here, I am afraid that you will no longer be able to take grain as you have. You may not be able to take any at all. That does not matter; the most important thing is that what has already been set aside remains safe."

"Of course, my lord," Greenwood nodded. "I will see to it."

"Please advise your men accordingly," Eamon added, "and I would be grateful if you would also give word of this to Captain Anderas."

"Yes, my lord."

Eamon looked at him. "Mr Greenwood?"

"My lord?"

"You are an exemplary officer. You serve an extraordinary captain and command excellent men. Be steadfast in your service, and you will go far." He did not add that he hoped one day to see the man in a different uniform.

"Thank you, my lord," Greenwood replied.

"Dismissed."

The draybant bowed and left. Eamon's gaze fell on the papers Greenwood had brought. For a moment he wondered if he should go and visit Anderas, but if the captain was ill perhaps he needed rest. He would see him in the morning.

The lamps and fires were lit as though they had willed it themselves. Eamon went to bed, seeing none of the household either on the stair or in the corridor. He wondered where they could possibly hide if they happened to be present when he passed. It was a mark of their skill – and the Handquarters' hidden places – that he knew it not.

He lay for a long time in his bed, reading, though his thoughts followed the volume with difficulty. In the tangled noise of his mind the servants gasped and paled, footsteps receeded.

> *And in the tide of later days*
> *These words shall live, and rend him praise.*

Just as they had opened it, they were the words that closed the Edelred Cycle.

He closed the book and let it rest on his hands while he thought. The following day the compulsory exit papers came into force. He had to see Mr Grennil again; he had to send a message to Hughan.

The following morning, Eamon rose and went down to the stables as he always did. He waited for some time, but Anderas did not appear. He asked the silent and downcast stablehand grooming Sahu whether he had seen the quarter's captain.

"No, my lord," the boy answered quietly.

Eamon waited, but Anderas did not come.

In silence and alone, he made his way back to the Handquarters. The captain had to be ill indeed if he had not come to ride and had sent no message.

As he reached the steps of the Handquarters hall he paused, and with a sigh looked back towards the college. His heart was full of misgiving; it was too unusual. He should go and see Anderas. It was early, but he was sure that the captain would be awake. What could have kept him?

He settled his mind and stepped down into the Ashen. A figure across the square approached him. The man walked sullenly. He reached the Handquarter steps, saw Eamon, and he bowed.

"Lord Goodman."

"Mr Kentigern," Eamon replied. He stepped towards him but Ladomer did not rise. Eamon's heart twisted with grief.

"Rise, Mr Kentigern," he said. Ladomer did so. "Did you come seeking me?"

"No, Lord Goodman," Ladomer replied. "With all due reverence and with your permission, I have come to see the head of your household. Lord Arlaith wishes to know how it is run and what of his own household he must bring with him."

"He will find his needs well served by my house," Eamon replied. "You may see Mr Slater. He will be more than capable of advising you."

"Thank you, Lord Goodman," Ladomer replied. "With your leave," he said, and moved to walk past. He had not met Eamon's gaze once during the conversation.

"Ladomer," Eamon called after him.

His friend paused, but did not turn to face him. "Lord Goodman."

For a moment Eamon did not know what to say; he did not know why he had spoken. But he could not bear how his friend now treated him. "Will you speak no other words to me?" he asked quietly.

Ladomer turned and bowed again. "Forgive me, Lord Goodman," he said, his tone frosty. "Congratulations on your new appointment."

"Ladomer," Eamon began, and stepped forward towards him, "does it mean so little to you? Do *I* mean so little to you?"

"I crave your pardon, Lord Goodman, but any right I held in regarding you for good or ill was waived by none other than yourself some weeks ago; it lies not with me to reinstate it, least of all now." His tone was angry and bore deep hurt.

"But you will serve me, Mr Kentigern," Eamon said gently. "Are you or are you not the lieutenant to the Right Hand? Surely your post will not change simply because the man himself changes? I would not have you serve bearing me such anger."

"I will not serve you, Lord Goodman," Ladomer replied, and at last he looked up. Eamon took a blow from the wrathful gaze. "When Lord Arlaith takes the East Quarter I am to be reassigned to duties in Etraia."

"Etraia?" Eamon stared at him and could feel anger in his voice as he spoke. "But men like you are needed here, not in some barren merchant province!"

"The Master sees me with different eyes," Ladomer answered. He matched Eamon's gaze with a startling formality. "I will not see you again, Lord Goodman. I doubt you will rue my absence much."

"Ladomer –"

"I wish you well with your new office," Ladomer answered. "Farewell." Bowing once more, he turned and left.

Eamon stared after him. Tears burned his eyes. So many years of friendship... Did Ladomer truly hate him that much? How could the lieutenant to the Right Hand not see why Eamon had spoken to him as he had done? How could the throned have posted Ladomer to Etraia?

He did not know. And, as Ladomer disappeared into the hallways of the Handquarters, he realized that he might never know it.

That morning the East Quarter brimmed with people, as all those to whom compulsory exit orders had been served – along with their families and some possessions – gathered in preparation for their departure. The first of the new Gauntlet arrivals were to come into the city the next day, so the billets had to be ready.

While Eamon had intended to find Anderas, he was called instead to oversee the final exit. There were a number of extra Gauntlet on duty at the Blind Gate, where papers were meticulously checked before each family was allowed, or in some cases encouraged, to leave the city.

Eamon waited in the shadow of the gates – where it was at least cooler – watching as the Gauntlet worked, and listening to the perpetual sound of hooves, feet, and wheels on the cobbles. Beyond the paved part of the road, the horizon was lined with thick dust where the traffic of the leavers cast it into the air. The skill and patience with which the officers handled the exodus impressed him.

He had not waited long when familiar faces appeared in the long line waiting permission to leave: the Grennils. They were gathered together in a cart, along with some of their belongings. Neithan entertained Damien with some story or other while they sat, and Mr Grennil sat at the head of the cart with his wife, with whom he spoke quietly.

Eamon stepped up to one of the Gauntlet soldiers. "I will speak with that man," he said, gesturing to Mr Grennil.

"Of course, my lord," the ensign replied. He went immediately over to the cart and summoned Mr Grennil down. Mr Grennil handed the reins to his wife, who looked worried until her husband gestured at the length of the line before them. He climbed down from the cart and followed the soldier back to where Eamon stood. Once there, Mr Grennil bowed.

"Lord Goodman."

"I would speak to you a moment, Mr Grennil."

Leaving the ensign outside, Eamon led Mr Grennil into the gatehouse. It was empty, for all its keepers were too busy with the exit. It was a small, ill-lit room crammed with papers, a small table and two smaller chairs.

Eamon closed the door and turned to Mr Grennil.

"I won't keep you for more than a moment," he said. He was amazed at how any and all pretence of being a Hand dropped from him the second the door was closed and they were away from other eyes. The gatehouse's small window was covered with a red curtain to keep out the bright sun. It cast a strange light on the sparse furnishings and ample papers.

"I heard rumours about your new appointment," Grennil answered. His face seemed grave as he said it. "Is it true?"

"Yes," Eamon sighed. "It is true." He wasn't surprised that news had gone about the quarter. He was gladder than ever that the Grennils were to exit the city before Arlaith took the East Quarter. He was sure that the disgruntled Hand would have found some way to strike at them for their hospitality towards him.

Grennil watched him sincerely. "I don't think that I would be able to bear it," he said, "but I am sure that you will do good, even there. You will be careful?" he added. The note of concern in his voice touched Eamon.

"As careful as I can be."

There was a small pause. "How may I serve you?" Grennil asked.

"I need you to take a message to the King," Eamon answered, leaning in closely. Grennil nodded bravely and Eamon marvelled at the man's courage. "First, you must tell him that I am to be made Right Hand. If there is anything he would have me do beyond what my own sense will tell me, he must send word to me, just as I will send word to him of whatever I can." Eamon did not doubt that, with the war brewing as it was, the day of battle between Hughan and the throned was near at hand. He felt it in the air, like a sound just beyond hearing.

"Yes," Grennil answered.

Eamon reached into the folds of his cloak and drew out a book. He met Grennil's gaze and spoke quietly. "There is something else you must tell him: it may be more important still."

Suddenly there was a knock at the door. Grennil looked up in alarm, but Eamon offered him a look of confidence. "Come in," he called, setting the book discreetly down on the table behind him.

The door opened and a shadow passed over the sunlit threshold. The familiar face of Captain Anderas appeared. "Lord Goodman?"

"I am here, captain."

"Lord Goodman, I must speak with –" Anderas began, and then halted as he saw Mr Grennil. An odd look passed over his face. "I'm sorry," he breathed, bowing. There was something stiff, almost stilted, in his tone and gesture. It worried Eamon. "I did not know that I was interrupting, my lord. I will leave."

"All is well, captain," Eamon answered. "You may stay. This will not take a moment." He gestured to Anderas to close the door. Grennil gave Eamon a confused glance.

"Lord Goodman –"

"Mr Grennil," Eamon answered, "Captain Anderas is a *friend*."

Grennil breathed a sigh of relief and then held his hand out to Anderas.

"It is a distinct pleasure, captain, to see you again."

Anderas looked surprised as he clasped Grennil's hand and looked across at Eamon. Though his look was tempestuous he said nothing.

"Are you well, captain?" Eamon asked. Fear crept into his breast.

"Yes," Anderas replied. His tone was icier than Eamon had ever heard it, but the captain said not a word more.

He cannot stay here, Eben's son. See his face? He can still betray you. Send him away – now.

Eamon closed his eyes for a moment, then looked back to Grennil and picked up the book again.

"I need you to take this," he said quietly. At his gesture, Grennil took the book into his hands. He looked curiously at it for a moment, then back at Eamon.

"The Edelred Cycle?"

"I have marked a page in it," Eamon replied, gesturing to where he had folded down a corner of the parchment. "This message is more important than the first. Unless your own life is in peril, you must not entrust it to anyone else."

Grennil nodded, and Eamon spoke again. "The King needs to know that Mathaiah Grahaven is dead," he said quietly. A look of realization passed across Anderas's face, followed by an odd scowl, but Eamon ignored it. He would answer Anderas, but he could not now. "Before his death, he was being tortured by the Hands and forced to read something called the Nightholt. The throned has this book, though how much or how little was transcribed using Mathaiah is something that I do not know. I know little else about it, but I fear that this book grants some power to the throned, and that it poses some great peril to the King. The passage that I have marked should be shown to the bookkeepers," he said quietly. "It speaks of a 'dark tome', and I believe the verse indicates something about the nature of the Nightholt and its relationship to the throned, but I do not understand it. The King and the bookkeepers will." At least, he *hoped* they would.

Grennil looked down at the book and nodded. "Very well, Lord Goodman," he said. As he answered he tucked the book deep into his jerkin. "I will deliver your message."

"Thank you," Eamon replied, reaching across and taking Grennil's hand warmly. "Take care of yourself; *good* care."

"And you," Grennil replied.

Grennil left. At Eamon's request, he was escorted back to his cart by the same ensign who had brought him. The door swung shut behind them, and Eamon was alone with Anderas. His heart beat with fear: the captain's face was stony and unreadable.

"You wanted to speak to me?" he said quietly. As he met Anderas's gaze a horrified, and almost disgusted, look grew clear on the man's face.

"He's a wayfarer, too?" the captain asked. There was a tone of betrayal to his voice.

Eamon frowned. "Yes," he answered. Anderas stared at him.

"How many others with exit papers are like him?"

"A number of them," Eamon replied truthfully.

"What about Cara? Is she a wayfarer, too?"

"Not to my knowledge. Anderas," Eamon said quietly, "what troubles you?"

"What troubles me?" Anderas's voice was bitter, and he laughed. "What troubles me? I believed that you did good in this quarter for the sake of this quarter. I even had this lofty picture in my head of you doing good in this quarter for the city. Now I see that you care nothing for either!"

"What?"

"You heard what I said," Anderas told him. "You care for nothing except the snakes that will raze this place to the ground when they come!"

"Do you truly believe that of me?" Eamon asked. A frantic look passed through Anderas's eyes, but the captain did not answer him. He stepped forward. "If all my care was for the wayfarers, Anderas, why would I bother seeking justice for all, and homes for the homeless? Why would I hoarde grain beneath the college?"

"To house and feed *them*, when they come."

"No," Eamon replied quietly. "It is to feed the people of this city when the siege comes. I love this city, Anderas."

"And you betray it even now!" Anderas growled. "You will betray it when you open its gates to him. He will not, nor cannot, love it."

"Anderas," Eamon said, "who has told you all these things?"

"Told me?" Anderas laughed bitterly. "Now I see what you think of me," he snapped. "You think me incapable of my own thought!"

"I think you far too capable of your own thought," Eamon countered, "which is how I know that these words are not yours."

"You are a traitor," Anderas retorted. Steel glinted in the captain's hand. "And you would have me betray myself! A fine pair we would have made: a Gauntlet captain and a Right Hand, traitors to the Master both, and I the more treacherous for letting you lead me astray with your poisonous words."

"I have never deceived you, Anderas, nor led you where your heart had not already been prepared to go," Eamon answered.

"You would lay the blame of treachery against me?" Anderas cried, blade in hand. "I will not be a traitor's pawn, to be moved and played by you!"

Eamon reached out and touched Anderas's shoulder. The captain could take his life at a stroke. Yet all that mattered to him was the anguish in his friend's eyes. He knew who had placed it there, and it stirred righteous anger in his heart.

"Anderas," he said. The captain did not meet his gaze. Eamon pressed his shoulder firmly. "Captain, *look at me*." The hand holding the blade shook. "Andreas!"

The captain looked at him in alarm. "There's a voice," Anderas whispered, his own – for it was his own voice again at last – rent with fear. "There's a voice in my head. It would have me –"

Suddenly he cried out in terror, clutching his palm where a red light grimly flickered.

Eamon set his hand over the captain's so that the red light struck them both. It burned him but he did not flinch from it. He knew that it could do nothing to him, and he looked Anderas straight in the eyes.

"Hence, voice of Edelred," he commanded. Though his voice was quiet, it struck keenly through the air. "This man is the King's and the King's grace is over him. By that grace I command you: hence."

A blaze of blue light arched from his palm to cover the captain's. The red fled before it and the frenzied fear in Anderas's eyes faded, leaving his tears.

There was a moment of silence broken only by a clatter as the blade fell to the ground. Anderas shook, and suddenly he wept.

"Courage, Anderas."

The words stirred him. The captain looked at him with renewed awe.

"Who are you?" he breathed.

"I am First Knight to King Hughan Brenuin, rightful lord over the River Realm."

"First… First Knight?"

"Yes."

"And that… that… *voice*?" he asked.

"Is the voice of Edelred, the throned," Eamon told him. He pressed encouragingly at Anderas's hand. "At our swearing, we gave him authority over us. He is a coward and a liar, and will do everything he can to set you against me, the King, and yourself."

"You hear it often?" Anderas still shook.

"Rather too frequently." Eamon looked curiously at Anderas. "You don't?"

"I've never heard it before," Anderas replied quietly. "Or at least, I don't think I have. At first I thought it was just my own thoughts. Then I was convinced it was some Serpent sorcery."

"It was no sorcery of the King's," Eamon told him. "This voice always lies, or twists what might be true. That is how it seeks to hold you. That is how it has often held me. I suspect you hear it now because you have given your oath to the King – and now it must redouble its efforts to master you."

Anderas looked up in alarm. "Does he… hear what I think?" he whispered.

Eamon shook his head. "I do not believe he can," he said. "I would have been lost long before now if he could. But his voice still carries power. It seems to know what makes us afraid."

"I was afraid," Anderas told him. "*So afraid*. This voice told me things, about you…"

"It lies," Eamon answered flatly. "You are covered by the King's grace, and by that grace you can command it to leave you."

"As you did?"

"Just as I did."

Anderas sighed, and was still for a long moment. "I should have come to you sooner," he said at last. "Then perhaps I would not have behaved like such a fool."

"I am afraid that I was the more foolish this time," Eamon answered. "I knew about the voice of Edelred – I have struggled with it since first I was sworn into the Gauntlet – and yet I said nothing of it to you. I am sorry that I did not. I assumed you knew."

"There is always more than one way to learn something," Anderas replied. A small smile touched his face. "I have always been one for learning things the hard way."

"Anderas, for men like you and me, men who gave their first allegiance to the throned and took his mark, being a King's man is difficult," Eamon told him. "It is made more difficult still when you serve in Dunthruik under the throned, and as difficult again when you hold positions where your authority can be worked for the King." He paused. "You will hear this voice often," he added, "and you must stand firm against it. I will not always be here with you, and it is when I am not there that it will strike hardest."

"I understand," Anderas said. He looked up. "And I will stand."

"You were right about one thing, though," Eamon told him.

"Really?" Anderas smiled.

"We *would* make a veritable sight if they found us out – the trusted captain and Lord of the East Quarter. Such good men... so *foully* led astray by the Serpent."

"They'd have more than a pyre for us set out if they found out," Anderas said, and laughed.

"Being tortured, breached, and more than lightly toasted doesn't worry you?" Eamon asked, surprised.

"Not if they toast using a very fine vintage."

Eamon stared at him incredulously. "I cannot believe you just said that."

"Must be the company I keep." Anderas grinned, then looked more serious. "You know, this city is full of good men."

"Yes," Eamon agreed, "it is."

"Being a good man in times like these helps, but it is not enough," Anderas replied. "I think that is what I finally understood when you told me who you are. It is not that you are good, rather that you are a King's man, which truly makes you what you are."

"We are both King's men," Eamon told him, pressing his hand with a smile.

"Yes," Anderas laughed. "We are."

CHAPTER XXXIV

After the East Quarter had been emptied of many of its ordinary citizens, the new Gauntlet officers and ensigns arrived. Eamon stood in the Ashen to watch them as they marched past, wondering how many of them had ever been to the city and how many of them would lose their lives in its defence.

He never saw Ladomer leave the Handquarters. His friend's words ran over and over in Eamon's mind that night as he tried to sleep. When he was not thinking about that he wondered about the Grennils, and whether his scant message would reach Hughan in time. And when he finally slept, his mind was burdened with images of the book he had torn from the tomb in Ellenswell and the memory of surrendering it into Ashway's hands. He woke from his dreams, alone and afraid, with only the dying fire in the grate and the starlight beyond his window to comfort him.

His last days as Lord of the East Quarter passed in a blur of paperwork and distant congratulations. Other than occasional meetings with Anderas, he felt very much alone. The silence of his halls haunted him and he hated it as much as he acknowledged its importance. He wondered whether it was not a taste of the solitude that he would reap when he became Right Hand.

You will not be alone, Eben's son, the voice of Edelred told him. *I will be there with you.*

It terrified him.

During Eamon's penultimate day in the East Quarter, he spent much of the evening with Anderas. The captain was a strong-willed man, resolute in his new allegiance, more determined than Eamon in his early days.

"It will be harder, Lord Goodman, when you are gone," he said.

"You will not just have the voice to contend with then," Eamon answered, "but Arlaith, too. You will need to keep all your wits about you."

"You would have me be as cunning as the Serpent?" Anderas laughed.

"And as innocent as a dove."

"And while I contend with the voice and with Lord Arlaith, you shall have the voice and the throned himself," Anderas replied. "I'm not sure which of us I envy the more."

"Neither am I," Eamon laughed.

Eamon walked solemnly across the Ashen to the Handquarters. The silence struck him from every side, blanketing itself around him and smothering him. He hated it.

As he reached the top of the stairs that led to his own rooms he heard the shuffle of feet, and whisper of voices within. The door to his chamber was slightly ajar. He recognized them at once: Cara and Callum, going about their duties.

As he set his foot onto the last step, his foot landed heavily enough to echo down the hall, but it did not help. With a deep sigh he walked to his door and pushed it open. Callum finished setting a small fire as Cara folded down the top sheet of the bed, her face all grace and concentration.

"If I were Lord Arlaith," Eamon announced, "you would now find yourselves at the receiving end of my deep displeasure."

The siblings froze and looked up at him. Their faces grew pale.

"Lord Goodman," Cara began, curtseying, "I am sorry, nobody –"

Eamon drove down the instinct to accept her apology, and struggled to force any trace of kindness from his face. "Somebody would be punished for it, were Lord Arlaith here," he said. "You must attend with greater care."

"But Lord Arlaith isn't here." Eamon turned to stare at Callum. The boy looked at him with an angry face. "*You* are here."

"But I won't be here the day after tomorrow," Eamon replied cuttingly. "If this were then, you would probably be taken to the Ashen and flogged, Callum."

Cara shuddered. Eamon did not apologize for his bluntness. They had to learn. Arlaith would set upon them for the smallest slight, simply because they had been part of Eamon's household. He could not let them walk indolently into Arlaith's cruel devices.

"But it's today," Callum answered boldly. "It's today, and you're here and we're serving *you*."

Eamon stared angrily at him. "Callum, you speak foolishly and out of turn."

"No I don't!" Callum retorted. Cara tried to pull him back, but the child was in full swing. He stepped forward angrily. "You should know what your servants are saying. No one in this house wants you to leave, Lord Goodman, not a single one of us, and because of Lord Arlaith we can't serve you to our full while you are still here."

Eamon was cut to the heart. "Callum," he tried again.

"You're robbing us of serving you," Callum cried. "That's mean when it's all we have to give you!"

Eamon glared. "Get out," he said quietly.

Callum froze, but did not move.

"Get out," Eamon said again. There was grief in his heart, for he loved his servants, and he saw the truth in Callum's words. "The household must go back to its ways of discretion, and better you relearn that under me than under Arlaith and suffer for it! Go," he yelled, "or I shall dismiss you for your own protection!"

Callum gasped and ran to the door, his sister close behind him. Eamon turned his back to their retreating figures. The strength of his cry still echoed in his ears. He did not hear whether the door closed or whether they ran down the stairs. His knees gave way beneath him. Suddenly he was on the floor sobbing.

He had to make them walk in fear and rob them of their final days of service.

Thus did Lord Arlaith rule the house even before Eamon departed.

He slept uneasily that night, but then he had slept uneasily all that week.

Eamon rose and looked out of his bedroom window. It was the twenty-ninth of April – his last day as Lord of the East Quarter. The next morning he would be made the Right Hand.

He glanced down at his ring. Callum's words rang in his ears. How would he leave the quarter? Would it be in the manner of his coming, doleful and weighed with grief? Was there not grief enough already in his house, without his adding to it? Would they not suffer enough when he was gone?

Take heart, Eamon. Take heart and stand.

At last, Eamon smiled. He would not bow to Arlaith, not now. He realized that the manner of his going was his to choose, and he would choose it.

He sought out Slater. The man was unbarring the various doors in the hallway ready for the day.

"Good morning," Eamon said. The head of his household started upon hearing his voice, and bowed at once.

"Lord Goodman," he said uncertainly.

"I know it to be short notice," Eamon told him, "but I want you to arrange a lunch."

"Of course, my lord," Slater replied. "For how many?"

"About fifty, I imagine," Eamon answered. "I want you to use all the best wear on the tables. The high table will not need to be set."

Slater masked his surprise very well. "Of course, my lord. For a menu?"

"The finest that you can find and choose with such short notice," Eamon answered. "It will be paid for directly from the Handquarters' purse." Slater bowed low. "One more thing, Mr

Slater: when everything is prepared, I wish you to come in person and advise me."

"Of course, my lord."

"What are you up to?"

"Is that a manner in which to speak to the Lord of the East Quarter?" Eamon asked.

"It's a fine manner in which to speak to you," Anderas replied. "Especially when you're up to something."

"I'm not up to anything," Eamon answered. They rode beyond the North Gate, and a strong wind careered across the plain behind them.

Anderas laughed. "Whatever else you may be, a poor liar you remain," he said. "If you could only see the look on your face, you would understand why I can't possibly believe you."

"Come to the Handquarters at lunch time," Eamon told him, "and then you'll see."

"So you *are* concocting some fresh madness."

"I never said that," Eamon replied. "But I will tell you one thing, captain: I shall sorely miss these rides."

"You shall only miss them sorely if you don't keep practising," Anderas answered.

"You are wise beyond your years, captain."

"As for myself, it isn't the rides I will miss," Anderas added quietly. "It is you. I will not be alone in that."

"We will endure this too, Anderas," Eamon answered. "The East Quarter will endure it. The city will endure it. I will endure it, and so will you, until the King comes."

Eamon was in his office when Slater came to find him. The man's knock at his door was tentative, but Eamon admitted him without hesitation.

"Mr Slater," he said with a smile, "is everything ready?"

"Yes, my lord."

"Do congratulate Mr Cook on my behalf. I imagine it was a morning of hard work."

"May I ask when the guests will arrive?" Slater asked. He looked anxious, and Eamon smiled.

"Shortly. But before they do, I would like you to summon the household."

Slater stared at him. "But, my lord, the dining room is –"

"I know, Mr Slater. There will be time before the guests arrive."

"Very well, my lord." Slater bowed and left. Barely able to contain his smile, Eamon set all his papers aside and stepped from his office.

He met Anderas in the corridor as he was on his way to the dining room.

"You're doing it again, my lord," the captain told him.

"Is there a second witness, captain, to your heinous accusation?"

"No, my lord."

"Then I fear you will have to obtain a confession from me."

The captain gaped at him. Eamon grinned broadly and fairly ran down the corridor to the hall. The doors stood open before him and he swept inside.

The tables were beautifully laid with a deep red cloth, and set with the Handquarters' finest tableware. The first course was laid out on the table, and broad platters of fish also. The smell of fresh bread filled the room. Although the high table had remained unset, it had been covered with a tablecloth that bore an owl and ash. Light spiralled down from the tall windows, showing the blue sky high beyond the glass.

Eamon laughed. It was perfect.

"Are you expecting someone to lunch?" Anderas asked casually.

"Yes," Eamon replied and laughed again. "Yes, I am."

"My lord?" called a quiet voice from the doorway. It was Slater, and beyond him the rest of the household gathered. Eamon marvelled that Slater could summon them all so quickly.

"Mr Slater! Come in – bring everyone in."

Nervously, Slater obeyed. Anderas watched the servants for a moment, and then turned to Eamon, wide-eyed.

"You aren't –" he began.

"This is going to be a spectacular example of that infamous Goodman style which you love so much," Eamon replied with a smile. "Observe it well, captain!"

As the servants filed into the hall, Eamon went lightly down its length to the high dais. There he stood and waited while the servants filled the space at the far end of the room. They looked nervously at the tables and then to the doors, as though they expected lords and ladies of Dunthruik to come in at any moment.

Eamon waited until he was sure that everyone was in the hall. He gestured for Slater to close the doors, and the man did so obediently. Lines of faces, people whom he had commanded to avoid him, now watched him anxiously.

He searched the lines of servants until he found Cara and her brother. "Master Tenent," he said, "step forward a moment."

Callum paled. Many of the servants in the hall did the same. The boy stepped forward and bowed.

"My lord," he whispered.

"You spoke unwisely to me last night."

"Yes, my lord," Callum answered.

"To speak to the Lord of the East Quarter, when he has not invited you to speak, or indeed, when he has expressly commanded you not to, is a folly that deserves punishment," he continued. The other servants grew even paler. Cara trembled. Callum remained, silent and still, in the hall before him. "You will not do it again. Is that understood?"

Callum nodded. "Yes, my lord."

"Callum," Eamon said. As he spoke his voice changed, and the boy looked up. "You must never speak to a Hand as you spoke to me. Though your speaking was out of place, I will not punish you."

Callum gaped. "My lord –"

"Don't interrupt."

Callum fell silent. Eamon restrained a smile.

"I will not punish you, Callum," Eamon told him, "for you spoke the truth, born from the heart of a true servant. I thank you for it."

Callum looked at him, his mouth open in awe.

Eamon smiled at him, and then looked back across the hall. "Just as I have spoken to Callum, I have spoken to you all once before about your service," he began. The servants looked at him in amazement. "Though I would not be wrong to repeat my high praise of it, I will not do so here. I will not speak of the depth of devotion that this house has shown me, even in these last few days.

"No, I will not speak of it. I scarcely have the words to express how dear it has been to me, and how much I will rue its lack now that I must serve the Master in another way, just as you will serve another master.

"The last week has been difficult for you all. But I had to test you, to be sure that you were ready to safely serve a man like Lord Arlaith. To do other would have been to send you out as sheep among the wolves.

"You have shown yourselves more than capable of that service. Indeed, you have set my mind at ease. I am confident that Lord Arlaith will find all that you have to offer more than satisfactory. You are ready to serve him.

"And so I wish to reward you."

He saw a couple of shocked looks, but he smiled. "You can see that there is a very fine dinner here," he said, a little more quietly. "I am told that Mr Cook and the kitchens worked very hard all morning to prepare it, and I thank them, as I thank you all. Mr Slater is worried that my speaking to you here, now, will interfere with the meal when the guests arrive. Of course," he said with a smile, "the guests are already here. And I must say that they are among the finest ladies and gentlemen I have ever met.

"This meal is for them. It can go no distance in thanking them for what they have done for me, nor in expressing how little I wish to leave them all behind. It cannot assuage the fact that some whom I would dearly love to be here are not, nor the fact that some of those who are here have suffered punishment for my sake. But it is all I have, and so I give it. House of Goodman," he said, tears in his eyes, "this meal is for you."

The room was deathly silent for a long moment. The servants stared at him and he understood why. How could they make sense of him? He had commanded their silence and now he revoked that by doing something no lord of Dunthruik had ever done. It flew in the face of the whole city and yet he smiled as he did it. Anderas leaned against a wall at the back of the room, smiling and shaking his head.

Slowly, Slater stepped forward. He stood by the nearest table and lifted a bottle of wine. He carefully poured a small amount into one of the glasses at the table and then raised it.

"To the Master's glory," he said, "and to Lord Goodman; well he bears that name."

There was a moment of silence as all eyes fixed upon the glass. Then a sudden cry was on the lips of the household:

"To Lord Goodman!" It was accompanied by rapturous applause that grew and grew.

Eamon flushed with embarrassment and came down from the dais. He felt their joy and sorrow in the air: joy that they had served him, and sorrow in his departure.

As he stepped down, Callum stood nearby. Cara was with him, holding her brother's hand. Worried that he had frightened the boy, Eamon went to them.

"Are you well, Master Tenent?"

Callum nodded. "Yes, my lord."

"I am glad," Eamon smiled. "Come and have something to eat," he added, gesturing to the tables where the other servants took their places.

"Lord Goodman?"

Eamon turned back to him. "Master Tenent?" he asked quietly.

"You won't forget us, will you?"

Eamon smiled at him. "No, Callum," he answered. "I won't."

Late that evening he went to see Anderas. The captain was in his own office, looking at some papers. His door stood partially ajar and, catching sight of him through it, Eamon knocked.

"Come in," Anderas called. He smiled as he saw Eamon, though it was a weary smile, as one who knew that he stood on the brink of a long, dark vigil. "Good evening, Lord Goodman."

"What are you doing?" Eamon asked. Anderas looked back down at the papers, then to Eamon.

"Nothing," he replied at last. "I am pretending to look at reports from Lieutenant Mers."

"Have you eaten anything today?" Eamon asked quietly.

"No." Anderas had not stayed for the servants' meal.

"At least you're honest, captain."

"A man must have at least one virtue to counterbalance his vices," Anderas replied wryly.

"Well, you shall eat," Eamon told him. "I have had your servant prepare something for you."

"Thank you…" Anderas looked up, utterly bemused. "My servant?" he repeated. "I don't *have* a servant."

"No?" Eamon feigned a surprised look. "That's very odd, because I encountered her just a moment ago. I said I was looking for the captain's servant, and she said that such was she."

"You sly, engineering rascal!" Anderas accused, then added, "I have a whole college full of cadets, ensigns, and lieutenants waiting for the chance to endear themselves to me –"

"A chance that you rarely give," Eamon countered, "because you are just and fair and would not saddle them with the unnecessary tasks by which most endear themselves to their captains, and because a man endears himself to you through his own merit."

"What do I need a servant for?"

"Encouragement," Eamon answered seriously. "Support." Anderas stared at him, and Eamon offered him a quiet smile. "When I was first sent to Dunthruik by the King," he said, "I was not sent alone. Mathaiah went with me. He was a source of strength and comfort. You will have need of both, Anderas."

"And who will strengthen you, up in the palace?" Anderas asked. "You will be utterly alone."

"I know," Eamon answered, terrified by the thought. "But I will be comforted in knowing that you are not."

At that moment the door opened and Eamon knew who would be there. The notion of asking her service had occurred to him a couple of days before, and she had answered him wholeheartedly. Mr Rose had willingly granted her leave to go with him when he had requested it earlier that day.

"Captain," he said, "this is Toriana. She used to find service in the house of Lady Turnholt, but since that house dissolved, has served under Mr Rose. She is utterly trustworthy and she will be a strength to you. She is of our number." She had been Lillabeth's support, much as Mathaiah had been his.

Anderas raised an eyebrow. "This city is crawling with wayfarers!" he laughed.

"If you know where to look," Eamon smiled.

Toriana came forward and curtseyed. "Good evening, captain," she said, and laid a plate on the table. Anderas looked at her, and his features softened at once.

"Thank you, Toriana," Anderas breathed. "You didn't just come because he told you to, did you?" he added.

"No, sir," Toriana replied with a gentle smile. "I came because he asked me to."

Anderas looked back to Eamon. "Thank you."

"I will see you again, Anderas," Eamon told him. "Even if I must wade through wreck and ruin to reach you. And this parting will not seem so terrible to us then. In the meantime, we must both find the strength to do what we must."

Anderas nodded firmly. "So we shall."

"Go with the King's grace, to love and serve him and his city."

"And you," Anderas answered.

The hallway that led to the throne room had never seemed longer to Eamon than it did that misty morning. The banners creased in the breeze over his head, almost as though they, like every man he met, bowed before him.

He came in silence to the great doors. The doorkeeper bowed deeply.

"Lord Goodman."

"Rise, doorkeeper, and let me pass."

The doors opened and he passed through.

Before him stretched the throne room, long and broad. At the far end stood the Master. The Quarter Hands, dressed in the fullest of their robes, waited near the door. They fell into formation, flanking Eamon: Cathair and Dehelt to his left, and Arlaith and Tramist to his right. Dozens of lesser Hands from the city and the nearest towns lined the hall before them.

They walked the length of the room in solemn procession. Eamon knew that the Quarter Hands walked with him and that the other Hands watched him, but he focused only on the iron gaze that drew him towards the throne.

When they reached the steps to the throne, the Hands knelt as one body, so that the floor at the foot of the steps became a mass of stone swathed in black. The Master stepped down towards them.

"Rise, my Hands."

They did so.

Only Eamon remained kneeling. His cloak and ring were taken from him, and in their places were set another cloak, this with a deep red trim, and another ring which bore on it a black eagle. The sight and feel of them turned his stomach.

The Master's hand fell on his shoulder. "Son of Eben, hold out your hand."

Eamon stretched out his right hand. It shook. He held out his left to support his palm as he turned it towards the Master. The Master set his right palm upon Eamon's own.

"You shall be my Right Hand."

Eamon's skin burned. Every sense in him heightened as red light cracked about their palms, meshing them together in a web of light. His senses reeled.

The Master held a dagger. Eamon could not help but stare at it, for its design was foreign to him. He had seen its like only a handful of times before – wielded by the Easters at Hughan's camp. On the dagger's blade he saw the same script that covered the Hands' Hall and the Nightholt. The horrifying darkness of the letters struck him with renewed force.

"Son of Eben." The Master's voice was as thunderous as a roaring ocean. "Receive the token of your office and of my pleasure."

The cool weight of the blade touched Eamon's outstretched palm. He gasped, and the Master smiled.

He saw with other sight. Another man knelt before the throned just as he knew himself to kneel, and that man was dressed in the same black cloak with the same red trim as now lay upon his own shoulders. About that man stood four other Hands. Eamon recognized Cathair and Ashway, both grim-faced; the other two he did not know, though he felt the strength of their presence. The throne room was dark. Candelabrum, as tall as they were intricately gilded, stood at either side of the dais. There stood the Master, his brow shadowed by his fiery hair, his face more terrifying for being darkened by searing rage.

"Did you hold to me through dark and fire only to turn now?" It was the Master who spoke and his voice cracked with ire. "It is a witless gesture, and will avail you naught."

"You had no right!" the man in the black and red cape called. Eamon started, for the defiant voice seemed somehow familiar. "You have no right and, while the house of Brenuin still has a single drop of blood, Edelred, you will have no right. The land itself knows what you have done and it reviles you, just as I do."

"Where is it, Eben?" The Master's voice shrilled banshee-like down Eamon's veins. He stared at the kneeling man aghast. Eben...

He saw the dagger, the same dagger that rested now upon his palm, on the floor before the man.

"Where is the Nightholt?"

"I destroyed it!"

Edelred's face warped with wrathful mirth. "Destroyed it?" he cried. "You have neither the wit nor ability for that, Eben Goodman!" He cast out his hand and rending lashes of red lightning tore through the air.

Eben fell back with an agonized cry and collapsed to his knees among the standing Hands.

The light stopped. Edelred watched as Eben writhed.

"Where is it?"

"I destroyed it! Even had I not, it would be no more mine to deliver to you than yours to possess." He turned bloodshot eyes towards the Master. "At last I have seen you for what you are, and this I tell you: the King's house will hold. And should my house live long enough to see the Star return to Allera, to see undone what I have so recklessly done, then my life is not spent in vain."

The Master picked up the dagger and turned it slowly in his hands before looking back to Eben.

"In striking bound, Eben Goodman," he said. "So is your house to mine, and through your house will I blot out your precious Star. So is your treachery, and my victory, complete."

The Master smiled, and as he smiled, the four Hands about Eben threw forth their palms. A hellish furore of red light blazed from them. Eben screamed and writhed as it tore through him.

"The King's house will hold, Edelred!"

Eamon blinked and his sight returned to him. The dagger was in his hand. Tears stung his eyes. Eben Goodman had been the first Right Hand. He had been murdered in the place where Eamon, last of his line, now knelt.

He swallowed and looked up at the Master. Still the man smiled. His fiery hair cast an eerie light over his face.

Chapter XXXIV

"Rise to my service, beloved of my right hand," he said. And Eamon rose.

Eamon Goodman's journey concludes in Volume III of
The Knight of Eldaran: The Broken Blade.

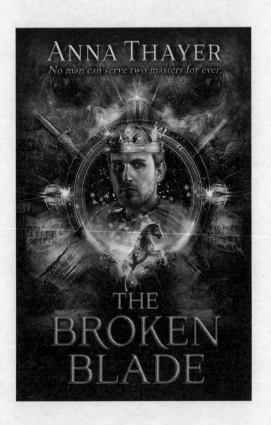